THE MIGRANT

A NOVEL

KATE FOX

IND PUBLISHING

ISBN 978-1-7771515-0-8 (paperback) / 978-1-7771515-1-5 (large print)/ 978-1-
7771515-2-2 (mobi) / 978-1-7771515-3-9 (epub)

~01.1v/72020~

THE MIGRANT

PROLOGUE

May 1, 2019
Eastern outskirts of San Salvador, El Salvador

The gunshot that split the night was more than a kilometer away—Carmelina hated that she could so accurately gauge the distance of the fighting—still, it was close enough that it would cause her mother to wring her hands and her father to grumble she should come inside. She ignored it and squeezed her young son's hand.

She lay on her back on the flat roof of the crudely built cinder block room in the side yard where her two older brothers slept. The heat of the day bled into her back, leaching from the rough cement into her bones. Beside her, two-year-old Ricky pointed a chubby finger to the sky. She treasured these moments alone with her son, solitary but together with a wide expanse of the world above them. At night, when the sky was so open, so vast, she could still feel a thrill of possibility, could still reach for the dreams that had almost been extinguished inside her.

"Mama," Ricky prompted, "that's the North Star, right?"

"You know it is. You ask me every time and you're always right."

He giggled. "That's because it's my favorite star."

"Your favorite? Why, *mijo*?"

"Because..."

Carmelina turned her face toward him, his little mouth pursed while he tried to put his thoughts into words.

"Because it's so bright. And open. It reminds me of *Sra*. Flores, friendly and kind."

"Do you miss her?" Their neighbor *Sra*. Flores, who'd always had a smile and small treat to offer Ricky, had died in one of the recent bus bombings. In a gang turf war over a boundary street, *Los Ochos* had targeted commuters. The bus carrying *Sra*. Flores had burst into flames, leaving sixteen innocent commuters dead and a gnarled mess of charred, twisted metal in the street.

Ricky shrugged. "I guess."

"You know," Carmelina said, "*Sra*. Flores is still here with us in a way. She can help you remember to always be kind and never give up on your dreams."

"Was she in a dream?"

She chuckled. "No, *mijo*, but she had a dream." Araceli Flores, widowed last year at twenty-five, had travelled into the city every day to study nursing. She, like Carmelina, had always had a textbook open on her lap, squeezing in study time during the commute. "In fact, she can teach us both something about determination."

"Deeter... ashun?"

"It means to keep following your dreams, no matter what."

"I want to be *in* somebody's dream," Ricky said.

"Oh, *mijo*, you're in my dreams all the time."

Another shot cracked through the humid air. This one only blocks away.

"Carmelina." Her father's reedy voice echoed off the cinder block wall of the patio.

She scrambled off the roof and shimmied down the rusted, exposed rebar, left behind after some long forgotten addition had fallen by the wayside when they'd run out of money. Landing solidly on the ground, a puff of fine dry dust billowing over her toes, she reached up for Ricky.

He stood on the edge, hands fisted against his slender hips, staring down at her. "Mama, don't leave me."

"I won't leave you, Ricky. I'm right here." She motioned for him to jump into her arms. Normally, he loved this part.

"I don't mean now. I mean like *Sra.* Flores. Don't leave me forever."

"Oh, *mijo,* I'm not going anywhere."

"Promise?"

She nodded and he let himself fall forward, arms extended, chirping as he flew down to her. She caught him and snuggled his warm body to her neck, breathing in the boyish scent of him.

"I'll never, ever leave you. Even when I die, you can always look up and see the North Star and know that we share the same sky."

"Carmelina?" Her mother stood in the open doorway, silhouetted by the weak yellow light of the kitchen. A small rectangle of it splashed into the yard, lighting the way like a flight path.

Another shot rang out—this time barely a block away—and was quickly followed by two more. She covered the distance to the door in a few hurried steps. Once she and Ricky were inside, her mother let the curtain to the small bodega patio drop back into place, shutting out the night, the stars, and the tiny spark of her tightly held dreams.

PART ONE
NO PLACE LIKE HOME

ONE

May 2, 2019
LC-14, Eastern outskirts of San Salvador

"Carmelina Diana Garcia Sanchez. That's quite a mouthful." The man above her barked a laugh out of the back of his throat, a raw twisted sound.

Eyes watering, Carmelina tried not to breathe in the musky scent of him. Was he joking about her name or boasting about his size?

Down the hall, the unsteady squeak of bedsprings was punctuated by the young girl's sobs. She'd recognized the girl, a school mate of one of her younger sisters, but she didn't know her. Dragging her across the room, Flaco had called her Britney. She'd stopped screaming when he back-handed her across the mouth, blood spurting from her lower lip, her pupils black and wild as she made eye contact with Carmelina before disappearing down the darkened hallway toward the only room with a door.

How many years had she spent down that same hallway with

Flaco? Two babies later, she'd been discarded, passed down twenty minutes ago like a worn-out sweater to his main lieutenant.

Her mother's voice rang in her ears as Flaco pushed her in Memo's direction: "Better the devil you know than the devil you don't." Until today, Carmelina couldn't have imagined a day when staying with Flaco would be a desirable option.

"Deeper," Memo grunted, his filthy fingers fisting the hair at the nape of her neck.

Memo. A cruel *bastardo* with a reputation for beating his girl-friends more than was usual. Two of the last three had disap-peared, the third still in critical care at the hospital. Behind the hands of the old women in the market, it was whispered that she'd tried to abort his baby. But Carmelina knew Memo had beaten her so badly—kicking her repeatedly in the abdomen and kidneys until the girl lost consciousness—she'd probably miscarried. Either way, if she was turned in, she'd end up in jail. Secrets were hard to keep in a town this size.

A tear trickled down Carmelina's cheek. Her life had gone from crap to disaster so quickly she felt dizzy. She reached for the leg of a nearby chair to brace herself and sent her mind away from the present moment. She wondered if her brother Diego would be home from his factory job early tonight. She wondered if her mother had enough money to buy chicken to go with the rice, and she wondered how long, after Memo finally let her go home later, she would have to stand in line to buy fresh tortillas.

Breathing heavily, Memo stepped back and pushed her away. "Make me a sandwich."

She wiped her face and rose on shaky legs, not bothering to brush the dirt from her knees. Eyes lowered, she crossed the room and entered the kitchen avoiding the hungry looks of the men seated around the battered dining table.

CARMELINA TWISTED OPENED the bag of rolls on the counter, split one and focused on spreading mayonnaise on it, ignoring the coarse talk of the men behind her, jeering and kidding Memo about Flaco's sloppy seconds. They joked but resentment laced their voices; she knew having Flaco gift her had cemented Memo's position as second-in-command, securing his place as Flaco's favorite.

"Be generous with the mayo, *chica*," Memo said behind her. "And my *cabróns* are hungry, too." A chorus of accord rose from the others.

Carmelina dumped the buns left in the bag onto the counter, split them, layered cheese and ham and sliced the chiles, then piled the *tortas* high on a plate and took them to the table for the men. *Men. Hmph.* Half of them were barely boys. One runner was the age of her youngest sister.

Memo slapped her ass as she turned away. "Where's the *cervezas*?" She pulled two six packs of beer from the fridge and placed them on the table, sliding them across the surface so he could easily reach one.

Flaco entered the room, zipping his jeans and fumbling with a large silver belt buckle. The younger boys sprang to attention. To a man, the rest of them straightened. The newest of the crew, a boy she didn't recognize—and the only one at the table without a 14 or *cadejo negro* inked on his face—jumped up to give Flaco his chair. Someone pushed the plate of food across the table, after sliding a handgun off to the side.

He looked over at Carmelina and jutted his chin toward the hall. "Go take care of my *niña*."

Escaping the claustrophobic kitchen, Carmelina started down the hall toward the wailing girl.

"Pop another one, boss?" one of the men asked.

"And shut her the hell up!" Flaco yelled.

Carmelina entered the squalid tiny room at the back and

closed the door quietly behind her, the clasp snicking into place. Soiled clothing, old food, and too many beer cans to count covered the floor. The one time she'd tried to clean it up, Flaco had thrown her out. A bare bulb hanging from the ceiling cast a sickly yellow light against the uneven cinder block walls. There was no window. The room was stifling, the stuffy air heavy with the musky scent of sex.

On the filthy mattress in the corner, the younger girl huddled against the wall, arms covering her chest, fists balled against her mouth. The swollen eye, Carmelina knew, would later turn a nasty black. She perched on the edge of the bed, her finger to her lips. "*Hermanita*, try to cry quietly."

She reached for the girl's hand, clasping her fingers. The girl's split lower lip, the blood already forming a dry crust, quivered as she tried to focus on Carmelina. Then she bridged the space between them and fell into Carmelina's arms.

"Shhh, quietly, *chica*." She rocked her against her chest, feeling a hundred years old, a thousand, a million years old. "I think you're a year or two ahead of my sister Claudia in school?"

"One year."

"You're thirteen."

The girl sniffled. Carmelina wiped a corner of the sheet across the girl's cheeks, gently dabbing the mucus away from her dripping nose. "What's your name?"

"Britney."

"Like Spears?" Carmelina asked. A tiny light sparked in the girl's dark eyes and she shook her head shyly. "Who's your mama?"

The girl mumbled her mama's name and turned away, reached for her dress, then pulled it over her head. She smoothed it down over her tiny scratched breasts, the capped sleeves covering some of the deep thumb marks in her upper arm.

She knew her mother. They lived on the other side of town beyond the main bus station. She was raising this girl and a younger boy on her own, the father long gone, north, disappeared, or dead. Like herself, the woman lived with her parents.

The girl was petite—she herself stood almost five-five—and slender with razor straight raven hair past her shoulders, whereas hers was wavy and often unruly. Still, looking at her it was clear Flaco had a type.

Britney retrieved her underwear from the floor. Little girl's pink cotton panties with blue teddy bears on them. With her back to Carmelina, she pulled them on over the dried blood that trailed down her pale inner thigh.

"Do you know my sister well?" Carmelina knew it was best to keep the girl talking, about anything really, anything to take her away from this moment, her present hell, to ground her in something outside of this room.

Britney turned to her. She shook her head, scrubbed her cheek, her tongue flashing out over the remnants of the shimmery pink gloss on her upper lip. It probably tasted like bubble gum. "I've seen her around is all."

Carmelina patted the bed. When Britney settled beside her, she reached for her hand. "She doesn't know about me. She's..." She'd almost said too young, but Britney was only a year older.

She tried another approach. "Look, we can't talk to anyone about being here."

Britney shook her head slowly, eyes brimming with fresh tears.

"Or what happens to us here." Britney's eyes grew wide and Carmelina was afraid the girl was going to scream. She squeezed her hand and leaned into her face, dropping her voice to a bare whisper. "Trust me, *hermanita*, it will be even more dangerous for you if you talk about any of it."

"I have to tell Mama."

That's what Carmelina had thought. But it had come back to bite her in the ass, in more ways than one. "Your family can't protect you from... this."

Britney's eyes hardened. "I'm never coming back here," she hissed.

Carmelina's heart broke. She bit her tongue, determined not to cry. At Britney's age, she'd thought the same. "You know what they say about us."

"About us?"

"About *niñas*." She lowered her head. "You can't refuse, Britney. They'll kill you if you say no. And maybe your mama, too." Britney's jaw dropped. Carmelina continued. "Remember the Hernandez girl and her mother a few years ago? You would have been pretty young."

"Murdered." Britney's tears flowed freely again. "Mama was good friends with *Sra.* Hernandez."

It had happened only a few days after Carmelina had found herself in Britney's position—a gruesome reminder that her options had been narrowed to her new life as Flaco's *niña* or no life. It had terrified her that her mother might also be killed. "I know you've heard the stories. Just--"

Footsteps approached down the hall. Memo flung the door open and stood in the opening. "We need more food. Bring her, too." He spun on his heel, not waiting for her to move. There was no need, he knew she'd obey.

She stood and pulled Britney to her feet, wrapping her in a hug. "I'll do anything I can to help you," she said, "but you have to keep this secret. I know it feels like the worst thing that could ever happen. But it's not. You're still alive. We need to keep you that way."

Britney started to sob again. Carmelina held her at arm's length. "Dry your tears and follow me to the kitchen. You can always talk to me, but be careful in front of the men. They don't like it when we talk together."

"Then how—"

"You live near the bus station. You can find me there most

mornings on my way to work." She pressed the pads of her thumbs below the girl's eyes to wick away the moisture, careful not to press too hard on the right one. The swelling was already closing the girl's lid.

Memo bellowed from the kitchen. "*Puta*, get out here now!"

Carmelina grabbed Britney's hand and hustled down the hall.

TWO

"*Mija*, you missed *comida.*" Lupe pushed a shock of jet black hair behind her ear, her forehead creased. "Are you hungry? I kept a plate."

Carmelina kissed her mother's cheek. "I'm sorry, Mama, I—" She choked down the sob threatening to escape her throat and turned away, busying herself placing the tortillas into the warmer. "It took longer than I thought."

Lupe lit the stove and slid a blackened pot onto the flame.

"I'll do that," Carmelina said.

"Sit. It'll only take a minute."

Carmelina pressed her palms against the surface of the battered family kitchen table, the wood worn as fine as butter, host to a lifetime of humble yet happy meals. Things were always tight but somehow her mother managed to keep them fed.

In the corner of the kitchen area stood the refrigerator. Once painted glossy ochre, the dulled paint sported so many scratches you could plot a route to Costa Rica, a huge dent in the bottom corner of the door a constant reminder of how drunk the men were when they dropped it off. Her father had won it playing cards when he'd had a job in San Salvador.

The dilapidated fridge chugged through the nights reminding her of a freight train—a comforting background that muted the familiar snores and grunts of her slumbering family. The sputtering when it restarted, after constant power outages, often woke her. She'd bolt upright in bed, eyes wide, ears straining, until she realized the rapid gunfire sounds were coming from the refrigerator. The gas burners were as fickle, flaring blue with gas or trickling to a sputtering flame without warning. Appliance warfare was alive and well in her family's kitchen.

"Eat." Lupe placed a plate in front of her. She'd been certain she couldn't eat, but the savory smells ignited her appetite, and she quickly cleaned her dish. Her mother chattered about a neighbor whose son had left for *El Norte* without telling his family. "Imagine," she said, twisting her mouth to the side, eliciting a familiar click. "Alejandro left for the United States and didn't even tell his own mother."

She recognized her mother's sadness for what it was: fear. There was no future here for Carmelina's generation. The factories paid little, farms were drying up in the droughts, the soil—and their livelihoods—literally blowing away on the wind.

Violence was getting worse. The gangs ran everything. These days, neighbors no longer sat outside their doors at night to socialize. One evening two years ago, the rival gang *Los Ochos* had driven down the street shooting everyone in sight. Her best friend's mother had been killed and the girl's father had moved the family away right after the funeral.

Not only had Carmelina lost her best friend, but her own father had taken a bullet to his lung. Unable to work, he continued to rock and wheeze his way through the days he had left, marooned in front of a small television set in the tiny back bedroom, his life deflated like a punctured balloon.

That night the gang hadn't found who they were looking for, but there'd been a lot of unfortunate collateral damage.

Gone were the days of children playing in the dusty street past sunset, the smell of *pupusas* cooking in the air, mothers and aunties sitting quietly with their husbands or laughing with neighbors. The street outside was quiet now, their neighbors cautious, subdued, wary of everyone who passed. Their own front door, for years open to the street to invite both a cross breeze and their neighbors and friends, remained closed. Day and night.

Carmelina no longer talked about her situation with her mother, unable to bear the sadness in her eyes. Lupe had also been good friends with *Sra.* Hernandez—she knew the score—and when she and her daughter had been killed, her mother had begged her wealthy sister for money to send Carmelina away. Her pleas, as was always the case with her sister, had fallen on deaf ears. Carmelina, fearing for her mother's life, downplayed things as much as possible and returned, daily, to Flaco and the *Casa Loca*.

Lupe, an *abuela* before her time, cared for Carmelina's children while she was out and, when she returned home—often bruised with swollen reddened eyes—tenderly rubbed arnica into her purpled and yellowed skin. Like stray dogs and roosters, the details of those bruises were left at the door.

"Has Diego already gone out?"

"Your brother's not home from the factory yet." Lupe rinsed Carmelina's empty plate under the faucet. "Why not go kiss your babies goodnight? Ricky's lids were heavy as lead before he dropped off hoping to see you before bedtime."

A pang of guilt gnawed her insides. "I know, Mama, I—"

Lupe put her hand up. "*Mija*, I'm just sharing information."

Carmelina smiled and slipped past the flimsy curtain that shielded the corner where she shared a cot with her children. Light from the yellowed kitchen bulb filtered through the cheap polyester material and shimmered in uneven, milky strips over her children. Chubby thumb in his mouth, Ricky slept with his back curled against the wall, his thick lashes feathering his cheek. That something she loved so deeply had come from such pain never ceased to amaze her. She brushed a thumb across his sweaty forehead, careful not to wake him. Beside him, in the basket that doubled as a bassinet, Katya slept, her limbs splayed out in an X. She'd never seen a baby so relaxed in sleep as this infant. Katya had been a difficult pregnancy, a very early birth, and a quiet and joyous baby.

Her healthy, happy children.

With no future.

IN THE SHOWER, Carmelina willed her aching muscles to relax, wishing she could dissolve like the soap she lathered over her skin and swirl down the damn drain and end up downstream, or float all the way to the Pacific. Anywhere but here. Selfish. She couldn't leave her children behind.

The sound of men's voices drifted into the small *bodega* patio outside the bathroom door. She dried herself, then dressed.

She stepped outside, threw her towel over the clothesline to dry, and went back into the house. In the kitchen she was greeted by the clatter of utensils.

"Diego." She smiled across the room at Diego. They looked so much alike, some mistook them for twins. Mouth full, he nodded back.

Kike quirked a brow. "Not happy to see your other older brother?" His thin lip twisted to a sneer only a mother could interpret as a smile.

"Of course I am." As Carmelina lifted his empty plate, Kike reached for her hand, his fingers circling the fine bones of her wrist. "I need more tortillas, little sister."

Ever the peacemaker, Lupe sprang up. "I'll get those."

"You sit, Mama. Visit with your sons." She refused to let Kike get a rise out of her. The chatter of her family soothed her while she washed up the last of the dishes, piling the drainboard high. They were never put away. The narrow single shelf below the counter was stuffed with pots and *masa* and large utensils. Besides, in the morning all the dishes would be needed again.

"Alex couldn't afford a coyote," Kike said.

"So dangerous without the coyote to guide him. Going all that way with no one to protect him or help him across borders?" Like a dog with a bone, her mother continued to worry over the neighbor's son. "El Norte," she scoffed. "Everyone goes to the USA and the USA sends them back. What a nightmare. Alejandro is only a boy."

Kike scoffed. "He's seventeen. That's hardly a boy. He shouldn't haven't left anyway. At seventeen he's old enough to man up and bring money home to his family."

Carmelina snuck a look at Diego. He was bristling. Eyes narrowed, mouth tight. Kike brought money to the family—when he felt like sharing—but expected Diego, two years younger at eighteen, to bring home every cent of his wages. Several times over the past couple of months, Kike had picked up Diego's pay envelope at the factory. He kept half the contents for himself, a pick up fee Kike called it, and put the rest to household expenses. That left Diego, who worked fourteen hour days, with only enough for a few cigarettes and bus fare in his pocket.

"Maybe if Alex had all the money he earned, he might have been able to pay a coyote to take him," Diego said. Kike hurled a fork into the middle of the table. It skittered across the surface until it clanked against the edge of Diego's plate. Carmelina felt the air suck out of the room.

Lupe cleared her throat and stood, her hands clenched in the hem of her apron. Kike's chair scraped back against the floor.

Here we go. Carmelina threw the dish rag into the sink. "Diego, I need a hand with something outside."

Diego stood, kissed his mother, and side-eyed Kike with a dark look. Carmelina grabbed his arm and dragged him toward the door.

"I hear El Flaco was in a generous mood today," Kike said. "Giving away his cast offs."

His laughter followed them into the street.

THREE

"Alex was supposed to go later." Diego leaned against the wall, hidden in shadow. He blew smoke out in a noisy stream. Canned laughter from the neighbor's television two doors down drifted into the small alley.

The night had opened the sky to an endless stretch of stars overhead. Last week the full moon had bathed this valley in shimmering silver but the new moon left the sky void of light save the stars. As a child, Carmelina had studied the sky, poring over picture books in the school library, learning the names of the constellations.

She was already teaching some of them to Ricky, delighting as his little eyes widened in wonder as she pointed out *The Bear* and *The Archer* overhead. "Bear," he would repeat after her. "Arker." Scanning the sky, she locked in on the north star, Ricky's favorite, probably because it was easiest to find. When she'd asked him, he said it was because it was the superhero of all the others. He wasn't wrong.

She huffed out a breath and eased herself onto an ancient wooden crate guarding the back door of the tortilla shop. Cigarette butts littered the ground at her feet. "I didn't hear what happened." She reached for Diego's cigarette.

"I overheard something on the bus home." Diego took another drag, his cheeks sucking in hard, the red tip flaring against the dark. His eyes narrowed. "You gave this up."

"Gimme. A puff won't kill me." She barely smoked anyway—who could afford tobacco on a regular basis—still, she was proud she'd given it up entirely both times she was pregnant. The nurse at the Natal Care Center had shown her a brochure filled with horrible images of what happened to babies when their mothers smoked or drank alcohol. *Great*, she'd thought at the time. *Like it's not enough that I'm bearing babies I didn't ask for and dropping out of school.*

For a while, she'd tried to keep up with continued studies at the Center, but, like most of the girls at the NCC, she'd had to let it go. Few girls in her neighborhood had finished high school. She planned to go back when her kids were older. For now, she studied English on her own.

She inhaled deeply, relishing the smoke filling her lungs before exhaling and passing the cigarette back to her brother. She let her head fall back against the wall. "Overheard what?"

"His cousin said *LC-14* turned up the pressure on him. Join up or pay the consequences."

"Do you think he's really gone north?" Her question hung in the air. So many people simply went missing. Their loved ones always hoped they had fled north but sometimes their bodies turned up in shallow graves outside of town. More often, they were never heard from again, leaving the family to wonder. Not knowing what happened to your child or brother or cousin was a cursed mystery as deep as the Lempa River.

"I pray he did. But Mama's right. It's so much more dangerous to go without the coyote." He spat onto the ground. "I'm gonna kill that *pendejo* Kike one day."

"Diego." She agreed with him. Kike was an asshole.

"You hate him, too."

"I know, but he's our brother."

"He's a bully." Diego shrank farther into the shadows as footsteps approached. A young couple turned into the alley, hand-in-hand. When they saw Diego and Carmelina, they pivoted away, scurrying back into the street.

"What's this about Flaco?"

She looked up into his face, creased with worry for her. He was the one person in the world strong enough to hear her truth. Only ten months apart, they'd shared everything since they were small babies. He'd made it his mission in life to try and protect her.

"He—" The sobs she'd suppressed for hours choked into her throat. Diego lowered himself onto the crate beside her, butting her hip to hip to slide over and make room. She inched to the side and dropped her head onto his shoulder when he wrapped his arm around her back.

"Get it out, little sister."

"He—he gave me to Memo." Diego's body stiffened. He wrapped her into a hug, both of his strong arms circling around her, and she slumped against the safety of his chest. When she was cried out, she took a deep breath and stared into his eyes. "What am I going to do, Diego?"

"We'll have to go. It's time anyway." Diego jumped to his feet and paced the ground in front of her. He paused to light a cigarette and leaned against the wall for several seconds, but he couldn't stay still.

"Katya is not old enough." They'd talked of this for so long. They even made a down payment for the coyote before she'd gotten pregnant with Katya.

"She'll survive the trip better than a lifetime without a mother." In the dusky light of the narrow alley, Diego's pursed lips looked almost white.

She stared up into her brother's face. "With Kike taking your pay, we'll never get enough money together."

Diego lit another cigarette from the tip of the last and tossed the butt into the dirt. She watched it bounce, the small spark leaping into the air before being snuffed out by the dust. They needed rain so badly. Each morning on the way to work, the fields stretching outside the bus window showed more signs of drought, the land parched and arid.

"We already gave Lagarto a down payment."

"That was almost a year ago. Will he still honor it?"

He shrugged. "I hope so. I'll contact him tomorrow."

"Even if he does honor it, we'll need so much more. You know the price has gone up. It's going to take us months."

"We need to reach *El Norte* before you turn eighteen. It'll be much easier for you as a minor."

"I won't be eighteen for almost eight months."

"That's not long, not really. Especially when you consider how much cash we'll need. Maybe we could borrow somewhere..."

"You know we can't. We've already looked at all those options."

"What about the women you work for?" Diego bit his lower lip and avoided her gaze. Was he really going to bring this up again? It hadn't gone well last time.

"What about them?" She had a string of small cleaning jobs in the city; it was never enough, but she was reliable and worked hard and often got more work by word of mouth. "You mean steal from them?"

Diego shrugged. "Of course not. Can you ask for money in advance? Or maybe they could pay you more for a while?"

She had asked them last time, knowing the answer before the words were out of her mouth. Worse than feeling like a servant cleaning rich women's toilets was the feeling she'd had in her gut that day. She hated the idea of having to beg again. She shook her head. "I did ask last time. Every one of them said no."

He grunted and flicked his cigarette butt toward the cinder block wall. "We'll make it work. I'll try for more shifts. It will add up."

Her cleaning jobs barely paid for food, and she was gone from before dawn until late into the evening. Most of the time, Flaco had someone waiting for her at the bus station, making her even later. She cringed thinking of the demands Memo might make on her. There was no time left in the day for her to take on more work.

Diego's job paid a little better but it was never enough, especially now with Kike taking most of it. Plus, they both needed to help their parents. It cost money to feed so many mouths. There was so little left over. So little to add up.

"It's going to take too long." Carmelina didn't need to remind Diego about Memo's previous girlfriends. One of them had been his childhood sweetheart.

He squeezed her arm. "We'll get there. I promise. Even if it takes months."

She whispered into the night, eyes fixed on a candy wrapper blowing into the alley.

"I might not have months."

FOUR

May 7, 2019
Natal Care Center

The sun was dipping behind the San Salvador Volcano as Carmelina hurried to her evening appointment at the Natal Care Center. She'd had to leave work early in order to make it on time and her mother had met her partway with Katya.

The NCC was a refuge, one of the few places she felt cared for and valued. It was a clean, efficient space filled with women, hope, and possibilities. A sign at the entrance said: *We respect all who enter.*

Large glass doors stood at the top of the short stairway. She pushed through them and stepped inside to a familiar murmur in the foyer. On Tuesdays, the center stayed open for evening appointments and night classes. As she made her way down the hall to the medical offices, she couldn't resist peeking in the doorways.

In one room, girls had their heads down writing furiously. A flash test perhaps. In the next, a girl at the back shot her arm high when the instructor asked a question. He caught Carmelina's eye as she passed and nodded to her. Science. It had been her favorite class. She shrugged off the pang of regret and kept walking. In her arms, Katya was starting to fuss. Carmelina's stomach growled. She hadn't eaten since morning, working through her breaks so she could catch the earlier bus.

The receptionist looked up, a wide grin plumping her cheeks. "Carmelina." Glancing down at the appointment book on her desk, she scratched a red check beside the time slot. "Wow, Katya is getting so big."

"Four months." Carmelina passed her to Gloria's waiting arms.

The older woman grinned into Katya's face, cooing at her. "I could do this all day."

Carmelina laughed. "You *do* do this all day."

Gloria chuckled. "Best job in the world." She passed Katya back, opened the top drawer of her desk, and extended a protein bar to Carmelina. "You look ready to pass out."

She took it gratefully. "Thanks, it's been a long day." She tore the wrapper and took a large bite.

"Aren't they all?" Gloria's eyes softened. None of the girls at the NCC lived what could be called easy lives: most having babies while they were still children, controlled by the gangs, or abused at home.

Behind her, a door squeaked open and the nurse poked her head out. "Carmelina, bring Katya in."

She edged past Gloria's desk, winking on her way by.

"So, how are we today?" Esther asked, tweaking Katya's cheek.

"Hungry and a bit cranky, I'm afraid."

"We talking about you or the baby?" Esther's gaze dropped to the bar in Carmelina's hands and she raised her brow, a smile tugging at her lips. "Put her on the table and have a seat."

Carmelina sat and ate. At moments like these, her bones aching like an *abuela's*, she found herself wondering how her mother had managed. With five children, her mother was in perpetual motion. She couldn't remember a time, as a child, when she'd seen her mother sitting, relaxing, even laughing much. Up before the family, she was usually the last to bed, even now. She was turning thirty-six in two months and already looked used up. If Carmelina felt like this at seventeen, with only two children, how tired must her mother feel?

"Any problems?" Esther held the stethoscope to Katya's small chest, before moving it around to her back. "She's gaining weight well, considering she arrived a month early." She popped her on the scale then returned her to the table and jotted a note in her chart. "She was six pounds at birth, gaining about a pound a month. That's great. She moving around much yet? Trying to roll herself over?"

"No. I've been trying not to worry about it, I mean, you said--"

"I did. We can expect her to develop a little more slowly, not unusual with premies. And she's still so tiny." Esther cooed and put her face close to Katya's.

"She's a happy baby. So much easier than Ricky."

"I remember." Esther chuckled.

"Maybe girls are just easier."

"Not always. Each little one has his or her own path." Esther ruffled Katya's feathery curls and turned to Carmelina. "What about you? How are you faring?" Her gaze dropped to the multiple round bruises on Carmelina's forearms. It didn't take a genius to figure out they were made by someone grabbing her.

"Fine. Same as always." Carmelina shrugged. Where to start? Esther meant well but there was only so much she could do.

"You know," Esther leaned back against the examination table, one finger clenched in Katya's chubby hand, "birth control is still an option. We've talked about it before."

They had. Birth control terrified her. Where would she hide it? If Kike discovered it, she'd never hear the end of it and he'd almost surely tell. Secrets and information were his favorite currency.

If Flaco had ever found out...

She'd given him his first son. He'd been proud as a peacock and insisted on being listed on the birth certificate as the father. As far as she knew, it was the first time he'd claimed a child. All the others had been girls. She'd also suspected it was why he kept her around, hoping she'd give him another son. Once she'd had Katya, it didn't take long for him to tire of her.

And now Memo. Memo, she was certain, would kill her if she gave him even the smallest of reasons. She shook her head slowly.

"Surely you don't want more children? I mean, not right now." Esther's brow shot up.

Carmelina sighed. "Of course I don't. It's just—"

"You know we have shots now. There's nothing to take with you, no pills to hide, I mean... keep track of." Esther's eyes locked on Carmelina. "The shot lasts three months. Nobody will ever know."

Three months. It was going to take her and Diego longer than that to gather the money they needed. In three months, she could come back in for another shot before leaving. Maybe she'd need two more shots before they left. Her heart sank calculating it could be six months before they could leave. Barring a miracle—a rich uncle they didn't know about, a winning lottery ticket—it could be that long or longer.

She'd heard of the shot. She knew she couldn't protect herself from being assaulted on the way north, but a lot of women took the shot to make sure they wouldn't also end up pregnant.

"But no period, right?" How was she going to explain that?

"Right." Esther watched her. "Maybe your friends have a solution for that."

Maybe. "I can't pay." She averted her gaze and looked at

Katya, who had fisted her hands against her sides, her lids growing heavy.

Esther unlocked a small cabinet on the opposite wall and removed a sealed packet. Snapping on gloves, she asked, "Arm or butt?"

Carmelina rolled her sleeve up, too embarrassed to let Esther see her bruised behind.

FIVE

May 10, 2019

Carmelina's breath caught in her throat. She coughed then gulped in air before she managed to choke out, "Fifteen thousand?"

She and Diego sat at the top of the post office stairs across from the small plaza she passed daily on her way to the bus station. The plaza had a tiny patch of scrubby grass, a handful of iron benches with most of the dulled paint scraped off, and a large mesquite tree at the south end. Legions of bougainvilleas paraded up the trunk and wrapped around the lower branches, a kaleidoscope of color poking out from the leaves. Most days the blossoms cheered Carmelina. Today they seemed to taunt her.

Diego had been waiting for her when she got off the bus, rushing her away down the street, while she looked over her shoulder for anyone who might be waiting for her. He steered her to a quiet, shaded spot on the stairs, insisting she sit down, before he gave her the news. At the far end of the plaza, kids screeched, chasing a soccer ball and kicking up dust.

"Lagarto said the price has gone up."

"Lagarto!" Carmelina spat his name and pressed her palm to her chest. Her heart pounded against it like a caged animal. "Why must we deal with such liars?"

Diego squeezed her knee. "It's not totally unexpected. I asked if he could give us last year's price. He said his expenses have gone up. On the plus side," he added, "he's going to honor our deposit."

"So we only need—"

"No, we still need fifteen thousand. On top of the deposit."

"Oh my stars." In her mind, a spinning calendar added up weeks and months. The numbers mounting higher than she could bear. She shifted on the stair, the hard cement unforgiving. "There's no way we'll ever save that much money, Diego. Even with your extra shifts. We'd need something to sell, something big, like land."

Diego scoffed. "Who has land?"

"You know very well. Mama's sister."

"You're kidding right? They haven't spoken in years."

"But maybe she'd reconsider now. Auntie doesn't have to sell the land. She could—"

Diego grunted. "What? Take out a loan against it? Her husband wouldn't let her do that for her own kids. Why would she do it for us? Anyway, she said no when Mama asked for her help to send you away, remember?"

Her heart sank. She remembered all too well. "What if we go on our own?"

Shaking his head, Diego put his palm up to her. "You know it's too dangerous. We've both heard the stories."

"Sure, we've heard stories from the ones who come back. What of the ones who make it?"

"You're not thinking straight. We've heard those stories too."

"A lot of people make it."

"And a lot of people are turned back. Right now, even Mexico is turning people away at the Guatemala border." A pleading note she rarely heard from him entered his voice.

Still, she persisted. "We were ready to go on our own before Katya."

He bit his lip. "But you had a safe birth. You didn't miscarry—"

She'd been terrified. The spotting, the cramping, she'd been certain she was going to miscarry or the baby would be stillborn. Her life would have been over. She could have been charged with homicide, sent to jail for decades. "My point is, we were ready to flee then."

"Your life was in danger then."

"My life is in danger now. We can make it."

"Or we might be killed on the way. Or forced into labor by the cartel. Or maybe kidnapped and sold to human traffickers." He paused. "You could be raped."

"I'm raped every damn night." Carmelina's lip trembled.

Diego winced. He grabbed her hand and brought it to his lips. "*Hermanita*, listen to reason. Do you think we're strong enough to walk almost five thousand kilometers?"

"Of course we are," she said. "We're young, we're—"

"What about Ricky? He's only two—"

"Three in two months."

"He'll have to walk most of the way on his own. I can help, but you'll be carrying Katya. How much does she weigh now?"

"Ten pounds. The nurse at the center said she's doing really well."

"Ten pounds will start to feel like twenty after a couple of hours marching in the heat."

"We can do it."

"It's a huge risk. I say we keep putting together money for Lagarto. It will take time, but we'll be assured passage."

"Ha. You can't believe that. Having the coyote won't guarantee anything." She turned to face him. "We have to find a way. Staying is not an option for me."

Her brother reached for her hand, the creases in his forehead deepening. "I can't lose you, too." She knew he still missed his girlfriend, the one Memo had *disappeared*. "We'll find a way."

"What about Chiapas?" she asked. "The Mexican government will take us if we can make it that far."

"The refugee camps there are huge. It could take months before we're processed."

"So what? We'll be alive. And they'll give us permission to work, help us get established."

He shook his head. "We'll face the same problems there eventually."

"Problems, maybe, but not the same. At least it's a small chance at a better life. How much will it cost to get us to Mexico?"

"*Chica! Oye*, Carmelina!"

Racing down the broken sidewalk, a young boy sprinted toward them, sailing nimbly over cracks and skirting the crumbling curb. He skidded to a halt at the bottom of the stairway, red cheeks puffing like a tin worker's bellows.

"You know this little upstart?" Diego laughed down at the young boy who was bent over, hands on his knees, sucking in air.

"That's Gallito, one of Flaco's new runners," Carmelina said quietly.

Gallito straightened, pushed a shock of red hair out of his eyes, and fixed Diego in a stare before turning to Carmelina. "You're late. Memo sent me to get you."

Carmelina filled her lungs, closed her eyes and held her breath a few seconds willing herself to submit. Better she stay under the radar until she had a fight she could win. She rose, dusted herself off, and bent to hug Diego.

He whispered in her ear, "We'll find a way. I promise."

"He's waiting," Gallito said. Twelve years old and already the cocky little rooster felt entitled to boss her around. She wanted to cuff him upside the head.

"Go," Diego said, pulling away.

She followed Gallito, hurrying down the street, subdued, a prisoner on her way to the executioner. At this moment in time, there was no escape. Before rounding the corner, she glanced back over her shoulder.

Diego remained at the top of the stairs, hands jammed into his pockets, his expression grim.

His look of helplessness mirrored how she felt.

SIX

May 11, 2019

"Shut that damn baby up!" Kike stomped across the floor and loomed over Carmelina, glaring down at her. "I worked all day and I don't need to come home to this."

"She's a baby. She's hungry. I just got home myself." The words were out of Carmelina's mouth before she had a chance to check herself. She was done having people order her around today. Done. She jumped to her feet, hand cradling Katya's head to her breast. The sour smell of stale alcohol on Kike's breath assaulted her nostrils. She lowered her gaze and sat again, focusing her attention to Katya.

"*Mijo*, where did you learn to talk to women this way? It sure as hell wasn't from me." Carmelina's father appeared from nowhere and stood nose to nose with his eldest son. Her father's breathing was labored and he seemed to shrink more into himself with each passing day. At twenty years old and almost six foot tall, Kike towered over him. "Be polite or be quiet."

Kike shrugged and ambled over to the only comfortable chair

in the house and parked himself in front of the television. "Whatever you say, Angel."

"My house, my rules," her father said. "And you can continue to call me Papi while you live in this house."

Rap music blared from the tinny TV speaker. Her father sat down across from Carmelina. She smiled at him.

"Good eater." He placed his hand on Katya's head, the fingers all bone, and lowered his voice. "You know better than to challenge Enrique when he's drunk."

"I know, Papi. That's why I sat down."

"I'll have another word with him tomorrow. When he's sober."

"Gracias, Papi." Katya released the pressure on her nipple. She looked down. The baby's lids were growing heavy. "Want to hold her?" Angel extended his arms and Carmelina passed the baby into his care.

Her father meant well but as his health had declined, he'd lost control over what Kike did, in the house or out of it. Kike was a bully. Had always been a bully. And now, he thought he ruled the household. When she was younger, Carmelina had hoped he'd find a wife and move away. But why would he? He had a roof over his head, someone to cook and clean for him, and people younger and smaller to push around.

And a job? That made her laugh. He talked about working when all he did was sit in the cantina and win a few pesos playing poker and eavesdropping on conversations so he could try to win favor with Flaco. Flaco hated him, a long-standing feud from grade school that had made them sworn enemies, and he rebuffed every attempt Kike made to join the gang.

At one point, Kike had threatened to join their rivals and Flaco had almost laughed him out of town. Unless he was prepared to move, aligning himself with *Los Ochos* in this neighborhood was a death sentence. How she'd love to see the look on Kike's face when he heard she was gone. The very thought of it made her smile.

"Where's Mama?" she asked.

"Lupita is lying down. She had one of her headaches." Her father tried to hide it but there was a note of concern in his voice. It was the third time this month.

"Again? That's not like—"

He flicked his wrist, waving her concern off. "I've asked her repeatedly to see the doctor, but you know your mother. I came up front to watch the kids so she could rest. You must have come in while I was checking on her. Your sisters are finishing their homework. Ricky fell asleep a while ago."

She nodded. "That boy can sleep through anything. Well, this one, too." Katya had drifted off in her grandfather's arms. "I'll put her down, then go check on the girls."

After settling Katya into her basket, Carmelina took a quick shower. When she came back into the main room, the television flickered against a dark backdrop with the music still blaring. Her father had gone to bed, Kike was gone. Relieved she wouldn't have to face him again tonight, she retrieved the remote and shut off the TV.

Across the room, the light was off behind her sisters' curtain. They must have finished their homework. She'd get an early night, too. She could use the sleep. As she turned away, she heard a low murmur from their corner. She tiptoed over to kiss them goodnight.

Claudia was twelve. Angie less than a year younger, at eleven. Like she and Diego, for two months of the year they were the same age, and they loved to tell people they were twins. As much as possible, they dressed alike, walked to school together, and even though they were in different grades, they had the same group of friends. They shared everything. Sometimes Carmelina envied their closeness and wished she'd had a sister closer to her own age. Not that she would trade Diego for anything in the world.

Smiling she reached for the curtain, her hand suspended in

space as she realized Kike was talking with Claudia. She held her breath and listened.

"But you'd like some extra money, wouldn't you, little sister?"

"Mama wouldn't like it," Claudia said. "She wants me to get good grades."

"It's only a couple of hours. Think of all the pretty clothes you could buy." His cajoling tone was one Carmelina had been intimately familiar with until she'd learned to see past her eldest brother's self-serving lies.

"Can Angie come too?"

"No." Impatience crept into Kike's voice. "It would be something just for you. You're pretty enough now—"

Carmelina pushed back the curtain. "Pretty enough for what?"

Kike turned and stared daggers at her. "That's between me and Claudia."

Claudia sat up, her voice bubbly. "Kike said I'm pretty enough to start running errands for some of his friends at the *cantina*."

"That's our secret, isn't it, Claudia." A hard edge crept into his voice and his eyes narrowed.

Carmelina sputtered, hands on her hips. "You're planning on pimping out your sister at the bar? She's twelve."

Kike rose from his spot on the bed, the springs creaking as he got up. He towered over her. "Nobody asked you, Carmelina." He pushed her out into the room, the curtain twisting behind Carmelina's back. Claudia's eyes grew wide.

"You need to mind your own business, *puta*. I know how you spend your time after work."

"Like I have a choice. I'm no whore, you bastard. You leave Claudia alone. She needs to be in school, not hanging around the *cantina* with a bunch of losers."

Kike's arm flashed out, the back of his hand cracking across her mouth. Carmelina's head snapped back. Drunker than earlier,

Kike's swing threw him off balance. He stumbled forward, bracing himself against her shoulders.

Carmelina shoved him off and he slumped onto the arm of the easy chair. "You can't take Claudia away from school. Stay the hell away from her."

Kike sneered, collapsing further into the chair. A glob of spittle sliding down his chin, he mumbled, "You'd be surprised what I can do."

A coppery taste tingled across her tongue. She wiped her lip and spun away.

"I keep waiting for you to surprise me, big brother," she said, "but you never do."

SEVEN

May 14, 2019

Just after seven o'clock, the sun weak and kissing the day a lingering goodbye, an exhausted Carmelina stepped off the bus. The woman she cleaned for had decided today was the day to clean all of the windows. From the outside. Shimmying up the rickety ladder to the second floor, she'd cursed her a hundred times. It was men's work. She had children at home who relied on her, she couldn't afford to fall off a decrepit ladder. Her job didn't cover her for sickness or injury. Seething, she'd kept those thoughts to herself. The exhaustion rolling through her came equally from biting her damn tongue as from physical exertion.

Warily, she scanned her surroundings searching for anyone sent by Memo. No one waited for her. Relieved, she set off at a leisurely pace toward El Flaco's, picturing herself as a small child —dragging her feet— which was how she really felt inside. A mangy black dog chased a hysterical scrawny chicken across her path as she left the dusty bus yard and stepped into the cobblestone street.

Tuesday nights were always hard. She longed for the days when her life was somewhat more carefree, for the days when she attended the night classes at the NCC. How she'd loved being in school and had never minded the homework. Head down, notebook on her knees, she'd completed most of it on her commute to work. She continued to study English—she'd need it when they went north—but self-study didn't give her the same satisfaction.

It didn't seem fair to have to leave school so young. But then, it's not like she would be able to carry on to university even if she did finish high school and anyway, not a hell of a lot about her life seemed fair. Normal, yes. Fair, no.

Someone hissed at her as she passed the dark opening of an alley. She averted her eyes. Most of the men on the street knew she belonged to Flaco—or used to, she reminded herself—and left her alone.

"Lina, *hermanita.*"

Stopping, she backed up a step.

"Don't turn toward me," Diego said. "Come in when there's no one to see you."

In front of her the street was empty. Shooting a quick glance over her shoulder, she determined there was no one behind her. She slipped into the alley. "What are you doing here?"

"Waiting for you, I..." Diego slumped against her. Supporting him, she guided him deeper into the darkness of the alley and lowered him against a wall. But not before she saw the pulpy mess of his face.

"What the hell, Diego? You're hurt."

"Thanks, Captain Obvious." His attempted grin made him wince, his hand clutching his side.

"What happened?" She pulled his hand away, stepped back in horror and gasped. Dark blood stained a large gash in his abdomen. "We need to get you to the hospital." She tried to pull him up.

"No, we can't. Stop. Let me explain."

"When did this happen? How much blood have you lost?" Using her body to shield the light, she flicked on her cell phone's flash light. Her breath caught in her throat. Blood stained his shirt and had dried in a snaking path to his belt. Dark brick red blotches marred his jeans.

"I don't know. A lot. We need to find someone to stitch me up." His face was paler than she'd ever seen it, his eyes rolling back in his head.

She slapped his face. "Stay with me, Diego. Get up, we need to go."

"Lina, I can't be seen."

"What about Jorge?" There was a doctor in town known to do some late night stitching.

Diego shook his head. "Too connected. I can't be seen."

If she needed to keep him under the radar, that left only one option.

Skirting the dark side of the street and ducking into doorways and alleys whenever they spotted a car or someone walking the street, they managed to make it in just over twenty minutes. She supported him through an alley that lead to a freight door often left propped open by staff while they smoked in the alley. Tonight it was closed. There was no handle or bell.

"I'll have to leave you here while I go in."

Diego's lips were rimmed with blue. He grunted as she lowered him to the ground. She sprinted around the side of the building and in through the front doors, down the hallway, past the classrooms, and skidded to a stop in front of Gloria's desk.

The receptionist looked up, surprised to see her. "Carmelina."

"I need to see Esther."

"Do you have an appointment?" Gloria's words trailed off when she spotted Carmelina's blood-soaked fingers. "Are you hurt?"

"Please, Gloria, it's my brother."

Her hand flew to her neck. "You can't bring him here, child. It's a women's center."

"I don't have a choice." She spun toward the door, her hand grasping the doorknob just as it swung open. It threw her off balance and she collided with the nurse. "Esther."

"What? Oh." She grabbed Carmelina's bloody hands, exchanging a look with Gloria over Carmelina's shoulder, then pulled her inside the exam room and shut the door.

"It's my brother. He's been stabbed. He's losing a ton of blood."

"What about the hospital? One of the teachers has a car. Where is he?"

"There's no time. He can't go anywhere public. Please, Esther." Carmelina's lip started to tremble. "He's in the alley, we can bring him in the back door."

"Ay, cristo." Esther took a big breath and blew it out between pursed lips. Flinging open the door, she crooked her head for Gloria to follow them. Five minutes later, they had Diego inside, prone on the examination table.

"We've got you, Diego," Esther said. "You're safe here."

With scissors she cut through the front of Diego's T-shirt and cleaned the dried blood, ignoring his grunts and explaining what she was doing as she went. She wiped the area around the gash with disinfectant that stained his skin a sickly burnt orange before expertly plunging a needle into his belly. "This will numb you."

Carmelina gripped Diego's hand. "I can help."

"Just stay there, keep him calm." From the cupboard behind them, Esther gathered sutures and tape. Twenty minutes later, Diego mercifully unconscious, the stomach wound was closed and Esther turned her attention to his face and hands.

"He fought back." She pointed out the stab wounds in his lower arms and hands. Carmelina hadn't even noticed. The whole sequence felt like a bad dream she was hoping to wake from. "What the hell happened?"

"I don't know yet, he needed all his energy just to walk here."

Esther placed a hand on her wrist. "He'll be all right. You did good."

She gulped, breathing in the metallic smell of blood laced with the disinfectant. "Thank you, Esther."

"We're not done yet." Esther cleaned and sutured a couple of the larger gashes on his arms and hands before turning her attention to his face.

Both eyes were swollen almost shut. Blood bathed his forehead, dried trickles inching over a map of broken blood vessels that marred his cheeks. His left earlobe dangled in shreds. His mustache stiff with dried blood and his nose bent, broken and crushed to one side. Carmelina looked away and stifled a sob.

Esther caught her eye and inclined her chin toward the stool at the end of the table. "Breathe, Carmelina. He'll be out for a bit. Sit down, you've had a shock."

From her perch, Carmelina watched while Esther patched Diego back together.

Was she shocked? Only because it was her brother. She'd seen worse. She didn't need to explain that. Esther had seen worse, too.

EIGHT

"Where are we?"

Diego's voice roused Carmelina and she rushed to his side. "We're still at the NCC."

"Right." He let his head fall back onto the table. "My head hurts."

"The nurse left something for the pain. Hang on." She retrieved the tablets from the counter, helped him sit up, popped the pills onto his tongue and held a paper cup of water to his swollen lips.

"Esther said you're going to be fine. You took quite a beating."

He stared at her through the slits in his lids, his eyes unfocused and bloodshot. He slumped back into the bed. "We need to get out of here."

"We're safe here for now. We need to wait until classes are over. Esther will find a car to take us home."

"Memo is going to be waiting. You should go."

"I'm staying."

"I'm sorry to be so much trouble."

"Don't say things like that." She caught herself about to punch his arm. An old habit. "What the hell happened to you?"

"It's a long story."

"Coincidentally, I happen to have some time." She tossed the paper cup in the garbage, then rolled the stool a few inches toward his legs so she was in his line of vision.

"It happened at work. I left the floor to get supplies. When I got to the supply room, the door was blocked from the inside. I tried to force it open. At first I didn't realize there was anybody in there, and then I heard the girl crying for help.

"When I got the door open, I saw one of my co-workers pinning down a young girl from the assembly line."

"Raping her?"

"He yelled at me to get out." His laugh was short and raspy. "As if. Maybe I should have."

Carmelina touched his arm. "No."

"I dragged him off her and the girl got away. He was pissed. He took a few swings at me."

"This is more than a few swings."

"I got a few good punches in, too. Bloodied his nose. After work, he and his friends were waiting for me." He shrugged. "They're all *Los Ochos*. I recognized a guy from shipping who's been trying to recruit me for months."

"You didn't tell me that."

"I said no, but now..."

"They ganged up on you outside?"

"Dragged me into an alley, kicked the shit out of me." He stared bleakly at her. "Well, you can see that for yourself. I'm sure they meant to kill me but a truck pulled into the alley and I was able to roll to the opposite side and escape. The knife was a last-ditch attempt to stop me.

"I took a different route than usual to get to a bus stop a few streets away so they wouldn't know which bus I got on." He rested and glanced toward the ceiling. "But it's only a matter of time."

"Until they figure out where you live?"

"When the factory opens tomorrow, they'll be able to find out everything they need. They'll come for me."

The night closed in around her, choking off yet another possibility. Jobs were scarce. If Diego wasn't working, they'd never get out.

He cleared his throat. "I know what you're thinking. I can't go back to work, Lina. They'll kill me."

"I get that."

"I need to talk to Lagarto again. See if he'll front me the money for the coyote. If he says yes, I'll leave tomorrow afternoon."

She placed a finger to her lip. Hurried footsteps approached on the other side of the door. They drew near, passed by, then faded to silence. "Talking to Lagarto is a waste of time and possibly dangerous. The less anyone knows, the better. We'll leave first thing in the morning. Like I said before, we go without a coyote, as far as Chiapas in southern Mexico."

"I've barely got a hundred bucks put away. You?"

"Sixty. You want to sit here and take your chances when they come looking for you? They might even come tonight." She couldn't bear the thought of losing Diego.

"It's too risky for you to come. I want you to go later. With the coyote."

Her eyes narrowed. Anger seared through her gut. "What you saved that girl from today? I go through that, and worse, all the time with Memo. And years of it with Flaco. I'm done."

Diego's voice caught in his throat and his eyes brimmed with tears. Remorse washed over her. She tried another approach.

"Look, do you know how hard it will be for you to pass the borders? A single guy on his own? If we look like a family, we'll have a better chance." She stared down at her nails, flicking at the dried blood that rimmed her cuticles. "I can't lose you, Diego. If you go north without me, I may never see you again."

A quick tap at the door interrupted her. The door opened and Esther slipped inside. "Almost everyone is gone now. We're bringing the car around back. Lina, help him up."

Esther busied herself putting together a packet of pills and extra bandages. She handed the bag to Carmelina. "He can take the pain killers as needed. Antibiotics morning and night. Make sure he takes them all. Keep the wound clean and dry, and try to have someone look at it in a few days."

The door cracked open and Gloria poked her head in. "All clear."

NINE

"Who was that who drove you home, *mija?*" At the door, Carmelina's mother wiped her hands on her apron, her eyes fixed on the taillights disappearing down the street.

Carmelina stumbled into the house supporting Diego.

"Is Diego drunk?"

"Yes, Mama," she said. "A little party at work."

Diego kept his head down, his face shielded by the baseball cap. They moved across the kitchen and through the back door to the small shed at the end of the bodega patio where Diego and Kike slept. Mercifully Kike was not at home.

She unbuttoned and helped him out of the shirt they'd given him at the center. Then checked his bandages before rolling a clean T-shirt on over his head and shoulders.

"I need a razor." He settled back onto his pillow and moaned.

"Worry about that later. You need sleep." They'd have plenty of time on the road for him to shave. Pulling the pill packet from her pocket, she passed him one. "Here, this will help."

"Bring me a razor. There's one on the basin outside. And scissors. And a towel." His words floated over her shoulder while she stepped outside.

She returned and dumped it all on the bed. "Your mustache?"

"It'll help a little, don't you think? And I'll cut my hair."

Diego was so proud of his long, glossy hair. With his mustache and scrub of a beard, he looked like Che Guevara, the Argentine revolutionary. The only thing missing was the hat.

"We can do it later. You should rest. They're not likely to show up here tonight."

"I don't want anyone to recognize me as we're leaving. Why take chances?"

A chill ran up Carmelina's spine. Fear? Excitement? A little of both. "So we're really doing this?"

"I don't see another way." He reached for the edge of the towel to pull the supplies toward him.

"I can help. It'll be faster if I do it." She picked up the scissors.

Diego placed his hand over hers. "No. Go spend some time with Mama and get organized. We need to leave here before five."

Carmelina pulled a light blanket up over his legs, spread the towel over his chest, and brought him a basin of water.

"*Hermanita*." She turned on her way out the door. "It's safer for you to go later."

She pursed her lips and tilted her chin upwards. "See you in the morning." The door clicked into place behind her and she went back to the kitchen to answer her mother's questions.

Lupe, standing at the counter peeling *nopal* for the morning, looked up when she came in. "Is he hurt? He looked hurt."

"No, Mama. He had more *cerveza* than usual, that's all. You know Diego, he can't hold his liquor."

Her mother chuckled. "He's nothing like Enrique, that's for sure. I sometimes wonder if he's even my son." Kike drank like a fish and all of her mother's brothers were proud of their ability to drink anyone in the *cantina* under the table. Long through the night and into the platinum light of morning went the parties when Carmelina's uncles tried to outdrink each other.

She laughed along with her mother. "He'll sleep it off and be fine in the morning." Guilt suppressed her laughter. In the morning they'd both be long gone and her mother's last memory of her son would be watching him stumble drunk across the room. Not to mention how she was going to feel when she found her grandchildren also gone.

It was late. The house was still and quiet. "Why are you still up, Mama?"

"Always something to do, *mija*." She turned to her, eyes clouded with worry. "Some kid named Gallito was here looking for you. Said Memo was waiting."

Carmelina shook her head. "Don't worry about that, Mama."

"You know I worry. My middle name is worry." She turned her focus back to peeling the fleshy cactus, but not before Carmelina saw the tears welling up in her eyes.

She hadn't meant to talk to her mother about Kike and Claudia but now she'd run out of time and wouldn't have another chance. "I need to talk to you about Kike. And Claudia."

"What about them? He teases her terribly."

"I'm not sure it's always in good fun," Carmelina said. "He's trying to get her to take a job after school."

Mama shrugged. "A little pocket money won't hurt her."

"At the *cantina*. You know what that could expose her to. She needs to be in school."

"I agree, she should be in school. I'll talk to Kike. I'm sure he didn't mean anything by it."

Carmelina sighed. She'd known this conversation would be a challenge. Where her first born was concerned, her mother had a blind spot. In her eyes, he was still a playful boy in a man's body. For Kike's part, he was cunning enough to hide the darkest side of his cruel nature from their mother.

"Where is Kike?"

"The *cantina*, I suppose." She rolled her eyes, and rinsed the knife under running water. "Your guess is as good as mine."

"Are the girls sleeping?" Sometimes Claudia and Angie stayed up late, giggling and reading with a flashlight under the blanket.

"I certainly hope so. I sent them to bed hours ago."

Carmelina took a glass from the shelf and poured herself some water. "Papi?"

"He went to bed early. Tired."

"I guess we've all had a long day." Carmelina yawned. Leaning into her mother at the counter, she circled her arm around her waist and rested her head on her shoulder. "And you?"

"Busy, like I said earlier."

"But our headache yesterday?"

"I should be the least of your worries—"

"You've had more than usual lately."

Lupe hushed her and kissed the top of her head. "*Mija*, you should get some rest."

"Yes, Mama, I will. I just wanted to..." Her words trailed off. All the things she wanted to say crowded into her head, but she couldn't raise her mother's suspicions. Someone from *Los Ochos* would come to the house looking for Diego tomorrow. She didn't want her family to have to lie. Better they knew nothing.

In the end, she said simply, "You do so much for us, Mama. I love you."

"*Ay, mija, te amo tambien.*" She kissed the top of her head again. "Go on, get some sleep. Morning comes early," she said through a yawn.

At the sink outside, Carmelina washed up and jammed her toothbrush in her pocket. Everything else she left. She went back inside.

She slipped behind her curtain. Ricky and Katya slept soundly. She stripped out of her clothes, slipped a shift over her head for sleeping, then stuffed clothes for the children and a couple of their favorite toys into a small backpack. For herself, she took only an extra shirt, underwear, and a pair of pants.

She pushed back against the tiredness that had seeped into her bones. The muted clatter in the kitchen confirmed her mother was still up.

She stole across the back of the room and peeked in on Claudia and Angie. They both slept. Quietly she edged in and perched on the side of the bed. She shook Claudia's shoulder, holding a finger to her lips when she stirred.

"Shhh, quiet. I need to talk with you."

"What is it?" Claudia looked up, her eyes crusted with sleep. "I have a big test tomorrow."

"I'm sorry, Claudia. Listen, *hermanita*, about the thing with Kike the other night--"

"You don't have to treat me like a baby. I'm not stupid." Claudia, at twelve, thought she knew everything.

"Keep your voice down. Mama's still up." She reached for her sister's hand. "I know how smart you are and I'm so proud of you. I want you to stay in school. No matter what. Don't let Kike convince you to do other things."

"Oh, I won't." Claudia shook her head solemnly.

"No, listen. Kike can be very... *convincing*. He can be mean. If he tries to talk you into anything, you go directly to Mama and Papa. Before he drags you away from your studies or from school. Promise me that."

Claudia's little face crumpled into worried creases, her twelve-year-old bravado sliding away like a cheap curtain. She sat up and flung her arms around Carmelina's neck. "You're scaring me."

"I'm sorry, *hermanita*. I need you to take this seriously."

"I do," Claudia whined. "I do take it seriously. That's why I need to sleep for my test tomorrow."

"Okay." Carmelina stroke her little sister's hair and pushed her gently back down onto her pillow. "And..." She paused. "Look after your sister." Her eyes flicked over to Angie.

Claudia scoffed. "I always look after her. You know that."

"All right, *hermanita*. Get some sleep." She laid her palm against Claudia's face, her cheek warm and creased from the pillow. "You know I love you, right, Claudia?"

"Of course, Carmelina. I love you... too." Eyes closing, her words faded as she drifted off.

Carmelina sat a few seconds more and watched her sister descend into slumber. Then she kissed her fingers and reached across Claudia's shoulder to press the kiss onto Angie's forehead.

After one final look, aware she was trying to memorize this moment for possibly a lifetime of replays, she turned away from her sisters and slipped out.

TEN

May 15, 2019

They stole out of the house, the only home she'd ever known, Carmelina nestling Katya close to her chest to muffle her murmurs. Ricky, wide-eyed and bristling with excitement at the secrecy of the adventure, clasped Diego's hand.

No light spilled from the houses they passed. The streets were empty. Against the distant horizon, wisps of mist obscured the top of the volcano. Milky light from the setting moon seeped through the clouds.

Hurrying along the cobblestone, Diego stumbled. She looped her arm through his.

"I'm fine." He shrugged her off but the pallor of his skin and off-kilter gait belied the pain he was in.

"You're not," she hissed. "And we don't have time to argue."

Together, they moved through the center of town, past the tortilla shop, the butcher shop, and the small dusty plaza. She took it all in, a snapshot of the life she was leaving behind.

By the time they reached the bus station, Diego was

exhausted, his breathing ragged. He scanned the yard. Satisfied there was no one looking for him, he limped to a spot in the shadows and waited with the children while she went inside to purchase tickets.

The ticket agent peered at her through half-closed eyes. He slurped coffee from a chipped clay cup and counted out her change with his free hand, pushing it and the tickets across the counter to her.

She returned to Diego. "The bus leaves in less than half an hour. I'll run over and grab *pupusas* and drinks."

"Mama, I wanna come with you."

"Stay here, Ricky," Diego said. "I need your help with the baby."

"I don't wanna." Carmelina heard Ricky whine as she strode across the yard to the food cart.

"Lina, you're early this morning." The woman tending the cart flashed her a smile.

"I picked up an early shift." Each lie came more easily. What was happening to her? She placed her order and passed the vendor a handful of coins. Her knees shook as she waited for the grill to melt the cheese. She'd waited so long for this day to become a reality, she expected to be nervous and excited. But Diego's fear was contagious and it was setting her nerves on edge. The sooner they got on the bus the better.

"Ready." The woman passed her the sack of food, grease already staining the brown paper. Carmelina thanked her and returned to the shadows.

Diego had managed to distract Ricky by having him collect an assortment of small pebbles. Her son crouched over them, Diego helping him count as he placed different sizes in new piles.

Diego motioned across the yard. "The bus is still locked. The driver is dragging his ass, smoking with his pals."

"We'll be gone soon enough."

"I'm hungry, Mama." Diego reached his hand up.

"We'll eat on the bus." She jammed the bag in the top of her backpack and took the baby from Diego.

"What is it?"

"Nothing."

"I know you, Lina. What's bothering you? Second thoughts?"

"No! It's only... Kike is pressuring Claudia to start running errands at the *cantina* after school. I spoke to her last night, but I'm worried. I don't trust him." She looked up from fussing over Katya and stopped speaking.

Diego's features were twisted. He looked horrified. Her heart skipped a beat.

"What is it?" She scanned the yard, eyes darting the area around the buses. "What?"

"If I tell you, you won't leave."

She forced herself to breathe. "You need to tell me."

Diego kicked at the dirt. "Kike is the reason you were with El Flaco."

"What do you mean? Flaco pulled me off the sidewalk one day after school." The day was etched in her memory. What she'd thought at the time, before she lived a couple of years subservient and under Flaco's thumb, was the worst day of her life.

That day she'd worn a new skirt Kike had given her. It was hot pink and she was so excited. Since their mother would never allow her to wear anything so short, Kike told her to keep it hidden in her locker and changed into it after school. She'd never owned anything so pretty. All her friends were jealous.

Hot lava roared through Carmelina. She felt her face flush. "Explain yourself."

"Kike set it up. He... he sold you to Flaco." Carmelina fixated on the rubbery way Diego's swollen lips moved as he spoke. It was easier than digesting the words. Her world stuttered into slow motion. "Remember that Christmas he had so much extra money for firecrackers?"

She did remember. Coming home, hurting and hiding in her bed with the covers pulled over her head, and those infernal firecrackers jangling her nerves each time one went off. And she... *she* was the reason he had them? Her childhood had been blown up so her sixteen-year-old brother could blast off some firecrackers?

Her gut twisted and she burned inside, a molten anger so hot she wanted to lash out at the nearest thing she could find. Then she looked down at her little boy playing in the dirt, at her infant cradled in her arms, and love pushed the hate away. But somewhere deep inside, she felt that molten lava harden and forge into something lethal.

"Why did you never tell me this before?"

"You were thirteen. He's your big brother. I thought it would break your heart."

"You're right. It would have. But no more secrets." She threw her arms around his neck. "You're the only one I can count on in this life. I need to be able to trust you."

"Yes, sister, count with me."

"The driver's there now. Let's go." Carmelina led the way across the yard, Diego following with Ricky. When they reached the bus, she fished in her pocket and extended his ticket. "I'm not coming."

"You have to come."

"I won't leave Claudia. Not now. The idea that she might have to live under Flaco's sadistic control—"

"No. You're already in jeopardy. We go north and we get Claudia out later."

"I'm sorry, I know it'll be harder to cross on your own."

"I'm not worried about me. You need to get away from Memo. And, you need to get to *El Norte* while you're still a minor."

"Claudia's twelve. I have to protect her."

"We can let Mama know."

"You know how she is with Kike. She won't see it until it's too late."

"But what can you do?"

"I don't know, but I have to try. I can't let her end up like me." Her memory supplied an image of a sobbing Britney pulling teddy bear covered panties over her bloodied thighs. "Once Flaco has her, Claudia won't have a way out."

"Lina, no--"

"I'll come later."

"It's not that easy. You know the road is dangerous for women, let alone single women." He lowered his voice and gripped her arm. "How will you manage alone with the two little ones? Listen to reason."

"I won't leave her. I can't." She stepped back, out of his reach.

Diego fell silent. Carmelina passed him her pack. "Take the food at the top. Your pills and bandages are in the front pocket."

"I'll get a job as soon as I get there," he said, stuffing the packets into his own bag. "I'll send money for the coyote. I'll set up a place, we'll all be together again soon."

"Promise you'll wait for me in Mexico. I'll come to Chiapas."

He nodded solemnly, his eyes brimming. "Chiapas."

Carmelina bit her lip. "Be safe brother. *Te amo mucho.*" She hugged him, careful not to press against his abdomen.

Ricky bounced up and down. "Bus, bus, bus," he chanted.

"Shhh, we're not going. Only uncle."

"You promised," Ricky yelled. "You said we're going on a big adventure."

Diego bent down to hug his nephew goodbye. He put his face nose to nose with him and spoke quietly. But his words were for Carmelina.

"They're here. Across the yard." He kissed Ricky on both cheeks, lowered his hat, then hugged Carmelina a second time, burying his face in her shoulder. "Be careful. I need to get on the bus."

Twisting her body only enough to slant a look across the yard, Carmelina saw two young thugs. One of them held a piece of paper. They were working their way through the yard, talking to passengers waiting for their buses.

"Go. *Cuidate mucho.*"

Diego tried to smile, the corners of his mouth too swollen to lift. "Love you." He put his foot on the stair, his ticket held up to the driver.

Ricky started to wail. "I want to go with Uncle Diego! You promised me. You promised. I'm going."

Carmelina clapped her hand over his mouth. "Get on," she said to Diego. People nearby looked their way. They were drawing too much attention.

"Ow."

Ricky bit her and resumed wailing. "I'm going with Uncle—"

Carmelina covered his mouth again. In the doorway of the bus, Diego's eyes were wild. Ricky kicked and bucked under her hand. She crouched and whispered in his ear. He quieted, put a finger to his lips, then planted a sloppy kiss on her cheek before slipping past Diego and darting up the stairs.

"Take him with you."

"Lina—"

"It's done."

"Are you sure?"

"Keep him safe," she said. "This way you'll cross easier."

"I'll meet you in Chiapas."

She checked over her shoulder. The men with the paper were only two buses away. "Go, brother. Don't lose my baby."

"I'll take care of him. I'll send money." Diego swiveled and disappeared into the bus. The driver shut the door behind him. Ricky's beaming face appeared in the window, he waved wildly down at her. Diego pulled him away, across the aisle to the far side. She started toward the front of the bus, to cross to the other side so she could wave as they pulled out, but someone grabbed her elbow.

"*Chica*, you know this guy?" A jagged scar ran down the man's cheek. He had hard eyes, thin lips. He thrust a paper in front of her face, a grainy black and white photocopy of an old photograph of Diego, probably pulled off Facebook. *Thank the stars Diego had shaved and cut his hair.*

"No." She shook her head, pressed Katya closer to her chest.

"You sure?" His eyes narrowed.

"I'm sure."

The driver revved the engine. She stepped back as the bus rolled forward. The two men moved on to the group of people standing behind her. The bus pulled away. She'd lost her chance for a final glimpse of her son.

ELEVEN

Tears streamed down Carmelina's face. She didn't bother to brush them away. Only an occasional car crawled past her in the pre-dawn light and she sobbed openly, periodically gulping in the humid morning air.

Her son was gone. In the moment, with Diego standing in the stairs of the bus, bandaged and bruised and vulnerable, it had seemed like the only way to keep him safe. Now the enormity of what she'd done flooded through her. Ricky wasn't even three yet. At first, it would all seem like a great adventure. But before long, he'd be crying for his mama and his *abuela*.

Diego is great with him. She struggled to grasp a calm thought in the panic whipping through her. She trusted Diego with her life, she could trust him with Ricky's.

Plus, it was true he'd do better at the border with Ricky in tow, and later, when she followed, she'd be able to move faster with only the baby to worry about.

Resisting the urge to stop and text him, she focused on putting one foot in front of the other.

There was time to get Katya home before she returned for her bus to work. Vision blurred, she retraced the steps she'd taken with Diego and Ricky barely an hour before.

As she neared home, she realized she had to get hold of herself and stop crying. Somehow she had to act like everything was normal.

Then it hit her. How would she explain to her family that Diego and Ricky were gone? The only choice was more lies. She had to buy them whatever time she could so they could get away. Every hour would count.

As the town woke and more neighbors crowded the bus station, it was only a matter of time until someone recognized Diego's photograph. Once they figured out who he was, it would take no time at all to find out where he lived and come knocking on the door. The best option was still for her family to not have to lie. Keeping them in the dark was the best protection she could offer.

The house sat in darkness, the low building squatting behind scrub bushes. Thanking her stars, she crept in the front door, easing it open to avoid the telltale squeal.

Weak light spilled in the window. A hush permeated the space. She knew her way like the face of her son. Creeping across the room, she tucked Katya back into her basket, fervently praying she wouldn't stir.

When she slipped off her backpack, she realized she'd forgotten to send Ricky's clothes and toys with Diego. Before sliding it under the bed, she dug for Katya's favorite toy and laid it gently on her belly, her breathing quiet and rhythmic.

Rousing herself, she moved away. She couldn't afford even a second more to watch her.

In the kitchen, she scrawled a note for her mother then hurried back out into the street.

TWELVE

Later that evening, sallow light spilled through the small front kitchen window as Carmelina shuffled up the path. The door swung open and she turned her face away, edging into the shadow.

"Carmelina," her mother hissed, "who are all these people coming to the house? They're looking for you, they're looking for Diego..." Her mother's voice faltered as Carmelina turned to her.

"Oh *mija*, what happened to you?" With a furtive look toward the street, Lupe grabbed her arm and pulled her into the house, locking the door.

Carmelina winced and leaned against the counter while her mother turned out the lights and tugged the front window curtain tight.

"Come, *mija*." Her mother gently guided her out to the patch of yard by the sink. She filled a basin with cool water and grabbed a cloth. "Sit."

Carmelina closed her eyes while her mother cleaned up her face and her arms. She clamped her hand over her mother's when she tried to lift her shirt.

"I'll do it."

She dabbed at the dried blood grateful to not look at the wounds again. Mama didn't ask who had hurt her.

"That kid Gallito was here looking for you again today. Twice. I suppose you know this already."

Her mother turned away, but not before Carmelina saw the moisture in her eyes. Her shoulders shook, then she spoke again.

"And two thugs I didn't recognize from around here came looking for Diego." She turned back, eyes darting over Carmelina's face. She bent toward her, voice low. "Where is your son? Where is my son? Why aren't they home yet? And that note you left—you expect me to believe Diego took Ricky to work with him at the factory? And, does this," she picked up the bloody rag from the basin, "have anything to do with it?"

Carmelina held her hand up. "Mama, please. Do we have aspirin? *Ibuprofeno?*" She had to tell her the truth. For Diego she could come up with a plausible story. He could be gone for the night with his friends or with a girl, but she couldn't explain away Ricky being out this late.

But how could she tell her and still keep them safe? She'd hoped to give them at least a twenty-four-hour start. How she wished she was on the bus with them, cuddling her son, on her way to a new life, her body and heart not bruised and battered.

She reached for the glass and tablets her mother passed her, swallowing them quickly while she chose her words.

"What I'm about to tell you now you have to promise to keep a secret."

"How can I agree to that before I even know what's going on?"

"Mama, it's important. Say you will."

"I'll consider it." Her mother crossed her arms.

"Diego wasn't drunk last night. He was wounded."

"Wounded how?"

"He saw something at work and intervened. Pissed some people off." It wasn't necessary to whitewash it. Still, there was no reason to delve into the details and worry her mother more. At this point, she still believed the less her family knew the better.

"Is he in hiding? Why would he have Ricky with him?" Recognition crossed her face and her jaw dropped. "He's gone to *El Norte.*"

Dumbly, Carmelina nodded, heart wrenching as she watched the knowledge that she'd likely never see them again crumple her mother's features.

"Why Ricky? Why..." Her words trailed off, her mouth opening and closing several times until she took a deep breath. "What changed your mind? I mean, look at you. Surely leaving with them was a better choice."

"I was ready to leave." She recounted the scene at the bus station, choking on her words when she got to the part about pushing Ricky on the bus.

"Smart. You probably saved your brother's life. That doesn't explain why you didn't leave with them."

"Kike."

"What does Enrique have to do with it?"

"I tried to tell you last night. He's pushing Claudia to work at the cantina after school."

Her mother waved her hand. "I told you, that's nothing. I'll make sure—"

"You don't understand, Mama. Kike *sold* me to Flaco."

Her mother gasped. "I don't believe it."

"Diego told me this morning. When I told him I was worried about Claudia."

Something dark flitted over her mother's face. "He wouldn't. Claudia's only twelve."

"I was only thirteen."

"No." She shook her head, the horror of Carmelina's words sinking in. "I don't believe it."

"Can't you send them away? Claudia and Angie."

"Where would I send them?"

"To school. To your sister. Anywhere he can't sell them."

"I'm sure Diego misunderstood. Your brother wouldn't sell you."

"And yet he did. How do you think I ended up with Flaco?"

Her mother dropped her head into her hands. "Ay, *mija*. I tried so hard to find a way out for you. My sister wouldn't help then, why would she help now?"

"But can't you ask? Do you really want Claudia to have my life? I'm seventeen, I've got two children, and no future beyond being someone's punching bag and a house whore."

"Don't talk about yourself that way. You have no control over that."

Carmelina sighed. She regretted not leaving. How long could she survive with Memo? She chose her next words with care, fighting to tamp down the hard edge creeping into her voice.

"It's true. Beyond dying or leaving, I have no control. But Mama," she grasped her hand, "Mama, you *can* control Claudia's future. And Angie's. Please, send them away. Talk to your sister.

She crossed her arms again, a gesture Carmelina knew well. There was no way she'd win this argument with her mother. Not this night.

"They're too young to leave. Who will keep an eye on them if not me? I'll talk to Kike."

"You can't tell Kike I told you about this. And you can't tell anyone, especially not Kike, about Diego and Ricky."

"How can I not tell your Papi something so important? And do you think Kike and your sisters won't notice they're gone?"

"Nobody will notice tonight. They'll just think they're sleeping. Look, they need time to get into Guatemala. Even there, they won't be out of the gang's reach."

Her blood ran cold as the truth of her words hit her. If they found Diego... Oh God. If they found Diego, what would happen to Ricky?

"Mama, please. We have to buy time for Diego and Ricky to get to safety."

THIRTEEN

May 23, 2019

The days stretched before Carmelina endlessly. Up early, bus to work, clean all day, bus back, time with Memo, home to eat, feed the baby, then fall into bed only to wake up and do it all again. And beneath it all, the gaping cavernous hole in her heart where Ricky should have been. In the night she would roll over, waking when his little body wasn't there for her to spoon. In bed, he was like a furnace in the night. Now she put extra heavy blankets over herself because at those moments, those moments when she woke cold and alone and remembered he was gone, she wanted to sit up and scream her head off.

Each day she compulsively checked her phone, waiting for some word from Diego. He'd promised to text. Her texts to him all went unanswered. She constantly topped up her phone, using money she needed to be saving to buy airtime, paranoid her minutes would run out and she'd miss a message from him.

In the meantime, she poured all her love into Katya. Her mother said she was going to smother the girl and shooed her out of the house in the mornings, laughing that she needed to give Katya a break. She wasn't wrong.

"*Mija*, Katya will be here tonight when you come back." Mama brushed a lock of hair off Carmelina's forehead before pulling her into a tight embrace. "Nothing will happen to her while she's under my care. I think you know that." Lupe raised a brow, a teasing smile tugging at her lips.

But Carmelina's sense of humor had left on the bus with Diego and Ricky. Every moment of her life now seemed like life or death. Nothing funny about any of it. No solace anywhere except when she had her own eyes on her daughter late at night.

Despite her worry, there was a hum of optimism buzzing through her, deep inside like a train approaching from a distance. When she tuned into it, it drowned out everything else. On the bus to work, she let it overtake her.

Diego would make it to Chiapas. He'd find a job and rent a small place for himself and Ricky. He'd send money. She'd be on the road before she knew it. It was just one more day of cleaning, one more day of Memo. She could do anything for just one day.

Her first job on Thursdays was *Sra.* Rodriguez. The señora, only a handful of years older than Carmelina, was a former Miss El Salvador, a Miss Universe runner-up—Carmelina had watched the competition on TV—and now a trophy wife for a municipal politician rumored to have strong ties to LC-14. Judging from appearances, Carmelina believed it. Money dripped from every corner of the house, from the garish antique chandelier that hung over the large foyer and wide spiraling staircase, to the fine linens in the bedrooms, to the rows upon rows of designer dresses and shoes in the former beauty queen's walk-in closet.

Marta, the full-time housekeeper, opened the back door to let her in. "The señora's waiting for you."

Carmelina glanced longingly at the coffee pot on the stove. The housekeeper ran a tight ship and normally every surface in the large kitchen gleamed until you could see your face in it. Today, it was a chaotic mess. Two girls she'd never seen before chopped chiles and onions at the far end of the large butcher block island. On the counter beside the stainless steel industrial sinks stood a tray piled high with small game hens. Freshly killed, blood pooled around the edges of the tray.

"She's in a bit of a state this morning. I'll keep coffee warm for you." Marta squeezed Carmelina's forearm and motioned toward the swinging door that led into the dining room. "In there."

Heavy expensive draperies flanked the large glass doors in the dining room that led to the inner courtyard. The doors were flung open, the señora talking with the gardener beside the ornate marble fountain. Streams of water spurted from the beaks of several intricately carved doves, the water cascading into smaller bowls below before it emptied into the pond at the bottom. Carmelina rarely entered the garden. Unwilling to interrupt the señora, she approached quietly but gasped in surprise when she spotted a flash of orange in the pond.

The gardener waggled his eyebrows and nodded in Carmelina's direction. *Sra.* Rodriguez spun, caught the look on her face, and smiled. "Lina, you've never seen the koi?"

Carmelina shook her head and approached the water. Plump orange and white fish swam through the crystal clear water, brushing up against green lily pads and pink and white lilies. It was like a fairy tale. "It's beautiful."

"It is," the señora agreed. "I'll be back in a few minutes," she said to the gardener. Carmelina followed her inside.

"We're having a *fiesta*." She clapped her hands, flashed an infectious smile of perfect white teeth, and flung open the doors to the china cabinet pointing to different shelves as she spoke. "I'll need those polished, and these crystal sorbet dishes, and of course, the silver goblets. They're Sr. Rodriguez's favorites."

Carmelina suppressed a grin. "I thought the señora was his favorite."

"Oh, you." She clapped again. "Let's get going, you can help set the table once we have the leaf in."

Standing in front of the cabinet, Carmelina cocked her head. The table seated twelve and the leaf expanded it to a comfortable fourteen or cozy sixteen. "How many of each shall I have ready?"

"Sixteen. Full house tonight." The señora winked at her before leaving the room. Apparently, "let's get going" didn't include her.

In the closet next to the pantry, Carmelina gathered the cleaning supplies she needed, detouring through the kitchen to pour herself a coffee. Needing energy after having tossed sleepless most of the night, she dumped two spoonfuls of sugar into the cup and filled it to the brim with heavy cream until it was cloudy white.

The hours passed. She polished each piece until it shone. When she was almost done, *Sra.* Rodriguez popped back into the room, as if on cue, with the gardener in tow, and supervised as they moved the leaf into the table. The large slab of mesquite was heavy as stone. Carmelina struggled.

"Use your legs," she said.

Grunting with exertion, Carmelina shook her head. She'd end up injuring her damn back doing this.

"Marta, we need help," the señora called out.

Marta backed through the swinging door, her apron and arms slimy with poultry guts. She turned and called the two girls. With the gardener on one side, Carmelina and the two girls on the other, they managed to slide the heavy leaf into place.

Mission accomplished, the girls returned to the kitchen, the gardener tipped his hat and slipped away through the garden doors. Carmelina, under *Sra.* Rodriguez's watchful eye, set the table for a formal dinner for sixteen. When she was finished, her stomach growled.

"You haven't eaten?"

When would she have eaten? She'd been in front of the woman all day and it was well past *comida*. In the kitchen, utensils clanked against dishes. She shook her head.

"Grab something in the kitchen and meet me upstairs in twenty minutes." She leaned against the buffet and brushed at a bit of lint on her stylish black skirt. "I'll need you to stay later today, in case we need extra help."

Carmelina froze. Her bruises from the last time she hadn't shown up for Memo, the night Diego had been hurt, hadn't even faded yet. Fear ripped through her. *No way.* "I can't do that."

"Nonsense. I need you here." The *señora* pressed her glossy pink lips together in a practiced pout that probably bought her some pretty nice trinkets, spun on her heel as if it was a done deal, and headed for the stairs.

FOURTEEN

The house swelled with noise and people as more vendors showed up with food for Marta and the two younger girls, more comfortable now that the señora was not watching, chattered non-stop between themselves despite Marta's warning glances which they either ignored or did not notice. Carmelina couldn't be sure which. The girls were perhaps twelve, maybe thirteen, and wore aprons they practically swam in. They were silly girls. Watching them, she thought of Britney, Flaco's new *niña*, she'd be a contemporary of them at school. And of Claudia. If she were out of the picture, if anything happened to her, who would protect Claudia? And Angie?

After a bowl of soup, eaten so quickly she burnt her tongue, she climbed the stairs trying out different arguments in her head to convince her self-absorbed boss she had to go home. She had to leave. She was not going to back down on that.

The spacious upstairs hallway was flanked by gigantic portraits in gilded frames of the politician's relatives. Their stern faces glared at her as she hurried along the red carpet. The Rodriguez family had long been involved in politics and it was unclear whether their wealth had come first or if their government roles had lined their pockets.

The final portrait, directly outside the door to the master suite, was of Sr. Rodriguez. She'd always thought him older, sixty maybe, but looking up at his likeness now she judged him to be mid-forties —the age of her father.

When she tapped at the door, it creaked open a few inches at her touch. She waited. A minute later she tapped again then stepped inside. From the bathroom came muffled sobs. Carmelina crept back toward the door. *No, wait.* She had to tell her she was leaving. Leaving without letting her know would almost certainly find her without a job when she returned next week. The money she was putting aside was adding up so slowly. She couldn't afford to lose her pay here.

Sucking in a breath, she walked to the bathroom. *Sra.* Rodriguez sat perched on the edge of the large enamel tub, trying to gulp back her sobs. When she looked up, she scrubbed her face with the heel of her hands, trying to wipe her face dry.

Carmelina's heart softened. She crossed the room, sat beside the señora, and put her hand on her knee. It was the most familiar she'd ever been with the woman and she buffered herself for any anger that might come from her impertinence.

The señora sniffled. "I'm so embarrassed."

"No need, señora." She reached for a tissue and pressed it into the other woman's hand.

"You... you should call me Gina."

"Gina." Carmelina repeated the name. "You know, sometimes my mother calls me Lina."

"Why would I know that?" Gina's features crumpled, confused.

"Short for Carmelina." She tried to coax her to the obvious conclusion. "Gina rhymes with Lina."

"Oh. How silly of me." She pressed the tissue against her eye, tears starting to flow freely again.

"Gina, it's okay." Carmelina's stomach clenched. How could she put her foot down now? But she must and the clock ticking in her head grew louder knowing how little time she had in order to be on the right bus for home.

Gina slumped against her shoulder. Not knowing what else to do, Carmelina put her arm around her and rocked, cooing to her as she would with Ricky. Ricky. If Memo killed her, who would take care of Ricky? And Katya?

Gradually the older woman calmed. She pulled back slightly and stared at Carmelina, her eyes wide. "I'm sorry, I... " She shook her head and dabbed at her tears again. "Did you ever meet my sister?"

She had. She was younger than Gina, almost as beautiful but not quite, though difficult to pin point why. The sister was a tall woman with full curves, plump lips, and raven dark hair. "Once. She was here for lunch one day. I remember she was very kind to me."

"She was... she was... " Gina dissolved into tears again. Finally she managed to say, "She was kind to everyone."

"I don't understand. Has your sister passed?" The Rodriguez house did not seem to be a house in mourning. Aside from the obvious—the party planning—nobody was wearing black, and there'd been no ribbon over the door.

Gina squeezed Carmelina's fingers so tight she had to resist pulling her hand away. "Go close the door."

When Carmelina clicked the door shut, Gina motioned her into the dressing room adjoining the bathroom. Carmelina had cleaned in here before, always awestruck that one person could wear, or own, so many clothes. Gina grabbed her hand and pulled her down beside her on a narrow bench.

"My sister is missing," she said simply. "Disappeared."

Carmelina let the words tick past waiting for Gina to say more. Disappeared in this town was a poor substitute for the other 'd' word, the big 'D': Dead.

The pause lengthened. Gina took a deep breath and explained.

"She had started to date one of my husband's... business associates. At first, she was excited by the glamor. She'd always been a little envious of me, I guess." She shrugged. "I married up.

"I knew the man and tried to warn her, but she wouldn't listen and blew me off. At first, she was so happy. Then it started. In the beginning, things only a sister would notice. She laughed less at parties, talked less, shied away, and became timid." She turned to Carmelina. "She was always more outgoing than me. So bubbly. Maybe you remember her from the Miss El Salvador pageant? She won Miss Congeniality."

Carmelina didn't remember. Who aspired to be Miss Congeniality? At eleven, Carmelina had wanted the crown.

Gina's lip trembled. "Everyone loved her."

She ventured a question. "How long has she been gone? Is it possible--"

"That she's gone north?" Gina rolled her eyes. "Normally we talk every day, sometimes a couple times a day. I haven't heard from her in over a week."

"What about your husband's... associate? Can your husband ask him about it?"

"He promised me he would. He said he's certain it's nothing, a lover's quarrel maybe, but... but this morning he told me my sister's boyfriend would be bringing a plus one." She swallowed hard. "He's done with my sister and nobody has heard a peep from her."

"I'm so sorry," Carmelina said. "I wish there was something I could do."

"There is." Gina grasped her hand again. "You can be here for me. Help me choose a dress, and stay around to help during dinner. I swear if there isn't someone else here who knows what I'm going through, well, I'm just going to go mad."

"What about your friends? Surely there's someone else you're close to."

"Ha. You see this mausoleum I live in? The wives of my husband's friends are all snobs and he forbids me from seeing my old friends." She stumbled on her words. "I'm a prisoner in this house. My sister was the only one I was allowed to spend time with."

Carmelina would never have guessed. From the outside, Gina's life looked so desirable. At least to Carmelina it did. She gazed around the room, at all the clothes, the expensive shoes and purses. Even the lush carpet under their feet would stick out like a sore thumb in the tiny cinder block home she shared with her family.

"And... " Gina sighed as if to say she'd gone this far, she might as well go the rest. She lifted the hem of her skirt and revealed dark purple bruises on her thigh. "He beats me. Usually where no one can see."

Carmelina's jaw dropped.

"What? You think it only happens to poor girls?" She sucked in her breath and rushed on. "Oh, that was unkind. I'm so sorry. See, like I said earlier, my sister was the kind one."

Gina's words may have been harsh but she was right: Carmelina had been shocked.

"I'm sorry. I didn't know." Carmelina's mind raced. She felt for Gina, of course she did, and feared her sister dead in a field some-where—her bones would turn up months down the road or maybe never at all. But she needed to get out of this house. If she didn't leave right now, she'd have to run like a demon to catch her bus.

She stood, turned, and lifted her shirt. Gina gasped and gingerly touched the bruises on her lower back. With her shirt still bunched in her fists, she turned and let Gina see her abdomen.

Tears flooded Gina's eyes again. "I didn't realize you were married. I mean, I always thought maybe, since you have the baby—"

"I have two children. And I've never been married. I'm someone's *niña*."

Gina reached for her but Carmelina stepped back, the cold reality of what the next few hours could bring solidifying her determination. "These bruises are from the last time I showed up late. Gina, I have to leave and I have to leave *now*."

"Of course, of course, I... I didn't know. I... Oh God, Carmelina." Gina stood and embraced her. It was surreal. This morning she'd been Gina's servant, now the woman was embracing her like a long-lost friend. Carmelina's knee started to shake. She had to go. Gina held her at arm's length.

"If you ever need anything, you come to me. Okay, Carmelina? You have a friend in me now."

Carmelina nodded and Gina leaned in closer, eyes wide and filled with kindness.

"I mean it. You come to me and I'll do anything I can to help."

ON THURSDAYS, when she worked for *Sra.* Rodriguez, she often went home a little depressed. The gap between the comfort in the *señora*'s home and her own... her life seemed so charmed. But today, on the bus on the way home, she tuned in again to that humming train of optimism chugging through her. With the señora's offer of help, she had one more thing going her way to help get her on the road. One more door that might open when she needed to leave.

FIFTEEN

RICKY GONE 14 DAYS

May 29, 2019

"Stop. Stop, you're killing me." Angie giggled uncontrollably, arms flailing, and tried to wrench away from her two older sisters. Claudia and Carmelina crouched over her, one on each side, tickling her belly, her feet, then, exchanging a look, they started under her arms. "Not under the arms," Angie shrieked. "Not under--"

"*Mijas*, I can hear you halfway down the street." Lupe stood in the doorway, arms laden with parcels. Everyone paused and stared at her wide-eyed. She laughed, dropped everything on the counter, and joined them, pinning Claudia's feet and tickling her soles.

"Mercy, mercy!"

"Are you sure?" Carmelina laughed and poked her fingers into Angie's ribs.

"No more," she stuttered, "I can't take anymore. Mama, make them stop."

Lupe laughed, a glint in her eye, and settled back on her knees. Pushing herself up, she dropped a hand on Carmelina's shoulder and squeezed. "Seeing you with your sisters reminds me of the girl you used to be, *mija*. Always so cheerful and positive." The corners of her mouth twitched downward at the unspoken ending of her thought.

These days Carmelina was anything but carefree. Still no news from Diego and not knowing was tearing her apart, the constant worry like a chigger burrowing under her skin. Countless times throughout the day, she reflected how angry she would be with Diego if she wasn't worried sick for their safety. Restless at night, she tossed and turned until her sisters complained and hissed at her, and the covers twisted around her legs like vipers.

"Claudia, Angelina, clean up and help me get supper ready."

"Mama," Angie whined. "I keep telling you-everyone calls me Angie now."

Lupe raised her brows at her youngest. "Now girls." Claudia and Angie clamored to their feet. "Hands first." The girls raced to the back to wash up.

After peeking in on Katya, Carmelina said, "Do you mind if I shower while she's sleeping?" Her mother waved her off.

Under a stream of lukewarm water—the decrepit and much-repaired boiler no longer held the heat—she tried to force the negative thoughts from her head. It had been over two weeks since she'd watched the bus carrying Diego and Ricky pull away from the station. Two long weeks with no news. Despite her numerous attempts to contact him, none of her messages had been answered.

Her imagination was her worst enemy. The thugs from *Los Ochos* had caught up with them. They didn't make it into Guatemala. Someone kidnapped them before they reached the shelter in Chiapas. The list of horrible, life-ending possibilities marched through her mind without end.

"Lina." Claudia banged at the door. "Get out here! Mama says come now!"

She shut off the faucet, wrapped herself in a towel, and raced to the kitchen in time to see Lupe replace the receiver onto the ancient phone that hung on the wall. Carmelina's heart sank. She couldn't bring herself to speak.

Lupe put her hands up. "It was Diego. They're fine."

Knees weak, Carmelina lowered herself into a chair. "Why didn't he wait to talk to me?"

"He was racing to get it all in before we were cut off. Maybe he'll call back."

"Are they in Chiapas? What took him so long?"

"Breathe, *mija*. He said his phone was stolen. They couldn't stop in Chiapas because he didn't have papers for Ricky."

"I packed Ricky's birth certificate, everything I thought he'd need." She replayed the scene at the bus, giving Diego the food, the hurried goodbye as the thugs looking for him drew closer. "Oh, no. They must still be in my pack."

"They managed to get a ride with someone and they're somewhere between Mexico City and Queretaro."

She and Diego had looked over the map so many times Carmelina could easily pinpoint his location in her head.

"And then where?"

"He was starting to tell me that when we were cut off."

"But how will it be any easier for him without papers for Ricky at the U.S. border?"

"I don't have any answers. That's everything he said, pretty much word for word. He said he'd email you soon. And," Mama reached across the table to squeeze Carmelina's hand, "he said not to worry."

Carmelina leaned back in her chair, the stress of the last couple of weeks draining from her body. Her shoulders dropped, her chest opened, the tightly knotted chain masquerading as her spine started to loosen, link by gnarled link. Relief surged through her. "They're okay."

"They're okay."

"Is Ricky having fun with Uncle Diego?" A glance passed between Carmelina and her mother. Angie was still so young.

"Of course he is." Claudia punched her in the arm and dragged her back to the counter to continue wrapping the *tamales*.

"They miss them, too," her mother said. "It's a huge relief to hear from them. Maybe tonight you'll get a proper sleep," her mother said.

Carmelina glanced over at her mother, ashamed she'd been so self-absorbed that only now she noticed the dark circles beneath her eyes. Naturally she was also worried about her son and grandson. She reached across the table and placed her hand over her mother's.

As the shadows grew longer they sat together, expectantly glancing at the phone every few minutes, while Carmelina struggled to take it all in. Getting to Mexico on her own had been one thing. So many hurdles to clear before she could make that possible and now, she no longer had to run a race, she had to prepare for a marathon.

How would she ever find the money she'd need to get all the way to the U.S.?

SIXTEEN

June 4, 2019

The natives are getting restless.

It was an expression Carmelina's father had used since she was a small child. Sometimes about his children as they kicked and pinched and poked each other crowded into a single bus seat on market day. Sometimes listening to the radio or watching TV. Although he used it widely, for a variety of situations, his expression or tone always made it clear whether he was joking or deadly serious.

The voice in Carmelina's head today was deadly serious. She stood at the kitchen counter, with her back to the men, making sandwiches. She'd discovered if she treated it like an assembly line, it went faster and lowered the chance of someone brushing up against her from behind or trying to cop a feel while Memo's attention was elsewhere.

Mayo. Mustard. Ham. Cheese. Chiles.

" *niña*. Stop making a hundred sandwiches. Make one for me, then finish for the others."

She slapped bread on top of the cheese, placed it on a paper plate and took it to Memo, keeping her eyes on her feet as she crossed to the table. He grunted and she turned back to the counter, putting sandwiches together and piling them onto a plate which she placed in the middle of the table. The men greedily snapped them up. Not one of them thanked or even acknowledged her.

At the counter, she shoved a bit of leftover ham and crumbs of cheese in her mouth. The cook at her Tuesday job had taken a dislike to her and had served her only watery soup for lunch. She wiped the counter and propped herself against the wall on the far side away from the men.

Flaco pushed noisily through the door with Britney on his heels. He nodded in response to the men's greetings and disappeared down the hall.

"When's he gonna pass her on?"

Carmelina didn't see who said it. The other men sniggered. Her thoughts flickered to Claudia.

"When will you pass your *niña* down, Memo? She makes a decent sandwich."

"Yeah," slurred the one they called Lobo. He clinked bottles with someone. "Bros are supposed to share."

Carmelina's blood ran cold. Traditionally, there were only two ways out of being Memo's *niña*. If she managed not to piss him off, and lasted long enough for him to get tired of her, he would pass her on to the rest of the men in the house to share. And that was the better of the two options.

"Shut up," Memo snarled, his attention on the television.

Earlier today, armed men believed to be with Los Tigres, kidnapped over fifty people off a bus bound for the U.S. border.

Carmelina's breath hitched in her throat and she stepped closer to the TV. Video footage showed several men dressed in black with automatic weapons surrounding a bus half in the ditch.

Authorities are still going through the transport company's passenger list, but at this time it's believed most of the people taken were Central American migrants.

"Assholes," somebody grumbled.

According to passengers left behind, no women were on board but it's believed some children were also taken.

The announcer's voice over the grainy video was so matter of fact, his tone imbued with a practiced gravitas. The jumpy cell phone video captured a string of men, hands clasped behind their heads, stumbling away from the bus toward several black SUVs. One of them held the hand of a small boy.

Heart racing out of control, Carmelina almost flung herself at the screen. It had been over a week since Diego called. The email he'd promised had never come. She struggled for restraint. Everyone had heard the story of what happened at the factory three weeks ago and knew Diego was missing, disappeared likely by the rival gang, but since he also wasn't LC-14, it was of no concern to them. Nobody knew for sure that he'd escaped to the north. And no one outside of her own family knew Ricky was gone.

"Niña, aquí." Memo grabbed her by the arm, guided her across the small living room, and positioned her over the back of the filthy couch. He kneed her legs apart.

After another story, the announcer looped back to the kidnapping. If she turned her head just so, barely an inch, not so much that Memo would notice, she could follow what was happening on the screen out of the corner of her eye.

But she could also see Lobo. He watched Memo, his dark eyes narrowed. She averted her eyes before he caught her looking.

She strained to hear the announcer over the rhythmic slap, slap, slap of Memo's flesh against hers. In the corner, a young girl she'd never seen before, gagged, her cries muffled. The man standing over her cracked his hand across her cheek.

"Memo, how'd you train that one to be quiet?"

"Flaco trained her," called out one of the other men.

Behind her, Memo tensed. Getting Flaco's hand-me-downs cemented his position; he was second in command. It also made him a target, as numbers three, four and five jostled for favor.

Carmelina had quickly learned that he also resented those favors. Despite his cruelty, he didn't command the same respect as Flaco. A day would come when he'd want to be leader.

Carmelina didn't miss Flaco but at times like these, she missed the small comfort of a closed door.

"I already told you once today to shut up," he said. The men laughed uneasily before falling silent.

A few seconds passed. Memo shuddered, his thumbs digging deeply into her hips before he stepped back. "Go on," he said, "get the hell out of here. Be on time tomorrow."

Eyes down, she tugged her skirt into place. Memo walked away and a chair scraped across the kitchen floor. She slanted a look over to see Lobo rising from the table. His tongue flicked over his upper lip. Frantic, she kicked her underwear off her ankle and toed the flimsy material under the back of the couch.

Memo was halfway across the kitchen, heading for the door. She closed the distance between them, skirted him as widely as possible so he didn't get angry for her cutting him off, and fled out the door to a chorus of the men's laughter.

———

THE STREETS WERE dark and lonely. Most shops had closed. This time of night she took a longer, more circuitous route home, street stall to street stall, hurrying toward the pools of light on every second or third corner.

There was always a risk she'd attract attention as she passed the stalls. Once two men followed her most of the way home until one of them recognized her as Flaco's.

Aside from the light, she knew the stalls offered little in the way of safety. If someone threw her in a car or dragged her away screaming or pushed her in an alley, nobody would help her. Nor would anyone come forward later. There would be no witnesses. But at some point, word would get to her family, and they'd have some idea what happened to her. Some closure. No need to look for bones.

A few blocks from the intersection that led to her street, she popped into a *tienda* and handed over her money for tomorrow's breakfast in order to top up her phone.

She breathed a sigh of relief when she finally reached home, closing the door firmly and sliding the lock into place. Everyone slept. The house still and quiet. She'd hoped for a note, praying her mother had also seen the news, praying there'd been another phone call from Diego, but the kitchen table stood empty except for a covered plate. She lifted the edge of the cloth to expose the *tamale* Mama had left for her. She practically inhaled it.

After checking on Katya, she sat at the kitchen table desperate for more information on the kidnapping. She used her phone to scour Facebook, Twitter, and several news sites. All she found was the same grainy video of the small boy clinging to the larger man's hand as they were led away at gunpoint into the black SUVs. She peered at the video trying to make out the color of the boy's shirt. Could it be Diego and Ricky?

Her phone pinged and her balance flashed on the screen embedded in a ticking clock.

She tried another search and found a link to a YouTube video posted seven minutes ago. She clicked over to the site. Hit play. The circle spun while the video loaded. And spun. She hit play.

Her phone pinged and a message popped up.

Please add money to your account to continue using data.

SEVENTEEN

June 8, 2019

The bus that serviced Carmelina's route into San Salvador was on its last legs and had been for a couple of years. Spewing diesel through a rusted exhaust pipe, fenders rattling and shaking like Elvis, it rumbled and jostled through the many stops, picking up children and young mothers, old ladies with baskets of fruit to sell on the sidewalks of the city and school girls in short plaid skirts with white knee-high socks, men and women heading to work and buskers hawking wares or singing songs, until it was ready to burst.

The driver, José Luis, a fixture for as long as Carmelina had been taking the bus, played the same tired *cumbia* playlist full blast. All windows that weren't broken or welded into place were permanently down. Those lucky enough to be seated beside one leaned into the humid morning air. Even with the slight breeze created by the bus's stuttering forward movement, it wasn't much cooler outside.

On a good day the ride took forty minutes and, if she was lucky and the bus wasn't running too far behind schedule, the

connecting bus into the affluent suburb where she worked took
another twenty.

Today she managed to secure a window seat. Wedged in
beside her was a mother with two young children about the ages of
her own. The baby drooled over her girl's shoulder, the toddler
stood between Carmelina's knees and her mother's, playing with a
sticky toy on her mother's lap. Occasionally she lifted the toy,
knocking Carmelina's forearm and leaving sticky fingerprints of
whatever syrup was on her hands.

Carmelina edged her phone out of her pocket. For days now
she'd compulsively checked her email waiting for the promised
update from Diego. No notifications. Regardless, she scanned
texts, WhatsApp, and FB messenger. Then the phone dinged and
a messenger notification flared on the screen.

*Lina, can you get somewhere to video chat with me? I can wait
twenty minutes. Please hurry.*

With shaking hands, her nerves combined with the constantly
rolling of the bus, she sent back a confirmation. They were almost
at the transfer point. Another ten minutes. That left her ten
minutes to get to the Internet cafe. Her knee started to tremble
against the back of the seat in front of her. She set the timer on her
phone and watched the minutes tick down. Nine. A taxi cut them
off, the driver yelled and blew his horn. Some of the passengers on
that side of the bus leaned out their windows to add their curses to
the bus driver's.

Seven. The bus crawled to a stop to let several people off.
They filed along the sidewalk below her window, disbursing as
quickly as ants under a magnifying glass. José Luis did not pull
back into traffic.

Six.

People stood shoulder to shoulder in the aisle, there was no
sightline to the front. Five. There were still eight blocks to cover
before the transfer point. Patience wasn't a virtue here, it was an

indisputable fact of life. Passengers murmured among themselves and checked their watches but remained quiet. The bus and its schedule was simply another reminder of a life Carmelina had no control over.

Unable to sit still longer, she stood and pushed her way past the girl and her children. Shoved and wedged herself through the aisle until she reached the back door, and pressed the button.

Three.

She pressed again, the bell dinged repeatedly.

"Baja," she yelled.

"The driver's not here," someone yelled back.

Heart pounding, she forced her way to the front of the bus, other passengers grumbling as she struggled past them. She leapt down the steps onto the sidewalk and dodged through the early morning throngs. Street stalls and vendors lined the street. Customers yelled orders over the heads of people closer to the counters. In front of one of the stalls, José Luis waited for his breakfast.

Four blocks ahead on the other side of the street was an Internet cafe. Ignoring the complaints of people around her she ran, dodging through traffic at the intersections, until she reached the small storefront.

In the doorway, she braced herself and struggled for breath. The woman behind the front desk nodded her toward an empty work station. Carmelina's fingers flew over the keyboard. Fifteen minutes had passed. She logged into her Facebook account, navigated to messenger, hit video, and watched it ring. Once. Twice. *Come on.*

"*Hermanita.*" Diego's face filled the screen.

She blew out air.

"Diego. Where are you? Are you both okay?"

"We're fine."

"Where are you? I saw the news about the kidnapping, and—"

He held a hand up. "We didn't go that way."

"How would I know that? You haven't been in touch."

Diego's mouth twisted. He looked tired, his cheek bruised, his hair—always his pride—matted to his head. Regret rippled through her.

"I'm sorry, I was just so worried. Tell me, where are you now?"

"We're in Juarez. I'm traveling with a few others and we've hired someone to get us across tonight."

"Tonight? Promise you'll text me when you get across."

He shook his head. "Still no phone."

"Can you borrow someone's to send a quick text?"

A shadow flitted across his face. "It's hard to know who to trust. I don't want anyone else to have your contact information."

"But I thought you said you're traveling with others."

"I am. Still..."

"What? Tell me."

"Nothing is straightforward on the road. It's hard to know who's a friend and who is setting you up. You'll see for yourself soon. By next week, I'll have a job and start sending money."

"So soon?"

"The guy I came up from Chiapas with has a cousin living in Texas. Says he can get us work right away."

"Did you get the scan I sent? Ricky's birth certificate?"

"I just printed it out." He glanced over his shoulder. "We only have a couple more minutes. There's someone here who wants to say hello."

Ricky's face filled the screen. He bounced on his uncle's lap and put his nose to the screen, planting a virtual kiss. "Mama!"

"Ricky." Carmelina fought to control the tremor in her voice. Relief and love and fifteen other emotions surged through her. "*Mijo.*"

"Mama, I'm gonna be three soon!" He waved four fingers in front of the camera.

Diego tucked one of his nephew's fingers down and whispered, "This is three. Like I showed you."

"Three, Mama! I'm gonna be all grown up!"

Her grin stretched wide. "Yes you are, sweet boy, next month. Are you being good for your uncle?"

"Yes, Mama. We're playing a hiding game and we have the most points of anybody."

"Lina, we have to go."

"Wait. Ricky, you listen to your uncle, hear? Do everything he says. Never let go of his hand."

"I'm sorry..." Diego's face filled the screen as he lifted Ricky from his lap. "We have to go. I'll be in touch with you as soon as I can."

"Wait. Diego. Promise me you'll let me know as soon as you're safe on the other side."

"I'll do the best I can. *Te amo, hermanita.* Pray for us tonight."

The call ended. She whispered to the screen, "I pray for you every night."

EIGHTEEN

June 15, 2019

"Diego promised he'd be in touch," Carmelina said, twisting a paper napkin to shreds. "I can't stop imagining the worst."

She and her mother sat at the table, ignoring the supper dishes the girls had stacked on the counter before heading to their bed to finish their homework.

Her mother's face fell. Carmelina kicked herself. She kept stepping in it. Why underline how much danger her son and grandson were in?

"Oh, Mama, I'm sorry."

"No, *mija*. I know what they're facing. Her mother's gaze strayed to the phone on the wall, then landed on Carmelina's cell laying on the table, never far from her hand. "Still no word. It's been a week."

"I know." They'd heard nothing since the day he was supposed to cross the border. Meanwhile, in northeastern Mexico, dozens of bodies had been uncovered in a mass grave in Tamaulipas. Authorities were trying to find a link to the bus kidnapping by *Los Tigres* but so far no one had claimed responsibility. She was so grateful Diego and Ricky hadn't traveled that way.

Mama twisted her hands, seemed to decide something, then spoke. "I talked with *Sra.* Lopez today. Alejandro was sent back. She met him at the bus yesterday morning. She said..." Her voice broke but she recovered quickly, lifting her head to look Carmelina in the eye. "She said the bus was packed, everybody that got off looked tired, hungry. Some government workers were there, gave them all two *pupusas* and shoe laces."

"Shoe laces?"

"Who knows. Some aid worker decided everybody needed shoe laces. Look, there's a cooperative effort now to send people back where they've come from. It's possible—"

"No." Carmelina shook her head and crossed her arms. "I'm sorry for Alex, of course, and for his mother, but—"

"It's possible they're on their way back here right now."

"No."

"When will you follow?"

"What?"

"I'm not stupid, *mija*. I'm sure you're not planning on having Diego raise your son in a strange country."

"I'm putting money away."

"You know how dangerous it is for women to go on their own."

"Diego will send money. We already have a deposit with a guy to pay for a coyote."

"Which guy?" One way or another, everyone in this town was connected. There wasn't too much her mother didn't know about.

"Lagarto."

"Hmph. *Mentiroso.* He's been a liar since before he learned to crawl."

"Mama." Carmelina chuckled.

"Just like his father. He was no good either. That *cabrón's* been gone over ten years and still hasn't sent a dollar home to his family."

Carmelina's laugh deepened. It was rare to hear her mother talk like this. "Are they sure he made it?"

"They claim he did." She cocked her head and grew serious. "Are you prepared for the worst?"

"Meaning what? No word again ever? Not knowing what happened?"

"That, and—"

She pointed her finger at her mother. "I can't even think about my son, or brother, as a pile of bones somewhere. Not right now." She pierced her mother with her gaze. "All I have right now is hope."

"And prayers," Lupe said. "We keep praying and we wait for their call."

Her mother could have her prayers. As far as Carmelina was concerned, she'd given God up when he'd abandoned her several years ago. Fair was fair. From what she'd seen, God provided only for the men.

The front door jiggled against the frame. Someone pushed against it, the knob rattled and turned in the wrong direction. They exchanged a look. Carmelina rose. Before she stepped away from the table, Kike flung open the door and stumbled in. He leaned over and brushed his lips across his mother's cheek, lost his balance, and grabbed her shoulders to right himself. The sour smell of cheap beer rolled off him in waves.

"*Mijo.*" Lupe waved her hand in front of her face. "You stink like the town drunk."

"Having a chat with your eldest daughter?" He skewered Carmelina with a resentful look. "Or should I say your favorite?"

"Mama doesn't have favorites, Kike. You're drunk."

He bellowed an ugly laugh. "Missing your brat, I suppose?"

Carmelina braced herself, palms down against the table top. Before she could open her mouth, Lupe stood up between them.

"Kike, that's your nephew you're talking about. Don't you have any shame?" She grabbed his elbow and steered him away. "Go take a cold shower."

"Hungry," he mumbled.

"I'll cook you something while you get cleaned up. Go." She pushed him out of the room and came back to the table.

"He's drinking more than usual these days," Carmelina said.

"Too much." She lowered her voice to a bare whisper. "I've been thinking about Claudia and Angelina, what we talked about. I wrote to my sister."

This was good news but she feared her mother didn't understand, or didn't want to acknowledge, the urgency of the situation.

"Why not call?"

She shrugged, the lines on her face etching deeper. "There's so much between us. We'd probably argue. Better she has a chance to take everything in, digest it, and answer in her own time."

"We're running out of time."

Her mother splayed her hands in front of her.

"Did you—"

"What? Apologize?" She puffed out a breath, dismissing her question. "I have nothing to—"

"Do it for Claudia," Carmelina said. "And Angie."

"Yes. Not in so many words, but yes, I apologized. She'll come through. We're still blood, after all. Like I taught you. Family first."

Carmelina embraced her. "Thanks, Mama. I know that cost you a lot."

"*Ay*, pride is overrated, *mija*." She stepped back and smiled at her. "Kike will be done soon. I better cook something to soak up the drink in his gut. Why don't you go help the girls with their homework?"

What she meant was, why didn't she get out of Kike's way and not piss him off more. Which worked for her. The less she had to see of Kike the better.

NINETEEN

RICKY GONE 35 DAYS

June 19, 2019

"I'll cut your tits off, *niña*."

Carmelina blanched. Her stomach hollowed out as surely as if he'd punched her in the gut. One of the older girls had lost her breasts and so much blood she'd almost died. That was months ago and in another *casa loca* in a nearby neighborhood. She'd heard the girl's family had sent her away, somewhere safe deep in the jungle near the Guatemalan border.

"Yeah, I thought that might get your attention." Memo grabbed her breast. "And it would be a shame, cause you have such nice tits. Nice plump *mamacita* tits. Oh, wait ..." he made a show of feeling the weight, "you need them now for the baby. So you better get smart, *niña*."

He trailed the knife down along the full line of her breast, bringing the cold blade against her nipple, and press until the knife pierced the swollen flesh and a drop of blood oozed out. He brushed his other thumb across it, then held it to her lips. Her tongue flicked out to clean it, her eyes never leaving his.

"Beautiful tits, *niña*." He squeezed her again, cruelly twisting and digging his thumb deep into her flesh, while, with his right hand, he sheathed the knife in his belt. "It would be such a pity."

He released her and strode to the door. "Get dressed and make me dinner. And hurry the hell up." He slammed the door on his way out. Flaco was gone for the night so Memo had taken over his room.

Carmelina collapsed onto the edge of the rumpled bed. Her entire body shuddering uncontrollably with fear. She fumbled for her clothing, blinking back tears.

She had zero doubt Memo would carry out his threat if she didn't keep him happy.

She'd already almost outlasted her time. He couldn't cast her off so quickly as he had the three *niñas* before her—Flaco would be insulted if he discarded his gift so fast—but he'd given her clear enough notice that her days were numbered.

What hell her life was shackled to Memo.

Not to mention Lobo, who was growing progressively cruder in his comments and gestures toward her. The brute gave her the creeps and continued to challenge Memo, spurring his anger to the forefront while Lobo jockeyed for second spot to the top.

Where was Mama's God now? Had he abandoned her too?

Gallito threw open the door and flicked his thumb back toward the kitchen. "Dinner. Now, Memo says."

And why should she pray to the same God who allowed young boys to be groomed into such hateful bastards? Still, she crossed herself, straightened her bra over the breasts she hoped to keep, and hurried to the kitchen.

TWO HOURS LATER, in the company of the final shards of fading light filtering through the trees, Carmelina made her way home, her mind still wild with fear—a tangible pinball of Indian rubber—so many possibilities and dead-ends bouncing around inside her head it was making her dizzy.

Along the street, vendors were closing up storefronts. The familiar rattle of the aluminum shutters and metal gates being rolled down into place surrounded her. Street lights flickered, silent sentinels preparing to burn and stand witness through the night.

Tomorrow was Thursday. Gina would be her salvation. If she gave her money, she could be on a bus in a few days. Better she go hungry to the border than be disappeared or bleed to death. A vivid memory of the cold steel of Memo's knife against her nipple lingered, and she placed her hand protectively over the small cut he'd inflicted.

Gina had said she'd do anything to help her. For now, she pushed other thoughts to the side and focused on that.

Her cell rang. She fished it from her pocket. Unknown. Out of country. "Hello?"

"*Hermanita.*"

"Diego?" She stood in front of a *farmacia,* the display window crowded with posters advertising painkillers, generic viagra, and cough syrup for babies at discount prices. She leaned up against a pillar, her back to the window, keeping her eyes on her surroundings. "Did you cross? Are you okay?"

"We're fine. We're in El Paso."

"Oh." Relief surged through her. She fell silent, forced herself to breath. "I was so worried."

"I'm sorry. I couldn't call before and I don't have long now, I'm using someone else's phone."

"I thought you said—"

"It's different here. Everything is different here. Listen."

"You're scaring me."

"We're fine," he said again. "But... We were picked up by *migra* the day after we crossed the border."

She struggled for words but found none, her tongue glued to the bottom of her mouth.

"I'm in detention. It's every bit as horrible as we've heard. I just got out of the *hielera* this morning. I don't know if I'll ever feel warm again."

"How long will they keep you?"

Diego scoffed. "As long as they like, apparently. Or they'll deport me back home." The wire hummed between them, a scratchy static as she waited for him to speak again.

When she couldn't bear it any longer, she blurted, "Ricky? How is he doing with all of this?"

"They separated us when they brought us in."

"What do you mean they separated you?"

"Sometimes they keep the children with mothers, but they refused to leave him with me. I'm in adult detention, men only."

"Where is he?" Carmelina's voice rose. A man walking a large pit bull on a heavy chain slanted a look in her direction.

"He's with the children. In a building where they keep the unaccompanied minors."

"But he's not unaccompanied. Didn't you show them the birth certificate I sent you?"

A muffled voice came through the line.

"Who was that?"

"Lina, I have to go. Listen, Ricky is nearby. He's safe. I'm working on getting a lawyer but... I won't be able to send money right away. Are you okay?"

Am I okay? You mean aside from having my life threatened by breast amputation a couple hours ago? And finding out that's the least of my worries 'cause my son has been taken from you, and is now somewhere alone? She swallowed hard and shoved the hysteria

threatening to bubble out her mouth farther down into her gut.
"Don't worry about me."

"Have you saved more money? Is there anyone you can ask to help?"

"Some, not much. Tomorrow I'm going to ask a woman I work for. Her sister is missing and she said she'd help me."

"Do it. Don't forget what we talked about. It's critical you cross the border here before you turn eighteen.

"And go back to see Lagarto. If you have to, beg him to get you a coyote. Do whatever it takes. All the horror stories we've heard are real. Don't try to come on your own. It's too dangerous."

"*Basta.* Enough." The second male voice was clearer now, louder.

"Diego, wait." She wailed into the phone. A woman exiting the *farmacia* looked over, caught the look of despair on Carmelina's face and quickly turned away, scuttling off in the other direction down the street.

The phone went dead.

TWENTY

June 20, 2019

"Gina's not here."

"What do you mean she's not here? You told me this morning she'd be back later."

"Yes, well...," Marta shrugged. "The *señor* sent her to visit her sister."

"Gina found her sister?"

The housekeeper had rolled her eyes. Advised her to mind her own business.

The whole conversation had taken less than a minute, yet Carmelina replayed it all the way home on the bus. For over an hour she flipped it, seeking answers in each curt response. It didn't matter how many ways she looked at the questions, the answers never came.

Had Gina's sister been found? Or had Gina also been disappeared? She hadn't noticed anything gone from her closets or bathroom, but then she hadn't been looking. The housekeeper had only told her the truth as she'd been leaving.

If she could count any of it as truth.

These days truth was an elusive thing she barely recognized.

The end result was the same. She was crushed. Her best chance at immediate money was gone.

LAGARTO TOED AT THE GROUND. "That's not really how a deposit works, *chica*."

"I realize that." Carmelina kept her tone even. She despised this man but for now he held all the cards which afforded him as much respect and deference as she could muster. "But circumstances change. If you can't get me a coyote, then I need the deposit back." She crossed her arms and stood up straighter. A scrap of dignity didn't come easily negotiating at the edge of a junk yard.

"I don't keep that kind of money on me." Lagarto was tall and lean with a long pointed nose and skin that scabbed and flaked on his forearms. He regarded her with heavy-lidded eyes. He resembled his namesake as much as a man ever could. It wasn't hard to see why the nickname had been pinned on him. Plus the whole lying thing. She didn't trust a word that came out of his mouth.

"Then loan me the money to go north." The conversation was becoming circular—he'd already said no to a loan before they started arguing about the deposit—but she was desperate. All she could think of was Ricky alone and crying for her. "I'm good for it."

"How?" He cocked his head to the side. "Your family has no land or you would have offered it sooner. No land, no vehicles, no rich relatives. You're poor as dirt. You expect me to believe you have something new for collateral?"

"No, but Diego is already there. Both of us will work. We'll pay you off."

He scoffed. "Diego disappeared."

"Yeah. He disappeared to *El Norte*."

Lagarto's eyes narrowed and his tongue flicked out over his top lip. "*Verdad?* You telling me the truth?"

Diego's whereabouts needed to remain a secret but it was a risk she'd have to take if she expected Lagarto to front her the money for the coyote. She nodded. "I am. Don't make me beg. Come on, you've known me my whole life. Diego, too. If we say we'll pay you, we will."

He held up a hand. "Even if I did have the money to loan you, I couldn't."

"Stop talking in riddles."

"You're not with Flaco anymore."

"So?" Her patience was running thin. This detour to Lagarto's had already made her an hour late for work. If she stayed late at work, she'd arrive late for Memo. It was a domino effect that wouldn't turn out well.

"You forget that Memo is my second cousin."

Carmelina's jaw dropped. She stepped back as if he'd slapped her in the face. If Memo knew she was planning to leave...

"I won't tell him. It would be bad business for people to find out I can't keep secrets. But..." he shrugged, palms up. "I can't help you either."

Memo. Everywhere she turned she was blocked.

If he wasn't going to help her, she wanted her damn money back.

"Then our deposit? Given the circumstances, you should be honor bound to return it." She resisted placing any emphasis on "honor". Sarcasm would not help her win this battle.

The deposit Lagarto was holding was enough money to get her most of the way through Guatemala. Together with the money she had stashed at home, she might get into Mexico, make it as far as Chiapas. There were resources there. Shelters. Other people traveling. Information about which routes were safer, which to avoid.

He spat on the ground, his eyes shifting to a rusted pile of wreckage off to the side, then he jammed his hands in his pockets and met her gaze.

"I'll see what I can do. Come back tomorrow."

CARMELINA HAD TO FACE FACTS. Ugly facts. Without Gina's money, and without Lagarto's connections, the possibility of hiring a coyote to guide her and Katya north had burst into flames. Now all that was left was ash.

But ash wasn't nothing. She would take that ash and forge it into something tangible and like a phoenix, she would rise. Diego had found a way, she would too.

That night, once the house was quiet, she dove deep into the Internet, browsing through Twitter and migrant Facebook groups.

What she discovered sparked a small glimmer of hope. Every three to four weeks, once enough people had signed up to travel together, a caravan left on foot from Santa Ana. The next one was estimated to leave by mid-July. That would give her time to plan the rest of her trip and have as much in order as possible.

Nervous about discovery, her conversation with Lagarto still fresh in her mind, she sent a private message saying her cousin wanted to join the caravan. She provided a fake name.

Seventeen days. She marked the date on her calendar and fell into bed, body thrumming with dread and exhaustion. But beneath her permanent state of fear, a seed of excitement and possibility was starting to grow. Salvation.

Finally, from the huge pile of shit her life was mired in, she'd found a twig of hope to cling to.

TWENTY-ONE

RICKY GONE 38 DAYS

June 22, 2019

Nestled in the corner of her bed, Carmelina remained fixated on her baby's sweet face, her heart full. Katya, finally sated, was drifting off to sleep. Her eyes became unfocused then her lids heavier as she fought against them until she relented and the land of dreams overcame her.

The thought of Katya growing up here was unimaginable. She wanted for her child what every mother wanted. *Una vida mejor.*

Ricky was smart. Carmelina was sure Katya would be too. She wanted her to have an education, be able to stay in school, to develop a career that would afford her, yes, a better life.

Moving carefully she placed the baby in her basket and tucked the soft pink blanket, finely embroidered with turquoise-browed motmot birds by her mother, over her chest.

"Lina?" From the other side of the curtain, Angie's voice came in a stage whisper.

She turned and slipped out, holding her finger to her lips. "What is it?"

Tears welled in her little sister's eyes. "Have I been bad?"

"What?" The question came out of the blue, taking Carmelina by surprise. "I'm sure you haven't. Why would you say that?"

"Because..." her lip trembled. "Because Claudia has new clothes and I didn't get any."

"Are you sure?"

"Claudia has a new skirt. I saw it when I was looking for my pen that rolled under the bed. She's hiding it under the mattress."

Oh, no, he didn't. Carmelina saw red. She crossed the short distance and slipped into the corner Angie shared with her sister, with Angie close on her heels. Claudia, cross-legged on the bed, looked up from the book she was reading.

"Is it true?"

"Is what true?"

"Do you have a new skirt?" Carmelina's hands went to her hips. It was a favorite move of her mother's. A vision of herself as an older woman flashed before her.

Claudia shook her head, her eyes darting to Angie.

"She does." Angie lifted the covers and tugged at a scrap of cloth peeking out from the foot of the bed.

"Careful." Claudia leapt from the bed and shoved Angie away. "You'll rip it, stupid."

"Don't call me stupid."

"Girls, shhh. Katya just went down. Angie, stand over there. Claudia, show me what you have."

With great care, Claudia removed the skirt from its hiding place and held it up to her waist. She pivoted. "See? It's cute."

Carmelina snapped it out of her hand. It was the same type of skirt Kike had given to her. "Kike gave you this."

"I..."

"Don't lie, Claudia." Carmelina turned, the curtain twisting over her shoulder as she pushed through it.

Claudia protested, her voice growing stronger. "All right, he gave it to me!" She followed Carmelina to the kitchen. "Traitor," she said to Angie.

"I'm no traitor."

"Girls." Lupe looked up from the chilies she was chopping at the kitchen table. "You'll make me old before my time."

Carmelina held the skirt out like an errant puppy and shook it. "Kike gave this skirt to Claudia."

Her mother's brows shot up. "That's nice. It's unlike him, but—"

"You still don't get it, do you Mama?"

"You won't speak to me like that in my own home, *mija*." Lupe stood and pointed toward the corner. "Claudia, Angelina, back to your bed."

"But Mama—"

"Claudia, now."

Claudia swiveled on her heel and flounced across the room, disappearing with Angie behind the curtain.

Lupe sat down and motioned Carmelina to take a seat. She lowered her voice. "I already talked to Kike. I told him Claudia would not be doing any work after school."

Carmelina dropped the scrap of flimsy material onto the table.

"What about your sister? Did you hear back yet?"

"I talked to Kike, *mija*. He's going to leave her alone."

"This is the same skirt he gave me."

"It looks brand-new."

"I mean it's the same type of skirt. The one I wore when he sold me, Mama."

"No." She shook her head. "Claudia's twelve."

"Mama, I was only thirteen. You know once Flaco has her it will be too late. Why take that chance?" Her heart was pounding. She sucked in a long slow breath and met her mother's eyes. "Can't you call your sister, Mama? Please."

Lupe took a deep breath and exhaled slowly. "She already answered. She said no."

"When?"

"Last week. The same day we got the news that Diego was in detention. I didn't have the heart to tell you." She rushed on. "But I will watch them like a hawk. No harm will come to them."

Carmelina bit her tongue. There was only one way to protect Claudia. And Angie. She'd have to take them with her. Her head spun. How could she possibly do that? She barely had enough money to take herself and Katya. But she did have a little bit of time to figure it out.

"When are you leaving?"

"In two or three weeks," she said.

"What's happening in two or three weeks?" Kike's voice boomed over her shoulder. She hadn't heard him come in. As usual lately, he reeked of drink.

"We're going to a special craft market at the church," Lupe said.

Kike scoffed, his dark eyes drilled into Carmelina. "I bet you're going to *El Norte*. It's only a matter of time until—"

"Are you calling your mother a liar?" Annoyance laced Lupe's voice.

That stopped him but not for long. He laser-focused his attention on Carmelina.

"From what I hear, you're past your sell-by date. Better not let Memo know you're going. Maybe a little birdie will tell him." He squeezed his elbows in against his rib cage and flapped his hands.

She jumped to her feet, grabbed the skirt and shook it in his face. "You gave this to Claudia. You can't sell her the way you did me."

He laughed. "Sell you. Ha. You've got an active imagination, girl."

Rage surged through her. Reason deserted her. "You better leave her alone or—"

"Or what?" Kike loomed over her and dug his fingers into her collarbone.

"Stop it, Enrique." Lupe grabbed his arm and tried to drag him away.

"What the hell is going on here?" Her father's voice roared over them all. He stepped between Kike and Carmelina, dwarfed by his son, and glared up into his eyes.

Lupe started to sob.

"Get the hell out of my house until you cool down." Angel pointed to the door.

For a few seconds, everything was suspended. Carmelina's breath hitched in her throat. It looked like Kike would disobey him.

But then he went, yelling to her over his shoulder as he did. "You learn to mind your own damn business, *hermanita*, or I'll kill you myself."

From his mouth, little sister sounded more like a curse. He didn't have to lift a finger to kill her and he knew it. All he had to do was let it slip in the cantina that she was leaving and Memo would take care of the rest.

Angel put his hand on her shoulder and pushed her gently into a chair. He motioned to her mother, "Lupita, come sit," then sat himself.

Trembling, Carmelina took a breath. "Mama, please. Please send Claudia and Angie away."

"What's this?" Angel's eyes darted between the two of them. "Send them where?"

"I want them to go live with Auntie."

"Lupita?" He looked to his wife, brow furrowed.

Mama shrugged. "I already wrote to her, she said no. They're fine here. In their own home. With their family."

"Papi—"

"Your mother knows best."

"Papi, you know she has a blind spot where Kike is concerned." Her eyes darted to her mother, but Lupe kept her gaze fixed on the table.

Her father slammed his palm on the table, the skin on the back of his hand dark brown and puckered, weathered like an orange peel left too long in the sun.

She stayed quiet. After a few minutes, her mother pushed the chiles across the table for her to continue chopping, and rose to fix a plate of food for her husband.

Carmelina picked up the knife and sliced through the pulpy flesh.

Fifteen days. As little as fifteen days to figure out how to take two more mouths to feed on the trip to *El Norte.*

She could no more leave her sisters behind than she could leave Katya.

TWENTY-TWO

June 27, 2019

Carmelina stood at the kitchen counter slurping sweetened instant coffee, and regretting her early departure from her warm bed. The neighbor's stupid rooster didn't understand the concept of dawn and had started crowing at barely four. On the upside, it gave her time to grab a bite to eat before rushing off to work.

Lagarto had returned her deposit. He'd pressed her up against the wall, claiming he needed to charge a small tax for giving her back the money. She'd kneed him in the groin, reminding him he was Memo's second cousin.

The cash was hard won. It still wouldn't be enough.

THE PHONE RANG, the sound shrill and demanding in the predawn light. She lunged for the receiver before it had a chance to ring again.

"*Sí?*"

"*Hermanita.*"

"Diego. Where are you? Are you okay?"

"I'm still in detention in El Paso."

"Did you find a lawyer?"

"Who is it, *mija?*" Her mother raced into the kitchen, forehead creased. Nobody called at this hour with good news.

"Diego." Into the receiver she said, "Did you?"

"I'm glad I caught you before you left for work. Is that Mama?"

"Yes. Is the lawyer going to get Ricky back?" Behind her, Lupe switched on the light. A soft lemon hue filled the room.

"Good."

"Do you want to speak to Mama? Speak to me first."

"I have bad news, *hermanita.*" He sucked in a long breath. Then his words came out in a tumble.

"There's no easy way to tell you this. A few days ago, Ricky was transferred out of the unaccompanied minors building."

Carmelina caught her mother's eye. She came over to stand beside her, arm around her shoulder. "Is he on his way back? Did they put him on a bus?"

"I don't know."

"What do you mean you don't know?"

"Nobody seems to know where he is."

"What? How the hell do you misplace a three-year-old boy?"

"Look, *migra* says he was transferred to a more permanent facility either out east or farther north, maybe even west, but..."

"But?" She held her breath, her hand clenched around the receiver. Her body thrummed like a thousand steel cords had snapped into place, holding her upright, rigid.

"They claim they've lost the records. I've called everybody I can—"

"Wait. When did this happen?"

"At least three days ago. That's when I found out."

"You've known for three days?" Her voice rose. Claudia slipped into the kitchen, rubbing the sleep from her eyes.

Diego rushed on. "I wanted time to find him. So I'd have some answers for you. I never dreamed they would lose him."

Lose him. The words ping-ponged through her skull.

"How can they not know?" Carmelina bit back the sobs closing her throat.

"Some kind of computer crash. At least that's the story, they—"

"Oh, my baby." Carmelina dropped the phone and fell to her knees.

Lupe grabbed the receiver twisting through the air like an abandoned child's swing. "*Mijo,* tell me what you know." She motioned to Claudia, pointed to a kitchen drawer. "Get me a pen. And paper."

"A pen? What?" Diego's voice came through the line, confused.

"I didn't mean you. Tell me what you know."

Claudia dug in the drawer, found a pen, flew into her room and returned with a notebook. She turned and bent so Lupe could use her back to write on.

From the floor, Carmelina watched through a film of tears.

Lupe scribbled furiously, her scratchings punctuated with questions: Who else? What was the name of that agency? Is there a website? What's the number?

Finally she stopped writing, handed the notebook to Claudia, and squeezed Claudia's shoulder.

"How are you, Diego?" Nodding her head, she listened. She turned her face away and her shoulders shook.

Carmelina stood, put her arm around her mother, and gently pried the phone from her hand.

"Diego."

"*Hermanita,* I'm so sorry. I'm doing everything I can from here."

"I know. Keep trying. We'll start calling from here. Let me know if you hear anything."

"Of course."

The distant sound of a buzzer coursed through the line.

"What is that?"

"Breakfast. I have to go line up. Don't lose hope, *hermanita*. We'll find him."

"HE COULD BE DEAD."

"Don't say that." Lupe turned from the counter and held out a cup of coffee. Carmelina took it and slumped into a chair. Claudia had been sent to wash up before breakfast.

"You've seen the news. Seven kids have died in those detention centers in the last six months. Who knows how many others are missing or unaccounted for?" She raked her nails down her cheeks, then wrapped her arms around her chest and rocked.

Lupe cradled her head to her breast. "*Mija*, keep the faith. We'll spend all day on the phone, we'll figure this out."

"No. I need to go to work."

"Today?"

It was Thursday. A plan was forming in her mind. "I need to see my boss's husband. He's high up in the government, maybe he can help me."

"Fine, you go. I'll make calls from here. Do you have phone credit?"

"Some." She tossed the last items she needed in her bag, shot a look at the clock.

"Take this." Lupe turned and dug to the back of the upper shelf where she kept a small tin with emergency grocery money.

"Top up your phone. Do as much searching as you can on the bus and call me if you have any new leads."

TWENTY-THREE

"Gina's still not home?" Carmelina stood in the kitchen, trying to keep her face open and friendly. She smiled at the housekeeper who seemed determined not to give an inch.

The woman raised her brow. "This again?"

"Just tell me. Has she been home since I was here last week?"

Marta huffed, shook her head, and turned her attention back to the mixture she was stirring in a large ceramic bowl.

"And the *señor*?"

"Don't you go bothering the *señor*." She slammed the wooden spoon onto the counter and stared at her with beady little eyes that had always reminded Carmelina of the neighbor's pig.

She took that to mean he was home. Turning, she grabbed the cleaning supplies from the closet beside the pantry and hurried through the house.

At the end of the wide hallway that extended off the foyer, ornately carved double oak doors led into the *señor's* office. It was off limits. The rules, clearly laid out and reinforced multiple times when she was new, were that the *señor* was never to be disturbed and this room was not to be entered for any reason.

Fuck that.
She rapped on the heavy wood.

AT LUNCHTIME, Marta pushed a plate of beans, rice, and beef in salsa in her direction. Carmelina ate in silence, soaking up the salsa with a rubbery tortilla. Apparently the miserable woman wanted to be sure she understood she didn't merit fresh ones.

When she was done, she took the plate to the sink, rinsed it, and placed it on the sideboard on top of a stack of dirty dishes.

As she crossed the room, the housekeeper spoke. "*Señor* says you're to see him when you're finished your lunch."

"You might have led with that." She rushed toward the door.

"Bet he fires you. I told you not to bother him." The woman's petty words chased her down the hall.

When she tapped at the door, Gina's husband bade her to enter and waved her to a large easy chair in front his desk. She perched on the edge, the stiff leather cool against the backs of her legs, hands folded in her lap.

He was a powerful man, a rich man, and—she couldn't help remembering—a man who had probably disappeared his wife. Early afternoon sunlight streamed in through the large window behind him, silhouetting his face, his features in shadow, and creating a halo around his head.

Would he be her salvation or her ruin?

Jabbing at a paper on his desk with his index finger, he cleared his throat. "I made a few calls. I'm afraid I came up empty." He lifted both hands, palms to the sky.

"There's nothing—"

"I'm at a dead end. There's nothing more I can do."

He came out from behind the heavy marble desk and walked around to where she was sitting. He leaned against the desk and crossed his right ankle over his left foot. She was surprised to see compassion in his face.

As if explaining why the sky is blue to a child, *just because it is*, he said, "I'm a municipal politician. I called my contacts with the federal government and one of them has a friend near the border. He called back before lunch and said there was some kind of computer crash, data lost, that kind of thing."

She opened her mouth but he held up his hand.

"It sounds like a cover up to me, too. I swear that government up there is crazier than ours."

He shrugged. "I'm truly sorry, Carmelina, but there's nothing more I can do."

In all the time she'd worked there, he'd never called her by name. Had barely acknowledged she existed. Never in a million years would she have believed there was a kind man beneath his polished and distant exterior. She almost wanted to ask about Gina.

"What are your plans?"

"What do you mean?"

"Do you plan to go north?"

"I..."

"Good. Keep your plans to yourself. It's safer that way."

He turned his back to her, stepped away, and opened a door in the large credenza that ran the length of the window. Shielding the opening, she heard him punch in numbers, then a small bell dinged.

He turned back to her, closed the distance between them and extended his hand, palm open. A stack of crisp bills, American dollars. Carmelina gasped.

"You look so much like Lupita it's uncanny."

Carmelina stepped back, shocked again. "You know my mother?"

"We were, uh, friends, school mates, long ago. She was a beauty at your age—as you are."

Her mouth dropped. There was too much happening at once, she couldn't find her words.

He pressed the money into her hand, closed her fingers over it. "Go on. I wish you all the luck in the world, and Carmelina? Stay safe."

She stashed the money deep in her apron pocket and backed toward the door, nodding her head. She was so flustered she half bowed. "Gracias, *señor*."

He put a finger to his lips and waved her off. "Go home early. Leave now."

TWENTY-FOUR

Head down and tucked into the shade of an overhang, Carmelina waited at the transfer point, clicking links to various U.S. Immigration and Homeland Security websites.

Thanks to Gina's husband, she'd be home early enough to avoid anyone waiting at the bus station for her, leaving her most of the afternoon to help her mother with calls. Today, Memo could go to hell.

She still couldn't believe her good luck. She'd been prepared to beg Sr. Rodriguez—had begged when she spoke to him before lunch, complete with crocodile tears, real ones. That her mother had once been friends with someone of his standing made her head spin.

"That's her." She glanced up when she heard a man's voice.

Two older guys advanced through the crowd milling around her waiting for their buses. They looked familiar.

"It's his sister."

Right. The guys looking for Diego at the bus station, the morning he'd left with Ricky. She backed farther into the crowd. How had they connected her to Diego?

They pushed their way directly to her. The taller one grabbed her arm and dragged her off to the side. Around her the crowd parted like the Red Sea, quick to sidestep obvious trouble.

"Where is he?"

"Who?"

"Your asshole of a brother. Diego. Where the hell is he?" He slammed her against the wall. Out of the corner of her eye, sunlight glinted off metal. Then she felt the point of the knife below her eye socket, pressing into her cheek. Warmth bubbled up around the blade as it pierced her skin.

"I don't know who you're talking about."

The smaller one laughed then leaned into her from the other side. "She's as stupid as he is. We found you on Facebook, *chica*."

She'd scrubbed her Facebook account of photos. Hidden all her friends and locations. So had Diego. It had to be Claudia or Angie. They didn't get it. Nothing she said to them could stop them from posting for their friends. In their preteen minds, they couldn't conceive of the reach they had or the predators who surfed their accounts looking for... well, looking for exactly this type of information.

The guy holding the knife to her face spoke again. "Where. Is. He?"

Offense was her only defense. "Why are you asking me? You killed him."

The pressure on the blade increased.

"Break it up!"

Over the thug's shoulder, Carmelina saw a policeman pushing his way toward them. The crowd didn't part so easily for him.

The two guys stepped back, jeered at her. "You got lucky this time, *chica*. But don't forget. We know who you are."

"And," added the other, "we know where you live."

"Go on, clear this area."

They slunk away.

The young cop looked two, maybe three years older than Carmelina. Barely twenty. A shock of light hair fell over his forehead. He grabbed her arm and steered her to a quiet spot away from the bus stop.

She was grateful but she didn't have time to fill out a report. She needed to get home. "Officer, I'm so grateful," she started.

"Yes, you are." He held his hand up and rubbed his fingers together in the universal sign for money. She looked over his shoulder. Nobody looked their way.

The wad of cash Gina's husband had given her rested against her pelvis, sticking against her skin, and locked in place by her underwear.

She reached into her bag, pulled out a small handful of notes, and pressed it into his outstretched palm. "Yes, officer. Gracias."

Disdain marred his handsome features. "That's not nearly enough."

She sputtered. "I'm a cleaner. That's every cent I made today."

He grunted and waved her away.

People were filing onto the bus, her bus. She queued up and managed to get the last seat open at the very back, beside an old man who coughed and hacked all the way home. At one point he passed her a soiled handkerchief motioning to her face. In the screen of her phone, she wiped away the blood that had trickled down her cheek.

On paydays, she always kept money aside for Memo. A habit, but one she almost didn't follow today since she planned to go straight home. But habit was habit, so she'd done it anyway.

Her simple routine had been her salvation and nobody had even guessed she had other money with her. She'd been so anxious to get home she hadn't dared count it, she just knew it was a lot. More cash than she, or any of her family, had ever had.

Her leg started to shake, her knee bumping against the seat back in front of her. She fixed her gaze on the familiar passing landmarks outside the window and counted off the minutes until she would be safe at home.

TWENTY-FIVE

Lupe hung up the phone. "Another dead end."

Carmelina glanced up from the table. "Why not take a break, Mama. How many hours have you been on the phone?"

"We're going to find him." She peered at the sheet of paper in her hand and dialed another number. After thirty seconds, she started punching in single digits, one every few seconds. "Damn phone menus."

Like other mothers and daughters her age, she and Lupe often butted heads, especially lately. But she had great respect for her mother. She looked soft and subservient, but underneath she was strong as steel. Though Angel was the Garcia figurehead, the family had known for years who really ran the show.

It was late afternoon, sliding into evening. The offices up north were starting to close. Again and again, Lupe was unable to reach anyone and left pleading messages begging someone to call back.

Claudia and Angie had been sent to their bed with sandwiches that Carmelina had quickly thrown together. They remained quiet, their innate radar for disaster keeping them out of the way.

A knock came at the door. Lupe peeked through the crack in the kitchen curtain and waved her hand to shoo Carmelina away. She scampered across the floor and slipped behind her curtain.

Lupe opened the door.

"Carmelina?"

"Did you still not learn any manners, young man?"

A pause. "*Disculpe. Buenes tardes, Sra. Garcia.* Is Carmelina here?"

"Please."

Behind the curtain, Carmelina stifled a laugh. Lupe was in a mood attempting to school Gallito. She hoped she didn't push him too far.

He repeated his question, speaking slowly and enunciating each word. "*Señora,* is Carmelina here, please?"

"She's sick." Lupe swung the door closed.

Gallito pounded on it. Lupe coughed and Carmelina heard the telltale creak of the hinges as she reopened the door.

"Young man—"

"Um, *señora,* her boyfriend will want to know how long she'll be sick."

"A few days, I suppose. Women's problems. You old enough to know about those?"

After a few seconds of silence, her mother spoke again. Carmelina could easily imagine the little rooster-headed juvenile thug-to-be twisting with discomfort.

"Tell her *boyfriend* she'll come see him when she's better. And not before."

The door closed this time with a definitive click. Carmelina crept back into the room. Lupe peeked through the kitchen window again.

"He's gone."

"I'm not sure that was wise," Carmelina said, returning to the table.

"I don't care. I'm sick of it, sick of all of it." She sank into a chair, and covered her face with her hands. "What is this world coming to, *mija*?"

The stress and fear of the day overtook her. She reached for her mother's hand and squeezed her fingers.

When she spoke, she kept her voice low. "I got some more money today, from my employer's husband. I think I should take Claudia and Angie with me when I go."

"You have enough money for a coyote?"

"No, of course not. He gave me some money, not a fortune."

Her brow crinkled. "Why would your employer's husband give you money? You mean like an advance?"

Carmelina bit her lip. "No, he gave me almost seven hundred dollars."

Lupe gasped. "For doing what?"

"I asked him to help me. I told him Ricky was missing and I had to leave." She squirmed in her chair, uncomfortable under her mother's disbelieving eye. "He said he knows you."

"Knows me?"

"Yes. Sr. Rodolfo Rodriguez. He called you Lupita."

Her mother's hand flew to her lips. "Rudy. I didn't know you worked for him."

She shrugged. "I worked for his wife. How was I to know he knew you."

Leaning forward, her mother lowered her voice. "Don't tell your father about this. He won't be happy about that man giving you money."

"Sr. Rodriguez said you went to school together."

Lupe flicked a hand. "Such a long time ago. It was barely more than a flirtation and then, of course, I met your father around that time."

"But you went to the same schools as someone like Sr.

Rodriguez? Mama, your family must have more money than you've let on."

Her eyes narrowed. "Yes, but I chose your father. And when I did—"

"They disowned you?"

"Not entirely."

And yet, it explained so much. Why she barely knew her maternal grandparents, the rift between her mother and her sister. How was she only putting this together now? "But Mama—"

"It's ancient history, *mija*. And it's disrespectful to your father to go on about it."

It wasn't hard to put the pieces together. When her parents met—so the story went—her father had newly arrived in the city from the campo and was working as a gardener.

"Wait. Papi worked as a gardener for *your* family?"

Her mother pursed her lips. "I said, this is the end of it."

She'd never dreamed he might have been working for her mother's family. Her mother had fallen in love with someone who her family considered beneath her. And when she'd chosen love over riches and social standing, she'd found herself cast out. She glanced around the small shabby home they all shared and wondered if she'd ever regretted her choice? She looked up at her mother to find her face a granite mask. Right, the end of that then, but there was still the question of her sisters.

"What about Claudia and Angie? Can they come with me? We'll join the group leaving from Santa Ana—we'll be safe going in a crowd."

Lupe lifted her head. "Safer maybe. But not safe. It's still much too dangerous. I don't even want you going."

"I have to go now."

"Your sisters won't want to leave. Claudia has a new crush at school, and you know Angie. She follows whatever Claudia says."

"But Kike—"

"I refuse to have this same argument again. We'll ask the girls."

She called for Claudia and Angie. They practically fell through the thin curtain, probably straining on the other side to hear every word.

"Sit down, girls. We have something important to discuss with you." Lupe looked to Carmelina. "Go ahead."

"I'm leaving soon," she said simply. "I want to take you with me."

Both girls shook their heads. Angie glanced at her mother.

She cleared her throat. "It's dangerous for you to stay here. In *El Norte* we can be with Diego and Ricky."

Angie's lip trembled. She spoke to Lupe. "I don't want to go. What if I get lost?"

"I won't let that happen," Carmelina said.

"Is it Uncle Diego's fault that Ricky is gone?"

"Of course not." Carmelina touched her sister's arm.

"Then how can you say you won't lose us, too?" Angie pulled away from Carmelina and threw her arms around her mother's neck. "I'm staying here with Mama."

Carmelina turned to Claudia. She was the key to convincing Angie.

"Claudia, this thing with Kike wanting you to work after school—"

"You did it." Her voice held a hard edge of defiance.

"I didn't have a choice. And Claudia—"

"I'm not going. And if you don't drop it, I'll tell Kike you're leaving."

Lupe gasped. "Claudia, tell your sister you don't mean that." Her eyes darted to Carmelina and her lips set into an expression of resolution Carmelina knew well. "Tell her."

"I'm sorry. I didn't mean it."

"Claudia, you have no idea, no idea, what's in store for you if you keep listening to Kike. Please, both of you need to come with me."

"No. I won't tell, but I'm not going either. You can't make us."

Icy tendrils of fear tightened around Carmelina's heart. It was true. If she couldn't make them leave, she couldn't save her. She tried again.

"*Hermanita*, it'll be years before you can leave on your own. Please."

Claudia stared defiantly at Carmelina.

Lupe cleared her throat. "Go back to your room, girls."

Angie slipped off her mother's lap. "Can we have a snack?"

"Grab some crackers and go back to your room."

Lupe drummed her fingers against the table top while the younger girls rummaged through a cupboard. When they were gone, she started to speak then fell silent.

Carmelina waited for the words, expecting them like blows: I told you so.

But what her mother said next surprised her.

TWENTY-SIX

Snippets of the conversations that had dogged her day crowded in on Carmelina through the long black hours of the night. Computer crash. Her boyfriend can wait. We know where you live.

Panicked, she bolted upright. She'd forgotten to warn her mother. In the utter chaos of the day, she hadn't even mentioned the two guys looking for Diego. Everyone was so used to seeing her bruised and abused, nobody had even mentioned the cut on her cheek. They'd learned if she didn't tell, it was better not to ask.

She hadn't even thought of it again herself. Their bullying and threats barely a blip on a day that had spiraled out of control.

Which led her to remember how they'd found her. She'd intended to talk to Claudia and Angie again about their Facebook photos. What else were they sharing that would come back to haunt the family?

But mostly, the phrase she could not quash, the one that shouted over and over in her head, cutting her to the core and wounding her repeatedly?

Diego's voice saying "I never dreamed they would lose him."

Lose him.

They'd lost her son. Misplaced him like a thrift store sweater. How do you lose a toddler?

She closed her eyes and pictured him the last day she'd seen him. Bouncing with excitement, eyes glowing, he had scooted up the steps onto the bus ready for the adventure. Ready for anything.

She thought she'd come to terms with letting him go with Diego.

But who could be ready for this?

She never should have let him go. What had she been thinking?

If she could turn back time, would she risk her brother's life to keep her son at her side? No. In the moment, with no other solution, she'd made the right decision.

But in hindsight? In hindsight everything looked different.

Was he alone? Cold? Hungry? Was he scared?

Her precious little boy. He'd be so frightened. Separated from the only person he knew, alone in a strange country, and left to fend for himself for over two weeks already.

He's not yet three! She squeezed the pillow to her face to muffle her sobs. Her beautiful, innocent, vulnerable son alone in the world.

If he was still in this world.

She couldn't go there. Her mother was right. If she imagined him already dead, she would spiral out of control.

She had to get a grip, pull herself together.

Ricky needed her.

She drew in a breath, forced it deep into her abdomen, and she saw once again her mother at the phone that afternoon. Hour after hour, punching in numbers, leaving messages, pushing on, refusing to give up.

She was her mother's daughter. Surely she'd inherited some of her strength. Something shifted deep inside her. It surged up from her belly and she wanted to roar aloud.

She was tired of being a victim. Flaco's punching bag and now Memo's. And at home, always under Kike's cruel watchful eye. Forced to grow up too fast, forgotten by the school system, cleaning other people's shit for barely enough money to buy *masa*.

Downtrodden? Perhaps.

Defeated? Hell no.

It was time to step up, draw on the strength she'd been born with.

Her son needed his mother.

He needed her.

Failure was not an option.

By the time the neighbor's rooster crowed, her mind was made up.

TWENTY-SEVEN

RICKY GONE 44 DAYS

June 28, 2019

Carmelina pushed back the curtain letting her eyes adjust to the darkness. She carried a small bag to the table. There in the dark, still as a statue, sat her mother.

"Mama, what are you doing up so early?"

"I'm a mother too, you know."

"I can't wait."

"I know, *mija*."

"Will you help me get Claudia and Angie ready?"

Lupe shook her head. "I've changed my mind."

"But you said last night it would be best."

"That's when we were talking about the caravan from Santa Ana."

"It would still be best. I have money now. I can pay for buses. We'll be fine."

Lupe shook her head again, resolute.

"How are you going to deal with Claudia's attitude?"

"She's twelve. She's going to push back on everything. It's part of being twelve."

"Still..." She tried a different argument. "If they come with me now, there's no chance they'll tell Kike."

Lupe stood. "I will put the fear of God into that girl, don't worry. If she doesn't want to be grounded for life, she'll stay quiet. Besides—" She held up a finger to quiet Carmelina's protests. "I've given this a lot of thought. If you take them now it's too much of a red flag. Kike will know you're gone. And you know I have little control over what he'll do once he knows."

She was right. At least she was acknowledging Kike was beyond her control, but leaving Claudia and Angie behind?

"Mama—"

"No. I've thought about it all night. It's safer this way. They'll slow you down. You'll move faster on your own with Katya."

"Could you take them to Santa Ana when they're ready to go so they can join the caravan?

Even as the words left her mouth, she knew the idea that two pre-teen girls could navigate safely to Chiapas and beyond on their own was crazy. Even if they did go with the group.

"I'll send money for them to come as soon as I can. Promise you'll keep them out of harm's way. Promise me, Mama."

"With all my heart, Lina."

Lupe walked to Carmelina's bed and collected Katya, cradling the infant against her shoulder.

"Don't wake her." Carmelina needed stealth, a crying baby would make her stick out from the shadows.

"Shhh, I won't." Lupe closed her eyes, her nose buried in the top of Katya's head as she breathed in her familiar scent. A tear trickled down her cheek as she settled the baby back in her basket on the table.

"*Mija*, they say that eight out of ten women on the road are—"

Carmelina shook her head. "It won't be worse than what I deal with here every day, Mama."

The inevitability of assault on the road was well-known. Border officials, police, cartel, the *polleros*, even other migrants became a threat to the women who continued to be treated like second-class citizens every step and every kilometer of the way north.

All she could do was hope it wouldn't happen to her. Or if it did, that she would live through it.

Her mother's tears flowed freely and she clutched her in a tight bear hug, like she never wanted to let go. She spoke into her ear, voice shaky. "You have protection?"

"I had the shot." It was almost two months since she'd had the birth control shot—she had over a month of protection left. With the money and only herself and Katya to worry about, she was confident she'd make good time.

Lupe sniffled and collected herself. "You'll have a head start at least. That cocky little rooster will tell them you're sick for a few days."

"I don't think Memo will be that patient. He might wait another day, two at the most.

"And what about Kike?" Her eldest brother was the bigger threat. If he could make a few bucks sharing information, she had no doubt he would.

"Leave Kike to me. Leave it all to me. I'll watch over the girls and I'll keep calling every day until we find Ricky. The minute I have news, I'll let you know." She paused before continuing.

"Also, I forgot to tell you that I took all of Ricky's paperwork and had notarized copies made. Just in case. So if you lose anything, I'll have backups here."

Reluctantly Carmelina pulled away, hefted her bag over her shoulder, and lifted Katya. "I'll stay in touch as much as I can."

"You take care of yourself and Katya, *mija*, and find our little boy."

Outside in the street, the milk vendor's cart rumbled past, wheels creaking in the still air. Once he reached the end of the street, four blocks away, he'd start working his way back, blowing his whistle to sell his wares.

The copper ribbon against the horizon confirmed daylight was not far off. Their neighbors would soon be stirring.

If she was leaving, the time to go was now.

Without a glance backward, she stole down the street.

PART TWO
FINDING TRUE NORTH

TWENTY-EIGHT

At this early hour, only three buses warmed up, spewing blue plumes of diesel into the still humidity. The smoke hung in the air like cartoon speech bubbles. Beyond the buses parked side by side all the way to the back of the yard at San Salvador's central station, one of the drivers used a discarded tire for a bathroom. An emaciated tan-colored dog, her teats brushing the tall grass near the fence, scrounged for scraps. Carmelina wondered absently if her litter was nearby.

"Carmelina."

She looked over her shoulder, hoping another passenger would answer the call. The yard was already filling with passengers, but not yet as busy as it would get later closer to the time she normally left.

Head down, she edged her way behind a couple of men smoking and arguing over last night's football game.

Her name rang out again. A woman calling her. "Carmelina."

She peeked out from behind the man's shoulder. Britney, Flaco's new *niña*, hurried across the yard toward her, waving frantically. Carmelina's eyes darted over the milling passengers and beyond Britney, looking for Gallito or one of the other men from the house. Her heart raced. There was nowhere for her to run.

The young girl reached her and paused to get her breath. "I thought I'd be too early. I thought you took a later bus."

"What are you doing here?"

"You told me if I needed to talk I could meet you here."

"Right. Of course." She stepped away from the men to a quiet spot. "Well, normally I do take a later bus."

Now what? One of her father's favorite expression came to mind: No good deed goes unpunished.

She'd told Britney to meet her here to talk. Why did the girl have to show up today of all days?

Another of her father's expressions came to mind: Timing is everything. She hoped to hell her good intentions and Britney's bad timing wouldn't ruin her chance of escaping.

"I've never met your baby." She reached out and stroked Katya's cheek. "Do you always take her to work?"

"No..." Carmelina's mind raced to keep up. She hadn't slept a wink, her brain was crammed with details and plans for the days ahead. "But I have an appointment at the NCC later and won't have time to go home to get her." She shrugged. "My employers can be picky about me leaving early."

"I bet."

Carmelina regarded Britney, waiting for the younger girl to explain why she'd come. Britney chewed her lip and toed at the ground.

"Why don't you tell me what's going on?" Carmelina's eyes darted over the waiting passengers again. She recognized a few people, but no one that set off any alarms.

"Flaco is..." She dissolved into tears and threw herself against Carmelina's free shoulder. "Oh, Carmelina, I have nobody. If I tell my mother what's going on, she'll kill me."

Not if Flaco kills you first.

"Don't you have a sister? A friend at school?"

"Nooooo." Britney wailed, her tears soaking Carmelina's shoulder. "And now, now..."

Behind her, the bus driver snapped the door open and people started filing onto the bus. She'd really wanted to get a good seat, so she could keep a lookout, but also so she could imprint the town on her mind as they rolled away. She would probably never see it again.

"Now what? Just tell me, chica."

She blubbered uncontrollably. "I'm pregnant."

Carmelina clasped her tighter. Son of a bitch. Flaco refused to use condoms. Why hadn't she taken time to talk to this girl before and help her find birth control?

She knew why. She didn't know her. Didn't know if she could be trusted. Birth control was frowned upon. Merely suggesting it could bring a world of misery down on her own head if Britney wasn't able to keep her mouth shut.

"They said..."

Carmelina glanced over her shoulder. Behind her, most of the passengers were on the idling bus. She resisted pulling out her phone to check the time.

"Who said?"

"The nurse at the NCC said my hips aren't developed enough. That, that, they might have to cut me open when the baby comes."

Carmelina hugged her tighter. This girl, with no one to help her, no one to love her. She wanted to pull her on to the bus and take her with her. Like she'd wanted to take Claudia. And Angie. And every girl she could find until all the buses in all the country were overflowing with girls and racing north to the border. Out of this godforsaken country and away from a life going nowhere.

The driver revved the engine. It wouldn't be long now.

"Trust the nurse at the NCC," she said. "Esther's a good woman and she'll help you."

She extracted herself from the young girl's arms. "I'm sorry, Britney. I have to go. My bus is leaving."

"But isn't that your bus?" Britney pointed at the bus two down that Carmelina normally rode to work. Torn, unable to come up with another cover story on the fly, Carmelina realized she'd have to get on her regular bus if she didn't want Britney to blow her cover.

"Be careful," she said to the younger girl. "Don't let Flaco know that we talked. It will—"

"Only make him more angry with me?" Britney's lip trembled. "I hate my life."

"I know, sweetheart."

Carmelina stroked her head, shushing her. Britney reminded her of a younger version of herself and she hoped, with all her heart, that she would be around in three or four more years to make her own escape.

But for now, like so many other things in her life, she needed to let her go.

She walked over to her bus and filed into the line of passengers boarding. As her foot hit the first step, Britney called out to her again.

"Can I come again? To talk to you?"

"Of course." The lie slipped over her teeth like cold liquid. Having to hold out such flimsy hope to the girl made her throat squeeze shut.

She climbed into the bus and found a seat near the back. She peered out the window. Britney had already turned away. She watched her walk through the yard. The girl's shoulders had drooped even lower, an air of defeat surrounded her. She knew she'd let her down. But there was nothing she could do for her now.

Carmelina's head was still spinning from yesterday's news and the chaos it had brought. It was hard to believe it had been barely twenty-four hours since Diego's call.

A month and a half had passed since Diego and Ricky had made this same exit. At least they'd been on the right bus.

She considered her options. If the timing was good, she might be able to intercept the Santa Ana bus if the driver let her out near the Pan-Am Highway interchange. But if Memo looked for her later, the driver would remember. The passengers would remember, too.

There was nothing to do. She'd have to ride into town, and then transfer to the central station and catch a later bus to Santa Ana.

To the west, a dark cloud of mist cloaked the summit of the Santa Ana volcano. It mirrored Britney's demeanor as she'd slouched away from the bus station and echoed her own spirits.

TWENTY-NINE

"She's my cousin." Julio winked, the ever-present toothpick rolling from one side of the bus driver's pink fleshy lips to the other. His mouth reminded Carmelina of the Mr. Potato Head toys she'd coveted in a storefront when she was a child.

The Guatemalan border official, leaning nonchalantly against the rail at the top of the stairs, tipped his hat back. "You have a lot of cousins, Julio."

Julio grunted an affirmation and reached to shake his hand, the quick exchange of bills practiced and barely perceptible. Carmelina would have missed it if she hadn't been sitting almost on top of it.

She'd been in the front seat since changing buses in Santa Ana. Having asked directions for the next bus to the border, the rotund driver had informed her he'd be driving the express bus to Guatemala City and she could stick with him.

Eager to avoid milling around the bus terminal in Santa Ana, and possibly being seen, Carmelina had hit the easy button and gone along.

After an awkward early lunch together, the driver drinking too much and asking too many questions, they'd set out, Julio insisting she sit in the front to keep him company and so he could protect her through Border Control.

She'd done worse for less. He kept reaching over to tap her knee, grinning like a lunatic when she fed Katya.

The official, tall and lean as a mesquite bean pod, his body bulging in odd places, towered over her. She tilted her head back and offered a weak smile.

"Where you headed?"

"Guatemala City."

"Nature of your visit?"

She offered the words Julio had coached her with. "To visit my aunt for a few days."

The man made a note on his clipboard and moved on to the next passenger. Carmelina exhaled. Her anxiety had built over two long hours while the bus crawled in the snaking line of traffic to the border.

The mid-afternoon heat was stifling. Diesel fumes from the tractor trailers and other buses surrounding them oozed in the open windows combining with the stench of body odor and fast food and something else underlying it that she couldn't quite identify, a lingering musty smell that seeped out of the filthy upholstery and cracks of the bus's interior.

None of it mattered. By some crazy lick of luck, she and Katya had secured safe passage across the first border. She offered up a silent prayer.

Julio stepped off the bus, lit a smoke and chatted through a window to the truck driver in the next lane. With his attention elsewhere, she checked her phone. She'd secreted it inside the fold of Katya's blanket with the ringer off.

No news from her mother. Still nothing from Diego. Dismayed, she tucked it away. Once the bus was moving again and she was safely on the other side, she'd send her mother an update.

Twenty minutes later, the official ambled back down the aisle, patting his overflowing pockets. She wondered how much her fellow passengers had paid. And how much she would owe the driver later.

Stepping down out of the bus, he clapped the driver on the back and they shook hands heartily before Julio clambered back onto the bus, adjusting his belt and dragging his pants up over his considerable belly. Winking at her, he settled back onto his seat, the worn springs squealing in protest.

A HEAVY HAZE clung to the horizon obscuring all but the summit of the volcano that dominated the city's landscape. Julio kept reaching over—he'd progressed from brief taps to familiar squeezes of her knee—and pointing: Pacaya. Pacaya.

He spoke to her like Spanish wasn't her first language. Short bursts. Mostly single syllables, rarely a sentence. And always with a gesture.

"Pacaya," he said again, jabbing his finger toward the large windshield.

Yeah, good. She got it. Pacaya. She'd grown up under the shadow of the Santa Ana Volcano. Pacaya wasn't her first rodeo.

Traffic slowed to a crawl as they approached Guatemala City. Behind her, passengers shifted in their seats.

South of Cuilapa, a multi-car accident had closed the Pan-American for over two hours. They'd milled around the bus, hunkered down in the meager strip of shade, patience growing thin. She'd averted her eyes when they finally idled through the accident scene, but not quickly enough. It surrounded them. Rivers of blood and mangled steel amid a sea of emergency responders.

In the city of Cuilapa a protest march delayed them another

hour, the traffic police laughing off the driver's concerns about his schedule.

The delays had put them solidly into rush hour. Guatemala City was ten times the size of San Salvador. She'd never seen anything like it. She kept thinking they were in the city only to realize they were still in the sprawl of the outer suburbs and slums. The bus rolled haltingly a handful of depressing meters forward, kilometer after kilometer, while around them drivers blew horns and jockeyed for minute advancement in alternate lanes.

Thanks to Britney and the circuitous express bus, she was hours later than she thought she'd be. She'd left in such a hurry, she hadn't thought about a backup plan. Her strategy was simple: keep moving.

The delays did nothing to allay her anxiety. Her pulse jumped in her throat. Picking up on her distress, Katya fussed constantly, kicking the blanket off, her small red face crumpled in discomfort.

Outside the window, poverty pressed up to the litter-strewn roadside. A shanty town of cardboard walls and heavy black plastic masquerading as roofs, hidden behind a parade of glossy billboards selling lipstick and gold watches. Mothers dragged dirty-faced children along the side of the highway. Old women struggled under bushels of sticks balanced on their shoulders.

How much longer until they reached the terminal?

She was lost without her phone. At one point while they'd been stopped for the accident, Julio had wandered off. She'd tried to text her mother, only to discover she had no signal. In the last minute rush to leave town, she hadn't thought to buy a package she could roam with.

Once she got off the bus, she'd buy a local SIM card. She needed to know if her mother had heard from Diego. Or if anyone from the different departments in the United States had called her back.

Her breath caught in her throat. She'd forgotten, yet again, to warn her mother that the thugs from *Los Ochos* knew where they lived.

Julio squeezed her knee. "Pacaya."

Yeah, yeah. She focused her gaze on the horizon and tried to push the panic that surged through her like hot lava back down into her belly.

Pacaya.

THIRTY

Bright white spotlights crisscrossed the dust-filled air like drunken disco lights and illuminated the yard of the bus terminal. Passengers filed off, grumpy and crumpled. Julio insisted she wait until everyone was off. When the bus was empty, he stepped down and opened the cargo door. Within seconds he was gone from sight as a sea of people pressed around him, all anxious to be on their way.

Finally, she stepped out of the sweltering metal prison and down onto the ground, onto foreign soil. El Salvador lay many kilometers behind her.

Heat leeched up from the pavement through the thin soles of her shoes. She'd have to buy shoes better suited for walking. Right after she found a SIM card.

For now, she needed to find the schedule for the next bus north. She edged to the side. Julio was still busy with passengers. Spotting the door to the terminal, she headed inside.

In the bathroom she splashed water on her face before changing Katya. She wiped her chubby arms and legs with cool water, Katya cooing and smiling up at her, then snapped her into a fresh onesie. Carmelina's clothes melded to her skin, damp with sweat. She wanted to change into her fresh shirt, but decided to wait until she had time to bathe properly.

As she stood under the large departure board reading the schedule, someone grasped her arm.

Julio didn't look happy about having to track her down. He put his thumb to his mouth, to indicate a bottle, and tilted his head back. "*Cerveza.*"

"I don't drink," she said, shifting Katya.

His eyes narrowed and anger started to bubble below the surface, his cheeks reddening.

"It's been a long day. Come on, we'll get a room, and you and the baby can rest." His fingers wrapped around her upper arm, and he started to step away, expecting her to follow.

She planted her feet firmly and tried to shake him off.

"I need to keep going."

This much was true. Fearful of Flaco and Memo's reach, she needed to keep pushing toward the Mexican border. She had no idea if they could find her in the sea of humanity that was Guatemala City, but standing in the main bus terminal made her an easy target.

It was also true that she had zero intention of sleeping with Julio.

"No." He shook his head and tightened his grip on her arm. "Better buses in the morning."

She cocked her head and smiled. "Julio, I'm so grateful for your help. I couldn't have asked more of my own father."

"Your father?" He loomed over her, his face darkening. His mouth opened and closed. She couldn't shake the image of Mr. Potato Head. "Look, chica--"

She pried his hand off her arm and backed away. "I have money. I'll pay you. Whatever you had to pay at the border."

"I don't need your money, *puta.*" His voice rose. People nearby glanced over, then quickly looked away. "I did you a favor. A big one."

"I'm no *puta,* Julio. You didn't have to help me." She strode through the open terminal in the direction of the wide front doors. With him yelling behind her, she spilled through and out onto the sidewalk. She broke into a run, weaving through the after-work crowds.

Half a block down, an alley led into a street market. She plunged into the chaos, entered a stall selling large bags, and hid behind a pillar to watch the street. A few seconds later, he walked by.

She returned to the end of the alley to peer into the street. He stopped in front of a street stall set up in front of a shoe store three doors down and yelled to the vendor.

The vendor yelled back. "A woman and a baby?" He gestured toward the passing crowd. Numerous women with babies or small children filed past them on the sidewalk, shoulder to shoulder with other *chipines* rushing home to their families and dinners.

"Salvadoran."

The vendor shrugged and turned back to his grill.

Julio stood staring down the street for several seconds before hitching his pants and ambling back toward the station. She shrank into the shadow as he passed then watched as he stopped again a few doors down. After a considerable pause, he crossed the street and pushed through the door of a cantina. *Ranchera* music blasted into the street. He disappeared inside, the door swinging closed behind him.

Sticking to the inside of the sidewalk, Carmelina returned to the terminal and scanned the schedule. The next bus left in ten minutes. At the far end of the ticket counter, a kiosk advertised SIM cards and pre-paid phones. Other travelers stood shoulder to shoulder and three deep demanding attention from the two harried employees.

For the hundredth time in the last two days, she had a decision to make. She chose Ricky. She chose forward.

She purchased a ticket from a disgruntled agent who didn't once look up from his smart phone as he pushed her change and ticket through the window. "Last one," he said.

She sprinted to the yard. An ancient woman with a battered cart milled near the departure gate and sold her an *atole*, the creamy rice drink foamy and hot, and a plastic cup of *elote* with *chile* and extra mayo. She added a large bottle of water to her purchase then climbed the stairs of the bus, juggling food in one hand, Katya in the other.

The bus was full. The young driver, a bright tattoo of a coral snake wrapped around his neck, glanced side-eyed at her ticket before he snapped the door shut. As the bus stuttered unevenly in reverse, Carmelina weaved down the aisle to the remaining empty seat, over the rear wheels, and settled in, her eye watching the street for the unfulfilled and disappointed Julio.

THIRTY-ONE

The bus bumped over endless *topes* for over an hour until it finally cleared the city and sped northwest on the open highway until it slowed again, lumbering up a steep mountain pass only to rumble down the far side like molten lava. Deep valleys plunged off the side of the road. The vehicle lurched and veered, swinging tight around the switchbacks.

Around one tight turn, the interior of the bus lit up with the bright lights of a tractor trailer coming directly at them. Many of the passengers prayed aloud. At the last second, the truck swayed to the inside, avoiding the head on collision, the sound of the trailer scraping against the cliff splitting the night

The driver slowed his roll, though not by much, and blew his horn repeatedly before swinging around the blind corners.

At the bottom of one pass, a large highway sign announced the distances to upcoming towns.

Carmelina cursed under her breath. The woman in the window seat turned and gave her a look, mouth twisting in disapproval.

She was traveling blind. Without a phone she was severely handicapped. She hadn't planned on doing this part of the journey on her own. Her whole plan had been to rely on the Santa Ana caravan. They knew where the roadblocks were and how to avoid them. At this point, she didn't even know where the next town was, let alone how far they were from the Mexican border.

Damn Julio. If he hadn't been an ass, she could have taken the time to pick up a SIM card, or even taken a later bus. But he did get her across the border. She was grateful for that.

The last of daylight faded. The bus lurched and swayed through the descending blackness. Not knowing how deep the gulches were or how closely they skirted the crumbling edge of the road was oddly comforting. Her lids grew heavy with the constant rolling.

Carmelina snatched much needed sleep, her slumber punctuated by Katya's schedule and the constant undulating forward movement of the bus.

Hours and kilometers stacked up, one upon the other like unleavened pancakes. Eventually, her seat mate softened. She offered to hold Katya while Carmelina fumbled in her bag for a diaper change.

When the woman handed her back, Carmelina scrounged up her courage. "Do you have a phone I could use?"

She shook her head. "*Lo siento,* no."

She had a phone, Carmelina had seen her use it. She held up her own phone and said, "Mine is not working."

"I'm out of minutes."

"I wanted to call my mother. She'll be worried."

Their tones were hushed in the quiet of the bus. The woman dropped her voice lower.

"You're heading to *El Norte?*"

Carmelina's mouth tightened.

"I ride this bus every week on my days off," the woman said, by way of explanation. "My mother is sick. She lives in a small village near the border."

"How much farther is it to the border?"

"About an hour." After a pause, she continued. "My phone really is out of minutes."

"Well..."

"There are several others on this bus going north."

"How do you know?" She'd boarded in such a rush, she'd paid no attention to the other passengers already seated.

"Like I said, I ride this bus every week." She leaned into her. "There's a checkpoint coming up soon. Isn't that why you really need the phone?"

Carmelina nodded.

"People pay the driver to let them off about a kilometer before the checkpoint. I suggest you have a few pesos in your hand and be ready to get off the bus when he stops."

"How much?"

"It won't matter. Everyone else has already paid. You'll be a bonus he's not expecting."

Carmelina fumbled in her bag and crumpled a small wad of bills in her hand.

"You only have a few minutes. Get your things ready."

As the bus slowed, Carmelina got to her feet.

The woman shoved a brown paper bag at her. "Go ahead, take it. I'm getting off soon anyway."

Several people flooded the aisle and shuffled to the front of the bus. The driver shifted, the bus lurching with each lower gear, and slammed to a stop on a darkened patch of highway next to a row of tall trees.

The passengers in front of her filed forward and down the stairs.

"*Andale, andale,*" the driver said.

She shuffled forward with the others, shoved the bills in his hand, and disembarked.

To her right, shadows disappeared behind the stand of trees. She followed.

THIRTY-TWO

June 29, 2019
Northern Guatemala

Carmelina counted seven other people. There was a young couple with a six-year-old boy named Beto she recognized from the Santa Ana bus. They'd chatted briefly when they were stranded on the highway south of Cuilapa waiting for the accident to clear. From south of San Salvador, they were traveling with the husband's brother, but had told her, as she had told them, that Guatemala City was their destination. The woman had introduced herself as Flora, her husband Manuel, and the brother-in-law was Jaime. Lining up facing them were three men she didn't know.

The small groups huddled loosely in the dark. She sidled up beside Flora's family.

The heaviest of the trio of men struck a match, lit a cigarette, and flicked the still burning match to the ground where it sputtered then extinguished.

"We know the way," he announced. "This is my third trip north."

"Yeah," said one of his friends. "We'll guide you to the border. We just need a few pesos."

"You're going anyway," said Flora's brother-in-law.

The man smoking barked out a laugh. "Indeed we are. And we're taking the quickest route possible. But you, *amigos*, could wander around this area for days without us. Trust me, I have been there and done that."

Trust. Carmelina didn't know who to trust. For all she knew, the men had boarded the bus for the sole purpose of luring them into some secluded area to rob them, or rape them, or even kill them. She'd heard the stories. People killed for a handful of pesos hidden in their socks.

She glanced over at Flora who shrugged, her hand gripping her son's.

"Leave them." The third man, shorter and slighter than his friends, spat on the ground. "Time's wasting."

The man smoking took a long drag off his cigarette, the tip flaring red in the night. Then he nodded to his friends and they turned and walked off.

"Wait," called Flora's husband.

"What are you doing?" his brother hissed.

"If they'd insisted, or tried to rob us, I'd be worried. But they didn't. I think we should pay and go with them."

"I do, too," Flora said. Beside her, the boy jammed his thumb in his mouth. He looked tired. He clutched a stuffed orange clown in his arms.

Carmelina found her words. "Me too. I don't even have a flashlight." Yet again, she asked herself how she'd found herself out this far so woefully unprepared? Her heart and panic had led her on a knee-jerk wild-goose chase without any rules.

They all nodded their agreement and Flora's husband called out again.

A light flickered several yards ahead. They walked toward it, negotiated a price they felt was fair, and walked on into the night.

They moved slowly through the jungle, ivy and branches lashing at their heads, legs, and torsos. Carmelina kept the baby cradled close to her chest, a flap of the scarf she'd wrapped her in protecting the back of her head from the foliage.

For a while she shined the light of her phone on the uneven ground. When it grew dim, she tucked it away to preserve battery, and promptly tripped over a root.

Flora's brother-in-law, Jaime, caught her arm from behind and righted her.

"Gracias."

"Just keep going, chica. These guys already have our money. They'll lose us if they can."

The jungle surrounding them seethed with life. Howler monkeys roared overhead, tracking them along the twisty path. Unknown birds called out, screeching in the night, the beat of their heavy wings whooshing through the trees.

Light began to seep through the dense canopy overhead, filtering down and making the path easier. They'd been walking well almost three hours.

The jungle air was still and cloying, her clothing stuck to her skin, her backpack glued to her spine. Moisture dripped off the large leaves as they pushed their way ahead.

Carmelina was exhausted, desperate for an energy boost. She thought of the brown paper sack she'd jammed into her pack and again offered a word of thanks to the woman on the bus who had helped her.

And for her good fortune to have company on this part of the trail.

And even for the accident and delay on the road south of Cuilapa where she'd had a chance to meet Flora and her small family.

As the sun rose higher and peeked through the leaves, leaving a shifting dappled pattern over the path they followed, Carmelina was feeling optimistic.

I'm coming, Ricky. Mama's coming.

THIRTY-THREE

The sun was well above the horizon when they sloshed through the shallow river, the second they'd crossed in the last hour. Carmelina's group hung together, always keeping the three men ahead within sight. The trio had picked up the pace once daylight hit, moving faster through the uneven terrain.

Each time the women suggested a brief rest, the men in the lead kicked the pace up another notch. There was no question now they were hoping to leave them behind. The path they were on was well-defined but they often came to forks in the trail. Despite the ruthless pace, their best hope was to keep up and keep going.

Through it all, Katya stayed silent. She'd missed a feeding yet slept through the humidity and uneven roll of Carmelina's gait over the rough terrain.

Despite her gratitude for Katya's demeanor, Diego's words floated back to her. Each passing hour the baby grew heavier. Carmelina's arms strained under her weight.

Flora's young son Beto struggled to keep up. Her husband and brother-in-law alternated carrying him, the youngster's head nodding into sleep on their shoulders.

Thirty minutes farther down the trail, they heard the rush of moving water. They approached the bank. Another river. This one swifter moving, deeper. Large boulders peeked out through the white rapids like shark fins. Carmelina's chest tightened.

Katya had wakened, hungry, and not worried about who knew about it. Her wails seared through the morning.

The three men shot glances back at Carmelina. Before they advanced into the river, the small skinny one looked back over his shoulder.

"Shut that damn kid up."

"She's hungry."

"We're all hungry. You're gonna get us killed. Shut her up."

"Guido." The large man shot his friend a look. "Keep up," he said over his shoulder.

Carmelina stepped into the water, it rushed and churned around her ankles. She took a deep breath and pushed forward. A few meters from the shore, she stepped on a rock, slick with moss and hidden from view under the frothy surface, and lost her footing.

She flailed, screaming. Jaime caught her, yet again, helping to right her. "I can't swim," she said, voice trembling.

"It's not deep. Take my hand."

"No, the baby." She held Katya tight to her shoulder.

Jaime grasped her by the upper arm and they moved together across the raging waters. At times, the water swirled mid-way up her thighs, tugging at her. Jaime walked down river, bracing her against the current. Flora and her husband, Beto on his shoulders, followed behind.

When they reached the far shore, the trio had already disappeared into the brush.

"We have to hurry," Flora said.

"I need to feed Katya."

"They're getting away," the husband said.

"I'll go." Jaime sprinted to the trail.

Carmelina collapsed on a fallen log, the soggy rotted wood crumbling as she settled her weight on it. Flora sat beside her and her husband laid their son on a patch of grass in full sun.

They were all drenched to the bone. Katya wailed anew. Carmelina stuck a finger in her mouth, hushing her. She couldn't be the reason for them all falling behind. If push came to shove, she was sure they'd simply leave her and Katya behind.

Jaime appeared from the trees, his mouth a thin line. He stormed over.

"They're not waiting."

He held his hand up as they all started to rise. "We won't catch them now. They said they've brought us far enough."

"But—"

He cut his brother off. "They gave me directions. Listen."

He repeated what they'd told him, where to turn right, where to pick up the trail, the spot with the twisted tree where it seemed natural to go north but where they needed to double back to the south for a ways in order to bypass a large gorge.

Carmelina listened while preparing Katya's bottle. "Should we write it down?"

"There's four of us, we should be able to remember." Flora pulled food out of her bag and passed a small packet to her son. Beto ate eagerly. Carmelina wondered if Ricky was being well-fed. Watching Beto on the trail, she couldn't help thinking what the journey would have been like for her son and Diego. Ricky was three years younger than Beto.

"If they even told us the truth," her husband said. "Jaime, are you sure of the directions they gave you?"

"What do I know? It's not like we have another option." Jaime exhaled loudly and sat on the ground next to his nephew.

Flora passed him some food. She offered a packet to Carmelina but she shook her head, remembering the paper sack from the bus.

Once Katya was full, she changed her diaper, and put her in dry clothes. She wrapped her loosely in a blanket and placed her on the grass to sleep. Starving, she opened the bag of food and ate every last crumb.

"How much farther? Did they say?" She looked up at Jaime.

He slanted a look to the trail.

"Well?" His brother prompted.

Flora screwed the top back onto the water she'd been drinking. "Jaime?"

Jaime threw his palms up and spat in the dirt.

THIRTY-FOUR

Onward. When life presents a single option, you take it.

They carried on. Marching through the hills under the punishing sun. As the hours passed, Katya fussed, Carmelina's stomach growled, her energy waning. They were short on food and water. The border couldn't come soon enough.

They moved forward on faith. Following the directions given to them, hoping to choose correctly at each fork in the trail. Within a couple of hours they were advancing blind, having reached the end of the directions the men had given Jaime.

They were headed for the Suchiate, the infamous river forming the border between northern Guatemala and southern Mexico. Rafts and small boats charged exorbitant amounts for the short trip to float migrants to the north bank. Desperation and demand had created a thriving market. Whatever the cost, the boat captains had learned the migrants were willing to pay it.

Cell service was non-existent. Nobody else passed them on the trail. Relying on the overhead sun to guide them, they pushed north.

"Let's stop here," Flora said. A flat outcrop of rock shaded by two large trees created the perfect place for a rest. The boy looked ready to wilt and curled up at his mother's feet.

Flora divided the small amount of food left, generously including Carmelina. Carmelina offered the last of her water to the group.

As they ate, she fed Katya.

"I'm surprised there's no one on this trail," Manuel said. He licked crumbs from his fingers, reached for the water and drank deeply.

"We're going the right way." Jaime extended his hand for the water.

"How can you know for sure?" Manuel pushed, reminding Carmelina a little of Kike and his knack for kicking up trouble. She could sense a rift of tension growing between the brothers, Flora occasionally acting as peace-maker with a joke or an anecdote about her family.

The battery on Carmelina's phone had long been dead. She wondered how her departure had settled with Kike. She could easily imagine his rage and subsequent rant, her mother trying to calm him, persuade him to keep the news to himself, for now, and not tell Flaco or Memo.

Katya fussed. Despite her efforts, she wouldn't take the bottle again. Whatever was happening here, the heat, the lack of food, the uncertainty as they moved forward, it was a better option than losing her breasts.

A horrible thought flooded her mind, arriving unannounced like a mudslide threatening to destroy her. What if Kike's anger prompted him to accelerate things and Claudia ended up in the *Casa Loca*? What if Memo took his anger at her out on Claudia? Panic surged through her. She forced herself to stay calm, think it through.

"I met a guy from Guatemala on the bus," Jaime was saying.

"He told me he was going north 'cause rainy season was so late this year their whole crop was wiped out."

If Kike sold Claudia, it would most likely be directly to Flaco. There was more money in that and he always got the fresh ones. Which meant that, at least for now, Memo wouldn't be able to touch her.

Manuel interrupted his brother. "I talked to that guy too. He said it like it was some kind of news. Water shortages aren't news. Fields blowing away like so much dust in the wind? Not exactly news."

But then, Carmelina thought, if Flaco had Claudia, that would mean Britney could be passed down to Memo. Britney with the narrow hips and baby growing in her belly. She wished again she'd talked to her about birth control.

She should insist Mama talk to Claudia about birth control. She couldn't imagine being able to convince her in person, let alone over the phone.

"Sure," Flora said, wiping her son's face with the edge of her dirtied peach-colored blouse. "But it's true that climate change is affecting more farmers, causing more food shortages."

"Same for us," Jaime said.

Despair seeped through Carmelina. It all felt futile.

Stop it. The one thing she couldn't afford right now was a sense of helplessness. Her mother would have to take care of Claudia and Angie. She'd promised she would keep Kike in check. There wasn't a thing Carmelina could do from here.

Her job was to get herself and Katya to the border in one piece. Never mind getting to the United States. Never mind getting through the entire country of Mexico.

Her job right this minute was to keep walking, keep moving to the border. The rest she would have to think about later.

"Why are you running?" Flora asked.

She shrugged. "*Una vida mejor.* A better life. Like everyone."

"You have anyone on the other side?" Jaime had a kind face, one of those faces that always seemed to be open, ready for a gentle word or warm greeting.

She realized she hadn't asked them the same questions. Why are you leaving? Who has your back?

It wasn't unusual to have spies among the migrants. People paid to find out if you had someone in the U.S. who would pay a ransom. People who could point you out to the cartel and the kidnappers.

She stalled. "In Chiapas, you mean?"

"No. In *El Norte*."

Carmelina had a reputation as a terrible liar. With more practice, it was starting to become easier. These days she lied more often, but her family always said the truth ran across her face like a neon billboard. She busied herself with Katya and took a moment to compose herself before she looked up.

All three of them studied her.

She shook her head. "No, without you I'd have nobody."

THIRTY-FIVE

The trail sloped down. In the hills behind them, the sun hung low on the horizon casting long shadows across their path.

Carmelina focused on moving forward. Her legs felt old and heavy reminding her of tree trunks laden with water. Katya fussed constantly. Manuel grumbled, their son napping on his back.

They were all tired and on edge with nightfall far too close for comfort.

Jaime led the way. They rounded a tight corner and Carmelina missed her footing as Flora crashed into Jaime's back.

"Hola *amigos.*" A small-boned man with a hooked nose leaned against a large moss-covered boulder, half his face obscured in shadow. He lifted a hand in greeting.

Jaime nodded a greeting and motioned to the path ahead. "We're on the right trail for the river?"

"*Claro que si,*" he said. "Another hour or so."

Manuel's forehead creased. "Another hour? I swear I can hear the water from here."

"Yes, an hour. The sound carries in the valley." He waved his hand around him like he was swatting off flies.

"Okay, thanks then," Jaime said. Carmelina saw him exchange a look with Manuel. "We're going to keep moving."

Carmelina side-eyed the man as they filed past. There was something about him that felt familiar. He was a funny little man, skinny as a rake. He looked straight at her and his lids closed over his eyes like heavy shutters. That was it. He reminded her of Lagarto—lizard-like and shifty.

She turned her gaze forward and kept moving.

Several paces behind her, Manuel followed with the boy. She heard the man step into the path, blocking Manuel's way.

"Flora," she said. Flora glanced over her shoulder, then got Jaime's attention. They all turned back toward Manuel.

"It's dangerous this way," the man said. "They'll be waiting for you on the other side."

"Who will?" Manuel let Beto slide to the ground and nudged him toward Flora. Then he squared off, widened his stance, and placed his hands on his hips.

The man shrugged. "Every day someone is kidnapped. Sometimes dozens of people simply disappear on the other side of the river."

"Then why go this way?" Manuel asked him.

"I'm not. But I thought you should know."

"It looks like you're trying to follow us."

"I'm not," he insisted. His hands and feet had not stopped moving, his eyes darted between each of them. Nerves? More likely he was on something. "Just trying to warn you."

"Well, thanks." Manuel's tone was a clear dismissal.

"It's not just kidnapping for money," he continued. "They'll take your women, sell them into the sex trade. The borders are jammed with a string of tolerance houses."

Carmelina had heard the term. In Guatemala prostitution was legal. In Mexico, they had so-called tolerance houses, a local euphemism for a brothel.

She'd once worked with an older woman whose daughter had been taken at the border, forced to work in a brothel. The woman's shame didn't prevent a flare of pride when she told how her daughter had returned home with enough money to build the family a cement house. On their own piece of land.

A couple of years later, an earthquake destroyed the little house and the girl, now a woman with children of her own, had left her babies behind with their grandmother and returned to Mexico to make more money.

The threat of being kidnapped or extorted or sold into the sex trade was real. Carmelina had heard the horror stories, they circulated among the people who returned like electricity: each recounting more charged and horrific.

Once they crossed this next border, they'd be walking into the most dangerous part of the journey.

"We know," Jaime said. He edged his way past Flora and Carmelina, shielding them with his body, and stood opposite Manuel, sandwiching the man between them. "What are you selling?"

"What?" He tried to conjure up a look of surprise but failed. "I'm just trying to help you out."

"Let's go," Jaime said. As he turned away, the man reached out and grabbed his arm.

"I know a place."

Jaime raised his brow.

He rushed on. "Gracias a Dios. It's a little town east of here. You can cross without paying anything."

"Go on," Manuel said.

"It's a land crossing. No controls. Completely safe."

Carmelina shuffled closer to Flora. Not paying to cross the ferry would save them all money. "Have you heard about this?"

Flora shook her head, her eyes fixed on her husband.

"I can take you there."

"And there it is," Jaime said. "For a small fee, I suppose."

Jaime turned his attention to his brother. "Why haven't we heard of this route before?"

Manuel shrugged and repeated Jaime's question.

"Most people take the river route. It's easier to get to if you're coming up the highway. Only a few coyotes and *polleros* know about Gracias a Dios."

He paused, pursed his thin lips. "Just because you haven't heard of it, doesn't mean it doesn't exist."

"How far is it?"

"It won't take long. And my fee to guide you will be less than what just one of you will pay to get across the river."

The brothers exchanged glances. It was starting to sound good to them. It was starting to sound good to Carmelina as well. She had a long way to go. Conserving her money now would pay off later.

Flora stepped into the mix. "How far is it?"

The man twitched, his head and shoulder reaching toward each other like lovers. "Another day. But I know a safe place you can spend the night."

Carmelina looked around the jungle. "There's nothing out here."

"It's an outdoor camp. A palapa to keep the rain off, a few hammocks."

She caught Jaime's eye. "We need to keep going."

"Included in the price. Very safe for your baby." The man stepped toward her, as if to touch Katya's head. Carmelina leaned back, out of his reach.

She caught Jaime's eye and repeated her words. "We need to keep going."

"Yeah. Thanks," he said to the man. "We're gonna pass."

"You'll be sorry." He edged toward Jaime. "Your money will be stolen. Your women will be raped."

Manuel took a deep breath, his chest rising, puffing himself up like a peacock. "Like my brother said, thanks. We'll take our chances."

"At least you could pay me a little for the information," the man whined.

"We didn't ask you for information," Manuel said. "Our thanks is all you're going to get."

The man's hand slipped behind his back. A blade flashed in the fading light. He waved it toward the men. Carmelina and Flora jumped back.

"I'm done playing nice." His eyes darted wildly between the two men. His whole body jittered like a bug stuck between two panes of glass. "Give me all your money."

Jaime stepped forward. The man lunged at him. Jaime easily stepped out of the way, throwing the man off balance, and Manuel jumped and pushed him to the ground.

They rolled off the path, a jumble of arms and legs. Jaime stepped over and stomped his foot down on the junkie's wrist. He screamed and released his grip on the knife. It fell to the ground and Jaime toed it away.

Manuel punched him in the face. Then again. And again.

"Stop," Flora yelled.

"Manuel." Jaime dragged his brother off the man, who lay prone in the dense underbrush, his face a bloodied mask.

"What if he's not alone?" Flora looked over her shoulder as if expecting someone to pop out of the brush.

"I don't think there's anyone else," Carmelina said. "He was high. Just looking for an opportunity to make a little money. There's probably not even a town called Gracias a Dios."

"Maybe." Flora wasn't convinced. "There might be others, waiting for him to lure us to his so-called camp so they could rob us. Or worse."

"We better get out of here." Manuel let Jaime pull him to his feet. They each grabbed an arm and disappeared into the jungle, dragging the unconscious man out of sight.

When they shouldered their way back onto the path, the jungle closing up behind them, Jaime again took up the lead, with Manuel at the rear.

Without a word, they carried on, picking their way down the path toward the river, pushing daylight.

THIRTY-SIX

Proceeding closer to their destination, the unmistakable sound of rushing water grew louder. Carmelina heaved a small sigh of relief. Encouraged, they picked up the pace.

The sun had slipped behind the hills and they moved forward through the fading twilight.

"Wait." In the lead, Jaime put his hand up, turned, and placed a finger to his lips.

Sure enough, over the birdsong and other jungle sounds, Carmelina heard the chatter of other voices.

It put them all on edge. They huddled together.

Flora whispered. "What if it's the guy's *compadres,* lying in wait to ambush us? I knew he was leading us into a trap."

"No." Carmelina shook her head. "Whoever it is, they don't care if we hear them."

At that moment, a woman's laughter rang through the air.

"See?" She hefted Katya, trying to relieve the strain on her arms.

"What do you think?" Manuel consulted Jaime, who shrugged.

"We keep going." Jaime patted the leg of his cargo pants where he'd pocketed the junkie's knife. "Unless you want to detour through the jungle. Thrashing through this, they're going to know we're here."

He was right.

Carmelina took a breath. "Fine, let's do it."

They forged on.

Less than fifty yards down the trail, a middle-aged couple sat on a pile of boulders.

The woman smiled widely. "Finally."

"You've been waiting for us?" Jaime stopped and the others gathered beside him.

"Not you specifically," the man explained. "We've been waiting a couple hours for someone else to come along."

Jaime cocked his head to the side. "Why?"

The man stood and Carmelina took an involuntarily step back. She noticed Flora did the same. All she could think about was the man they'd left behind them, unconscious in the jungle. Maybe he hadn't been operating alone.

He threw his hands open in front of them and spoke quickly. "We're not a threat. We're waiting for others who want to go to the other side."

"I don't—"

The woman interrupted Manuel. "What he means to say is, we're waiting for others who want to cross the Suchiate. Into Mexico," she added, as if it wasn't obvious already, even with them standing on the trail leading to the river.

Manuel looked to the others before responding. "You have a boat?"

"No." The man jabbed at his chest with his thumb. "I'm Vicente. This is Verónica." Verónica smiled.

Vicente continued. "We heard you can negotiate a better deal across if you come with a full boatload."

Finally, something that made sense. And yet, Carmelina didn't quite trust it. She turned to Manuel, eyes narrowed, and turned her chin to the side.

"Give us a minute," he said.

Carmelina crab-walked to the side until she was confident they were out of earshot. She kept her voice low.

"Doesn't this feel a little too convenient?"

"It does." Flora looked to her husband as she spoke.

Manuel shrugged. "I don't know. Might be simple economics."

Carmelina gestured to the sky. "The sun has set, it's getting dark... Would you be sitting up here having a laugh, hoping someone would show up, or would you be hurrying down the trail while there's still a stick of daylight?"

The others nodded. Jaime pursed his lips. "Then what?"

"I don't know," she said. "I think we proceed with caution."

"They're going in the same direction. I don't want a repeat of what happened earlier. If you don't mind, I'd like to avoid a hard no."

"Fine with me." She agreed with Jaime. The last thing they needed today was more trouble.

"Why don't we ask them to lead the way and we can try negotiating together? What do we have to lose?" Jaime kept his eyes on Carmelina.

She nodded. The others agreed. They returned to Vicente and Verónica. Jaime asked what it was going to cost.

"We don't know for sure," Vicente said. "Only that if we have a full boatload, it'll cost less."

"How many is a boatload?" Flora gripped her son's hand.

"There are all different sizes of boats and rafts," Verónica said. "We find one we all fit in and try to make a deal."

"We want to search you first for weapons," Manuel said. Jaime shot him a perplexed look. They hadn't agreed on that.

Carmelina took a breath. The energy in the air shifted, became charged. She sensed another conflict looming.

"Fine," Verónica said. She pointed to Carmelina. "She can search me."

"And you," Vicente said, nodding to Jaime, "can search me."

A minute later, satisfied the couple was not armed, they prepared to continue.

"How much longer to the boat, Mama?" Beto asked.

They all looked to Vicente and Verónica.

"About fifteen minutes, I think."

Flora grinned down at her boy. "Not much longer."

"I'm tired, Mama."

"I know," she said.

"And hungry."

"Sí, Beto, we're all tired. We're all hungry. Hang on, we're almost there."

Jaime looked over to the trail. "You first. We'll follow."

Vicente and Verónica led the way. Carmelina shifted Katya's weight again, cursing the deep ridges cutting into her shoulders, then fell into line behind Jaime, then Flora, with Manuel bringing up the rear.

In the final shards of daylight, they wasted no time making their way along the last leg of the path to the Suchiate River and the fabled southern Mexican border.

THIRTY-SEVEN

The trail ended at the slick bank of the river. Mud oozed up around their ankles where many had trekked before them.

Downriver, a man poled a raft piled high with boxes of *cerveza* across the water, fighting the current. This route, popular with migrants, was also heavily used by merchants looking to avoid custom duties on varied goods that flowed both north and south.

Darkness approached, a not-so-timid lover, reaching her slender fingers into each remaining crevice of light.

Silhouettes of small groups huddled on the shore greeted them. Vicente and Verónica kept moving.

"*Amigos*, come on my raft, good price." A young guy about Carmelina's age perching on a make-shift raft hissed as they went past. The platform of the raft consisted of weathered planks lashed to enormous inner tubes.

Continuing along the shore, Carmelina noticed only these cobbled together rafts, nothing she'd ever label a boat. She spotted a head bobbing across the water. The river was not so wide you couldn't swim across but the current looked swift.

"Hey *amigos*," called another man, "you going north? I can take you."

Vicente and Verónica pushed forward. Carmelina glanced back at Manuel, a question forming on her lips. Any of the rafts they passed could have taken them.

"Shill," hissed a guy lounging on the bank, his shorts glistening with mud. When he caught Carmelina's eye, his eyes angled toward the front of the group.

After passing four or five rafts, the couple came to a stop. To Carmelina's eyes, the one they now stood before looked identical to the others. They huddled around it. A middle-aged man, the waistband of his shorts enveloped by his belly, huffed as he labored to a standing position. Beads of sweat popped on his reddened cheeks. He shook Vicente's hand.

"We're looking for passage," Vicente said.

The captain pushed a ball cap back on his head, his gaze shrewd, appraising them. "Five hundred each."

"No," Vicente said. "We're a full load. We want a group discount."

"Discount!" The man guffawed into the air. "This ain't Costco, my friend."

His large belly shook. He jabbed a finger toward the boy and then at Katya. "Six adults, three thousand, and the kids ride free."

"Now look here," Verónica started.

"Shill." A wiry shirtless man scampered past. Verónica shot him a dirty look.

Manuel spoke up. "It's late. There won't be many more cross-ings tonight. We can pay fifteen hundred to take us over."

"Nah." The rotund captain shook his head. "I live on this side. I'll have to come back empty."

"Twenty-five then." Verónica's voice had taken on a needling quality.

The captain grunted.

"We'll talk it over," Manuel said. He turned and the group followed him a few steps away. "I think we should talk to some of the other boats."

"This is the best one," Vicente said. "Why waste time? It's getting dark. We can probably get him down another five hundred."

Carmelina caught Manuel's eye. "I think we should talk this over together."

Manuel looked at Vicente and Verónica. "Why don't you see what you can do to get him down more while we talk?"

Reluctantly, the couple backed away.

"You think it's too high?" Manuel addressed Carmelina.

"Did you hear those two guys? These guys might be shills. How would Vicente know this is the best boat if they'd never been here before?"

"Right," Flora said. "Why don't we talk to some of the others?"

The brothers agreed. As a group, they turned back toward the last raft they'd passed.

"Hey, ho!" Vicente quickly closed the distance between them and grabbed Manuel's forearm. "I got him down to two thousand. Come on, that's just over 300 each."

"We're gonna talk to someone else."

"Ay, it's late. You're wasting precious time."

"So be it," Manuel said, shaking off his grip.

"Ay, *cabrón*," Vicente said. "You're putting me in a difficult position."

"You're welcome to come with us if you want," Manuel said. "But we're going to talk to this guy."

The young guy he'd pointed out stood shin deep in the water, leaning on his pole. He wore baggy board shorts in a fluorescent orange floral pattern, his black T-shirt ripped and faded. Gold chains of various weights and lengths hung around his neck.

"You all going?" he asked. He fixed a look on Vicente and Verónica. "I won't pay you."

"*Pendejo.*" Vicente uttered a low growl. Verónica shook her head before turning away with him.

The young man laughed. "Those two sit up on that hill all day guiding people down to their friend's raft. For a fee, of course."

"And what's your fee? To take us across?" Jaime crossed his arms over his chest, his voice laced with frustration.

"It's late," he said.

"We don't have to go with you." Jaime waved his hand along the shore. "We can keep shopping."

"Ay, slow your roll, cowboy. I was gonna say I live on the other side. I'll take you all for a thousand." He took a breath and added, "I'm Chuy."

Carmelina let out a breath, her gaze landing on the water flowing by. To the north, across that darkened water, the Mexican border teased and taunted her. Finally it seemed within reach. Except, to get there, she had to cross the river.

"But, I can't take you right away."

"You just said yourself it's late." Carmelina wanted to sit. To eat. She wanted to get across the river to a phone. If she didn't go now, she might lose her nerve.

"Trust me, we need to wait a little bit longer."

She exchanged a glance with Jaime. "For others to come? You need a full load before you'll go?"

"No." He shook his head. His eyes narrowed. "You don't know? How long have you been on the road?"

They all shrugged but remained tight-lipped, none of them willing to provide specifics about anything.

"So." He lowered himself to edge of his raft, his feet planted in the murky water. "Mexico sent in the National Guard yesterday to guard the border. I can take you across but they'll pick you up and drive you straight back across the bridge." He jabbed his thumb in the air toward the west.

Carmelina felt sick. This crossing was supposed to be easy, trouble-free, and then a quick walk into Ciudad Hidalgo where they could get food, water, maybe find a room for the night. They all needed rest.

"You said you could take us."

Carmelina recognized the edge in Manuel's voice for what it was—another impending confrontation.

"I can and I will," the guy said, his words calm and measured. "Look, there's a lot of them, truckloads, but they're still pretty disorganized over there. Relax for now, you guys look exhausted, and let me explain to you how it's going to work."

THIRTY-EIGHT

Overhead a million stars twinkled against an endless sky. A bare sliver of a pale crescent moon rested on its side over the eastern horizon.

They lay shoulder to shoulder with their backs flat against the rough-hewn planks. Around them only darkness. The only sound was the soft swish of water against the inner tubes beneath them, punctuated by the soft plunge of Chuy's pole as he navigated.

According to Chuy, the best time for the crossing would be during shift change at midnight. Floating along with the current, they'd heard a lot of activity and then, gradually it lessened as the new shift took their posts and the earlier shift completed their goodbyes.

From along the far shore came the muted chatter of men. A flare as someone lit a match. The red tip of a cigarette bouncing along disembodied like a firefly in the night.

After some time, even fewer voices reached them from the shore. Carmelina peered into the night but there was nothing to see. Flora lay to her right with Beto wedged between them. Katya nestled on her chest. She prayed she'd stay sleeping and silent.

Jaime, knowing she couldn't swim and picking up on her anxiety, had insisted she be in the middle, far from the edge of the raft. He flanked her other side. The only way she'd drown was if the raft capsized and they all went over. Even then, Jaime had said, looking to Chuy for confirmation, the water was not deep.

The raft floated farther and farther eastward on the river. She fixed her gaze on the Big Dipper and the North Star. It was hard to believe that less than two months ago, she'd lain on the roof at home with Ricky giggling beside her and carefully repeating each name while she pointed out the constellations to him.

Her heart hurt as if cold fingers had reached into her chest and grabbed her life force.

Almost three full days had passed since Diego had called with the news. Almost seventy hours. She'd been keeping track. Somewhere out there, as far as she knew, Ricky was still alone. Still missing.

Her fear of the water below the rough raft was overshadowed by her determination to get to the other side. To find a phone. An Internet cafe. Anything that would allow her to contact her family and get news of her son.

Chuy steered the boat hard to one side with a long pole. It was easy to be disoriented in the dark, but it felt like they were heading toward shore. He worked hard against a rip of current, heaving with exertion, the long pole occasionally clacking against the wood at the back.

To her left, Jaime shifted, lifting himself on his elbow. Chuy shushed him and pressed his hand in the air. Jaime lay back down, his back flat, his body a comforting presence against her side.

Several minutes later, they bumped up against a partially submerged tree. Chuy grabbed one of the dead branches, moss trailing to the surface, and held the raft in place. They rose and fell as the current continued beneath them.

"I'm going to drop you there." With his chin, he indicated to the left.

Carmelina could hear the leaves rustling along the shore, the quiet slap of water against the bank.

"We'll settle up here."

He waited while Manuel counted out the money. Carmelina had already given Manuel her share.

Chuy folded the bills into a plastic bag and jammed it deep into his front pocket.

"Don't forget. When we land on shore, stay quiet. Get inland as fast as you can. Once you hit the highway, head west and it will take you back to Ciudad Hidalgo."

They whispered their thanks. He tipped his chin and minutes later they were at the shore. Manuel leapt first, his foot gliding on the slippery wet bank. He righted himself and helped Flora and his son off.

The raft bobbled and tipped against the bank.

Jaime shook Chuy's hand, then extended his hand to Carmelina.

She took it and set her foot down onto Mexican soil. Her knees trembled with relief. The river was behind them.

One more border crossed. One more milestone reached.

But she knew it wasn't over yet.

THIRTY-NINE

RICKY GONE 46 DAYS

June 30, 2019

Bienvenidos a México.

How Carmelina had longed for this greeting. She'd seen those words in giant man-high colorful letters on photographs of signs she'd found on the Internet when she and Diego had been researching their trip north. Here there were no signs, no one to greet them, no kaleidoscope of bright, primary colors. Only darkness.

They stuck to the shadows—it was all shadow—and remained quiet, the ominous threat of the National Guard hanging over their heads.

For a while, they used the river to navigate. As long as they kept the sound of rushing water at their backs, they were heading north. Once that noise faded, Carmelina relied on her knowledge of the stars to guide them.

Before they crossed, while they were waiting for Chuy to deem the time right, they'd bought water and *pupusas* from a girl on shore. The quick meal hadn't filled her—it wasn't nearly enough to counter the tiredness clawing at her from the last twenty-four hours since they got off the bus—but it had given her enough energy to keep going. It would sustain her. For now.

A truck rumbled down the road. They heard it before before they saw it, the headlights slicing through the night. Crouching, they watched it pass.

"Now we know where the highway is," Jaime said.

"Can we rest?" Flora let Beto slide to the ground. He crumpled into a heap, resting his head on his arms. "I need to pee." She disappeared back the way they had come.

Carmelina sat cross-legged on the ground and took a swig of water. Katya stirred but didn't wake. Jaime and Manuel stood off to the side with their backs to her talking quietly.

It was so tempting to simply lie down, curl herself around Katya, and let sleep take her. Her lids and limbs had grown so heavy—rest beckoned like a gentle lover. She'd been on the move for over forty hours with only a handful of fitful naps on the bus the night before.

Chuy had been clear that they'd need to keep moving if they wanted to enter Hidalgo before morning. With so much activity at the border, darkness was their strongest ally.

"Mama?" Beto lifted his head, looked around and spotted Carmelina. "Where's my mama?"

"She'll be right back." Carmelina had no idea how much time had passed. Had she nodded off? She opened her mouth to call out to the men.

But before she could get her words out, Flora's scream split the air. Both men spun toward Carmelina and a look of panic passed over Manuel's face.

"Flora's not back yet?"

"She didn't, I didn't—" *How was this her fault?*

Manuel and Jaime took off in the direction of her scream.

Carmelina rolled up on her knees and closed the distance between herself and Beto. She pulled him close and put a finger to his lips.

Manuel yelled for Flora. Jaime raced back to Carmelina. "Do you have anything for light? Is your phone still working?"

"No, nothing. Go."

"We can't see a thing."

"Jaime." Manuel's voice was frantic.

Jaime spun away, his back swallowed instantly by the dark.

Carmelina peered into the night, holding her breath. She strained to hear more, to hear anything above the sound of Jaime and Manuel's feet pounding against the ground.

There. A strangled cry followed by what sounded like a slap. Or a punch.

"This way," Jaime said.

"Flora!" Manuel called for his wife.

A shot cracked through the air. Carmelina jumped to her feet. Adrenalin ripped through her but she was helpless, tethered to the children. She couldn't leave them alone.

A man yelled, pain seared his voice. Shouts of men laced over Flora screaming freely. She tried to distinguished voices, piece together how many she was hearing, but in the cacophony it was impossible.

Hurriedly, she tied Katya back onto her chest and prepared to run with the boy if necessary. Her heart pounded in her chest, and the blood surging in her ears provided a backdrop to the chaos of sound reaching her from somewhere nearby.

They weren't far away. But there was nothing she could do. She waited, her body coiled with panic, ready to bolt farther into the night.

FORTY

Heavy footsteps pounded against the dry ground. Someone was coming. Carmelina grabbed the boy's hand, hushed him and veered away from the path. She crouched behind a large shrub. It wasn't much of a hiding spot but at least she wasn't directly in the open.

Eyes peeled, she waited, her breath choked in her throat.

Jaime appeared first.

Manuel followed, barely slowing as he entered the open patch of ground she'd just deserted. He carried a limp Flora in his arms.

"She's not here." Jaime made a full turn. "I'm sure this is where we stopped."

"Keep going," Manuel said.

"Wait. She's here. Beto, too."

"I'm here." Carmelina stepped from her hiding place. "What happened?"

Flora's face was covered with blood, her head lolled against her husband's chest.

"Come on." Jaime scooped up Beto and hissed at Carmelina. "Run."

She raced across the open field toward the highway, the hairy fingers of an unknown devil clawing the air at her back. Another truck rumbled toward them. They crouched until it passed.

"What's going on?" Carmelina asked.

Manuel held a finger to his lips. The second the truck had rolled past and the road was in darkness, he rose and ran on, his gait uneven as he sped across the scrub and cracked ground, Flora's arms flapping at his sides like some kind of boneless sea creature.

"Wait," Carmelina pleaded, her breath short and ragged.

"Keep going." Jaime tossed the words over his shoulder. "Come on."

They ran on into the night. Katya woke and tried to push herself away from her mother. When she started to cry, Carmelina clapped her hand over her mouth. Her muffled cries accompanied them for the next hour as they continued west, jogging along the south side of the highway.

Another truck rolled toward them in the distance. This time it came from the east. They hunkered down behind a patch of thorny shrubs.

The truck labored, gears grinding, then crested a hill, the headlights creating a prism of light on the ribboned highway. It was followed by another, and another, and still another, until they counted five trucks in total.

Jaime let out a low whistle. "I'll bet that's the National Guard."

"Are we being chased?" Carmelina couldn't push much harder. They needed to slow down. "What the hell happened back there?"

"Not here," Manuel said. "We need more cover." He rose and they followed until they came to a large tree surrounded incongruously with a spattering of gigantic boulders. Like a cargo truck had broken down in the middle of nowhere and simply dumped its cargo.

Manuel drew them around the back, the rocks providing a shelter from the highway, and gently laid Flora on the ground. He leaned over her, patting her face.

"Is she all right?" Carmelina knelt at her side.

"Get away from my wife." Manuel's eyes narrowed but he didn't look at her.

Jaime put the boy down. "They raped her."

"What? She was only gone a few minutes. And where did they come from? Wait—you said they, right?"

"Two guys. They must have seen us when we came through. When I got there—"

"Shut up." Manuel's nostrils flared. "Shut the hell up."

"I'll get some water." Carmelina put Katya down and asked Beto to watch her. She wet the corner of her shirt and dabbed at Flora's face. Blood had spurted from her nose. Her lower lip was split. Her clothes were torn.

"I said--"

Jaime cut him off. "Manual, let her help."

"She's helped enough."

"Manuel," Jaime hissed.

Carmelina continued cleaning Flora's face ignoring the tinder box of energy seething from Manuel. She spoke quietly, her tone neutral. "I heard a gun."

"I shot the bastard," Manuel said.

"He pulled the gun right out of his hand and shot him. You should have seen him."

Carmelina looked between the two brothers. "And the other guy?"

"Jaime beat the crap out of him."

She looked up at Jaime. His hands were covered with blood. "Were you injured?"

He shrugged. "He pulled the knife away from me and I got a nasty slash on my palm. I'll be fine."

"You don't look fine."

Jaime's eyes narrowed and he slanted a look toward his brother. Carmelina let it go and said, "I don't understand why we're running."

"Anyone could have heard the shot," Manuel said. "If they're not alone..." His words trailed off.

Flora stirred as Carmelina cleaned her face.

"We need to keep moving," Manuel said. "Anyway, it's better if she just stays unconscious for a while. When she wakes up, she's going to freak out."

He slid his hands gently under his wife and hefted her into his arms.

Jaime picked up the boy. Carmelina grabbed Katya.

They trudged on.

She lost track of time. Lost track of distance. One foot in front of the other.

She kept her mind focused. Get to town. Get to a phone. Find Ricky.

Kilometer after kilometer they pushed on through the night, tracking the thin slice of moon overhead until it dissolved into the sky. Just how far east on the Suchiate had Chuy taken them?

In the distance, a handful of weak halos of light and the faint chorus of barking dogs announced Ciudad Hidalgo's presence. They walked toward it.

Flora woke and sobbed against her husband's shoulder. After what seemed like forever, her sobs subsided, her silence punctuated by pitiful mewling noises. Carmelina's heart broke for her.

They crossed through lumpy pasture land dotted with slumbering cows so emaciated their hip bones stood higher than their resting heads. The placid creatures watched them lazily as they passed. The appearance of more fences and a tiny cinder block building with a corrugated tin roof and sun-weathered Coca-Cola sign announced the edge of town.

A dark purple strip defined the horizon giving notice that daylight would not be far behind. Somewhere nearby a rooster crowed.

They hurried on.

FORTY-ONE

The scissors clattered against the bottom of the stainless steel dish. The doctor tossed a scrap of bloodied gauze in on top and shoved the dish to the side. Surveying the stitches across Jaime's palm, he nodded slowly and grunted.

"That's a nasty gash. You're lucky it didn't damage your flexor tendon. You might have gone through life not able to bend your fingers."

Jaime's eyes flared wider.

The doctor raised his hand. "You're fine. Those injuries can bleed a lot but once the stitches are out, you'll be back to normal movement." His gaze shot toward Carmelina. She sat stiffly on a straight-backed chair in the corner, Katya sleeping against her shoulder.

"Have your wife change this dressing daily. If it gets red or inflamed, if you see any puss or discharge, you need to get back to a doctor. Got it?" He cocked his head and waited for Jaime to acknowledge him.

Jaime nodded.

"So," the doctor rinsed his hands in the sink, "that's it then. Unless there's something else?"

Carmelina leaned forward. "I was hoping to get a morning after pill."

The doctor's brow shot up and he looked back at Jaime. "Morning after?" he said to Carmelina. "You're not on any kind of birth control?"

"We use the rhythm method."

"I see." His eyes left Carmelina and he looked again at Jaime before turning back to her. "Do you want to speak to me in private? Without your husband?"

She shook her head. "No, that's not necessary, I—"

He stepped closer to her. "Were you assaulted? Is that why?"

"No. No, of course not."

"Doc, we used a condom and it broke, that's all." Jaime stood. "We want more kids but at this point, while we're on the road..." He walked over and put his good hand on the back of Katya's head.

The doctor looked down at Carmelina. "A lot of women come through here. If you were assaulted, I can examine you for injuries."

"I'm fine. It's like my husband said, the condom broke and we don't want to take any chances. At least, not while we're traveling."

"I see." He stroked his chin, his eyes fixed on her. "I could give you a shot. It'll last three months."

Carmelina hesitated. She had over a month left on the shot she'd had at the NCC, plus she really needed to walk out of here with a prescription for Flora. Flora, still in shock, had refused to come to the doctor and seemed to be in complete denial. "I don't think so," she said. "I'm deathly afraid of needles."

He grunted, turned away and scrawled a note on a pad sitting on the counter to the side. He peeled the sheet off and passed it to

Carmelina. "Give this to the nurse and she'll give you what you need.

"How's the baby? Want me to have a quick look?"

Carmelina nodded. She rose and put Katya on the exam table. The doctor did a quick peek and poke and asked her several general questions: Yes, she was eating well. Yes, she was getting enough rest. No, she didn't seem to have a fever or skin irritations.

Katya flashed a sloppy, toothless grin up at the doctor. He smiled back. "Heathy girl," he said. "Keep doing what you're doing."

"Thanks, doc." She scooped Katya back into her arms.

The doctor put his hand on the door knob. When Jaime thanked him, the doctor turned back to them.

"How do you plan to get to Tapachula?"

Carmelina exchanged a look with Jaime.

"A bus," Jaime said. "Otherwise we'll walk. Thirty kilometers? Should be about five hours to walk."

The doctor shook his head. "Things have tightened up here the past couple of days. Big brouhaha. Immigration is sending people back if they don't have papers. I'm guessing you came into town before it was light."

He paused. "Do you have papers?"

Carmelina held her breath. There didn't seem to be a good answer, so she stayed quiet.

The doctor jammed his hands in the pockets of his lab coat and his eyes shifted back to the notepad on the counter. After several seconds had passed, he seemed to have made a decision.

"I know someone. He drives a delivery truck. He can take you all the way to Mapastepec."

"Thanks," Jaime said, "but we're going to Tapachula."

"The shelter there is full and they opened another one farther up the highway. Look, my friend can take you."

"Why would you do that for us?" With all the stories of

express kidnapping and sex trafficking, Carmelina found herself looking for hidden danger in his offer.

He reached his hand out and let Katya grab his fingers. "Because I can," he said simply.

Carmelina looked to Jaime.

"My brother and his wife and child are waiting outside for us. Will he have room for us all?"

"I think so."

"How much? Should we pay your friend or pay you?"

He shrugged and threw his hands open. "It's my brother-in-law. Give him a little money for *cerveza*. Wait in the alley behind the *farmacia* next door. He'll pick you up there. He drives a red pickup with a white metal box on the back."

With that, he flung the door open and walked down the hall toward the back.

Jaime and Carmelina exchanged glances and returned to the front. They had waited at the door before the clinic opened and been first in line. Now the waiting room was crowded with people.

Carmelina got in line behind another woman. "Why didn't you tell me about that wound? I could have patched you up."

"Manuel wouldn't have stood for any delays. Anyway, it turned out all right."

"Yeah, except--"

"Next." She stepped up to the counter and passed the note with the doctor's scrawl to the nurse. The woman grabbed a key ring, stood and walked through a small doorway. From behind a partition came the jangle of keys, and the click of a drawer or door closing.

When she returned, she passed a small packet to Carmelina and turned her attention to the next person in line. She'd barely glanced up at Carmelina.

"WE'RE VULNERABLE HERE," Manuel said. "Sitting ducks."

They huddled in the narrow alley that ran along the side of the *farmacia*. To one side, rancid garbage overflowed from the battered bins and refuse best left unidentified dripped down the exposed, crumbling brick wall.

Flora sat on a slimy pallet, rocking back and forth, her arms locked around her son. She hadn't taken her eyes off the ground or expressed any interest in the conversation.

The alley ended at a tall brick wall. The only opening was to the street.

"What if he's working with someone? What if they kidnap us? It happens all the time here." Manuel stalked across the narrow passageway, jittery with nerves.

"They might only kidnap the women," Carmelina said. The words sounded dead on her lips. She'd hoped saying them aloud would take away their power, but it had not. "You know, for all the brothels we passed on the way in here."

Manuel huffed and wiped a hand across his sweaty brow. The humidity building in the closed space was punishing even at this early hour. Waves of heat rose off the metal garbage bins. "I don't know. I don't know."

"Look, whatever we choose right now will be risky." Jaime squared off in front of his brother. He widened his stance as if grounding himself. He stood stock still and spoke slowly. "If we take a bus, we risk being seen on the way to the station. Or maybe we'd be dragged off the bus later and taken back to the border."

Manuel shook his head and continued pacing.

"If we walk, we have seven hours ahead of us, in this heat, on the open road."

"That's too risky," Manuel said.

"Both things are too risky," Carmelina said. "We could rent a room and wait for nightfall. Get some rest while we consider our options."

"I say we keep going."

Flora's voice surprised them. They all turned to her. Her face devoid of emotion, she avoided Carmelina's eyes, and blinked once at her husband before speaking again.

"We can't sit in this alley all day. He could be setting us up or he could be a good person. I have to believe..." She faltered as she sobbed, the rest of her words caught in her throat.

Carmelina moved to her side and squeezed her hand.

Keeping her eyes on the ground, Flora whispered, "I have to believe there's still good people in the world."

FORTY-TWO

Carmelina inserted the local Mexican SIM card she'd purchased in the *farmacia* into her phone and checked the screen. A signal. She dialed home and pressed the phone to her ear. Street noise crowded out the repeated ringing so she pressed her palm over her other ear.

"Come on." It was almost ten o'clock. Her mother was usually home from the market by now.

"Bueno."

"Angie? Angie, it's Lina."

"Lina. Where are you? We've been so worried."

"I'm in Mexico."

"How is Katya?"

"She's fine. Angie, I need to speak to Mama."

"She's not back from the market."

Just her luck. You could set your clock on her mother's schedule but today she was running late. "Papi?"

"Asleep in his chair."

Any minute the doctor's brother-in-law could arrive and cut

her call short. She glanced down the alley at her new friends. "Put Claudia on then. Wait, why aren't you in school?"

"It's a holiday, silly."

"Well, let me talk to Claudia."

"She's out. Kike took her for breakfast."

Carmelina's heart pounded in her ears.

Angie dropped her voice to a low whine. Carmelina strained to hear. "Why doesn't he take me for breakfast too, Carmelina? I'm just as pretty as Claudia."

"Angie. I do *not* want you going for breakfast with Kike." What happened to her mother's promise to look out for Claudia and Angie?

"Does Mama know Claudia is out with Kike?"

"No, she'd already gone to the market when Kike got up. They left me here on my own, Lina."

How could she explain to Angie that she was the lucky one and not Claudia?

"Angie, please. Listen to me, this is important. Do *not* let Kike buy you things or take you for breakfast. Understand? Tell me you understand."

A man passing by the alley swung his head toward her. She turned her back to the street and saw Manuel and Jaime staring at her.

She lowered her voice.

"Angie?"

"You're not the boss of me, Carmelina. You're not even here."

She sucked in a breath and exhaled slowly. "Angie, please trust me on this. You know I love you and want the best for you, right?"

The line hissed between them.

"Angie?"

"Yes," she said, her voice small and solemn.

The rest of Angie's words were drowned out by the blast of a horn. A red cargo truck rolled up along the opening to the alley.

"Angie, is there word from Diego? Any news about Ricky?"

"Yes, but..."

"Angie, please. I don't have much time."

The horn blew again. Jaime strode past her to speak to the driver of the truck. Manuel and Flora edged their way down the alley, their son between them.

"He talked to Mama. I don't remember."

Flora tugged her arm as they passed her. "Come on."

She turned. Jaime gestured for them to hurry.

"Tell Mama I'll call back. Angie, write down this number." She reeled off the digits, ended the call and rushed to the back of the truck. Jaime grabbed her hand and helped her up. As her foot left the ground, the driver released the brake and pulled out into traffic.

THE TRUCK BUMPED along the main road through Ciudad Hidalgo, swerving potholes, the driver liberally blowing his horn and cursing at other vehicles, at people, at stray dogs and livestock, and perhaps at the air itself. A band of tension across Carmelina's forehead tightened each time the horn blew.

"He'll make several stops," Jaime said. "He said not to worry and to stay out of sight. Sometimes his stops are a few minutes, sometimes much longer."

"What's he delivering?" Carmelina asked.

They huddled together in the back of the small truck, completely enclosed by the truck's metal box. The heat was unbearable. Sweat rolled down Carmelina's forehead. Although she'd removed all of the baby's clothing except for her diaper, the baby continued to fuss.

Jaime shrugged and looked around the empty space. "Whatever it is, it must be in the back of the cab."

"Did you give him the money?"

"No. I will when we get there."

"He was okay with that?" Manuel shifted, trying to get comfortable.

"He said to wait." Jaime glanced at Carmelina. "He said if his brother-in-law vouched for us, that's good enough for him. You have a good ticket to ride there." He tilted his chin toward Katya.

Carmelina laughed. "I guess."

After some time, the road smoothed out, the constant lurching ceased, and the driver slowed for fewer speed bumps. She guessed they were on the highway. Exhausted, she rested her back against the side of the truck, fighting to stay awake, her head nodding with the heat and fatigue and the steady hum of the tires against the pavement. She kept hearing Angie's voice: *Claudia is out with Kike.*

She snapped awake. The truck slowed, the driver jerking the transmission roughly into a lower gear. The others were also awake, vigilant. Jaime crawled to the back and peered out through a narrow slat in the door.

"Roadblock. Looks like... three buses pulled over. The buses look empty. Everyone is on the side of the highway, standing in the ditch. There's five, no, six vans from Immigration. Some of the agents are checking papers...

"And, now they're taking people over to the vans. That guy yelling sounds Honduran, he has two women with him, plus they're taking two young Guatemalan guys and a bunch of little kids." He looked over his shoulder at them, eyes wide with worry.

Carmelina raised Katya to her shoulder and held her close, praying she wouldn't stir. Her little face was cherry red. She blotted perspiration from her cheeks with the dampened hem of her shirt.

Manuel and Flora stared at Jaime's back. Beto slept curled at his father's side with his head on Manuel's leg.

The air in the enclosed space thickened with the heat and their sweat, their fear palpable.

The driver tapped twice, lightly, on the back of the truck cab.

Jaime's head swiveled and he held a finger to his lips.

From outside came the low rumble of voices. Carmelina held her breath. It couldn't end here. She bit her lip and resisted rocking. After several minutes of chatter, someone slapped the side of the truck twice. Flora clapped a hand over her mouth, her eyes wide.

Then the truck advanced. As they inched down the highway, the voices of the people pulled off the buses filled the air.

Immigration agents shouted orders. Women and babies cried. Men yelled that they deserved freedom. Someone yelled that they weren't going back.

"It's a mess out there. Now they're pulling over another bus."

Long minutes later, the voices faded behind them. Jaime turned and sat heavily, rubbing his knee, his features pinched with strain.

The truck resumed its rhythm along the highway. Carmelina breathed a sigh of relief, the tension in her shoulders released, her body melded into the unforgiving floor of the truck beneath her.

FORTY-THREE

The highway rolled by beneath them. The mid-morning sun beat mercilessly down as they traveled north, the back of the truck like a sauna. After the scare on the highway, Carmelina remained lost in her own thoughts. What if they'd taken the bus?

She was forced out of her head when the truck slowed again. As they crawled along, the noise outside grew louder and stronger until she realized it was the sound of people singing, or chanting.

Jaime moved to the back again. "Looks like a fairly large caravan. I think we're approaching a town."

Shouts of anger surrounded them. Carmelina coddled Katya, impatient to know what was happening outside.

"I can't see anything." Jaime spoke at normal volume, his voice almost drowned out by the shouting that surrounded them.

"Oh."

He ducked down, away from the crack. Someone banged on the back doors. The truck continued to edge forward. The back doors rattled but didn't open. Jaime grabbed the inside handles tightly, Manuel scrambled forward to help him.

Someone climbed over the bumper and onto the roof. People

slapped the walls of the truck. From all sides came angry yelling and noise. So much noise. Flora's son covered his ears, his eyes wide.

The truck started to sway. They were pushing on the sides from outside, rocking the vehicle.

The driver blew the horn.

"Away from there. Let the traffic through."

"Police. They have a bullhorn," Jaime said. "They're pushing the crowd back."

More banging on the roof as someone jumped off. Then more shouting as the police tried to control the crowds.

"Go," someone shouted. The driver increased his speed and they rolled forward.

Flora clutched Carmelina's hand. At the back, Manuel and Jaime held tight to the inside handles.

The noise outside was deafening. Chanting, yelling, a woman screaming, babies crying.

"They have the road into town blocked," Manuel said. "How many people are out there?"

"Hundreds," Jaime said.

"What?" Carmelina scooted forward and wedged herself between the brothers.

People stood shoulder to shoulder along the sides of the road, an ocean of other migrants spreading back into the ditches and along the sides of the road. Most were Central Americans but also Africans, Cubans, Asians. They funneled toward the branch in the highway that led into a town.

Several police trucks and a double line of police with shields blocked the entrance to the town. The white spires of a church rose behind them, and beyond that, an enormous rock on the horizon. Carmelina had seen a poster of this rock, *La piedra de Huixtla*, in a tour guide window near the doctor's office.

"We're in Huixtla," she said.

The sea of migrants undulated and surged, an unruly tide of humanity pushing forward and then back.

Carmelina held her breath.

The truck kept rolling. Minutes later the driver picked up speed, leaving the throngs behind as he continued north along the highway.

After about twenty minutes, the truck slowed and bumped over uneven ground. The truck jerked to a stop and the front door opened. The driver jumped out.

"One of his stops?" Manuel said.

Jaime shrugged.

The handles of the back door turned and the driver flung the doors open. He stepped back as hot air whooshed out.

They were on a small dusty track. Large trees overhung the vehicle. Sunlight filtered through the canopy of leaves, but the air remained still, close, cloying.

The driver addressed them. "That was a shit show."

Carmelina had her first look at him up close. He had large brown eyes, a wide forehead, and wore a thick gold chain around his neck. She gazed over his shoulder. Was this some kind of ambush? From where she sat, there was nothing to be seen behind him.

"What was that?" Jaime rocked up onto his knees.

"The police in Huixtla are barring a caravan from entering town. After the big caravan a few months ago—thousands of people—it's just too much. The town doesn't have the resources to deal with that many extra people."

Carmelina shifted uncomfortably. Was he denouncing the police or the migrants?

"What will happen once they block them?" Jaime said.

"Lots of photographs for starters. There was a ton of media there. Our government is bowing to pressure from the United States to stop the flow of migrants to *El Norte*."

He sneered then spat on the ground. "If Mexico doesn't slow things somehow, they're threatening to impose tariffs. I thought the U.S. Government was bad. Now my government is just as bad.

"On the upside," he said, "they were too busy for standard roadblocks, so we snuck through undetected."

He waved his hand toward the trees. "Pit stop. Take a few minutes to stretch and get some air. We still have a ways to go."

Jaime and Manuel jumped out. Jaime turned back and extended a hand to Carmelina. She climbed down, waited until he helped Flora and Beto down, then headed for the bushes.

FORTY-FOUR

Carmelina checked her phone. They'd been back on the road almost an hour. She felt like she would melt into the floorboards of the truck, the metal unforgiving in the blaring heat of the late morning.

Jaime and Manuel sat together against the tailgate, talking quietly.

She saw her chance. She shifted closer to Flora.

"Did you take it?"

Flora pursed her lips but held Carmelina's gaze.

During their stop, when she and Flora were in the bush out of sight of the men, she'd given her the packet with the morning after pill. Flora was shocked Carmelina would expect her to take such a thing.

"I'm married," she'd protested. "We want more children."

"But do you want someone else's child? Surely you don't want to take a chance that, that.... *pendejo* got you pregnant?"

"Manuel would kill me if he found out."

Maybe not. Aloud she said, "He doesn't have to know."

"Wasn't Jaime there when you got it?"

"Yes, but—"

"Those two share everything. He'll tell him."

"I don't think so."

She explained Jaime had backed her up with the doctor. For the life of her, she couldn't understand Flora's reluctance. She put it down to trauma. She knew from her own experiences it was difficult to think beyond the present, and the immediate horrible past, when something like this happened.

"Look, take the pill and if he finds out, you can deal with that later. But if you don't take the pill now, it will be too late. You won't have another chance."

Now, she peered into Flora's face. The truck leaned hard to one side as they went around a tight corner. "Did you?"

Flora's lip trembled.

Carmelina whispered, one eye on the men. "None of this is easy, Flora." She unscrewed the top of her water bottle and handed it to her.

Flora's eyes brimmed with tears. She reached into her shirt, tore open the top of the packet, and dumped the small pill into her hand. She glanced nervously toward the back of the truck. Manuel and Jaime paid them no attention. She popped it onto her tongue, accepted the bottle, and took a long drink. Carmelina watched her swallow.

Flora's cheeks reddened and she stared down at the floor. She spoke so softly Carmelina had to lean closer to hear her. "I heard it could happen, I just didn't expect it to happen to me."

"I think you should see a doctor when we get to the shelter."

"For what?"

"In case he hurt you. Maybe they can give you something, you know, in case he had an STD."

Shaking her head, Flora looked away. "No. I want it behind me."

"You don't want to report it?" Even as the words left her mouth, Carmelina realized how foolish she sounded.

Flora barked out a soundless laugh. "Report what? You think they're worried about that here? Or worried about us?"

She was right. Carmelina clamped her mouth shut, feeling naive. For a second she'd actually thought crossing a couple of borders could change the reality of her life.

"Besides," Flora continued in a whisper, "my husband shot that asshole. He's dead. How would we explain that?"

"WHAT'S your plan once we get to the shelter?" Carmelina and Jaime talked quietly. Flora dozed, nestled into the shoulder of her husband.

"We're going to apply for humanitarian visas." Jaime dabbed at the sweat beading on his forehead.

"For Mexico? I thought you were going all the way to the States?"

"Yes, but..." His eyes narrowed as he looked at her. "Sometimes I think you just got on a bus and ran without doing any planning at all."

"That's partly true. It's complicated." She shrugged. "Tell me about the visa."

"Basically it gives you papers to be in Mexico legally. You should get one, too."

"I can't stay in Mexico," she said. "I have to get to the U.S. as fast as I can."

"Our plan is to keep moving too. Basically, the visa means we'll be able to take buses and not worry about being deported. It's safer."

They fell silent. After a few minutes, she said, "What will happen to all those people they took off the buses in Tapachula?"

"I don't know. I suppose they'll be sent back."

"To Guatemala?"

"Maybe. Or maybe all the way back home."

"I can't imagine that." She shuddered at the thought of being sent home after all the distance she'd already covered. Plus, if they sent her back, Memo would be waiting. He'd surely kill her.

"We got lucky today," Jaime said. He blotted his forehead again.

Carmelina took a drink of water and offered some to Jaime. He shook his head and reached for his own bottle.

"Don't you think it's odd we haven't stopped to make any deliveries? I thought the doctor said he was a delivery driver."

"Yeah." Jaime paused before continuing. "He told me he had to stop for deliveries. Some quick, some longer. Remember? I told you when I got in."

"Right. But aside from the roadblocks, he didn't make any stops."

"What are you thinking?"

"The worst, apparently. I mean, what if he is setting us up to be kidnapped? Or robbed?"

"If they rob us they won't get much. You?"

She shook her head. "Same. I have a bit left for food."

She resisted the urge to pat her belly where her cash rested. The plastic against her skin was hellish uncomfortable in this heat, but it was the only place it felt secure. She'd had an awkward moment in the trees with Flora, fumbling to get her underwear down and not reveal her stash. Fortunately, Flora had been busy with her son.

"They could kidnap us. I mean—"

Jaime touched her leg. Aside from taking her hand to help her at times, it was more familiar than he'd ever been. Familiar, yet it was comfortable. It had the desired effect, to make her stop talking and focus on the present.

"Let's not get ahead of ourselves. I don't know why he didn't stop and I agree it seems suspicious, but short of jumping out of the truck while it's hurtling down the highway, there's not a lot we can do."

Jaime glanced toward Manuel and Flora. "Besides, let's not ratchet up the tension if we don't have to. There's been enough drama."

"Sure." Carmelina leaned back.

They were sitting ducks.

FORTY-FIVE

A series of *topes* announced their proximity to the next town. As agreed, the driver kept going until they'd cleared the town. A couple of kilometers later, he pulled over.

They clambered out beside a string of roadside taco stands. Carmelina spied a liter bottle of water on one of the counters. Jaime pressed money into the man's hand and thanked him. He wished them well and sped away.

People milled around the taco stands. Carmelina took stock and heaved a sigh of relief when she realized there was no one watching, nobody lying in wait. No deals waiting to be made.

They headed south on foot, back toward Mapastepec where, according to the doctor and his brother-in-law, the new temporary shelters had been set up. The brother-in-law let them off to the north so they could avoid any roadblocks walking in from the south.

After half an hour on the highway, skirting the trees and staying in the shade, Carmelina spotted people walking from the other direction and turning off the highway onto a smaller road.

Without discussion, she and her friends fell into step behind them. A fine dust kicked up from the road as they plodded forward.

"You heading to the shelter, mama?" A young black man in a bright yellow cotton shirt kept step beside her. His shirt sleeves clung to his skinny arms, the sharp bones of his shoulders tenting the material near his neck.

She nodded. "You?"

"Yeah. It's ahead, there." He pointed in the distance. She couldn't see anything. "It's in a big sports field. Not much there."

"You've already been inside?"

"Sure, mama. Just went to town for the day. Good luck to you." He picked up his pace and strode away. She watched his back until she lost sight of his yellow shirt when he slipped past a trio of large women in flowing clothing walking with bundles on their heads.

Farther along the road, things slowed down, and people bunched up closer together until they were eight and ten deep across the road.

"What's going on?" She stood on tiptoe but there was nothing to see but an uneven cobblestoned swath of heads.

Manuel grunted. "Looks like this is the line to get in the shelter."

"Can we stay together?" Carmelina hated the pleading note in her voice but she was reluctant to give up her new friends. There were so many people here it made her nervous. She didn't want to be alone.

"Of course. You'll go where we go." Flora smiled and Carmelina relaxed.

Hours passed slowly under the blazing sun. They shuffled forward. At different times, skirmishes broke out ahead of them as people tried to cut the line. No one was having any of that. Occasionally shelter workers and volunteers passed among them handing out water, promising they'd be given food once they were processed and inside.

The sun started its slide down the sky toward evening. Carmelina kept a scarf over Katya's head, shielding her from the low-hanging sun. To the east rose foothills and mountains. Somewhere to the west was the Pacific. The musk of salt drifted in on a breeze that barely stirred the heavy air.

Humanity pressed around her. She bowed her head and bided her time, grateful she'd have a safe place to lie down for the night.

"KEEP YOUR BACK TO THE FENCE," Jaime said. He laid the blanket he'd been given on the ground beside hers. Anyone wanting to get to Carmelina and Katya would have to go over him. Beside them, Manuel and Flora had set up the same way.

The huge open grounds offered no shade. The lucky ones had erected tents. Others had fashioned shelters from sticks and palm fronds. From one end of the space to the other, blankets and bodies and make-shift shelters filled the large field for as far as the eye could see. They'd been lucky to find a spot up against a fence.

The bathrooms reeked like open latrines, the plumbing over burdened by demands on a sewer system built to accommodate barely a third of the numbers crammed into the fields.

Nevertheless, there was running water. And there were showers. After waiting in line for over an hour, she and Flora had been able to shower under bare lead pipes that stuck out from the cement wall. Under a slow but steady drip of tepid water, she managed to bathe both herself and Katya. She emerged, hair wet, feeling like a new woman.

Roaches played hide and seek near the floor drains and tiny

geckos scuttled up the wall in the fading light as she and Flora rinsed out clothing for the children. By the time they returned to their spot in the field, they were ready to bed down for the night.

Carmelina's limbs trembled with exhaustion. She'd barely managed to cobble together a handful of hours of sleep since she'd left home. She couldn't wait to lie down.

As she tucked Katya in for the night, her phone rang. She stood and gingerly picked her way to an open spot of ground a few yards from her friends.

"Diego?" The number was unknown, not a Salvadoran exchange.

"Si, *hermanita.*"

Tears of relief sprang to her eyes. "Diego, do you have news?"

"Good news. The officials tracked Ricky. He's in a facility in Tucson. That's in Arizona," he added.

"How far is that from the detention center where you are?"

"About four or five hours by bus from El Paso, I think. Where are you?"

"We got to Mapastepec this afternoon."

"Right, north of Tapachula. We went through there. Who is we?"

"Friends I met on the bus. We crossed the border together." She bent into the phone. "How is Ricky? Have you talked to him?"

"No, I'm still in detention. Tomorrow I have a meeting with my lawyer. She's going to help me apply for asylum and put in the papers so they can reunite me with Ricky."

"I can leave here in the morning," she said. "I'll go straight to Arizona."

"No, listen. It's a family facility, so I might be able to travel there and join him. It's not urgent now that we know where he is."

"How do you know? You haven't talked to him. He's still a little boy all by himself in a strange country." She swallowed, hard.

"Let's wait until I talk to the lawyer. I'll call you tomorrow night." Diego paused a beat. "Have you talked to Mama?"

"No. I called but she wasn't at home." Carmelina kept her eyes fixed on Katya who slept with her little fist jammed against her mouth, a trail of spittle sliding down her chin.

"I called too. She gave me your number." He paused again. Carmelina heard him draw a deep breath. "Kike has... accelerated things with Claudia."

"I know, I spoke to Angie."

"Bastard."

"Mama said she spoke to Kike."

"We know that won't change anything." Frustration laced Diego's voice.

Bile rose in Carmelina's throat. With every fiber of her being, she wanted to kill Kike.

"I only have a bit of money on this phone, Lina. Listen, tomorrow night I'll update you on Ricky."

"Okay. Tomorrow we're going to apply for humanitarian visas so we can travel legally to the border. Then I can get on a bus and be there in a couple of days."

"Maybe it would be better if you waited there and we figure out a way to get Claudia and Angie there to meet you."

"I've been thinking about that," she said. "I—"

Three small beeps and the line went dead. Diego was out of minutes.

She returned to her spot and stepped over Jaime. He snored softly. Flora and Manuel and their son were a jumble of arms and legs. Even in the oppressive heat, they curled up together.

It had been three days since she left. That meant the Santa Ana caravan could be leaving within the next couple of weeks.

In the morning, before Lupe went to market and when Kike would most likely be sleeping off a hangover, she needed to call home and convince her mother to get Claudia and Angie to Santa Ana. They could join the caravan and she would wait for them here.

If Ricky was in a safe place and Diego could get to him soon, then she needed to do what she could to get her sisters out.

FORTY-SIX

July 1, 2019
Mapastepec, Chiapas, Mexico

"Mama, there might not be another chance."

"I'm not sending those girls on their own all the way across Guatemala and into Mexico. They're my babies."

"They're your babies who are being exploited and sold, Mama, by your own son. I thought you were going to look out for Claudia."

Her mother huffed into the phone, a low growl. "*Mija*, you will not speak to your mother this way."

"Angie told me Kike took Claudia for breakfast. I know how he works. It's the same routine he used with me. Look," she breathed deeply through her nose, trying to still the tremor in her voice. "Have Claudia show you the Facebook page. You can talk to the organizers yourself. All you have to do is put them on a bus to Santa Ana."

Freedom for her sisters was a ninety-minute bus ride. Or so she tried to tell herself. She shoved the other realities aside: the deportations she'd seen in Tapachula where they'd dragged people off buses and the roadblocks in Huixtla barring entry into the town; and all the trouble she herself had gone through as they'd walked to the Suchiate River—not forgetting the battered junkie and the dead rapist they'd left behind.

Claudia was twelve. Angie was only eleven and seemed much younger than that. How could she, in good conscience, subject them to such a journey?

One word. Memo. Memo would destroy Claudia's innocence, wreck her body. If he was feeling particularly vengeful, he would kill her.

"Mama, I'm begging you to talk with Claudia again and look at the caravan page. I can wait here for them. I will wait until the caravan reaches here. There's safety in numbers."

"You don't know what you're asking me to do."

"I do know and I wouldn't ask if I thought there was another way to keep them safe." Carmelina cradled the phone against her ear and watched her friends shuffle forward. She kept pace with them a few yards to the side.

They'd been in line to apply for visas since before daylight but the line still snaked ahead of her for a long way. People nearby were already grumbling.

Someone behind her jostled up against her. She lost her balance and tightened her grip on Katya. Her phone dropped to the ground. She scrambled for it, picked it up, but the call had been disconnected.

"THAT SOUNDED HEATED." Flora raised an eyebrow, a question mark in her voice.

Carmelina shrugged. "A disagreement with my mother."

"Is she worried about you?"

"Yes." Carmelina didn't want to get into this. With so many balls in the air, trying to explain it to someone else would add to her stress, not relieve it. "How long do you think we'll have to wait in this line?"

Flora shrugged, clearly put off by her reluctance to confide in her. Carmelina felt a pang of guilt. She didn't want to hurt Flora's feelings but despite having traveled for several days now with Flora's family, she didn't know a whole lot more about them than when she'd stepped off the bus.

In the counseling room at the NCC there was a poster, a teddy bear with a bandage on its mouth, with the caption "Secrets can kill you." Perhaps. She couldn't help feel that the rules were different on the road. It seemed prudent to keep your secrets to yourself.

Katya fussed and, glad for the distraction, she turned her attention to feeding her. Flora returned to her conversation with Manuel.

Fifteen minutes later, Jaime joined them, his hand freshly wrapped.

"All good?" Carmelina asked.

"Doc gave me a shot and checked the stitches. I have to keep an eye on it. But as I was leaving, a couple guys came in who had just got out of the line. They were in line for over two hours and they started near the front."

Manuel rolled his eyes. "Not much we can do but wait."

BY THE TIME Carmelina got to the table, her stomach was growling and she felt woozy from the heat. She was faint with hunger. The woman gave her several sheets of paper and told her what to do with the forms once they were filled out.

Carmelina only half listened. The agent repeated the same

thing she'd said to Flora and Manuel and Jaime. Before she had a chance to even ask a question, she was edged out of the way by the press of people behind her.

It didn't matter. Plenty of others had asked questions and the answer had been the same: Come back with the forms filled out.

"We're going to grab some tacos and find a spot to fill these out." Flora waved the papers. "Just think, in a few days we could be on our way."

"Hey, mama. You got your forms." Carmelina's young friend in the yellow shirt was back. She couldn't place his accent but it had a Caribbean flair.

"We did. They said it'll be a few days though."

He laughed. "A few days, mama? That's what they tell everybody."

"What do you mean?"

"I've been here for over a month. My friends have been here over two."

"Two months? Why tell us a few days?"

He shrugged. "I don't know, mama. Pretty sure they'd have a riot on their hands if they flat out told us the truth."

"What is the truth?" Carmelina asked. They all waited for his answer.

"The rumor is that Mexico is no longer giving out the humanitarian visas."

"Then why do we have application forms?"

Mr. Yellow Shirt threw up his hand, his palm as pink as Carmelina's neighbor's pig. "Don't shoot the messenger, mama. The States are growing angry with so many migrants traveling freely to the northern border. Mexico is slowing things down. Unofficially, that is."

"But—"

"Gotta run, mama." He pointed to the east. "Good tacos over

in that direction. Try the *chorizo*. Or *campechano*. They run out early so don't be late."

Carmelina watched him go, the tails of his bright yellow shirt flapping behind him.

Accompanied by Manuel's grumbling, they made their way across the field, stood in line for tacos, and then sat cross-legged in a circle on the ground.

Carmelina devoured three *campechano* tacos, salsa dripping out the sides. The combined meat tacos were so good she wanted more, but the lineup had grown since they'd sat down.

"Delicious," Jaime said, licking his fingers.

"What now?" Manuel rolled his napkin into a tight ball. "Why even bother with these stupid papers if they're not giving the visas out?"

"He didn't say they weren't giving them out." The flicker of hope in Flora's voice made it sound like a question.

"Well he should have." A woman sitting behind Manuel turned and spoke to them. "They've only given out thirty or forty visas in the last few weeks. You have a better chance of winning the lottery."

FORTY-SEVEN

July 2, 2019

"Did I hear you say something about the train?"

The brothers fell silent. Carmelina saw a look pass between them.

"How's Katya?" Flora asked while Carmelina settled into a spot beside her with a loud sigh. She felt as if her whole day had been spent standing in line. After lunch, the baby had started to fuss. Her temperature was high so she'd taken her to the medical tent.

"She's picked up a bug of some sort." She brushed a bit of fluff off Katya's cheek.

"Not surprising with so many people here," Flora said. "Will she be okay?"

"The nurse gave me some drops and said to watch her fever. If she's not better in two days, I'm supposed to take her back." She glanced around to each of their faces. Jaime kept his head down and wouldn't meet her gaze.

She asked again. "Were you talking about the train?"

Jaime slanted a look at Manuel. Flora cleared her throat and made a show of looking for her son in the gaggle of kids who kicked a stuffed sock nearby. "Goal," one of the boys shouted.

It was Manuel who finally answered her. "We're thinking we'll take the train north."

Carmelina's mouth dropped and she shook her head. "The Beast? No. It's so dangerous." Her gaze went to Beto. "I've heard horrible stories."

Manuel shrugged. "For every bad story, there's probably hundreds of stories of people who made it north without any problems."

"Clinging to the top of a train?" Instinctively she tightened her grip on Katya.

Jaime lifted his head. "We can't afford to wait around for the visas to come through."

"But it might only be a few days. We can't take the information we've heard secondhand as gospel."

"Why not?" Flora's face pinched. "You're taking second-hand news about the train as gospel."

Carmelina felt as though Flora had slapped her. She breathed in slowly and leaned back. "I'm not, Flora, but don't you think it's risky to try to get Beto on the train?"

"All I know is—"

Jaime cleared his throat and looked up. He looked first to Flora. She stopped talking. Then he addressed Carmelina.

"Taking the train will be faster."

"But you're the one who said getting the visas would be safer, so we can take the bus."

"Things don't look good for the visas. We talked to more people while you were at the doctor. A lot of people have already been here over a month. A month. Some have been here two months. All they get are empty promises from Immigration to come back tomorrow, and then come back tomorrow. Always *mañana*."

"Surely they won't make everyone wait here without giving us some kind of real answers."

Jaime shrugged. "All I know is, once we hand in those applications, we're in another line up. It could take weeks to get to our names."

"Even then there's no guarantee." Manuel reached for Flora's hand. "There's something else. In place of those visas, they're giving out regional visas."

"What is that?" Carmelina studied Manuel as he spoke.

"It gives you the right to stay, work, rights to services like medical, but you have to stay in this region. You can't go farther north."

Flora released her hand from Manuel's. "This is what I'd like to do," she said. "We're safer here than El Salvador. We could make a good life here."

"For now," Manuel said. "Then what? *Los Ochos* has people everywhere. They might have someone here in Chiapas, we can't know that for sure."

"You're running from..." Carmelina bit her lip, let her question hang.

Manuel clamped his mouth shut.

"What my brother means is, staying here is a short-term solution. It might be better than El Salvador, but not by much."

"We could stay long enough to make some money. If we live nearby, they might change the rules for the humanitarian visas. We can live in peace and have enough food and wait for things to change," Flora said.

Manuel laughed. "Change. Working for five bucks a day and still looking over my shoulder is not much of a change if you ask me."

"I agree," Jaime said. "If we go north, we can get real jobs, make enough money to live, and send money home too."

"You left family behind?" Carmelina asked.

This shut things down again. Nobody wanted to reveal who might be left behind able to pay a ransom. Stories of cartel spies in the migrant shelters and even walking with the caravans on the road were rampant.

They didn't trust her. Fair enough, she didn't trust them. At least not with that kind of information.

"You could get a regional visa, Carmelina. If you stay, I can try to convince my husband to stay."

"We're not staying, Flora." Manuel stood and stalked away.

Jaime put his hand up when Flora started to rise. "Leave him."

He looked at Carmelina. "We need to keep pushing north. The truth is..." His face reddened and he glanced away from her. After a pause, he continued in a lower voice. "If we wait for the visas, we'll run out of money, and won't have enough for the buses anyway."

Carmelina's mind raced. She mentally flicked through the bills she kept close to her. She might have enough to pay the buses to the border. For all of them. But she needed that money for Claudia and Angie. She was certain her mother wouldn't be able to send them with enough money to pay their way.

"But the train? There's no way I can go on the train with you."

"We'll help you with Katya," Flora said.

"I won't risk it." The Beast was famous for extracting high prices from those that rode it: slicing limbs, taking lives, kidnappings, robberies. The list of horrors seemed endless. And clinging to the top of a freight train for eleven hours with an infant? Madness.

"Didn't you hear about the women who were abducted a couple of weeks ago?"

Flora bit her lip, worry etched in her face. Carmelina continued.

"The cartel chased the train and took five women. You know those women are going to be sold. End up in some brothel or worse."

"The conductor must have been involved," Flora said.

"Sure," Jaime said. "If there's money to be made."

"Anyway," Flora said, "there's no guarantee the same thing wouldn't happen walking along the highway."

Carmelina met Flora's gaze. "Flora, please. Can you take a couple of days to think about it? At least until we pass in our papers tomorrow and find out firsthand exactly what's going on?"

Jaime and Flora exchanged glances.

"Please. Wait until tomorrow to make any decisions."

Her voice sounded whiny to her own ears but there were worse things than having to beg her friends to wait for her.

The grainy news clip video of the white trucks chasing the train flashed through her mind followed by the seedy looking brothels they'd passed when they'd first crossed the border. It would be her life with Flaco and Memo all over again. Except there would be no going home at night.

FORTY-EIGHT

The sun dipped lower in the sky. Another day almost done. Across the sprawling open fields, people were gathering and settling in for the night. In another hour, the large spotlights would light up the field leaving corners of black around the far edges.

Katya's forehead was warmer and she fussed more. She was miserable. Carmelina wished she could do more for her. She kept a wet cloth on her forehead and gave her the drops on schedule. She walked with her around the edges of the field, trying to soothe her. Occasionally Katya dropped into an uneasy sleep which never lasted long.

At one of these moments, when Katya was sleeping, she pulled out her phone. Still nothing from Diego. She'd tried calling the number from last night and received the dreaded message that the number was not available.

With Katya against her shoulder, she continued her tour of the shelter while she called home.

"Mama?"

"*Mija*, how are you today?"

"I'm okay, Mama. Katya is a little sick."

For several minutes, she answered her mother's questions and took her advice on board. Many of the things she'd already tried.

"Mama, have you heard from Diego? He was supposed to get back to me last night."

"No, but it's only eight o'clock."

"It's been two days with no news."

"Try to be patient, *mija*. I know you're worried about them."

Worried. That was an understatement.

"Mama, did you get the information on the caravan?"

The line hissed between them and Carmelina's heart sank. "Mama?"

"I won't send them, *mija*."

"But Mama, you must."

"I won't, Carmelina. I had a talk with Claudia. She knows how important school is. I also spoke with Kike."

Carmelina choked. She wanted to throw up. She could not get her words out. She froze in place. Someone called out to her. She was blocking the light. She stepped forward. She loved her mother, and respected her, she was a smart woman, resilient, creative, able to stretch a meal for four into a feast for eight, but when it came to Kike the woman had a blind spot so large you could drive a truck through it.

"Did you hear me, *mija*? Kike said you had it all wrong."

"I'm sure he did." In her head she composed her next argument but she knew she'd only be banging her head against the wall. She'd lost this fight. For now. A tear rolled down her cheek at the thought of Claudia taking Britney's place in Flaco's room, or worse, being passed immediately to Memo.

On her shoulder, Katya woke with a wail.

"I have to go, Mama. If you hear from Diego, ask him to call me."

"*Cuidate mucho, mija.*" Her mother said something else but Katya's cries drowned her out. Carmelina ended the call.

"I'LL COME WITH YOU." Flora placed her hand on the baby's forehead. "She's burning up."

Carmelina had returned to their spot to gather fresh clothes for Katya. It was still early and everyone was still awake.

"She hasn't stopped crying since she woke up."

Carmelina grabbed her small pack and hurried toward the medical tent with Flora. Everything was in darkness.

"They're closed."

They switched direction and entered the barren bathroom.

Together they stripped the infant and held her under cool running water. In time, she stopped screeching. When her forehead felt less warm to the touch and her cries subsided to small sobs, Flora dried her and Carmelina wrapped her in a fresh scarf.

The brittle fluorescent light overhead flickered and sputtered each time a moth made a kamikaze flight into the long tubes. The concrete floor was grimy from heavy traffic.

"Let's get out of here." Flora led the way. They found an open spot on the stadium risers and sat in easy silence for a while, Katya drifting off to sleep on Carmelina's shoulder.

"Thanks for your help."

"Sure," Flora said. "You know, I'm really sorry about Manuel."

"I understand," Carmelina said. "He's looking out for his family."

Flora placed her hand on Carmelina's knee. "No, I mean... he's determined to keep going. We're leaving in the morning."

"But I thought—"

"He and Jaime fought about it but his mind is made up. I'm really sorry. You're welcome to come with us and ride the train."

She looked at the babe in her arms. "You know I can't. Not with Katya so sick."

Flora splayed her palms open. "I really am sorry."

And the hits just keep on coming. No news from Diego. Katya burning up. Claudia and Angie marooned at home.

Wait.

"What if I could help you?"

"Help how?"

"You know earlier today when I was on the phone?"

Flora nodded. It had been an awkward moment between them.

"I was trying to convince my mother to send my younger sisters. They're in trouble there." There was no need to say more. Trouble for girls in their country didn't require further explanation.

"She said she would try. Tonight she told me she won't send them."

"I'm sorry."

"Thing is," she took a deep breath and plunged on, "I have enough money to pay their bus to the north. Now that they're not coming, I could help pay your bus. At least for two of you. Do you think you'd have enough to pay the other ticket?"

"You would do that for us?"

Carmelina nodded. "Of course. We've come this far together, we should stay together. Would you have enough to pay the other bus fare?"

"I think so. I mean, it'll be faster so we'll need less money for food."

"Will you talk to Manuel?"

Flora looked at her slyly. "I'll talk to Jaime first and then we'll talk to Manuel together. To be honest, I'm terrified to get on that train with Beto."

"Why don't you go ahead then and I'll give you some privacy so you can talk?"

"I can't believe you'd do this for us, Carmelina. This will be amazing."

She put her arm around Carmelina and rested her forehead on her free shoulder for a moment before hurrying away across the field.

Carmelina watched her go, grateful for a friend amid the throngs of strangers. To the far left of the field, she thought she spotted a flash of yellow.

And then it was gone.

FORTY-NINE

RICKY GONE 49 DAYS

July 3, 2019

Carmelina slept uneasily, rising often to consciousness to check on Katya, then falling swiftly into vivid dreams.

On a cracked sidewalk, Kike towered over Claudia. Claudia wore a cute skirt and white knee-high socks, her face a mask of surprise.

A long freight train roared down the sidewalk toward them and Claudia and Kike flung themselves into the street only to almost be run over by a white pick up truck. The truck screeched to a halt and several men wearing black bandanas over their mouths jumped down and grabbed Claudia.

Kike stood to the side laughing. The truck pulled away and one of the men flung a handful of change into the street. Kike bent to gather it out of the gutter, ignoring Claudia's calls for help. Her screams pierced the night.

"Hey, shut that baby up." Someone shook her shoulder roughly. "We're trying to sleep."

Carmelina came to, her arms tightly wrapped around Katya. The baby wailed in protest. She loosened her grip and sat up.

Mind fuzzy, she wondered how they had reached her without waking Jaime. As her eyes adjusted to the dark, she realized the spot beside her was empty. Jaime was up somewhere. She turned to look behind her but there was only a pile of gray blankets marking the spot on the ground where Manuel, Flora, and Beto had been sleeping.

A serpent of fear twisted through her, jarring her fully awake. She reached for her pack. Baby clothing was jumbled in on top. It had been emptied and hastily stuffed again. She laid Katya on the blanket beside her, and dumped the contents out on the ground.

The small gold crucifix she'd tucked into an inner pocket was gone, along with a small roll of bills she'd kept there for quick purchases—and as a decoy for anyone attempting to steal from her. When they'd first arrived at the shelter, she'd secreted herself in a bathroom stall and divided her money into smaller packets as a safeguard from losing it all. Frantic, she pried beneath the stiff cardboard at the bottom of the pack and walked her fingers along the hidden seam. She'd secreted three separate rolls of bills there, rolled as tightly as cigarettes. Thankfully, they were still there.

She breathed in, her belly expanding against her shirt. Her hand flew to her stomach and touched bare skin under her waistband. The packet of money she'd been carrying against her pelvis was gone.

Carmelina jumped to her feet and scanned the yard. Under the glare of the spotlights lay row upon disorganized row of sleeping bodies. She grabbed Katya from the strip of darkness where they slept and raced along the perimeter of the field.

Surely they couldn't have gotten far. How could they have packed up so quietly that she hadn't heard them?

At the main gate, reality slapped her in the face. She was wasting her time. Nose pressed against the wire, she peered through the fence. Illuminated by the full moon, the silvery barren landscape and empty road that stretched through it was empty, confirming her fears. They were gone.

———————

THE MORNING SUN beat harshly down on her head. Too agitated to sleep again, she'd been one of the first in line. The immigration agents weren't due until 8 a.m.

Last night's conversation with Flora played on a continuous loop through her head until she wanted to scream. Why had she offered to help? Why had she trusted them?

Through a mental fog, she replayed that scene and the subsequent scene at their spot against the fence before they'd gone to sleep. Manuel too proud to thank her—or what she'd mistakenly interpreted as pride. Jaime's shy glances. Flora's overly-friendly gratitude. Before sleep, she'd enjoyed some tea Flora had bought for her from the far side of the field.

She realized now she'd probably drugged her. It explained how they'd managed to rob her, why she hadn't heard them leave, and also her wildly vivid, crazy dreams.

How could she have been so stupid? The one thing she knew, that Diego had burned into her consciousness from the first time they'd talked about going north, was that no one was her friend. No one could be trusted.

Stupid stupid stupid. Not only was she alone now, but her money was gone too. She couldn't buy her way north even if, by some miracle, she got the visa.

A man and woman in uniform made their way across the field. Different officers from the day before. Several people approached them but the man put his hand up, told them to wait for their turn.

After ten minutes of shuffling paper and setting up at the table in front, the line started to move.

Three applicants later, Carmelina stepped to the table. She presented her papers, duly completed. The woman smiled at Katya. "Pretty baby."

The small word of kindness almost dissolved her. She forced her tears down and said thank you.

The woman flipped through the pages. "You forgot to sign here." She flipped the page around and passed Carmelina a pen.

She signed. "What's next?"

"Your application will be reviewed and then you'll have an interview."

"How long will that take?"

The woman's smile flattened. "There's a bit of a backlog."

"But how long?"

She shrugged, avoiding the question. "I can't say." She pointed to a wall of paperwork tucked under an alcove that Carmelina hadn't noticed before. "We post the schedules there. Keep checking that wall for your name and it will tell you the date for your interview."

"Is there nothing we can do to speed it up? My baby is very sick."

"Did you see medical?"

"Yesterday, yes, but—"

The agent held her hand up, her kind demeanor and patience sliding off her face like rain. "Everybody's in a hurry. Everybody's application is urgent." She tilted her head. "Do you want to consider a regional visa? We can get you set up with one of those in a few days."

A few days? Then how long were the other visas? Was it like everyone was saying? A month? Longer? How could she survive in this shelter with so little money for over a month?

"That's not an option for me." At this point she had nothing to lose, so she said, "My son is in the system somewhere in the States.

It's his birthday in a couple of days. He's only three. I need to keep going."

The woman's eyes softened. "We'll do our best," she said. She stamped the application before placing it in the basket beside her.

"Next."

FIFTY

In the small alcove, Carmelina stood staring at the paperwork on the wall. Multiple sheets plastered the cement like wallpaper hung by a blind person.

The sheets at the top were curling from the humidity, the tape brown and cracked. Someone had torn a sheet down from the corner. A blank spot of crumbling concrete stared back at her.

She tried to make sense of the sequence. At the top of each sheet was the date they'd been printed. They didn't seem to be in chronological sequence, the agents clearly adding pages wherever they could find an open spot on the wall.

Rows upon rows of names and dates swam in front of her eyes. Here was one that had an interview tomorrow. Here was one with an interview next week.

She crouched, ran her finger down along the side of the pages. Two or three pages would have the same interview dates in fifteen minute intervals. Fifteen minutes would decide her future.

At the bottom of the wall, she knelt to better see the small black print. The dates were almost six weeks out. Her friend in the yellow shirt had been right.

"See your name, mama?" As if she'd summoned him, he appeared at her side. She turned and accepted the hand he offered to help her up.

"I just put my papers in this morning."

He slapped a sheet with the palm of his hand. "This is me right here. Interview in three weeks. I've already been here longer than that."

Katya stirred.

"You looked tired, mama."

"I didn't sleep well." Not exactly a lie. "My baby is sick."

"I'll walk with you over to medical."

"They gave me drops. Her fever has gone down."

"Doesn't hurt to be sure, mama. Unless you have something better to do than stand in another line?" He flashed her a bright, toothy grin, his smile infectious.

Carmelina laughed. "I suppose I could stand around and watch other people stand in line."

When they reached medical, he reminded her about the tacos and wandered off, thin arms swinging freely at his sides like a man without a single care in the world. Again, she watched him until the yellow was swallowed up by the crowd.

WAITING FOR THE DOCTOR, she considered her options. She simply couldn't stay long enough to get the visa. It was out of the question.

Striking out on her own was also not an option.

She considered the Santa Ana caravan, the one she'd hoped Claudia and Angie would be with.

That group would be leaving Santa Ana in six days. If they didn't run into any problems, they would be in the area within a week, two at the most. She could continue north with them.

Having a plan, any plan, helped her push her despair aside. The last thing she could afford to do right now was give up. They might have stolen her money, but they could not take her hope.

———

WHEN THE PHONE RANG, she almost lost the call fumbling the phone from her pocket.

"Diego?"

"Si. How are you?"

"Never mind that," she said. "What's happening with Ricky?"

"Lina—"

"I just mean, I don't want the call to cut off."

"Fair enough. It's not good news. But it's not bad either."

"Tell me." She was tenth in line at the medical tent.

"First, Ricky is in a facility run by the church in Tucson."

"That's the same thing you told me last time. Why didn't you call me earlier?"

"No phone," he said simply. "The lawyer says Ricky is definitely there. That's the good news."

"And the bad?"

"I won't be able to get out for a while."

"Define a while."

"She doesn't know. She thinks I have a strong case to be reunited with Ricky. Yesterday she took a lot of information and she's going to file the papers today."

"So Ricky is still on his own."

"Yes."

"Can you call him?"

"We tried yesterday but they said they're still putting the records together and couldn't find him."

Carmelina fought down panic. "Couldn't find him?"

"Hang on. They had a lot of people arrive at one time and

they're still sorting things out. The lawyer thinks she'll know some-thing for sure the next time she comes, and then we'll call Ricky on her phone."

Carmelina took a breath. "Good. When will that be?"

Diego paused.

"Diego? When?"

"At the end of next week."

"Next week? Can't she do it before that?"

"I'm doing the best I can, Lina. So is she. She's working with a lot of other people. We have to wait for things to work their way through the system."

"To hell with the system."

The woman in front of Carmelina turned halfway toward her, then faced forward again. Frustration was no stranger to this crowd.

"You know I'll do everything I can. My lawyer is great. You'd like her. You sound stressed. Talk to me."

She bit her tongue. "Ay, Diego..." Her voice trembled. She swallowed, collected herself. "Hang on."

Earlier she'd chatted with the man behind her, a Honduran with a nasty looking boil on the side of his neck. She turned to him. "Can you save my place?" When he nodded, she stepped away and lowered her voice.

"I was robbed last night."

"What? How?"

"The people I was traveling with."

"Oh, Lina."

"I let my guard down. Mama said she wouldn't send Claudia and Angie."

He huffed over the phone.

"They were leaving to take the train. I thought I could help them and we could all go by bus together to the border."

"Ay, Lina."

"Go ahead, tell me I'm stupid. I already know it."

"No, *hermanita*. Did they get everything?"

"No." She glanced around. "But they got most of it."

"I'm so sorry. Are you okay? Did they hurt you?"

"No, I'm fine but pretty sure they drugged me before we went to sleep."

"*Pendejos.* I wish there was some way I could help. What are you going to do now? How long until you get the visa?"

"More bad news there. It's going to take another month, maybe longer. I'll run out of money long before then."

"You can't come on your own."

"No. I'm going to wait for the caravan coming from Santa Ana and go with them."

"That's a good plan, sister. Smart. How's Katya?"

"She has a fever. I'm in line at the medical tent."

"I have to go. I'm running out of minutes. I'll call you soon, okay?"

FIFTY-ONE
RICKY GONE 51 DAYS

July 5, 2019

Two days later, Carmelina stood in line for tacos tossing her baby in the air. Katya giggled wildly with each toss, landing happily into her waiting arms.

"Hungry, mama?" Her friend in the yellow shirt appeared beside her.

"You have a habit of doing that," she said.

"What?"

"Showing up without warning."

"I'd have thought my shirt was enough of a warning." He ran his hands down the front of his body and out to the sides, a clear imitation of a runway model showing off a new dress.

She laughed. He always brightened her spirits. "What's your name?"

"It's Yonas, mama. How shall I call you?"

"Carmelina." They shook hands.

"Pleased to meet you, mama."

She laughed. "Where are you from?"

"Eritrea. It's in Africa."

"Africa. You're a long way from home. I thought I detected a Caribbean accent."

"Nope. And yes, a long way from home."

"Are you traveling with friends?" She'd never seen him with anyone.

"There's a few of us that came up through Panama together."

"I heard that's rough through there. On the border."

"Yeah, Darien Gap." A shadow flitted across his face. "We lost a couple people through there. A robbery got ugly."

"People you knew?"

He raised a brow, his face suddenly closed. "Did you try the *chorizo* yet?"

"I've been eating the *campechano*, as you recommended."

"An excellent choice," he said. With a flourish, he stepped aside and she stepped up to the counter.

He joined her again when she sat down. "Where are your friends, Carmelina? I haven't seen them around."

"They couldn't wait," she lied. "They're taking the train north."

"The Beast?" His eyes flared open. "One of the guys traveling with us took the train a couple years ago. He said it was horrible then and even more dangerous now. He's prepared to wait as long as he has to for the visa."

She took another bite of taco, savoring the *tomatilla salsa*, one of the best she'd ever tasted.

"And you?"

Mouth full, she continued chewing and pointed to her lips. There was zero chance she was going to tell anybody about anything. Yonas was friendly, and she liked him, but she didn't plan to make the same mistake twice.

"Some of my travel buddies are itching to go," he said. "There's a group of Hondurans, Guatemalans, Cubans, all planning to hit the road sometime after the weekend." He poked at the taco on his plate, pinched a stray pile of onion and cilantro and stuffed it back into the tortilla.

"Today's Friday. Will you go with them?"

"Thinking about it. I've been here a long time. Might be time." He quirked a brow. When she ignored the obvious question, he used his taco to mop up the salsa on his plate then pushed the whole thing in his mouth, eyes closed in obvious pleasure as he chewed. When he opened them, he looked at her.

"Was I right about the tacos, mama?"

"You were right."

Without another word, he popped up and disappeared into the crowd.

WITH HER BELLY FULL, Carmelina wanted a nap. Instead, she set off through the front gate and walked into town to look for the Internet cafe. She found it tucked away down a side street, half a block from the bakery. Every chair was filled.

The young guy at the desk held up five fingers and motioned her to an empty row of chairs against the wall. Did that mean five minutes or that she was fifth in line? Before she had a chance to ask, the guy picked up the phone.

Five minutes later, a young girl left her spot in the corner, and the young guy waved Carmelina over. She went immediately to Facebook and the Santa Ana caravan page. They still didn't have a firm date for leaving.

She spent another few minutes looking at her timeline which helpfully reminded her it was her son's birthday. *Gee, thanks Facebook—as if missing his birthday hadn't been burning a hole in her heart since the moment she'd opened her eyes today.*

Then she took a quick peek at Claudia's timeline before

checking her email. There was a message from Diego. She opened it with trepidation.

Hermanita, he wrote, *the lawyer sent me a note. She was able to talk to someone at the facility in Tucson.*

Carmelina's heart fluttered.

I am sorry to tell you this by email.

Oh no. No.

Ricky is not at that facility. Once again, they can't confirm where they have sent him. The lawyer assured me she is going to stay on top of this until she gets an answer about where he is.

Hermanita, try not to worry. Please wait for the caravan. I will call you as soon as I can put more money on my phone.

The clacking of keyboards around her faded to a steady drone. A loud buzzing filled her head. The words on the screen in front of her danced like crazed drunks at a party. Heat balled into a searing force in Carmelina's belly and ripped up through her body.

"No." She slammed her hands against the battered plastic table. People around her looked her way but she was barely aware of them.

She pounded the keys, punishing the keyboard. Her words violently tumbling onto the screen.

They will not lose my son again, Diego. Do everything possible. Keep pushing. I have faith in you.

I won't wait for the Santa Ana caravan. I heard of one earlier today that is leaving from here after the weekend. So don't worry. I won't be alone, I'll be with them.

I am coming.

FIFTY-TWO

RICKY GONE 60 DAYS

July 14, 2019
Northeast of Ixtepec, Oaxaca

The wide expanse of sky overhead was crisp, ironed flat like a fine blue linen. Wisps of cloud skittered along the horizon. The crowd marching around Carmelina had fallen silent. The first few days the road paralleled the coast, barely rising above sea level.

Now the road climbed into the mountains, the beginning of the caravan snaking up into the jungle before her.

She'd hoped it would be cooler as they wound farther north from Ixtepec and away from the humidity of the coast. No such luck. People mopped at their foreheads. Most of the men had removed their shirts. The older woman beside her, flanked by two children about ten, struggled on, her face red. She'd heard the children call her *abuela*. Carmelina guessed her to be her mother's age. She'd yet to see the children's parents.

Katya had developed an ugly heat rash. Multiple small red spots blistered her skin wherever it came in contact with material. In her discomfort, she wept and kicked against her.

As Diego had predicted, the baby grew heavier with each passing kilometer. Her arms ached, and the scarf dug deeply into her shoulders. She flinched. A pinched nerve sent a spasm of pain down her arm.

"Are you all right?" the woman beside her asked.

Carmelina nodded. She'd kept to herself since leaving Mapastepec. Even though she knew she should make some women friends—nothing shouted "vulnerable, kidnap this one" like a woman with no obvious ties—but she was gun shy following her experience with Flora's family. "How old is your baby?"

"Six and a half months." She shifted her to the other side.

"Can I make a suggestion?"

Carmelina looked at the woman. She had a broad, open face. Her eyes twinkled despite her obvious exhaustion. "I guess."

"What are you carrying in that backpack?"

Her eyes narrowed. The woman held up her index finger. "Don't tell me, it's not important. But is it heavier than the baby?"

"No, it's mostly clothes. A couple small toys."

"Why not carry the baby in the backpack and use the scarf to sling the clothes?"

"What? I can't put my baby in a backpack." The woman was delusional.

She laughed. "Have you seen the baby carriers that woman have on their backs? You could cut holes in the corners of the pack for the baby's legs. It would distribute her weight better."

Carmelina tried to picture it in her mind. "She's overheated already with just the scarf."

"You're right, it would make her warmer," the woman said. "I'm Bonita."

"That's my grandmother's name," Carmelina said. Instantly she regretted it.

"She must be a wise and wonderful woman." She winked and

smiled widely. "If you like, we can look at the pack together when we stop later. Are you on your own, dear?"

"Are you?"

"Yes," she said. "With my two grandsons. But I'm an old woman."

"Not old," Carmelina said. "You look like my mother's age, mid-thirties?"

"Almost forty. My grandsons are eight and nine."

That's what she'd thought for the boys.

"You're wondering about their parents."

"It's none of my business," she said.

"It's fine," Bonita said. "I'm glad to have someone to talk to. It'll help pass the time."

She spoke to her grandsons. "Boys, run ahead and get in line at the store so we can buy more water."

She pressed a coin into the older boy's hand and the two brothers ran off, their gangly limbs akimbo as they sprinted through the crowd.

"Their parents are already in the States," she said. "They crossed over a few months ago. They were lucky. They came through when Mexico was still giving out humanitarian visas to anyone who asked for one."

"Have they arranged for you to join them?"

"Not exactly. Right now they're in southern California, waiting for their amnesty hearing. But I wanted to get the boys to the border before things get tighter."

"What do you mean by tighter?"

"The U.S. government is doing everything they can do to prevent more people crossing. They're talking about closing the border." She glanced at Katya. "You know, right now it's easier to get across the border and to stay across the border, if you have a child with you."

"I've heard that." No way she was telling this stranger about

Diego and Ricky. For all she knew, she was a spy that would tag her for a kidnap ransom. *Paranoid much?* Maybe. Maybe not. Better safe than sorry.

"What I'm trying to say, dear, is that you need to keep a very close eye on your child. I've heard of children being taken by other travelers so they'll have an easier time of it at the border."

Instinctively, Carmelina wrapped her arms tighter around Katya, who immediately—and loudly—protested against the pressure and extra warmth, her little fists punching the air.

"I don't want to scare you."

"I appreciate the warning," Carmelina said. They came up alongside the small tienda where the boys waited in the lineup to get inside.

She would need water soon too. She was torn. Keep walking and put some distance between herself and Bonita or stick around and get water. She decided to err on the side of prudence. Digging in her pocket for coins, she stepped toward the line.

"The boys will get what you need," Bonita said.

Carmelina passed her the change and, after Bonita told the boys what to buy, they moved into a small slice of shade at the side of the building.

"Take your pack off for a minute," Bonita said.

Carmelina shrugged out of it and Bonita showed her the idea she had for converting it to a carrier for Katya. It wasn't a horrible idea, but it would mean rearranging Katya each time she needed to feed her, and slinging her belongings across her front. "I'll think about it," she said. She wasn't sure she'd be able to close up the scarf enough to secure her things. And the canvas of the small backpack was heavy. At least the scarf was cotton and somewhat breathable.

The boys arrived with large bottles of cold water, the condensation dripping off them. Carmelina pressed the cool bottle against Katya's skin then took a long drink.

FIFTY-THREE

"Hey, mama." Yonas sidled up to her.

"Yonas, I almost didn't see you."

"That's because I changed my shirt, mama." He twirled. A loose lime green shirt tented around him. "What do you think?"

"I think you'll be harder to find in a crowd."

"But not impossible to find. That's the important part." He laughed and fell into step beside her. "Sorry I missed you the last couple of days."

She was growing increasingly fond of Yonas and his quirky ways. And she was grateful to him for telling her about this caravan. Every day she was closing the gap between herself and Ricky. If he hadn't mentioned it, she might still be in Mapastepec waiting for the people from Santa Ana. "Been staying busy?" she quipped.

"I volunteered to sweep at the back."

"Sweep at the back?"

"There's almost five hundred of us now, so when we roll into a town, we leave a bit of a mess. Some of us stay behind in the mornings to help pick up the garbage, keep things clean, you know? Sort of like, if we leave things clean, they'll be more likely to welcome us in the next town."

"That's really smart. Maybe I can help."

"I don't want you at the end of the caravan, mama. Better you stick here in the middle." His speech was rapid fire and she wondered for the first time if he might be on something.

"Did you find the burritos?"

"Burritos? You always know about the food." She laughed. "How do you manage to stay so skinny?"

"I'm not skinny, mama. I'm lean and mean, a real macho machine." To demonstrate he lifted his arm and flexed a small bicep. It popped like a bead on a chain. He wiggled his eyebrows and hips.

She laughed with him. "I didn't find the burritos."

"They're delicious. Two guys from a few hours south of here. I think they said Tierra Blanca. They're driving an old beat up Blazer pulling a taco stand. Watch for them, mama." He winked and ducked away. Before she knew it, he and his lime green shirt had blended in with the crowd.

She chuckled and wondered what someone from the Red Sea would know about burritos. So far Yonas hadn't steered her wrong.

AN HOUR LATER, she crested the top of the hill they'd been trudging up and started down the other side. At the bottom, the lights of a small town sparkled in the dimming light. She'd been on the road almost sixteen hours.

A few kilometers back, unable to continue, Bonita and the boys had stopped for the night. Bonita said they would rise early and catch up to the caravan in the morning.

Finally, after a long nine day wait Diego had texted with news. Bad news. Ricky was still missing. She'd been separated from her son for two months and nobody knew exactly where he was.

Carmelina pushed on.

As the caravan approached the town, police lined the road, asking the travelers to stay on the shoulder. They walked closer together, some in the ditch, the line stretching longer as the width of the caravan narrowed.

The lights grew brighter. She pressed on. Her stomach growled. A truck rumbled down the hill beside her. It sounded like a freight train, the engine an uneven growl, metal bits clanking.

It pulled alongside her and she recognized the Chevrolet Blazer Yonas had talked about. It was two-tone blue. Or rather, it used to be. So much paint flaked off the bottom panel it resembled a dairy cow. The top half, some sort of vinyl covering, had also seen better days. Thin strips of ragged vinyl hung down the sides as if it had been peeled like an orange.

Two large men shouted to each other over the noise. An old hit by Chicago blared out the open windows. She recognized the tune. A younger, more likable Kike had played the album often when she'd been a child and still loved him.

Thick exhaust belched from the rattling truck and left a haze in the air as the truck continued down the hill toward the town, the horrible clanking of the taco stand chasing it like a noisy demon.

The police funneled the caravan toward the town square. By the time she arrived, it was already crowded. She found a place in a corner, near a family, and spread her blanket on the ground. Mariachis played somewhere in the distance. From the far side of the square drifted the fragrant smell of grilling beef. Mouth watering, she followed her nose.

Parked up against the curb was the Blazer. The two men, clearly brothers, stood stooped in the taco stand. In the small space, they both looked like giants. The one taking orders had a bulbous nose covered with a topography of veins. A drinker. He smiled easily but his resting face hardened into an angry mask.

Taking Carmelina's order, he explained there were two options. Burrito with beef or burrito with beef. He meant this to be funny.

"Burrito with beef is fine."

"*Con todo?*"

"What's everything?"

"What's everything tonight, Carlos?"

The other brother looked up from the pile of cilantro he was chopping, a shock of brown hair fell across his forehead. Brothers, yes, but this second brother, Carlos, had the open face of a laughing child.

"Cilantro, onions. Of course beans and cheese. You like cheese, *chica?*"

Carmelina nodded. "Yes, then, *con todo.*"

Carlos threw the ingredients onto a large flour tortilla, rolled it, wrapped it in foil, and passed it to his brother.

The brother passed it to her. "A hundred dollars."

"Good one," she said. He didn't look like he was joking. She waited for him to smile. Behind him, Carlos shrugged.

"Fifty *pesitos.*"

She handed him the coins and pushed back through the crowd. A man got up from a bench as she approached and she settled into the small space he'd left and unwrapped the end of the burrito. It was stuffed full. She bit into it. Delicious. She was gaining confidence in Yonas and his deep love for Latin food.

Once she was done, she balled up the foil, licked her fingers and leaned against the back of the bench, grateful for the support.

Business at the burrito stand was booming. The lineups never dwindled. The angry looking brother, the blonde one, took the orders and called them out in a singsong voice to Carlos. Carlos slapped it all together, rolled it into foil and presented it with a flourish. They worked fast but not fast enough.

A young man in his thirties stood in line waiting. From the side, his profile reminded her of Jaime, the same haircut and frame, but this man had a dark tattoo that snaked up the left side of his neck and onto his cheek. His small earring flashed in the light of the bare bulb that hung from the taco stand. Carmelina knew that if she looked she'd find an extension cord running out to a pole somewhere on the edge of the square.

Her eyelids drooped. She forced herself up and wound through the crowd back to her blanket. After a friendly word to her closest neighbors—the smallest security to somehow make it through the hours to come—she tied her backpack to her thigh and settled down for the night curled around Katya.

FIFTY-FOUR

July 15, 2019
North of Tierra Blanca, Veracruz

The following night, after another punishing day on the road during which neither Bonita nor her grandsons made an appearance, Carmelina found herself in the plaza of another town standing in line for another burrito.

"*Con todo?*" the angry one asked her, his bushy brows weaving together above the bridge of his bulbous nose.

"What is everything today?" She smiled, hoping to see another glimpse of the smile that would transform his face.

Hands constantly moving, eyes scanning the large crowd behind her, he shouted to his brother. "Carlos?"

"Same as last night, Paco."

"So yes, with everything." She piled her change on the counter and edged over to stand in front of Carlos. He grinned at her, the lock of hair falling over his right eye. He had the most amazing, warm eyes.

"*Con todo.*" A man shouldered up to the counter beside her, his upper arm rubbing up against hers. Out of the corner of her eye, she recognized the tattoo and earring of the man she'd noticed in line last night.

"Good burritos, right *chica*?" When he smiled, gold glinted from his mouth.

"The best," she said.

"So wait," he turned back to the blond brother, "did I just hear that your name is Paco?"

Paco tilted his chin up. "That's what my mother calls me."

"And this is your taco stand?"

Paco's brows drew together again, his forehead furled.

"So this is Paco's Tacos?" The man started to laugh. "Paco's Tacos?"

Paco grunted. "You gonna order or not?"

"*Oye, chica*, your special *Paco's Taco's* burrito is ready." With a comic flourish and a wink, Carlos handed over her food.

Earlier today, passing by Tierra Blanca—another major train town where the two lines from the Pacific and the Atlantic joined to run north through Veracruz—their numbers had grown. Rumor had it the northbound train had stopped running and many, tired of waiting over a week, had abandoned the rails and decided to try their luck on foot with the caravan.

She'd kept an eye out for Flora and her family but hadn't spotted any of them, and she wondered whether they'd bothered with the train or if they were already at the U.S. Border thanks to bus tickets paid for with her money.

The plaza overflowed with people, both travelers and locals alike. With nowhere to sit, she leaned against a tree, eating the large burrito while Katya gurgled against her shoulder.

Over the heads and shoulders of the continuous throng of people standing in front of the taco stand, she had a good view of Carlos and Paco. They worked without pause, limbs moving like machine parts. For some reason, each time Carlos waved a large burrito in the air, she thought of Pinocchio, his wooden limbs propelled by taut strings.

The sun had slipped behind the mountains only moments ago. They'd stopped early, the next town too far up the highway to reach before nightfall. As the road wound higher into the mountains, the pine forest marched up to the side of the highway—the occasional peek-a-boo view through the tall trees revealing lush deltas and a parade of volcanoes.

She pulled her phone from her pocket, a compulsion she couldn't resist. She verified the ringer was on. If Diego or her mother contacted her, she would hear it. Her mind looped between worst-case scenarios and miraculous news that Ricky had been found. Which was reality? The waiting was torture and all of it was out of her control. Being suspended in such uncertainty, perpetually in limbo, threatened to drive her mad.

After she fed Katya and watched the baby's lids grow heavy, she made a decision. Before she had time to change her mind, she rose and approached the end of the stand where Carlos was busy chopping onions. The knife sliced down repeatedly against the metal counter top.

"Need help?"

He glanced up, smiled. "We can't pay anyone."

"I can work for free."

Paco slanted a look in their direction. "Two more with everything," he shouted.

She rushed on. "I need something to stay busy. Please. I have experience."

His brows waggled, his chopping never ceased. "What kind of experience?"

She rolled her eyes. "The kind that means I can cut an onion while you're wrapping burritos."

"I don't know." He glanced over at his brother. "You've already been on your feet all day."

"Come on, free labor. Save me from myself."

He put the knife down and looked straight into her face. After thinking it over a few seconds longer, he opened the door at the end of the cart and extended a hand to help her up.

The hours passed. It was hot and steamy in the cart but she was grateful for the company, happy to keep her mind busy. She tucked a sleepy Katya into an empty plastic dishpan and placed the container under a shelf. It was a relief to know she was safe without constantly having her in her arms.

She chopped mountains of onions and mounds of cilantro that disappeared as fast as she could create them. Carlos kept the meat moving on the grill, occasionally stirred a large pot of beans, and constantly ladled beans and meat and handfuls of everything else onto the large tortillas.

Carmelina fell into a rhythm. Once she had a stockpile of cilantro and onions, she ripped sheets of foil from the roll so they were ready for Carlos. By the time she'd stacked those an inch high, it was time to chop again.

From time to time, he nodded and waggled his brows at her, but mostly the two brothers spoke little aside from relaying orders and keeping things moving.

Beneath the counter by Paco, a huge white pail slowly filled as he tossed change into it. Fifty pesos times how many burritos? It added up to a lot of money.

He caught her looking and gave her the stink eye. Carmelina lowered her gaze and concentrated on cutting the onions.

FIFTY-FIVE

July 16, 2019

Carmelina was delighted to discover the burritos were almost as delicious cold as they were hot. Carlos had tried to press some bills into her hand, which she'd refused—a deal was a deal. In lieu of money, he'd given her two large burritos for the road and told her she was welcome back the following night. If she wanted to, that was.

She wanted to. It had kept her mind off things, and when she'd finally gone to bed, she'd instantly drifted into a dreamless sleep.

The afternoon temperature could only be described as sweltering. An inferno. A hellfire of air and transport trucks spewing diesel fumes as they plodded up the long hills on narrow roads with steep shoulders that dropped into ditches filled with a kaleidoscope of plastic and other litter.

It seemed the higher they climbed, the hotter the sun. She'd been grateful for a break and rested in a patch of shade with Bonita. They'd arrived late last night, Bonita told her. She finished off the half burrito Carmelina had shared with her, the other burrito had been quickly devoured by the young boys. Now they raced between the trees behind them, shouting, their voices swallowed by the heavy foliage.

Bonita balled up the foil and removed her weathered shoes. Large blisters covered her heels. From the bag over her shoulder, she pulled a tube of arnica, applied it liberally to her skin, and extended it to Carmelina.

She shook her head. Her skin had toughened to the point that her shoes no longer chaffed against her heels or her toes.

Other migrants marching past greeted either Bonita or Carmelina.

"It's going to rain soon," Bonita said.

Carmelina looked at the strip of sky visible through the towering trees. A truck geared down, brakes squealing, diesel belching up in a blue-charcoal plume.

"Are you sure?"

"Maybe not today, but rainy season is usually here by now. Everybody's been talking about how dry everything is. How late the rains are."

She didn't need a reminder. The air was pregnant with moisture. On one hand, a good rain would leave things fresh, at least for a few hours. On the other, walking in the rain, and dealing with wet shoes and clothing would create another layer of difficulty.

Finally she said, "It'll be cooler."

"We need to move faster. Things are getting tighter at the border." Bonita checked over her shoulder for the two boys. "I'm thinking of taking a bus."

The bus wasn't an option for Carmelina. For one thing, her money wouldn't stretch that far. For another, choosing to leave with the caravan meant she remained undocumented. At any point, Immigration could pick her up and either detain or deport her. She couldn't risk being kept in a Mexican holding cell. Not when Ricky needed her.

"What do you think?" Bonita prompted.

"I think we still have a couple of weeks before the rains start. We'll be north of Mexico City by then."

"I have a little money," Bonita volunteered. "A little extra, I mean. Enough for you to come with us."

Carmelina held her breath. Once again, her mind jumped to worst-case scenarios. Why would Bonita offer to help her? She barely knew the woman.

"I enjoy the company," Bonita said. "And I think there's safety in numbers, especially for women. I'm not worried about myself, but I worry about the boys."

She lowered her voice. "There's so much sex trafficking. They could easily disappear me, take the boys, nobody would be the wiser."

"They're only what? Eight, nine?"

"It's a cruel world we're living in these days." Bonita carefully rolled her socks over the arnica soaked bandages on her feet, then winced as she gently pushed into her shoes and tied the worn grayed laces in double bows.

"And you," she made eye contact with Carmelina, "you're about the same age as my daughter-in-law. You're pretty. They could easily nab you. Who would even know you were gone?"

The words chimed through Carmelina's head like a warning bell at full volume. She wanted to jump up and run screaming into the crowd. Instead, she took a deep breath, forced her shoulders down, and busied herself with Katya.

"Yonas would know."

"Who is Yonas?"

"My friend."

"I haven't seen you talking to anyone else."

The bell rang louder. How *had* Bonita and her grandsons managed to catch them after being almost a full day behind?

"You haven't been around all the time. Where were you yester-day? You never did say."

"I did say. We got up early, walked all day, and caught up. We got in very late." She fanned her face. "I'm running on empty today."

"There's a lot more walking to do." Carmelina pushed herself up off the ground. "I think I'll get going again."

"Carmelina, I... thanks for the burrito." Bonita floundered, her cheeks reddening. "I'm not someone you need to be worried about."

"Oh, I'm not," Carmelina lied.

"My offer is genuine. If you change your mind, you're welcome to come with us. I'll pay your bus fare."

Carmelina nodded, hefted Katya against her chest, and stepped out of the ditch onto the scorching surface of the paved road. Her legs ached, her soles of her feet felt like pulp, but at least her belly was full.

Adjusting the straps of the backpack, she pointed herself forward, to the north, and walked on.

FIFTY-SIX

For a moment—the briefest of moments before the anger and betrayal rushed in—Carmelina missed Flora. At least she'd had several days of what she now saw had been only an illusion of safety. In the end, the people she'd thought were her friends had robbed her despite her offer to help them.

She checked over her shoulder and scanned the crowd. Somewhere behind her was Bonita and her grandsons. Had her offer to pay her bus fare been genuine or was she a cartel spy? Bonita was right. Being on the road on her own made her vulnerable. Nobody would even know if she went missing.

A memory of Flora squeezing her hand outside the bathroom the night Katya had been so sick, bathing the baby together like sisters. Her offer to take them along with her had been genuine. She had enough money, it was better than traveling alone.

Was it possible Bonita's offer had been genuine as well?

Trust remained a fragile orchid in the garden of Carmelina's soul. Something she no longer even tried to nurture. Weeds of distrust and past experience choked out the smallest glimmer of human kindness. Ahead of her stretched punitive days of walking and unknown possible pitfalls at the border. Having someone at her side would be a blessing. Not for the first time, she wished things had gone differently and she'd traveled to the border with Diego and Ricky.

It had been two days since she'd heard a word from him. A text from her mother earlier confirmed that she also hadn't heard anything. Lupe continued to make the calls north, trying to track Ricky. Not one of the people she'd left messages for had even called her back.

Ricky. Her fears for her son multiplied on a daily basis. Was he getting enough to eat? Was he cold? Was someone, anyone, looking out for him? Were there bullies where he was being held?

She'd seen the news reports. Kids in cages at the border. Was he in a place like that? With only cold concrete to sleep on? Punishing overhead lights left on twenty-four seven? The media said they didn't even let the kids brush their teeth, or shower.

The idea of it all strengthened her resolve. She would make it to the border if it killed her. She pushed her fear aside. Ricky needed her. She breathed deep, filling her lungs, and tried an exercise the counsellors at the NCC had taught her.

She swept the worst-case scenario from her mind and pictured her son smiling and happy. He was tucked into a comfortable bed, a fuzzy blanket rolled up to his chin, his chubby little hand holding the hand of a kind woman who read to him from a picture book.

The woman closed the book.

"Again," he said.

She smiled kindly at him and stood up.

"Just once more," he pleaded.

"Tomorrow," the woman said. She bent and kissed his forehead.

There. Someone was caring for her child.

As the woman stepped away toward the door, Ricky spoke again.

"Mama, please."

Mama? Had he already forgotten her? Fear ripped through her again.

"Hey, mama, you're making good time today."

Snapped out of her thoughts, Carmelina turned and focused on Yonas. Once again, he wore the yellow shirt. "Yonas."

He hustled along beside her. "Carmelina, you're practically running. You know this is more a marathon than a sprint, right?"

"It's a race for me," she blurted. She bit her lip. Too much information.

"What's got you in such a hurry today? Hot date later?" He grinned.

"No food tips today?" She tried to change the topic.

"Nah, burritos still the best thing going unless there's something new at the next stop."

"Still on clean up duty?"

"You bet. Last out. Suits me. Then I get to see all my pals as I walk to the front." He winked. "Hey, I saw you last night. You're helping out with the burritos."

She shrugged. "Yeah."

"You think they need someone else? I could use a little work," he added, almost as an afterthought.

"They're not paying me. Like you and the sweeping, it keeps me busy."

"All right, mama. Gotta run. But I'll see you later." He weaved away, quickly blending into the crowd.

CARMELINA SQUEEZED past the broken turnstile into the toilets at the Pemex. When she'd seen the signs on the highway, she'd expected the service station to be busy. What she found was the opposite.

The OXXO was long closed, the windows of the convenience store smashed out, metal shelves overturned or missing. The gas pumps stood unmanned, hoses strewn on the ground. Weeds sprouted through the cracks, a chaotic map of green on the soiled, oil-stained cement.

The bathroom reeked. The taps were broken, the sinks a grimy black mix of mold and built-up dirt. Gingerly, she pressed one of the stall doors open. She clapped a hand over her mouth and stepped back.

It had been a long time since water had run here. Rancid blots of once wet tissue peppered the floor around the toilet. Streaks of feces lined the concrete wall.

Her bowels protested loudly. She checked the other stalls, hoping against hope to find one she might be able to use. She'd be better off outside in the woods.

Behind her, she heard a commotion as someone pressed through the turnstile, hissing her name.

Her belly clenched and her eyes darted to the corners. She was trapped here.

Bonita burst into the small space, her grandsons close behind her. "They're coming," she said.

"Who?" Carmelina looked over Bonita's shoulder but her view out the door ended at the turnstile.

"Cartel. White trucks are coming up the highway, scooping up women and young girls."

"I didn't see anyone."

"They just crested the hill, they're coming from behind, from the south. I heard the screams. Carmelina, you need to get out of here." Bonita pointed to a small rectangle over a sink. "Through there."

Carmelina stood her ground and looked at Bonita. The woman could be leading her into a trap.

"Carmelina, please. Go. I'll hold the baby."

So that was her game. "You already showed your hand," Carmelina said. "Remember, you were the one who told me about people stealing babies."

"I'm not going to steal your baby." Frantic, she looked over her shoulder toward the door. "Please go. Take my boys." She held her hands out for Katya.

Outside, Carmelina heard the sound of roaring engines and tires rolling into the yard. A young girl screeched like she was being killed.

"Boys first." She'd be crazy to go out the window first and leave Katya with this woman.

"Boys, go."

Agile as monkeys, the boys scrambled up over the sink and dropped down the other side.

"Let me help you." Bonita reached for Katya. Carmelina shook her head.

"Check the toilets!"

"For the love of God, girl." Bonita grabbed Katya out of Carmelina's hands and pushed her toward the sink. Carmelina scrambled up, using Bonita's shoulder for leverage. She turned and took Katya and dropped her three feet into the waiting arms of Bonita's eldest grandson.

Hands on the sill, she turned back to Bonita. "What about you?"

"I'll never fit. I'm too old for them to bother with. Go. I'll meet you later."

The turnstile rattled. Carmelina dove head first out the window.

FIFTY-SEVEN

Carmelina dangled down the outside wall of the building, her foot snagged on the window hardware. The youngest grandson pulled on her arms and tried his best to support her. Bonita pushed her foot loose and Carmelina dropped to the ground with a thud.

The grandson carrying Katya was halfway to the tree line. The younger boy helped Carmelina up and they raced after them.

"There's only me," she heard Bonita yell behind them. "There's no one else here."

"Get out of my way, woman." A loud crack echoed out the window. Bonita screamed in pain.

The grandson with Katya turned back toward his grandmother's cries. Carmelina waved him forward and he disappeared into the trees. She dove into the brush and rolled, the other boy beside her.

Breathing hard, she peeked back toward the building. A man's head popped into the small opening, his nose and mouth covered by a black bandana. His head swiveled as he scanned the edge of the woods.

"Go around." He yelled to someone and his head disappeared.

Katya started to wail. Carmelina took her from the boy and smothered her cries against her breast. She motioned the boys to stay quiet and follow her. They scrambled farther back into the brush. She weaved to the north, following the tree line.

Several yards away she spotted a fallen tree, the roots rising high into the air. She dropped into the hole left by the root ball. The boys jumped in beside her.

She picked up a handful of dirt and smeared it on her cheeks. The boys followed her lead. She pulled some loose branches over them and huddled down into the hole as far as she could.

"I don't see anyone." Someone thrashed through the brush near where they had entered.

Carmelina put her finger in Katya's mouth. The baby fussed. She reached for the edge of the scarf to cover Katya's face. There was a large chunk out of it. In the scramble to get through the trees, she'd torn it. She prayed it would not lead them to her.

The man slashed at trees and branches, cursing loudly. The boys, wide-eyed, stared at Carmelina. The younger boy shuddered with fear. She pressed a finger to her lips.

Not far away, another man yelled. "Leave it. We're full anyway."

The man retreated, crashing through the underbrush.

"Hurry up, *gordo*."

"*Ay, callate, cabrón.*"

She stayed in the hole, cuddled together with the boys until the smell of the earth seeped into her nostrils and all she could taste was dank foliage, until the wet of the earth seeped into her clothes and the boys shivered beside her.

From the highway, came a chorus of people screaming, shouting, crying.

When all fell silent again, when the only noise overhead was birdsong and distant voices, when the youngest boy started to weep uncontrollably, she chanced it and stood up.

The woods were empty. The boys clambered up the muddy side of the hole and then helped her out, the older one holding Katya as she pulled herself out using one of the roots.

She led them north, parallel to the highway, staying a few yards inside the tree line.

After several hundred meters, she edged closer to the edge of the jungle. The caravan had grown stronger each day and pockets of people still trudged past. She knew it would be dangerous to stick out. She needed to get herself and the boys back to the caravan where they could lose themselves among the crowd.

"*Abuelita*," the youngest boy said, pointing.

Ahead on the highway, at the edge of the ditch, stood Bonita. She alternated between watching the people filing past her and casting furtive glances into the woods.

Carmelina continued to follow the tree line, staying out of sight, until they were alongside Bonita. She stepped partially out of the foliage and waited for Bonita to spot her. When she saw her, she waved and gave her a thumbs up.

She let the boys go. They raced ahead of her toward their grandmother and flung themselves into her arms. When Carmelina reached them, they enveloped her and Katya into their hug and they stood, together, on the side of the road weeping with relief.

———

"IT WAS HORRIBLE," Bonita said. "I heard they took about twenty women."

Carmelina put her hand to Bonita's right brow. The blood had dried in clumps where the man had hit her in the bathroom.

"I can clean that for you."

"We need to keep going," Bonita said. "I blocked the window for as long as I could."

"You were very brave. We might not be here if not for you."
Bonita had risked a lot to warn her. She'd heard stories of the traffickers selling babies for five thousand dollars. "Gracias."

"It's me who should be thanking you, for keeping the boys safe.
They also took young girls and some boys. One man said his
daughter was only eight. He fought them. You should have seen
him. He was a mess. They smashed the side of his face with the
butt of a rifle.

"One of the women tried to escape over the side of the truck as
they were leaving. They let her hang there, dragging along behind
the truck..." Bonita sobbed, pressing her eyes shut tight. "The
screaming..."

Carmelina swore under her breath and grabbed Bonita's hand.
She prayed the girl would make it. "We should rest," she said.

"No, they might come back."

The idea of being taken and sold into sex trafficking terrified
her. At seventeen, she'd be considered middle-aged and only have
a few years left before she would be discarded. Released back into
the public, if she was lucky. Sold into labor elsewhere if she was
not. She'd heard a lot of the women who worked the fields through
Guatemala were sex and labor slaves, laboring in the fields under
the hot sun all week, and being passed around to drunks on the
weekends in the brothels.

They fell silent, each lost in her own dark thoughts, the two
boys subdued, sticking to their sides like glue. The road climbed,
the air grew thinner, the sun beat down on them.

All around them, the group buzzed with news of who was
taken. How many. How young. The daughter of a friend. A
cousin. Someone's pregnant wife.

Someone started to sing. Others joined in. Soon a chorus of
voices surrounded her, lifting in song to chase away the demons.

Out of the corner of her eye, Carmelina saw a flash of blue
beside her. A man called her name. She grabbed for Bonita's hand,

her gaze automatically sliding to the ditch and gauging the distance to the woods.

"Ay, Carmelina, it's Carlos."

It was the battered blue Blazer with the clattering taco stand. The robust singing had drowned out its arrival.

The truck rolled to a stop and Carlos waved her over. "Ride with us," he said.

Not a chance. I barely know these guys. They could sell me, too.

FIFTY-EIGHT

"I'm fine, I can walk."

Carlos leaned out the window. "It's too dangerous. They already grabbed a bunch of women today."

"I'll stay with my friends."

Bonita came to stand beside Carmelina, the boys hiding behind their grandmother.

"They're coming back," Paco said from behind the wheel. He jutted his chin. Sure enough, the white pickups were cresting the hill about a kilometer away and moving fast.

Carmelina's gaze shot to the woods.

"Come with us," Carlos said. "We're not going to hurt you."

"You might sell her," Bonita said. Carmelina braced herself. Carlos was a big man. At this point, he could get out of the truck and simply scoop her up.

Carlos's mouth dropped. "We... good grief, Carmelina, would you let us help you?"

People ahead of them were starting to run for the woods.

"Get the hell in before they see you and come after all of us," Paco growled. "All of you, there's room. Jaysus, get in!"

Bonita grabbed the back door and ushered the two boys in, then got in herself. Carmelina slid in beside her and slammed the door shut.

The truck pulled away, rolling at a normal speed, as the convoy of white pick ups roared toward them.

Bonita pushed the boys down onto the floor and flung herself face first over them. Carmelina stretched out flat on the seat.

Looking in from the outside, all anyone would see was the two men driving the truck and the taco stand.

CARMELINA BRUSHED a tear from her eye with the back of her hand. She was up to her elbows in a mountain of chopped onion.

"Fresher than last night, yeah?" Carlos caught her in the act.

She laughed. "A bit."

"We're good on that for a while. How about getting more foil ready?"

"On it." She bent to check on Katya, sleeping soundly and tucked back into the plastic dishpan under the bottom shelf.

Not only had Carlos and Paco given them a ride and got them out of danger, they'd also insisted Bonita and the boys eat with them before they started setting up for the night. Bonita could not stop thanking them.

She'd had it wrong about Bonita. If it hadn't been for her warning earlier, who knows where she'd be now? And she owed a debt of gratitude to Carlos and Paco.

Finished with the roll of tin foil, she patted the top of a good size pile. Carlos tipped his chin, his arms in constant motion, as he wrapped and delivered burritos. Tonight *con todo* consisted of the same *con todo* as the night before, and the night before that. The heap of onions resembled an ant hill more than a mountain, she picked up the knife and pulled onions and cilantro from the blue wash bin where they'd been soaking.

The knife sliced cleanly through the onion in a satisfying way. Her instructions had been to half it, then peel the skin off the half, then dice. It worked famously.

Carlos cleared his throat. She glanced over and he slanted his eyes to a man standing in front of Carmelina across the counter.

"I'm happy to see you, mama. I thought you might have been caught up in the trouble earlier."

"No, Yonas, I'm too old for them." She tried to make a joke but neither of them laughed. Carlos turned away, listening to another order from Paco.

"Horrible thing," Yonas said. "I'm glad you're okay. And the little one?"

"Sleeping like a trooper."

"Do troopers sleep?"

Carmelina rolled her eyes, sliced through another onion, and pushed it onto its side.

"You make good time," she said to Yonas. "Always getting from the back to the front again. That must be the thing that keeps you thin."

"My motor mouth keeps me thin, mama. The faster I talk, the faster my metabolism runs. I couldn't put on weight if I ate nothing but lard morning, noon, and night. Trust me, I've tried." He winked.

"Ready." Carlos handed Yonas his burrito.

The man pranced in place licking his lips. "Thank you, sir."

Carlos nodded and started rolling the next one.

"You take care of yourself, mama. Keep your eyes open."

Carmelina watched him go then refocused on the onion.

"You know him?"

"Seen him around is all. He told me about this caravan. At first I was planning to wait for another one to arrive from Santa Ana—

that's in northern El Salvador," she added. "But I decided to join this one."

"I see him around a lot," Carlos said.

"He's a joker. Always manages to make me smile."

Carlos's brows shot up.

"We working here or what?" Paco grumbled and barked out another order.

Carlos went back to work, Carmelina pushed the chopped onions to the side and started on a large bunch of cilantro.

———

"YOU SHOULD GO AHEAD," Carlos said. "Get some rest. We'll finish cleaning up."

He pushed the scraper across the grill in a practiced motion, scooping the last of the grease and the burnt bits off the grill. Savory smoke rose as he tossed water onto the hot surface.

In the corner, his head below the counter, Paco perched on a stool—comically small for his large frame—counting the take for the night. Piles of peso coins marched along the shelf nestled against stacks of bills. Knowing he didn't yet trust her, she kept her eyes off their prize.

"I don't mind," she said, wiping the stainless counter with a damp cloth. "Katya's asleep for now." The truth of course was more complicated. Or perhaps it was simpler. Surrounded by the two large men, enclosed within the stainless steel taco stand, provided her with a sense of security. She felt less vulnerable. Safer.

"You'll be dead on your feet tomorrow," Carlos said.

She shrugged. "I won't sleep a whole lot tonight anyway. Besides, Bonita and I, we're getting on a bus tomorrow morning."

"Hey."

They both looked up from their tasks as a man approached the counter. Paco shot a look at his brother.

"Sorry, you've missed us for tonight," Carlos said.

"I'm not hungry." When he shrugged, his single earring shimmered in the light.

"We're all out." Carlos splayed his large hands. "Sorry."

"A good night for you guys then."

Carmelina recognized him from the last two nights. The man who she thought resembled Jaime. Except Jaime didn't have the kind of tats this guy did running up the left side of his neck onto his cheek.

In the corner, Paco nudged a dirty rag over the shelf, his movement deft as he quickly covered the stack of money.

"We can only buy supplies we have money for. Once we cook that, we're done for the night."

"Really good business here," he said, his eyes shifting to Carmelina. "Hey, I remember you from the other night. Good burritos, right?"

"Yes." She did her best to control her voice, keep it even, hoping he wouldn't hear the tremor that had started in her toes.

"*Mira*." Paco stood and the guy swung toward him. "We don't make a shit ton of money here. We make enough to buy supplies for tomorrow, enough to pay gas to the next town, and enough for the propane to cook. All we're doing is working our way north."

The gold in the man's mouth glinted when he grinned, but it was an ugly smile. "We're all heading north."

FIFTY-NINE

"Maybe we can help you out," Carlos said. Under the counter, he made a gesture to Paco to back off.

It was late. Anyone nearby with enough room to stretch out was horizontal. At the far corner of the plaza, a laugh arose from a local taco stand where a small group of men clinked their beer bottles.

"I'm César." He extended his hand. His jacket sleeve rode up to reveal an expensive-looking gold watch. The back of his knuckles were covered in ink. Carmelina had seen enough bad tattoos to know they'd been done in a clubhouse. Or in prison.

She regretted not leaving when Carlos had tried to send her away.

Carlos shook his hand, introduced himself and his brother. Carmelina was grateful to be excluded.

"I don't need handouts," César said, his hand smoothing the hair over his ears. It was heavily gelled and jet black.

"A business arrangement then," Carlos said. "I heard you talking about how good our burritos are. I'm sure you're contributing to our success, recommending us, helping us get new customers. That's worth something."

"*Si*," Paco said, nodding. "That's definitely worth something to us, César. We don't want any trouble."

"You misunderstand me, my friends. I'm not here to make things difficult or take your money. I'm here to make things easier for you. Simpler."

Although his words were smooth, Carmelina quaked at the tone in his voice. Under the shelf near her feet, Katya started to stir, a sign she would soon wake.

Carlos turned toward her. "You should take the baby and head out," he said. "You don't need to be here for this."

Carmelina bent to retrieve Kayta. When she stood, César met her gaze and put his hand up.

"Hang on." César pierced her with a look. "I like the girl. You've been a whole lot faster the last couple nights."

"She's not really part of our crew," Carlos said. "I'd rather not include her."

"Hmm. I guess that would have weight if I'd asked you what you wanted." He leaned in, placing his elbows on the top of the counter. "Let me explain how this is going to go. I need someone who can prepare a lot of food fast. From what I've seen, you fit the bill."

César stepped back and circled to the end of the taco stand. Paco reached for a baseball bat she hadn't noticed before, tucked below the bottom shelf near where he kept the money.

"I wouldn't if I were you." César pushed the back door open and entered. With a flick, he displaced the corner of his shirt to expose the gun tucked in his waistband. "Gunfight 101, right? Don't bring a bat to a gun fight." He chuckled at his own joke.

Carmelina pressed back against the counter, head down, arms tightly wrapped around Katya. Things were going sour very fast.

"Put the baby down," he ordered. "Help these guys finish packing up. Then we're all gonna take a little ride."

THE BLAZER LABORED up the endless hill, belching and backfiring like an unruly dragon. The taco stand trailing behind rattled so loudly, Carmelina worried the whole thing would fly apart. She imagined long sheets of battered stainless steel flying into the ditch, onto the windshields of the traffic behind them, and she fantasized that a traffic catastrophe would get them out of the jackpot they were in.

She sat frozen in the backseat with her backpack at her feet. Katya slept on the seat in the space between her and Carlos.

Paco drove, César riding shotgun, the little *pendejo* literally sitting in the passenger seat with his pistol aimed at Paco. Paco had barely said a word. If she'd thought he looked angry earlier, now he looked ready to explode. Perspiration beaded his forehead, his eyes fixed steadfastly on the oncoming traffic.

Carlos stared out the window. All his attempts to negotiate with César had been wasted breath. If she knew him better, she might guess what was behind the large, furrowed forehead and calm brown eyes.

He'd fought hard, repeatedly and without success, to have her left behind. Now, even though he was larger and stronger than César, there was no way he'd make a move that might endanger his brother.

The kilometers rolled on through a moonless night.

"Won't this piece of shit go any faster?" César fiddled with the radio, dialed in a station he liked, and *ranchera* music blasted out of the tinny speakers.

Without taking his eyes from the road, Paco pursed his lips and twisted his head to the far left, then the far right.

"A man of few words. I like that. Still, this truck is a piece of shit."

It was difficult to know where they were. The road climbed and plummeted, twisting through the mountains. They passed a sign for Orizaba. She recognized the name—it was on their route so they were still heading north. But having walked so far, the distance marked on the sign didn't seem to have any meaning for her.

They swung around a tight corner. She shifted in her seat, bracing herself at the last minute with her hand on Carlos's thigh to avoid disturbing Katya. Was Paco planning to dislodge César's weapon, somehow catch him off guard?

"Don't lose that stand over the side of the road." Voice silky, he didn't lift his gaze from the screen of his phone. "Without the stand, I have zero use for any of you."

They sailed down a hill, the muffler of the decrepit truck rumbling beneath them. Lights glimmered in the distance. Lots of lights. The whole sky lit up with the lights. As they drove closer, the shape of tall buildings and church steeples sparked against the horizon.

The poorly aimed headlights lit up a road sign that announced Puebla. That name was familiar, too. Another town would have been on their route. It was one of the places she and Bonita had planned to change buses. At least she was still going in the right direction.

Somehow, in that moment, it wasn't much consolation.

SIXTY

They skirted the city of Puebla, the traffic heavy on the *periférico* bypass despite the late hour. Paco kept to the slowest lane, yet horns blared behind and around them, angry cargo truck drivers shaking their fists as they jostled between vehicles and blasted past.

Paco focused on the road. Undisturbed, César laughed, lit a joint, and turned up the music. The speakers boomed out *Corrido de Chihuahua*, César singing along at the top of his lungs while the interior of the vehicle filled with the sweet, cloying smell of pot.

Carmelina cracked the window. César shot her a warning glance over his shoulder.

"For the baby," she said.

He dragged deeply on the joint, held the smoke, then blew it over the seat in her direction. It billowed into her face. She sat still as stone. He laughed again but a few seconds later, a stream of smoke was sucked into the exhaust-filled air when he rolled the front window down a couple of inches.

Gradually, traffic thinned. They were back on the highway, a convoy of trucks and late night travelers, the city behind them.

"Where are we going?" She mouthed the words to Carlos.

He shrugged. "I don't know," he mouthed back.

She was left to her own devices, her mind a terrible, writhing thing filled with worst-case scenarios. What did he mean when he said he needed cooks? Who were they supposed to feed?

And what would Bonita think when Carmelina didn't show up to sleep where they'd agreed? Would she notice or would she wake up in the morning to find her not there? Would she feel abandoned? Worry about whether Carmelina had been disappeared? She was likely the only person, aside from Yonas, who would even miss her.

Yonas. She imagined his quick smile, his ratty yellow shirt tails trailing behind him as he vanished into the crowds. Where would he think she had gone?

People joined the caravan daily. They'd set out from Mapastepec with only a few hundred people. Now their numbers had swelled closer to a thousand, especially with the surge of people joining them after giving up on the train.

Flora. Her adorable son, Beto. Jaime and even Manuel. Their betrayal still cut her. But she knew it was nothing compared to what might lie ahead.

Because what lay ahead could not be named. And she'd learned—experience was a merciless teacher—that a danger that could not be named, could not be clearly seen, could grow to enormous, frightening proportions, bolstered by a mind not kept busy enough.

Right now, trapped in the smoky backseat of this lumbering vehicle, her only hope two brothers who were nearly strangers to her, Carmelina's mind sparred with the festering, unknown monster lurking in the shadows.

A monster yet to be disclosed.

TIME ROLLED ON. Carmelina shifted in her seat, striving for a position to relieve the pressure from her full bladder.

Carlos raised his brows in a silent question.

She mimed her need and he nodded, pointing to himself.

"How much longer?" he asked, addressing César.

"In this tub? It could be a while." César's head rested against the back of the seat, his eyes partly closed.

"We need to pull over for a minute."

"For what? There's nothing here." Outside the window, a chain of closed up shops and market stalls huddled in the darkness like tall turtles.

"I need a toilet," Carlos said.

Paco glanced into the rearview mirror and made eye contact with his brother. "Me, too. And a quick stretch."

"There's nothing here." César flicked a hand at the window. "Keep going."

"Two minutes, man. There's room here for us to pull over."

"Jaysus, Mary and Joseph. You people are like a drip of water I can't shut off." He grunted and waved the pistol toward the side of the road.

Paco pulled the vehicle onto the shoulder, and parked in front of one of the darkened stalls. César exited and motioned Carlos and Paco out. Carmelina gathered Katya. Before she could climb down, César skewered her with a look. "Not the baby."

"She needs to be changed."

"Later, when you come back."

Reluctantly, she laid Katya back down on the seat. The baby cooed and gurgled up at her.

"There." He pointed to the side of the stall. "Stay where I can see you."

Modesty was a luxury Carmelina hadn't enjoyed in a long time but she wished she was wearing her skirt. Despite her urgent need to urinate, she was shy about having to drop her pants and

squat in front of Carlos and Paco. Sensing her discomfort, the two
brothers turned away and pissed against a nearby shed.

César smoked a cigarette, the tip flaring in the dark. Cars and
trucks whizzed past them, the constant stream of headlights
strobing between the row of darkened stalls.

Carmelina buttoned her pants and clambered back into the
car. She pulled Katya onto her lap, hoping to change her while the
vehicle was still. Not that it mattered, Katya was used to constant
motion, it was simply easier if Carmelina didn't have to anticipate
the rolls through the turns.

The brothers got back into the vehicle, their shoulders lower
than when they'd climbed out. Dejected. There'd been a spark of
hope when they'd stopped. She'd hoped to run into the night but
without Katya, it wasn't an option. The men had probably hoped
to overcome César.

César had remained vigilant. He hadn't dropped the gun or his
attention for a single second. He'd left them with no wiggle room
at all.

With his back against the open passenger door, and his pistol
aimed steadily at Paco, he pissed onto the shoulder, dust rising in
the dashboard light, the biting scent of ammonia drifting into the
truck.

Carmelina lowered her gaze and busied herself with changing
Katya.

SIXTY-ONE

"You'll sleep out here in the truck. Don't think about going anywhere."

After collecting their cell phones and the knives and large utensils, César left them. Carmelina was dead tired. Paco's eyes drooped. Carlos rooted around in the back of the Blazer, digging out blankets.

Traffic coming in to Mexico City had been at a standstill. It had taken hours to lurch forward, yard by painful yard, through the relentless congestion.

Approaching the city, Carmelina was overwhelmed. She'd never seen anything like it. Guatemala City dwarfed in comparison. It sprawled in every direction, lights marched up hills and into the crevices of valleys and mountainsides. Brightly lit billboards lined the roadways, large towers dotted the landscape. Planes flew overhead. At one point, a helicopter dipped over the highway above them, so low the rotors were easily heard over César's music.

If she was able to slip away from César, how would she ever find her way out of this?

"Over twenty million people," Carlos whispered.

César had found a late night rap station. He drummed against the cracked dash, his hands beating out a staccato rhythm that didn't complement the song in any way.

Finally they exited the highway into a residential area. Street after quiet street wound up the side of the mountain, a virtual maze, lined with brightly colored cement walls that seemed to grow out of the edge of the sidewalk. Bursts of ochre, mustard, rich royal blues, deep greens, earthy golds and sunflower yellow, flashed by under their lights.

Near the end of a dead-end street, double metal doors opened and a man guided them in. The truck and taco stand came to rest under a large party tent.

In the corner of the yard, by another gate, two men sat in the halo of an overhead light playing dominos on a makeshift table of plywood supported by two overturned paint pails. Their rifles leaned casually against the soft lavender of the concrete wall beside them.

"Let's get some sleep." Carlos passed Carmelina a blanket and pillow, then climbed into the front seat.

"What do you think they want with us here?"

"I don't know. But whatever it is, I'm guessing they're gonna get it."

Carmelina stretched out over the back seat with Katya nestled beside her. It felt so good to be horizontal, her head resting on the small pillow. She sat up. "Wait, why am I lying down and you two have to sit up?"

"We're used to sitting up," Carlos said. "We alternate in the back. Anyway, there's more leg room up front. It's fine."

Paco huffed, then snorted, already asleep. A few seconds later, his rhythmic snoring filled the small space.

"We'll get out of here," Carlos said. "We'll see our chance, and we'll get out."

He turned to her, his eyes kind. "You're one of us now. We'll take care of you."

July 17, 2019
Northern Mexico City

"Up!"

Carmelina's eyes flew open. Someone banged on the outside of the truck and yelled again.

"Up!"

The party tent shielded them from the sky above. It was barely light but hard to guess the time.

"Up!"

Apparently it was time to get up. The banging on the roof increased. A small man with a goatee and two teardrops tattooed under his left eye wrenched open the driver's door. Having been slumped against it, Paco rolled out onto the ground.

He landed with a thump in the dirt. "What the hell?"

The little man toed him in the kidney with his metal-tipped turquoise cowboy boot, the bright leather polished to a high gleam. "Get up. Time for breakfast."

He went around the front of the truck, flung open Carlos's

door and tossed a pen and notepad in his lap. "Make a list of what you need. Hurry up."

"Breakfast for how many?"

"Burritos for a hundred."

"What kind do you want?"

The man edged himself closer to the door. He narrowed his eyes. "I want the kind that cook fast and don't cost a shit ton. Beans, rice, lots of filler and some kind of cheap meat. Got it?"

Carlos scribbled out a list of ingredients.

Paco got up and brushed himself off. "We need propane," he said. "We're out."

"*cabrón!* Go check the propane tanks. Bring me one that's full."

One of the guards at the back gate shuffled off out of sight along the far wall.

List complete, Carlos passed the notebook back to the man. He took it and strode away after the guard. Several minutes later, they reappeared, the guard hoisting a thirty pound propane tank on his shoulder.

"Where you want it, Goat?" The man with the goatee indicated a spot on the ground and the guard put it down.

Goat stroked his goatee. "You have anything on hand?"

"A few pounds of rice." Carlos took a deep breath, sleep still heavy on his face.

"Start with that. Get the grills hot and ready to go." He glanced into the backseat and fixed on Carmelina. "You waiting on room service, *Princesa?* Get the hell up and get this show on the road."

He stomped away. The guard drifted back toward his post at the gate.

Paco hooked up the propane while Carlos dumped rice into a large stock pot. After feeding Katya, Carmelina brought her back to the taco stand and tucked her into the plastic dishpan under the shelf.

"Want to leave her in the truck?" Carlos twisted the top of the large bag, shoved it back into a pail, then pressed the lid down to secure it. "She might be more comfortable there."

"I'm not letting her out of my sight." She turned away, opened the bin with the rags soaking in bleach and laid them out on the counter to dry. She turned back to him and lowered her voice. "Did you see his tattoos?"

"The teardrops? It could mean something else."

"With *LC-14* around home it usually means the number of murders they've committed."

"These guys are *Los Tigres*," Carlos said.

"So does it mean the same thing?"

He expelled a breath. "As far as I know."

Carmelina rearranged the rags, aimlessly shuffling them on the counter. "You figure there's a party about to show up here for breakfast?"

A snort from behind her made her turn. "I doubt it," Paco said, edging past her.

"But the party tent?"

Paco surveyed the area around them. There were no shadows outside the sides of the white tent. He dropped his voice anyway. "My guess is we're feeding people being held inside the house."

"Oh." Carmelina put two and two together. It added up to a big pile of stinking shit.

THE TENT WAS DESIGNED to shelter party goers from the sun, or possibly, depending on the time of year, from the rain. It was wide enough to park two or three vehicles side by side and long enough, from front to back, to completely cover the old Blazer and the rickety stainless steel taco stand.

The high concrete walls and gates they had passed through last night shielded them from prying eyes outside on the street. The tent shielded them from anyone passing by overhead. Like a drone. Or a helicopter. Or a low-flying plane.

Judging from the distance between the front gate and the back gate, they were on a very large property. And if the gates they'd seen on their way in were any indication, a very wealthy neighborhood.

The grass lay brown and wilted. According to Carlos, July was normally the rainiest month of the year, but so far the rains had not come. The parched lawn had been beaten down, tracked by tires and trampled by countless feet. From nearby came the sound of running water. Perhaps a water feature or fountain.

"We need water." Paco grabbed two large twenty liter containers, stepped out of the stand, and headed to his left. He didn't make it to the side of the tent before the guard sprinted across the grass.

"Whoa there, cowboy. Where you headed?"

He lifted the jugs. "We need water."

"I'll bring you a hose. Get back in the stand."

Paco backed up, turned toward Carmelina and Carlos and lifted his brow. He waited, leaning against the rear edge of the stand.

The guard returned, dragging a long black hose with a shut off valve.

"This is potable?"

"You need drinkable water?"

"Some. This is fine for cleaning and washing vegetables. Can you find us a *garafon* of fresh water?"

The guard narrowed his eyes and shuffled off. Paco filled the jugs and brought them on board. The knifes and utensils had been returned and Carmelina laid everything out on the counter, along with the containers. All she needed now were the supplies and she could start chopping.

The large pot of rice simmered on the element, a low whining indicated it would boil soon. Without worry of running out of propane, Carlos had the flame on under the grill, warming things up.

"They might be a while," Paco said, pointing his chin toward the grill.

"He said be ready. I'm ready. It's not my gas."

"Hmph. I guess without customers I won't need to take orders."

"You can cook, wrap, or help chop," Carlos said.

"I'll cook. What did you ask for?"

"*Chorizo* and *costilla*."

"Pork rib? I thought they wanted cheap."

"They want fast, too. *Costilla* and sausage today, chicken tomorrow."

"You think there's going to be a tomorrow?" Carmelina's stomach plummeted as she asked the question, knowing full well what the answer would be before Carlos uttered the words.

"I think there's going to be many tomorrows."

SIXTY-THREE

RICKY GONE 84 DAYS

August 7, 2019
Express Kidnap House, Northern Mexico City

The rains came, arriving late but with a vengeance. By early August, the yard had turned into a sea of mud. The guards slipped through it. It lapped at the tires of the Blazer, seeped under the taco stand, and wilted Katya's skin until it was the texture of prunes.

The party tent kept them dry while they worked. From early morning until late into the night, they cooked and chopped and wrapped burritos. At first, it was a hundred burritos in the morning and a hundred more at night.

Now they cooked a hundred and fifty in the morning. Goat, the one with the goatee and teardrop tattoos who bought the food, constantly admonished them to use cheaper supplies. More rice, more beans, less protein, he said.

Later in the day, after a brief siesta, they cooked a hundred and fifty more. They never saw who they were cooking for. Occasionally, yells or anguished screams leaked out from the inside of the house and Carmelina would cover her ears.

Once in the night, when a piercing cry woke her from a fitful sleep, Carmelina sat up to see them dragging bodies across the back lawn. When she told Carlos in the morning his eyes widened and he placed a finger to his lips.

Their role was clear. Cook. See nothing. Shut up.

Carmelina chopped until the inside of her thumbs blistered and broke, the skin reddened and raw. Then it would scab up. Eventually the new skin would harden and she could chop without pain again.

Some part of her hand or her fingers was always bandaged.

Katya grew larger. She outgrew the plastic dishpan and Carmelina salvaged a cardboard box from the supplies and kept her in that. She was more alert. At night, she flailed her little arms and legs, trying to crawl but there was nowhere for her to go. If they weren't in the taco stand working, they were in the truck sleeping.

A bucket in the corner of the tent served as their toilet. She'd hung her tattered scarf in front of it but it offered little privacy. She held her bowels until night time or early morning. When the bucket was full, or particularly ripe from the sweltering heat, Carlos or Paco got permission from the guards to empty it out through the back gate.

Behind the back gate ran a dirt alley that bordered the properties on one side of the street. The homes and concrete walls ran in each direction as far as the eye could see.

On the far side of the alley stretched grassland and brambles. Carlos and Paco thought if they could ever get out, under cover of darkness, they might be able to run fast enough, and far enough, to get away. They'd have to stay out in the open a long time though since looping back into the neighborhood would be too risky.

It wasn't much of an escape plan. It didn't matter. They were never left unattended. Two men flanked the back gate at all times.

They rarely saw César. Carlos figured managing the food was below his pay grade. Or maybe above it. He could be a scout, spending most of his time on the road.

They saw a lot of the little man with the teardrop tattoos and the ugly goatee. Goat was a prick with a Napoleon complex. He took the orders for supplies and bossed them around. He bought the rattiest cilantro, moldy onions, beans so old and hard all the water in the world wouldn't render them edible, and often, meat tinged with green that Paco cooked forever striving to burn the bacteria out of it.

He consistently bought the wrong size diapers for Katya, a discount brand that made her skin break out. She scowled and fussed through the night. Without skin cream or Vaseline or even *arnica,* Carmelina had to use the *manteca* they used for cooking to soothe Katya's raw skin. It helped but the roaches, attracted by the smell of the pork lard, sought the baby out while she slept in her box on the floor.

The elastic in Carmelina's skirt had stretched and the waist-band rode low on her hips. Her pants were just as loose—she threaded a piece of twine from the rice sack through the belt loops to hold them up. Her face, when she dared to look in the side mirror of the truck, was gaunt and sallow. The lack of exercise, stress, and steady diet of rice and beans—she often wouldn't eat the meat—was taking a toll. She recognized the same stresses and loss of vibrancy in Carlos and Paco.

At night, she wept quietly into her pillow. They'd taken her phone. She had no idea what was happening with Diego. Desperate for news of Ricky and feeling more powerless than she'd ever felt in her life, she even prayed—she prayed to every Saint she'd ever been acquainted with.

She was losing track of how long it had been since she last

talked to her brother. Under the shelf in the taco stand, she used a pencil to etch the days on a rudimentary calendar. They'd been here three weeks already and it was a few days before that when she'd talked to Diego. Twenty-four days then since the last news.

Eighty-four days since Diego and Ricky left. Eighty-four days without her son. Worse, since early June he'd been on his own and lost in the damn system. She could only hope Diego had left El Paso and gone to collect him by now.

She also had other, more pressing concerns. One of the guards had started to pay too much attention to her. He watched each time she slipped behind the flimsy scarf to void her bladder. She often waited until the pressure was unbearable, hoping he'd go off shift or slip away for food or a drink.

Once, he stopped by to compliment her on the burritos. A few days ago, he intercepted her on the way from the truck in the morning, his fingers gripped the top of Katya's head, his thumb resting casually against her breast. His smile revealed a mouthful of rotted teeth. His rancid breath caused her to close her mouth tightly.

Carlos had a sharp eye. Not much got past him. He told her it would be better if they pretended to be a couple. So they hatched a plan. They started to flirt in the taco stand as they chopped and wrapped, and Paco gruffly told them, in good fun, to knock it off. Paco made jokes about having to sleep in the taco stand so his brother and Carmelina could have their privacy in the truck.

The guard watched them both carefully and his demeanor grew churlish and petty. Paco had to take the bucket to the alley because the guard once tripped Carlos. Another time he shoved him so hard from behind that Carlos face-planted into the muck, the bucket emptying before him and soiling his shirt and hair.

It had been three months since Carmelina's birth control shot at the NCC. Not only had she no recourse if the guard chose to assault her, she also had no protection against a pregnancy.

Stretched out on the saggy backseat of the old truck through the long hours of the night, these things weighed on her mind as keenly as the worn springs pressing into her back. She tried to focus on the noise around her, as familiar now as her own baby's breath: the rain pelting against the vinyl tent overhead, Paco's snoring, Carlos's murmuring—he talked in his sleep, sometimes whole sentences that prompted her to cobble together some kind of story to distract herself from her insomnia and torturous thoughts.

Carmelina wished she could escape the truck, the tent, her mind, and the melting, punishing heat of the endless rainy Mexican summer.

SIXTY-FOUR

RICKY GONE 126 DAYS

September 17, 2019

"You. We need help with the burritos."

Carmelina looked up, the knife she held mid-slice through a large onion. Goat stood at the counter, his finger pointed in her direction.

"Hurry up, get out here." He gestured for her to exit the taco stand. She wiped her hands on the rag she kept tucked into her waistband, glanced down at Katya, then stepped around front.

Goat was not tall. It was the first time she'd been so close to him. It felt odd to not have the barrier of the stainless steel counter between them.

"Here." He pulled one of the bins piled high with burritos down off the counter and plunked it into her arms. He grabbed the other, tipped his chin toward the house, and turned away.

Carmelina's heart climbed into her throat. She glanced up at Carlos then hurried after Goat. Out of the tent. Across the yard. Two more men perched like ravens on each side of the back door. They scrambled to open it when Goat approached.

Without acknowledging them, he passed through and she followed him into a large kitchen.

The smell hit her first, a solid punch to her senses. Her nose twitched. Stale beer, the sweet stench of pot, rancid food. Empty bottles and fast food containers covered the counters and the large square table that dominated the center of the room.

Six men played cards. Stacks of peso coins in the middle of the table. Only one glanced up when they entered, his right brow rising before he turned back to his hand.

In the corner of the kitchen a thin woman with a blackened eye looked up from the rag she was pushing along the counter. Carmelina recognized terror in her eyes. Another woman, barely visible behind the first, washed dishes.

Goat guided her down a dark hallway that led to the right wing of the house. A heavy silence dogged their steps. Here the air was pungent. The bitter tang of ammonia, the nose-tickling stench of perspiration and unwashed bodies. She held her breath. Her arms ached under the weight of the bin.

Two more men sat at the end of the hallway, smoking, the window behind them open. One of them tipped his chin to Goat.

Goat cracked open a door. It was dark inside. Stale air wafted into the hall. Carmelina glimpsed a square of pale greenish light— a window covered with a tarp or garbage bag. He tossed burritos, two at a time, to the other side of the door. In all he made eight tosses. When he closed the door, there was a scramble of shuffling from inside and lowered voices. He hit the door once with the side of his fist and the voices ceased.

Sixteen? Carmelina calculated there were sixteen people in that small room.

The performance was repeated five more times on the lower level. Three more in the wing they'd started in. Twice near the large double doors that opened onto the front foyer. A large bunch of white, red, and bright green balloons were tied to an ornamental planter that stood against the wall.

At the bottom of the wide staircase that led to the upper level, he took the bin from her and jutted his chin toward the kitchen.

She scuttled back down the hallway, anxious to pass through the kitchen and back to the tent unnoticed or at least undisturbed. The men playing cards in the kitchen was too familiar, reminiscent of Flaco and Memo and the hell she'd left behind. Chest tight, she crept through the kitchen, eyes fixed on the back door.

Someone coughed, but no one spoke to her. She pushed through the door, past the two guards there, and fled back to the taco stand under the intense watchful eye of the guard at the back gate.

"TAKE A BREATH," Carlos said. She knelt on the floor of the taco stand, forehead pressed to the floor beneath her, a rag pressed to her mouth to muffle her sobs. Tears streamed down her face. Her body shook violently.

"Breathe." Carlos crouched beside her and placed his large hand on her back and breathed loudly, in then out. The warmth of his hand between her shoulder blades radiated outward. She snuffled and gulped her sobs back into her throat, focused on his breathing and tried to regulate hers to his.

"I—"

"Don't talk. Breathe." He rubbed her back in a circular motion. Her mother had done that when she was a child. She blinked, focused on a stray stalk of cilantro that had fallen under one of the shelves, forced herself to breathe. In. Out.

"The guards are watching. Carlos, stand up."

Paco was elbow deep in a bin of water, washing up. Once everything was washed down, they'd eat breakfast—their burritos sat on the side, wrapped tightly. Then they started the whole routine again. Chopping, cooking, wrapping.

Carlos rose. Carmelina shifted her focus to his large work boots. The leather on the toes curled back to reveal the plate of metal beneath. The heel of the sole was uneven, the back worn down to almost nothing.

She pushed herself to a sitting position and scrubbed her face with her palms. Stretching, she grabbed a sheet of paper towel and used it to blow her nose. She blew again, so hard she made a honking sound. Would the smell from inside that hellhole ever leave her? She blew once more before tossing the towel in the trash.

Carlos offered her a hand up. She slipped her hand into his and rose, brushing the dust from the back of her pants.

"We're almost done here," Paco said. "Why don't you take the baby and go eat? Carlos will go with you."

Grateful, she nodded and collected Katya.

Carlos grabbed the burritos and drinks. "Come join us when you're done?" he asked his brother.

"Be there in five."

Carlos led the way back to the spot they normally sat to eat beside the truck. It was shaded and out of the direct sight line of the guards. He put the food on the improvised table and watched while she settled Katya and then sat down on one of the wooden crates.

Carlos sat across from her. She raised her gaze to meet his.

And the tears began to flow once more.

"YOU WERE RIGHT," she said, looking over at Carlos and Paco.

They exchanged a worried look.

"Finish eating," Paco said.

They insisted she eat before talking, claiming the food would settle her stomach. She chewed slowly, forcing the food down her throat, not sure that it would help.

When she was done, she spoke again.

"I saw six rooms, each filled with people. There are more upstairs."

"How many people?"

"I don't know. He barely cracked the doors open. The smell..." She puffed out a breath. "The smell inside is horrible."

"I'm sorry you had to see that," Carlos said.

"I've seen a lot in my life," she said. "And I knew, I mean, we all knew what was probably going on inside. But the conditions those poor people are being held in..."

"All the windows are covered, there's no fresh air, the house is sweltering. Imagine this heat," she waved her hand around her, "multiplied by, I don't now... it must be over a hundred degrees inside. Probably even hotter upstairs."

The men waited for her to continue. She glanced over at Katya. The baby stretched out on her belly on a blanket, struggling to pull herself forward with her chubby arms.

"It was horrible," she said again. She felt drained, her muscles liquefied, a kick-back to the stress.

"Are there more men inside?" Paco leaned forward.

Carlos slanted a look at him.

Carmelina flicked her wrist. "It's fine. Yes, six men in the kitchen. Two outside the back door. I saw another two down one of the hallways. There's a wing to the right of the kitchen. Is that ten?"

"There's probably more upstairs. Anyone by the front door?"

"Right, yes. Two more in the front." She paused.

"What is it?"

"Something odd. There was a huge bunch of balloons in the front. Green, white, red balloons."

"Independence Day," Paco said.

"Right," said Carlos. "What's the date, Lina? According to your calendar?"

"Um, September 17." She dropped her head into her hands. "We've been here over two months already." *Two months with no news of Ricky. Over four months since she'd seen his sweet face.*

Paco nodded. "Independence Day was yesterday."

"That's ironic." She looked up. "Sorry."

"Don't be sorry," Carlos said. "What you saw inside confirms what we already knew."

"It's a kidnap express house." Paco's brow furrowed. "The authorities only catch a fraction of them."

Carlos scowled at his brother. "Or not so express, based on the rising number of burritos."

But Paco's unspoken thoughts were not lost on Carmelina. They hung in the air as tangible as the cloying smell from the house lodged deep in her nostrils.

They might never be discovered or rescued.

SIXTY-FIVE

RICKY GONE 169 DAYS

October 30, 2019

Over the next six weeks, Goat roped Carmelina into helping him more days than not. The routine was always the same. They covered the rooms downstairs together and then he took the second bin upstairs sending her back outside with the empty one.

She kept her head down, did as she was told, and padded back through the kitchen.

In the third week, she'd had to step around a large pool of blood seeping out from below the last door at the far end of the hallway. Goat's nonchalant attitude and obvious dismissal of the mess had shocked her so much she'd looked up.

Then wished she hadn't. The wall along the left side of the hallway was spattered with blood and chunks of gray matter. She blanched, noticed the two men at the end of the hall staring at her, and quickly refocused her gaze back to the floor.

Carlos and Paco were convinced there were fewer hostages than burritos, based on the number of men inside. She thought otherwise, explaining the volumes of fast food containers strewn about the kitchen. For the most part, the men were bringing in their own food.

Without fail, Carmelina scratched a sad inventory of the passing time into the wall under the counter using the same knife she used for onions once the pencil was ground down to a nub. Almost three and a half months since her last contact with Diego. One hundred and sixty-eight days since she'd laid eyes on her son.

Some days her desperation threatened to swallow her whole.

ONE MORNING when Carlos was writing out the supply list, the burrito count went down by twenty. Later that day, assisting Goat, she noticed the room at the far end of the hall stood open.

The heavy scent of bleach and *Fabuloso* filled the air. Two women, so thin their shoulder blades stuck out from the thin material of their dresses, scrubbed the floor by hand with stiff brushes. Great swirls of sudsy pink water lapped up against their fingers.

The youngest of the two cried freely as she worked. Goat kicked her in the shin and told her to shut up. She coughed and fell silent, her body still shaking with her sobs. Neither woman looked up.

Carmelina kept her eyes down. This explained the lower count for burritos.

At the end of the sixth week, something happened that surprised her.

They proceeded through the kitchen as usual. In the darkened hallway, Goat's eyes narrowed as he peered closely at her face, clearly assessing her. It made her nervous. She looked away. Goat was like a mad dog. Staring at him could only provoke him.

"Look at me," he said, his voice a low growl.

Reluctantly she met his gaze. He stared at her for several

seconds, then said, "You know what to do. Do it and then go back outside."

He pivoted and strode toward the front of the house leaving her in the hall. For several seconds, she simply stood there, the muscles in her upper arm protesting under the weight of the bin.

She moved forward. A few inches past the first door she put the bin down and cracked the door open. By now, she thought she'd be used to the smell. She was not. Two by two she tossed the burritos in.

"It's the girl," she heard a man whisper.

"Ask her," someone else whispered.

She tossed in two more burritos and reached for the door handle. A cell phone slid under the door as she went to pull it shut. She toed it quickly toward the bin. It wedged there between the wall and the bin.

Glancing over her shoulder, she checked on the two guards. They were playing cards. One blew smoke rings toward the window.

She reached down, her back to the guards, and snapped up the phone. Miraculously she had the presence of mind to check the ringer was off. Later, when she recounted to Carlos and Paco how she came to have the phone, this is the part she would remember.

She jammed the phone into her pants, lifted the bin and proceeded down the hall to the next door. She threw in sixteen burritos. At the third door, she threw in eighteen.

That left her with a surplus in the bin. Goat hadn't said so, but clearly she was meant to do the rooms in the front also.

Those front rooms off the foyer were larger and held more people. She could always hear shuffling and low murmurs when the doors were open. A new guard sat on the lowest stair to the upper level. He was built like a beast. Heavy thick brows framed a broad prominent forehead. He reminded her of an evolution poster they'd had at school. Back before Flaco, when she still had time for school and her biggest worry was having her uniform pressed and her homework done.

The man's mouth twisted into a sick facsimile of a smile when he saw her. Ogled her was more accurate. His oily gaze trailed down her body and his hand cradled his crotch. His thick tongue flicked out over large, rubbery lips.

As quickly as possible, she tossed the burritos into the two rooms and spun away, walking ramrod straight toward the kitchen.

She didn't make it.

"AREN'T you a sight for sore eyes?"

As Carmelina entered the narrow passageway that led from the foyer back toward the kitchen, the brute tackled her. He wrapped his large hands around her abdomen and slammed her into the wall. His breath heated her neck, rancid curls of it breaching her nostrils. He ground his pelvis against her, hands roaming up her ribcage to her breasts. He squeezed both breasts so hard she bit her tongue.

The coppery tang of blood in her mouth snapped her into action. She had a phone down her pants! They'd think she was helping the hostages. If they found it, they'd beat her or kill her. Or they'd throw her in one of those rooms and forget about her.

She bent her knee and brought her foot down as hard as she could on the top of the Neanderthal's foot. He yelped and released his hold on her. She spun away, ducked under his arm, and raced down the hall.

The men gathered around the kitchen table watched her go. The large man yelled and lumbered after her. Carmelina fled through the door to the back yard.

"Let her go," one of the men said. "Plenty more where that came from."

The enormous man's protests were quickly drowned out by the laughter of the other men.

Now she had one more reason to dread going inside for meal delivery. But for now, she had the phone. She prayed it would have a balance, at least enough to send a text to her mother. She wanted, no, needed... she needed to have news of Ricky.

SIXTY-SIX

"Make your call," Carlos said. "We'll keep watch."

Carmelina crouched on the floor of the taco stand and punched in her mother's number. The phone rang five times, then six.

Come on, pick up.

On the seventh ring, her mother answered, breathing heavily.

"Mama, it's Carmelina."

"*Mija,* where are you? We thought you were--"

"I know, Mama, and I'm sorry. Please, listen. I only have a minute."

Carmelina was surprised to find the phone still working. When she'd turned it on, the battery was only two-thirds depleted and the screen saver had a message: *Call my family. Gracias, José.* The contact list held only one name and number. Carlos showed her how to text Telcel, the Mexican cell carrier, to get the balance. The text pinged back showing fifty pesos of airtime on the account.

She had a choice to make. Use the airtime to find her son or call José's family. She'd sent a text to José's single contact:

José alive. More news later.

Then she called her mother.

"You're scaring me," Lupe said. "What's going on, why are you whispering?"

"Mama, did Diego find Ricky?"

Silence.

"Did he?" she pressed, the urgency she felt lacing her voice.

"*Mija,* I haven't heard from you in over three months, we thought you were dead."

"Mama, please!"

"Diego is working on it. Ricky is still somewhere in Arizona."

"Diego's not with him yet? It's been months." Her throat squeezed closed.

"I--"

"Can you give me Diego's number?"

"You don't have it?"

"I lost my phone."

"Then how are you calling me?"

"Mama." Her frustration sizzled across the line. Paco tapped lightly on the counter top and looked furtively toward the back gate. Carmelina's heart threatened to pound out of her chest.

"Hang on, it's here somewhere."

In her mind's eye, she could see her mother scanning the list of numbers they kept taped to the wall by the phone.

Come on. She had no idea how much an International call would cost or how fast the airtime would be used up. Or if Paco would give her a sign to end the call.

"Here it is." Mama rattled off the number and Carmelina scratched it on the bottom side of an empty carton, using the pointed handle of the spatula.

"Thanks. I'm sorry but I have to go," she said.

"*Mija—*"

"*Te amo,* Mama. I'm safe," she lied. "I'll call soon."

With her mother's protests ringing in her ear, she ended the call. She checked the airtime balance again. Still some pesos. Fingers poised over the phone, she glanced up at Paco. When he nodded she punched in Diego's number and sent a text:

Call this number with any news, brother. C.

The phone vibrated in her hand. She stared down at the text.

Mijo, where are you?

She looked up at the brothers. "The contact was José's parents. Now what?"

"What did they say?" Carlos asked.

"They're asking where he is." She held the screen up toward him.

Carlos raised his hand, stroked his chin thoughtfully. She'd been noticing him doing so more often, a habit of his. He was a deep thinker.

"That's a tricky one. If you say he's being held hostage, it will seem like you're asking for ransom."

Carmelina hadn't considered that. "What do you suppose José would want me to say? I can't imagine how he was able to hang onto this phone." Relinquishing their own phones had been one of César's first demands when they'd arrived at the property.

"He must be new here," she said. "Otherwise, the battery would be dead."

"Not necessarily. It was off, right?" When she nodded, Carlos continued. "A phone only loses five to ten percent charge over a month's time if it's turned off. It's possible he's been here a few months."

Paco stepped sideways from where he'd been staying busy, casually wiping down the counter. To anyone watching from the outside—the two guards at the back gate were always watching—they were still doing post-breakfast cleanup.

In a low voice, without looking away from what he was doing, he said, "Ask them to call the police. Then go into maps and send them a location."

"How would I do that?" Carmelina stared at the phone. It wasn't a smart phone but an older basic cell phone. "I don't know that it has an Internet connection."

Carlos extended his hand and she passed it up to him. With his hands below the counter, he played with the buttons. "You're right. There's no data on this cell."

He glanced over at his brother. "Any other ideas? We don't have a clue where we are."

"I wonder if the phone company could pinpoint the call? Don't they do that on television? Triangulate the signal from the cell towers or whatever?"

"Maybe." Carlos didn't sound convinced.

"My mother is really worried," Carmelina said. "Whatever we say to José's parents, we can't scare them unless we can also offer some kind of solution."

A low rumble in the distance announced a coming storm. Dark clouds crowded the sky. More rain was on the way. By October the rainy season should have ended but perhaps because it had started so late, it was lingering because recently, rain was plentiful.

Solutions, however, were not.

SIXTY-SEVEN

"That's a local number." Carlos peered over Carmelina's shoulder. They had the text from José's parent open, trying to decide what to say.

"Mexico City?"

"No." Carlos dropped a hand onto her shoulder.

He'd been touching her more often, in a casual way, a familiar way. No one but her family had ever touched her without wanting something from her. She welcomed it. A tangible reminder of her humanity in the cesspool of her current life.

"It's Cuernevaca, I think." He read the area code aloud and turned to his brother. "Cuernevaca?"

Paco nodded and looked to Carmelina. "It's about an hour south of the city. There's a lot of money there. José might not be a migrant. He might be a wealthy businessman."

"That would explain why they're being held so long." Carlos let out a long, slow breath.

"I'm not following." Carmelina tucked the phone back into its hiding spot and Carlos helped her up.

"With the migrants, they call their families and demand

money before they're released. Either family back home, or family in *El Norte*."

"Sometimes both," Paco interjected.

Carmelina's heart thudded against her chest. "My mother's number is in this phone now."

"It won't matter," Carlos said. "If they want your family's number, they'll make sure you give it up. One way or another."

The image of the blood seeping under the door in the house flashed into her mind. She shook her head to clear it. "So what about José? If his family's in Cuernevaca, you think he's Mexican?"

"This happened to a friend of mine from Torreon," Paco said. "The family was quite wealthy. Basically they grab you and keep you until they extract every penny the family can get their hands on. Sometimes it takes weeks, sometimes it takes months. In her father's case, they held him over nine months."

Carmelina's hand went to her throat. "Did he—"

"Did he live? He did."

When Paco opened his mouth to continue, a look passed between the brothers. As clear a "shut up" as she'd ever seen not spoken aloud. Whatever the story was, it was too grueling to be told. Fine with her. Her fear and current situation were enough to deal with.

"So how do we respond to that text?"

"I have an idea," Carlos said. "I think we—"

A commotion at the back of the house interrupted him. The two guards at the back gate abandoned their post and bolted across the yard.

"What the hell?" Paco leaned over the counter, listening.

Carlos jumped to the ground, made his way to the corner of the tent, and edged his forehead past the white vinyl wall.

"Cheater!"

"I didn't cheat, asshole. You're a shitty card player. You couldn't—"

A sickening thump was followed by a dull crack.

"You broke my nose."

Jeers from the other men filled the air.

"Everybody shut up." Carmelina recognized the voice of the guard from the back gate. "Keep it down."

"He did cheat," someone grumbled.

"Yeah? Just cause I'm new here, you think I'm a cheater? What is wrong with you assholes?"

"What the hell is going on out here?" Goat's distinctive voice cut through the chatter. Everyone fell silent. "And what the hell are we paying you for?"

"We tried," the guard said. "It was—"

"Next time try harder." Goat clapped his hands. "You, get your things and get out of here."

"He stole money from me, Goat. He's been cheating."

"Jaysus. You guys are in charge, not me. Why are you all such whiny babies?"

"Watch yourself," someone said.

"Yeah," another voice chimed in.

"Fine, sorry boss. What do you want me to do with this big asshole?" Goat said.

Carmelina jumped down and crept up beside Carlos to peek out. "That's him," she whispered.

"José?"

"No. The gorilla that attacked me inside."

"Get him out of here. He can leave by the front door."

Carmelina recognized the man giving the orders from the card games in the kitchen. She never would have pegged him as the boss. He had a bleached streak of yellow running down the center of his closely cut black hair. The men called him Skunk.

"Sure, boss." Goat waved his pistol at the big man. The man's hands, covering his nose, were awash with blood. He cast an evil eye at the man who had punched him. After a look of disgust at the rest of them, he held his head high and led the way back into the house.

Carlos and Carmelina crept back to the taco stand.

"Why not just send him out through the back gate?" Carmelina said. "It's closer."

Carlos cocked a brow. "Have you seen anybody leave by the back gate? Anyone still standing, that is?"

She shook her head. "So cheating was enough to get him fired, but not enough to get him killed."

"Word to the wise. Don't cheat at cards." Paco rolled his eyes. He held up several wrapped burritos and motioned to Carlos to grab the drinks standing on the counter. "Enough excitement. Let's go eat."

SIXTY-EIGHT

After the men encouraged her to eat a little to maintain her strength, Carmelina was resting with Katya. Carlos napped nearby. Paco's snores from the front seat of the Blazer confirmed he was deeply asleep.

The phone vibrated against Carmelina's abdomen, tickling her skin. After a quick look around the yard to ensure nobody was watching, she pulled it out and peered at the text. Her heart fluttered. The text was from Diego.

Been so worried, hermanita. Lawyer found Ricky. Confirmed he's in Tucson. But they might be moving him again next week.

I'm still in detention and can't get to him. But the lawyer has filed the papers.

Carmelina tapped a message back:

Filing papers for what?

To ensure they keep Ricky until a guardian comes to get him.

How long can they hold you? It's been four and a half months already.

Almost five. Lawyer can't say. Court system overloaded. Lots of delays.

So he's still alone?

I'm sorry. If we had family in the U.S., we could send them to get him.

She stared at the text. How was she going to get out here?

Mama thought you were dead. We've been so worried.

Kidnapped to cook for cartel. Don't tell Mama. Will try to escape.

No! They'll kill you. Have they asked for money?

Not yet. I need to get to Ricky before they send him somewhere else.

Carmelina watched her text. The words pulsed on the screen, waiting to be sent.

Ping.

A message popped up telling her to top up. She'd depleted the balance. The phone was out of airtime.

Carmelina gulped and gripped the cell so hard her knuckles turned white. What was she going to do now?

KATYA PULLED herself forward on the blanket. Every day she was more mobile. Carmelina wanted to start her on solid food, but she could hardly feed her burritos. For now, she'd have to continue with rice and water. Goat refused to buy enough formula.

Carlos roused from his siesta. He scrubbed the sleep from his eyes and shuffled to the bucket they kept for washing up to splash water on his face.

The late afternoon heat was oppressive. The heat would build through the day until the rains tamped it down for a few hours. Carmelina felt sleepy herself and would welcome a nap. However, she was much too agitated to sleep.

Carlos settled on the ground across from her. She looked at

him for several seconds and then made a decision. She had to confide in someone.

"I need to get north," she said.

He nodded.

"They're moving my son next week."

His brow creased. "Ricky?"

They'd overheard her. Hard not to. "I have a three-year-old. He's in detention up there."

"What?"

She sucked in a breath. The more people that knew, the more vulnerable she would be, the more it would expose her to extortion.

It didn't matter. Based on what Carlos and Paco had said, she was convinced their captors would extort money from her at some point anyway. But right now, she needed help figuring out how to get to Ricky.

"He traveled north with my brother five and a half months ago. It's a long story." She patted Katya's mouth with a cloth and settled her back onto the blanket. The baby burped and produced a sated grin, her eyelids sliding closed.

"He's not with your brother?"

"They separated them soon after they were picked up."

Carlos cursed under his breath. "I had no idea you were carrying this. What a strain."

She pulled in another deep breath and her lip trembled. A sob rose in her throat. She gulped it back down.

Carlos laid his hand on her shin. "Let it go," he said.

She sucked in air, drew it deep into her lungs, and tipped her chin up to meet his gaze. "No," she said, shaking her head. "I can't fall apart. Not when my son needs me. I need to figure out a way out of here. Will you help me?"

Carlos glanced over his shoulder at Paco. His brother's head lolled against the back of the driver's seat in the Blazer. The snoring confirmed he was still asleep.

"We both will," he said simply. "But Lina, we haven't seen a way out yet. Things are locked down pretty tight. Do you have any kind of plan?"

She shook her head, staring into his eyes. "No, but there has to be a way."

CARMELINA SHOOK HER HEAD. "NO. NO," she said a second time, for emphasis. "That will put you in too much danger."

Paco shrugged. "We're big boys."

"You should come with me."

Carlos put his hand up. "We've been over this. It's too risky to get us all over the gate. It will take too long."

"But—"

"No. We've already decided," Paco said.

"But, where would we get enough of anything to knock them out?" She cocked her head. So far it was the best idea they'd had—putting something in the burritos to put the two guards at the back gate asleep.

"I don't have all the answers. Look, usually by the time we go to sleep at night, the guards are left on their own back there."

"That's true," Carmelina said. They drank and played cards, but Carmelina had sometimes been up to use the bucket at night, and noticed them both sleeping.

They both looked at Carlos when he cleared his throat. "Have you seen anything inside?"

"You mean like more guards? We've gone over that. I already told you where they're all posted."

"No, I mean... with that many people locked up inside, they must be using sedatives or something in the water."

"You think?" Carmelina hadn't considered that. It might explain how they kept everyone subdued. Although, the threat of dying a horrible death probably worked for most of them.

"Could you have a look next time you go in?"

She scoffed. "It's not like I have the run of the house. Goat goes upstairs, I deliver to the downstairs rooms, and then I get the hell out as fast as I can."

The day the gorilla groped her continued to hang over her head, and each time she crept back through the kitchen, she could feel the men's eyes on her. Unlike El Flaco's house, back at home, there were no *niñas* hanging around here to keep the men entertained.

"Doesn't it surprise you that they don't have girlfriends or prostitutes coming in to entertain the men?" she asked.

"Too risky," Paco said. "The fewer people coming and going, the better. But I think Carlos is onto something. I'll bet they have a stash of drugs in there somewhere, something they put in the water to keep people quiet."

If there was a stash, she had to figure out where it might be. Maybe in the kitchen or in one of the rooms the men used for sleeping? She'd never been upstairs, had no idea what might be up there, and knew it would be impossible to gain access. The front door was always guarded.

Still, for now, drugging the guards at the back gate was their best shot. If only she could find the drugs.

SIXTY-NINE

RICKY GONE 170 DAYS

October 31, 2019

"This is all we have," Paco said. Using his hand as a funnel, he released a stream of coins into a small plastic bag. "There's enough here to get on a local bus and buy some airtime and a cheap charger for the phone. You remember the plan?"

"Yes. Find a place to buy airtime—"

"Any OXXO or Guadalajara Farmacia. They'll sell chargers, too," Carlos interjected. "OXXO is everywhere. You only need twenty pesos of airtime."

"Shouldn't I buy more?"

"You might need money to eat or take a bus. Send a quick text to your brother and then call José's parents."

She inhaled sharply and filled her lungs. When she exhaled, she felt a bit calmer.

"Pay close attention to where we are," Paco said. "Once you leave, you're our only hope."

"Paco." Carlos slanted a dark look at his brother.

So, no pressure. She nodded gravely. "I know. I'll take care of it."

Silence stretched between them, tight as a circus high wire with tension. "I still think this is a bad idea. What's going to happen to you once I'm gone?"

Carlos put his hand over hers. "We're big boys. Find José's parents. They'll help you get in touch with the authorities. And then go and get your son."

ONCE CARMELINA HAD KNOWN what to look for, it had been easy to spot the drugs. They sat on the kitchen table, next to a mound of poker chips directly adjacent to Skunk's elbow. Getting them, however, had been another story.

After she completed the evening delivery of burritos, she stumbled into the table on her way through the kitchen, brushing a pile of things to the floor. She crouched over the items.

"*Cuidado*, stupid girl." Skunk stood, his beer dripping off the table into his lap. He lashed out, landing a kick in Carmelina's kidneys. She grunted, black spots danced in front of her eyes obscuring her vision of the things strewn about on the floor.

On her knees, she frantically stuffed the small bag of pills down her pants, and unfolded herself, her hands filled with poker chips. "Sorry. Please forgive me, sorry." She scooped up more of the colorful plastic discs and a beer bottle rolling into the table leg and placed it all back on the table.

Skunk stared daggers at her. She bit her tongue and lowered her head. "Sorry," she mumbled again.

He lashed out once more, the back of his hand making solid contact with her cheek. She squealed with pain. Again, spots danced in front of her eyes. A wave of nausea threatened to put her back on her ass.

"Get the hell out of here." He flicked his hand toward the door, dismissing her.

"Why don't I have a fresh beer?" he said menacingly into the silent room.

Carmelina heard a chair scrape against the floor behind her as she fled. "Coming right up, boss," someone said.

The metal door clanged shut behind her.

UNDER THE STARLESS NIGHT, the two guards in the back were intent on their card game. Except for the halo of light on their table, the yard was dark. The full moon was waning, occasionally peeking out from behind dark storm clouds. The burritos Paco had delivered to them earlier sat to the side, untouched.

In this neighborhood, they rarely heard anything. The properties were huge and in the early days she'd expected to hear children playing or families enjoying a barbecue, couples fighting or screwing or laughing. Something. But there was never a peep. The nights remained as quiet as the days.

"When are they going to eat?" Carmelina's leg shook, her knee bouncing. Each minute that ticked past ratcheted her anxiety higher. "What if they notice inside that the drugs are gone?"

Carlos and Paco exchanged a look. Nobody spoke the answer aloud. It wasn't necessary. If they suspected her of taking them, they'd likely kill her. Skunk was already annoyed with her.

For the next while they sat, without speaking, beside the truck until Carmelina couldn't take it any longer. "Maybe if we go inside. Make it look like we're going to bed for the night?"

Carlos put his hand on her knee and squeezed gently. "Sure. It's time anyway."

They went through the motions, following their regular routine before bedding down for the night. Teeth brushed, last trips to the bucket in the corner, Carlos stripped off his pants and pulled on a pair of gym shorts for sleeping.

As Paco climbed into the front seat, he said, "They're eating now. They should be out in about half an hour."

For the next thirty minutes, the world around Carmelina slowed to a crawl. Each second ticked past in its own sweet punishing time. Her things were ready to go. Katya was fed and deeply asleep. That part at least, timing-wise, had worked out well.

Emotions were high. They didn't speak, each of them lost in their own thoughts. After so many months together, leaving them felt like losing a limb. Being alone in the world again terrified her.

When she thought she could bear it no longer and might lose her nerve, Carlos turned and gave her a sign.

It was time.

SEVENTY

Carmelina cowered in the shadows. The street stretched to her
right. The sole streetlight at the far corner stood dark, a lone and
ineffectual sentinel. At home, in her barrio, non-working street-
lights were the norm. Rocks or bullets were often used to break the
lights.

She imagined it was the same here. Even in this upscale
suburb. Criminals rarely wanted to be seen. At home, the dark
made her vulnerable. Tonight, it would work in her favor.

Once she'd cleared the alley and circled back to the street,
she'd tucked herself in the recessed wall of a front gate. She dare
not stay here long. If a car drove by, the chances of her being seen
were high. If the gate of this home opened, she'd have nowhere to
hide.

The properties on the street were large, the gates widely
spaced apart. She searched for the next gate that might offer her
refuge and spotted one mid-way between where she stood and the
lonely streetlight on the corner. It was a long way for her to be out
in the open and she'd have to cross the street to reach it. Aside
from the obvious danger of being seen by her captors, on foot she'd

stick out like a sore thumb in this area. Not only because she was a poorly dressed, skinny migrant with a baby. But because, in a wealthy suburb like this, people drove.

She chewed her lower lip. The other option was to backtrack to the alley and cross the barren field that stretched behind the properties. At some point, she'd have to run back into civilization. But how long would that take? And what if she lost her way out there? With her gone, Carlos and Paco were at risk. The clock was ticking and people were counting on her.

The gate, then. Decision made, she patted the phone in her pocket to ensure it was secure, and eyeballed the distance again. Her mouth dropped as a figure swung around the far corner. Arms akimbo, the lean young man strolled down the street. Something about him seemed familiar. She shrank farther back into the shadow.

If he was going to the house, he wouldn't come down this far. She estimated the house she'd just escaped from was three or four gates up on the side where she stood. She was going to have to pass it to get to the other gate. Thankfully, although the inside was heavily guarded at all times, they never posted guards in the street.

She held her breath while the figure advanced. He was in no hurry, his relaxed gait, even in silhouette, screamed he didn't have a worry in the world. As he strolled past one of the gates, a sensor light flared over his head.

She gasped. Hope charged through her. She'd recognize that yellow shirt anywhere. She lifted her arm to wave to him, opened her mouth to call out, the juicy "Yoh" of his name on the tip of her tongue.

The squeal of rubber against the cobblestones silenced her. She flattened herself back against the concrete wall as a black SUV careened around the corner. The daytime heat leeched out of the stone and into her backside. Yonas, midway down the street, stood pinned in the headlights. The vehicle braked and skidded to a heavy stop.

It was too late to warn him. She watched, her heart pounding.

The driver rolled his window down. Ranchera music drifted into the street. Yonas stepped out of the bright light and edged to the side of the vehicle. Carmelina held her breath. The driver killed the headlights.

The back door of the SUV opened. Carmelina waited for some thug to step out and tackle Yonas, but no one got out. Yonas approached the driver's window. The music died. A match flared and the driver bent his head over the flame. It was Goat.

They'd scoop Yonas off the street.

No, wait. What was Yonas doing here?

Goat's ugly laugh grated through the quiet of the empty street. Yonas fist bumped him. "*cabrón*," he said.

The hope within Carmelina was snuffed out. She breathed deep, forcing the bile charging up her throat back into her belly, back into the bowels of her soul, where all the other betrayals of her life rubbed elbows in uneasy proximity.

The pieces fell together.

Yonas touching base with her at the shelter in Mapastepec. Yonas, always popping up, always friendly, never staying long. Yonas, Mr. Congeniality, Mr. Casual, who seemed to know half the people at the shelter, and most of the people on the road. Who stayed behind, and traveled the length of the caravan each day.

Now she knew how he covered that much territory every day.

Yonas was a scout for Goat and her captors. Her heart, already cracked, broke a little more. Was there no one on this damn journey that she could trust?

No doubt he'd been working with César. She'd never seen them together but, at least one night at the burrito stand, he'd appeared only a few minutes before César.

Why had she not seen him around the house? A scheduling

thing perhaps. When they'd been brought in, it had been after midnight. It was most likely they brought new people into the house under the cover of darkness and she was inside delivering burritos in the morning and early evening.

A sinew of hatred threaded its way up through her chest. He had tagged her as vulnerable. Picked her out from among the crowd to what? Live this life, stuck behind a wall, cooking burritos forever? She was glad she hadn't told him anything about herself.

And now she regretted telling so much of her story to Carlos and Paco. She needed to get the hell out of here. Put as much distance between this place and herself as fast as she could.

In the middle of the street, the men continued to talk, their low voices reaching her, their words indistinguishable. Yonas leaned casually against the front panel of the car, his thin arm draped over the side mirror. They passed a joint between them. A large man Carmelina hadn't seen before clambered out of the back seat and joined them, hands in the pockets of his baggy jeans.

Come on. Get the hell out of the street and out of my life.

The minutes ticked by. She wanted to pull the phone from her pocket, check the time, but couldn't risk the small flare of light. Anyway, it didn't matter. They would leave eventually. They couldn't stay in the street all night.

After more time passed, she reconsidered her decision about going around the back. If they stayed much longer, Katya would wake, possibly hungry, and begin to fuss. But there was no way for her to retrace her steps without being seen. For now, she was pinned here.

A cacophony of laughter in the street drew her focus back to Goat's vehicle and Yonas. The third man walked across the street and tapped on a gate. Now she knew exactly which one it was.

The mechanical grinding of the gate opening filled the street. Goat held his hand up, Yonas fist-bumped him again, and stepped back from the SUV. Goat pulled away and through the gate into the property, a square of light falling across Yonas standing several yards away.

The gate closed. Yonas turned on his heel and, with his distinctive swinging gait, walked to the gate directly across the street, slid a key into the door beside the large gate, and passed through into the property.

What the hell?

The tall sunflower-colored wall, covered with *bugambilia*, was topped with a foot of nasty-looking razor wire. A dim light shone from within. She held her breath and strained forward, but there was nothing to hear. After several minutes, the light went out.

Convinced Yonas was not coming back out, she set her sights on the recessed gate two doors past the gate he'd just entered, and bolted down the street.

SEVENTY-ONE

RICKY GONE 171 DAYS

November 1, 2019

"I don't understand," the woman said. "Who are you?"

Carmelina sat on a bench, partially hidden behind a shrub, in a small plaza. Rosy pre-dawn light tinged the horizon. It wouldn't be long until the sun was up.

She explained it all to the woman again, speaking quietly into the cell and doing her best to be patient. Then she said, "I don't have much money on this phone."

"Hang up, I'll call you back. It won't cost you anything if I call you."

She gripped the phone tightly. What if she didn't call back? This was her lifeline. "But—"

"I'll call you right back," the woman said.

Carmelina glanced around. There was no one nearby. She disconnected the call, flicked the ringer off, and watched the screen for the call to come in.

When she picked up, it was a man's voice. "I'm José's father. Tell me what you just told my wife."

She repeated the story a third time. Katya was starting to squirm. She struggled to hear what the man was saying.

"You're not calling for ransom?"

"No, sir," she said. "José gave me his phone and asked me to call you."

"How is he?"

"Like I said," a tinge of impatience laced her voice, "I don't know. I didn't see him at all. All I know is that he's alive."

There was a long pause. "You were also being held inside?"

"Yes, sir."

"Could you find your way back to where José is being held?"

"Yes." She'd paid attention to the street names on her way out through the maze of the suburb.

"Tell me where you are. We'll come and get you."

CARMELINA FISHED in the plastic bag of change and counted out coins to pay for tacos. She poured a liberal amount of salsa over them and walked back to another bench in the park.

The neighborhood was waking up. People filed through the park on their way to work. On the far side of the plaza, people queued up for a bus. Mothers with children in tow, scurried past, on their way to school.

Carmelina kept her head down. Occasionally she would rise, walk with purpose as if she was going somewhere, and circle back to another bench. She knew she was being paranoid.

A long hour and a half later, an impeccably dressed distinguished looking couple, probably in their sixties, walked through the park and stood in front of the gazebo. From their well-tailored clothes to their haircuts, their wealth was obvious. They glanced around nervously, the woman's arm laced through her husband's.

After several minutes, the man punched a text into his phone.

Carmelina's phone pinged. It was José's parents.

"WE NEED TO CALL THE POLICE," Carmelina said. The SUV barreled down the hill. As they veered around corners, she spotted glimpses of a large city nestled in the green bosom of an enormous valley.

José's father, Ernesto, sat in the front seat, and his bodyguard drove. The bodyguard had been watching them as they waited for Carmelina in the plaza. He was good at his job, Carmelina hadn't seen him at all. But then, she hadn't been watching for anything like that.

Estella, José's mother, sat on the back seat beside her, cradling Katya in her arms, and cooing down at her. The baby gurgled and smiled up at her.

The bodyguard and Ernesto exchanged a look. Ernesto turned to look at her. "The police might be in on it. We have another plan."

"What is it?"

"We'll tell you once we get to the house."

"How do I know you're not just kidnapping me now? Maybe you're going to sell me, or sell my baby?" Carmelina's voice rose. After all the waiting at the house, walking and creeping into town, and waiting for them to arrive, the last hour had moved much too fast. The stress of the last twenty-four hours crashed down on her.

Estella reached for her hand and squeezed her fingers. "Ay, niña, you can trust us. We won't harm you or the little one."

Ernesto cleared his throat. "Trust us, Carmelina. We've dealt with this kind of thing before. You've nothing to fear from us."

They sped around another corner. Short of jumping out of the car into traffic, there was nothing she could do. She slumped back against the seat. Estella held her hand and offered her a reassuring smile.

The road signs announced their entrance to Cuernevaca. The driver wound his way through mid-morning traffic and into an upscale neighborhood. Even Carmelina's richest clients at home hadn't lived in neighborhoods this wealthy.

Again, the tall walls, the razor wire, the spacing of the gates on the enormous properties, announced security. And money. Apparently, her captors knew how to pick a wealthy businessman from the crowd.

This thought didn't calm her. She knew from the set up of the house that she was dealing with organized criminals. Sure, day to day, the men guarding the gates and crowding the kitchen table appeared to be ordinary thugs, but somewhere at the top, someone had a plan and was pulling the strings, dancing the lower echelons of the organization like evil little marionettes.

The bodyguard pulled up to a gate. It slid open and he drove through to a vast cobblestone courtyard. A large fountain with cherubs dribbling water from their mouths stood in the center of a circular drive. He navigated to the front entrance and jumped out to open the door for Estella.

A maid opened the door and rushed outside. Clearly, the staff had been expecting them.

"Go with her," Estella said. She passed the baby toward the maid, but Carmelina stepped in and grabbed Katya mid-air.

"I'll take her," she said.

Estella nodded and turned to the maid. "You have a bath ready for *Sra.* Carmelina?"

"*Si, señora,*" the woman said, with a quick nod of her head.

"Gaby will take you upstairs. She'll show you your room and bring in a bassinet for the baby," Estella said. "Once you've had a chance to bathe, come downstairs and we'll have lunch together."

SEVENTY-TWO

After a luxurious bath, in a huge tub with ornate golden fixtures—
the whole house was like something out of a glossy magazine—
Carmelina put on the clean clothes Gaby had laid out on the four-
poster bed for her. They didn't quite fit, but the material was
expensive, and it felt amazing to get out of the shabby clothes she'd
worn down to bare threads.

Pressing her hand down on the edge of the bed, her fingers
disappeared into the large puffy comforter, like they were being
eaten by a cloud. The bed was soft, yet firm. The pillows called to
her. She longed to simply crawl in and go to sleep. She wanted to
sleep for a week. In the lacy bassinet, Katya slept soundly.

At the back of the wide hall outside her room, she descended
the service stairway, and found herself in the largest private
kitchen she'd ever seen. Stainless steel appliances and counters
gleamed. A large, mesquite table dominated the middle of the
room. Several kitchen staff chopped food at different stations
around the room. A man wearing a chef's hat glanced up from the
sauce he was stirring, his bright blue eyes piercing her with a look.
The corners of his mouth crinkled.

"This beautiful girl looks lost," he said, speaking directly to her. "I think the *señora* wants you to join her in the dining room." He indicated a set of double doors on the left.

She almost dropped into a curtsy, resisted the urge, nodded instead and hustled out through the double doors into a formal dining room. The table was laden with food.

"Come join us, Carmelina." Estella motioned for her to take the seat across from her. Ernesto sat at the head.

Carmelina placed Katya and the bassinet on an empty chair and sat down.

Estella passed her a bowl of beef in green salsa. "I'm sure you're hungry."

Carmelina spooned food onto her plate. Beef, Mexican rice with large chunks of tomato, a salad of *nopal* cactus and savory onion. One of the kitchen staff replenished the fresh corn tortillas and set the tortilla warmer down next to her plate. For a second, she stared at the bounty on her plate. Then, unable to resist the tantalizing smell of the food, she ate.

When she raised her head several minutes later, a worried look creased Estella's face.

"*Lo siento,*" Carmelina said, her loaded fork in the air. "Did I do something wrong?"

"Don't be sorry, my dear," Ernesto said. "Eat, please."

Estella patted her lips with a peach-colored linen napkin. "It's only... seeing you so hungry makes me realize José must be starving also."

"Oh." Carmelina set her fork down. "Everyone is fed twice a day. The burritos we make have protein in them." Not great protein, she neglected to say. The cheapest protein Goat could get his hands on, but still, it was protein.

Feeling guilty, she placed her napkin beside her plate and folded her hands in her lap, her appetite gone.

"Please, dear, eat," Estella said.

"*Gracias*, it's delicious but I'm too tired to eat more right now."

She turned her attention to Ernesto.

"You said you had a plan?"

ERNESTO HELD A FINGER UP.

Two of the kitchen staff pushed through the door, cleared their plates, and removed the bowls of food. Someone brought in a steaming carafe of coffee and filled each of their cups. Lastly, the chef pushed through the doors and, with a flourish, gently set a flan down in front of the *señora*.

He winked at Carmelina. "For your beautiful guest," he said, eyes sparkling.

Carmelina, surprised by such kindness, broke into a smile. She laughed. And that surprised her too. Her voice sounded like one of her younger sisters. She hadn't sounded so light since she'd been a girl.

"Thank you, chef," Estella said. He disappeared through the double doors.

While Estella served the flan, Ernesto spoke. "We can't rule out the possibility that the police might be working with this group. It's happened before."

"José has been kidnapped before?"

"Thankfully, no, but we have friends who have been through this. Many times, unfortunately." He waved his hand in semicircle, she supposed to indicate his wealthy neighbors. "Our best approach is to pay the ransom for José."

"I don't understand."

"We want to be sure we get our son out. If we go to the police, they could move everyone to another location. Or kill them." His voice was quiet.

"But my friends are there. The ones who helped me escape. With me gone—"

"I know it's difficult, Carmelina. We do have a plan though, and José's captors have been texting us for some time now."

"You knew he was there?"

"We did."

"But, what about the texts between us earlier?"

"We didn't know who you were. We thought it best to play dumb." Estella passed Carmelina a generous slice of flan. "We wanted to be sure."

"You mean José had two phones?"

"Apparently so," Ernesto said.

"But why?"

Ernesto shrugged. "I have no idea. But it's given us an opportunity. I mean, here you are. And Katya. You're both safe now. Plus, we know where José is being held. This is huge."

"We've been sending money for three months, they just keep asking for more."

"Three months?" Right, Carlos had said they'd hold the wealthy Mexicans hostage until the money dried up. "You still haven't said what your plan is."

SEVENTY-THREE

RICKY GONE 172 DAYS

November 2, 2019

The SUV glided silently through the night. The windows were darkly tinted. She knew no one could see in, yet she hunkered as low as possible in the back seat, her body shaking as they approached the street.

"It's the fourth gate down," she said. "On the left."

Ernesto took several photos with his phone, then nodded to his bodyguard.

The driver made a U-turn and navigated back out of the suburb.

Carmelina let out a breath, releasing some of the stress in her limbs.

"Good job," Ernesto said. "This will help so much."

They drove back down the mountain. Estella had stayed at home. Beside her on the back seat, sat an average looking woman with jet black hair. Carmelina thought she looked about five years older than herself, early twenties. She was dressed well, but not in a flashy way. If you passed her on the street, you wouldn't be able to describe her five minutes later. Ernesto had introduced her as Ana.

The driver pulled into a well-lit express bus station. Ernesto turned to Carmelina.

"Ana is going to take you to the border," Ernesto said.

"Now?" Carmelina's heart jumped into her throat. She glanced at the clean, express buses lined up at the station. "I don't have the money for that."

"Don't worry about that." Ernesto pressed a thick envelope into her hands. "Ana knows what she's doing. She'll get you to the border and introduce you to someone who can get you across. She has enough money for the trip. That," he indicated the envelope he'd given her, "is to give you a start once you get there."

Tears pricked behind Carmelina's eyes. "I can't take this. It's too generous." *Ricky*. She could be in *El Norte* within a couple of days. She made eye contact with Ernesto. "Thank you. Please don't forget your promise to me."

"I won't." He reached for her hand. "You've probably saved our son's life. I promise I'll do everything I can for your friends. Paco and Carlos, right?"

She nodded. Ana opened her door and motioned to Carmelina. Carmelina gathered Katya and the bodyguard exited and opened the door for her. He stepped around to the back of the vehicle, pulled out a leather duffle bag which he passed to Ana, and turned to Carmelina. "The *señora* packed fresh clothes for you. Also some items for the baby."

Carmelina nodded, mute, too emotional to speak. She turned to follow Ana into the station, but Ernesto blocked her way.

Without warning, he flung his arms around her and wept.

"*Vaya con dios*, Carmelina. Thank you for finding my son."

November 3, 2019
North of San Luis Potosi, San Luis Potosi

"I don't understand why we came this way," Carmelina said.

"Once again, because it's the shortest route to the border." Ana crossed her arms and stared out the window. "Trust me, it's only another routine security check."

The bus hadn't moved for a while, stopped in a line of traffic. Carmelina's heart pounded in her throat, anxiety flooding through her body.

From Mexico City, they'd traveled up Highway 57 through Queretaro. As they'd hurtled down the highway through the night, she'd begged Ana to get off the bus in San Luis Potosi and take the route to the northwest. Carmelina wanted to go via Zacatecas and north through Torreon and Chihuahua toward El Paso where Diego was in detention and where she could be closer to where Ricky was being held.

"For one thing," Ana had explained patiently, "it's a much longer route. For another thing, you don't want to be waiting in

Ciudad Juarez. It's much too dangerous. You do know it's one of the most dangerous cities in the world, right?"

"But..." Carmelina let her words trail off. She didn't know how to explain how important it was for her to go west, without revealing too much information.

Regardless of how much Ernesto had paid Ana, Carmelina didn't dare to trust anyone right now. If Ana knew she had family on the other side, even if Diego was stuck in detention without a peso to his name, she might try to make a few extra bucks by passing her over to another express kidnapper near the border.

It even made Carmelina nervous that Ana had seen Ernesto give her the envelope of cash. Still, at this point, Ana was her only hope.

"Also," Ana continued, "my contacts are here at the border, not in Juarez. These days, it's almost impossible to cross in Juarez. You have to trust me."

From San Luis Potosi, the bus headed north toward Saltillo but had only covered a few kilometers when they'd come to a stop almost twenty minutes ago.

"This is just another run of the mill security roadblock."

"And if it isn't?" Carmelina lowered her voice. "You know about the mass graves. All those people *Los Tigres* pulled off the buses."

"Shhh." Ana shushed her and look around, her forehead creasing. "Don't say that out loud."

Between the seats, Carmelina could see an older couple in the seats behind them. They appeared to be sleeping, the woman's head resting on her husband's shoulder.

Ana leaned her head closer to Carmelina's, her lips brushing against her ear. It tickled.

"I have a boss who pays the tariff to *Los Tigres*," she said. "You're safe until we get to the border. I've already paid your way."

"What do you mean until?"

"At the border, I'll introduce you to someone else who will take you over. As the *señor* explained before."

The thought of being passed off to someone new made Carmelina nervous.

"What happens after Saltillo? We go on to Monterrey and Laredo?"

"No, it's tough there right now. We'll travel through Monclova and up to Piedras Negras on the border with Texas. I know a guy who can get you across there."

The bus rolled forward. Carmelina leaned into the aisle to try to see the road ahead of them. All she saw was a long line of slowly moving traffic edging past makeshift shelters selling dried snakeskins. Across the open landscape to the east, the sun was rising.

"They're not going to drag us off the bus, Carmelina. If we were closer to Victoria, or Reynosa, I might be worried. But here, trust me, it's some sort of security stop. Maybe even an agricultural control stop."

Ana leaned her head against the window and closed her eyes, ending the conversation. Her breath steamed the window in small wisps.

There was nothing more for Carmelina to do but wait it out.

THE SUN HAD SET by the time they pulled into their final destination. Piedras Negras was a larger, grander town that she'd been expecting. They'd been on the bus over twenty hours. Ana led her to a nearby hotel and left her there to bathe while she ran out to get hot food. Standing under a lukewarm shower, with Katya in her arms, Carmelina wondered if she'd ever see her again.

Twenty minutes later, after Carmelina had dried and fed Katya, and was in the process of snapping her into a brand-new pink onesie from the supplies Estella had generously sent, Ana sailed through the door with food. Carmelina's mouth watered as the rich smell of *lengua* tacos and *gorditas* stuffed with *rajas*, *championes*, and Oaxaca cheese filled the room. She hurriedly snapped up Katya's onesie and laid her on the bed to sleep.

Ana set the food and a couple of Cokes, the bottles sweaty with condensation, on the small bedside table wedged between the two matrimonial beds. Without ceremony, the two women tucked into the food, both of them making appreciative noises. Ana wiped at a stream of salsa dribbling down her chin and, when she met Carmelina's gaze, she put her finger to her nose. Carmelina reached up and found a bit of cilantro stuck to the tip of her nose. The two women started to laugh.

Once she started, Carmelina couldn't stop. She put her food down and clapped a hand over her mouth. She laughed until tears streamed down her eyes. Ana laughed, too, tumbling sideways on the bed and curling into a fetal position. Carmelina hugged herself, the muscles in her belly aching. She couldn't remember the last time she'd laughed so hard. All the tension she'd been carrying eased a little. She let herself fall backward on the bed, head resting on the thin pillow, and stared at the ceiling until her breathing slowed and she was calmer. She turned her head and looked over at Ana who gave her a sheepish grin.

"It's going to be all right, Carmelina. I promise you."

She stretched out her arm and Carmelina slipped her hand into hers. The two women stayed that way for some time, their fingers laced together, hands swinging freely in the chasm between the two beds as the evening shifted into night.

SEVENTY-FIVE

November 4, 2019
Safe House, Piedras Negras, Coahuilla

The heat in the small enclosed space was stifling. A large window at the end of the room had been boarded up. No light, not a hint of fresh air pierced it. The built-up essence of perspiration practically bubbled in the still air, creating an effervescent distasteful tingling in Carmelina's nose.

There were two single men, three small families, and one other single woman, a little older than Carmelina. In all, five men and five women. The coyote had told them they should travel as family units. In other words, he wanted the two single women to pair up with the two single men. The men's eyes had raked over Carmelina, making her squirm.

This close to the border she didn't see the point. On the other side, she'd have her baby. Why would she want to help some stranger have a better shot at asylum? It wasn't as if they wouldn't look at their documents, figure out who was who, and who was actually related. Diego was Ricky's blood relative and it hadn't helped him one bit.

On the way to the safe house the previous morning and before saying goodbye to Ana, she'd topped up the phone Ernesto had given her and called her mother to let her know she was okay and would be crossing into *El Norte* soon. Her mother wailed into the phone that Claudia hadn't been home all night. *She's only twelve, mija,* her mother had cried. Carmelina had nearly bitten her tongue off, biting back the words. *I told you so.*

And Kike, she'd asked. What does Kike say. Mama had fallen silent.

It shattered her, but she'd known it was coming. She hated feeling helpless in the face of it.

Afterward, she texted Diego. He didn't have more news. He promised to text her if he knew anything, but once she crossed the border she wasn't sure if her number would even work. She'd probably need a new SIM card. At least she had enough cash to get one.

"WE'VE BEEN HERE FIVE DAYS," one of the men complained. A small child bounced on his lap.

The man who brought them food stood in the middle of the room with a large sack of fast food. His gaze shifted to each of them in turn, his brows raised.

Carmelina lowered her head, clutching Katya closer to her body. She'd been here two days. The other single woman, Dora, had arrived the same day as Carmelina.

"You hungry or not?"

The Honduran man in the corner nodded. He had a small family, an infant and two toddlers. Carmelina had thought her journey was difficult with the baby. At least there were two of them to manage it.

He reached for the food but the man released his fingers and let the bag fall to the floor. The drinks inside toppled and gushed out, the bottom of the bag broke open and loosely wrapped packets of food tumbled onto the dirty cement floor.

"Keep your strength up," he huffed. "We'll go when the boss says conditions are right and not before."

He slammed the flimsy cheap door behind him. The solid sound of the padlock sliding into place was followed by his footsteps moving away down the hall and then down the stairs to the lower level.

One of the women moved forward to salvage the food and parcel it out. Starving, Carmelina ate the soggy burger without thinking too much about where it had been.

"We've been here over a week," one of the single men said.

"What's the delay?" Dora asked.

"It's about the river," one of the single men said. "My brother crossed a few months ago. They have to wait for the river to recede so we don't drown on the way over."

Dora's mouth dropped. "I don't know how to swim."

"Me either," Carmelina muttered. At least crossing the Suchiate, she'd had Jaime looking out for her. "How deep is it?"

"Don't know," the man said. "But the currents can be fierce when the water is high."

The wife of the Honduran cuddled her children closer in a protective way. "I'm sure there's a raft or something. We can't cross the river with the little ones."

"I wouldn't count on it," the first man said. "In this hellhole, I wouldn't count on anything."

Carmelina finished her burger, threw the wrapper back into the empty, torn bag, and stepped over her companions to the bathroom. Mercifully it had a door. It probably hadn't been cleaned since she'd been a baby bouncing on her father's knee. She avoided touching anything inside. But there was running water and the toilet still flushed.

She pulled her phone out. Still nothing from Diego. She sent another text.

Someone banged on the door. "I need the toilet."

She put her phone away, flushed, quickly washed her hands—which she wiped dry by smoothing her hands over her head—and stepped back out into the room. The man almost knocked her over in his rush to the toilet.

DORA LOOKED up at her when she returned to her corner. They'd talked a lot over the last couple of days. She was from northern Guatemala. A squat, cheerful, darker-skinned woman who could have made a living as a poster model for Guatemalan tourism. Carmelina wasn't ready to trust her, but she did like her quite a lot.

Dora had arrived only a few hours before Carmelina. Her face had lit up when Carmelina had walked in with Katya, and she'd immediately bonded with her. While Carmelina was grateful for the company she kept rhyming Dora with Flora. She shook it off. Lina rhymed with Gina and that had worked out well for her.

Based on what she'd seen in the house in Mexico City, their conditions, while not luxurious, could have been much worse. They were fed regularly, they had a quasi-working bathroom, and twice a day, the man came and took them up onto the rooftop where they could sit in the sun and enjoy the fresh air. It was early November and the worst of the heat was behind them. Still, without shelter from the sun, she felt like an egg on the hot cement roof, ready to be fried. They never stayed long, reluctantly returning to the small room.

She wasn't a captive. Ana had explained she would be kept out of sight because she was undocumented. This close to the border she was prey for Mexican immigration officials, the police, the cartel, and any small hood opportunist who might spot her.

It was hard to frame it that way, but Ana had insisted that securing a place in this house was a favor she was cashing in. Carmelina didn't doubt that Ana had paid well to get her safely over the border. While not ideal, it was a lot better than anything she could have managed on her own.

"I'm surprised they haven't asked for more money from us," Dora said. They stood in a thin slice of shade on the roof, sheltered beneath a large water tank.

Carmelina wiped Katya's forehead which was bright red with the heat. "My coyote already paid."

"Mine, too," Dora said, "but it's not uncommon for the men in the safe house to ask for more money."

"Safe house?" Carmelina barked out a laugh. "Is that what this is?"

The wife of the Honduran who had spoken out earlier approached them, attracted by Carmelina's laughter or seeking to share the only shade on the roof, it was difficult to say.

She smiled and they shifted so she could join them. "I'm Maria," she said, shyly.

Dora nodded and pointed to Carmelina, then herself. "That's Carmelina, I'm Dora." She peered at her, a beat too long. The woman shifted her weight.

"You don't talk much. Inside, I mean," Dora said.

"I'm busy with the babies," Maria said. "My husband, well, he likes to speak for the family." After a pause, she said, "I'm sorry you don't have someone to speak for you."

Carmelina and Dora exchanged a glance.

"We're doing okay on our own," Carmelina said.

"Are you?" The woman's brow creased. "I think their suggestion that you pretend to be a family with the two other men is a good idea."

"Can't hurt," Dora said.

"Do you know about the assaults? Especially near the border?" Maria's eyes darted between the two of them.

"We know." Carmelina lowered her voice. The man who brought them upstairs stood smoking and staring over the horizon from the far corner of the roof. "It happened to my friend while she was traveling with her husband. Being married won't protect you."

"I know. It's just..." Maria swallowed and met Carmelina's eye. "You know, a lot of babies are stolen. And small children. Be careful. Having a child with you can make things easier once you cross. For your asylum application."

She talked in a stilted way, each sentence stuttering out of her like a train jerking down a track, like her voice was something unfamiliar she needed to tame.

"I've heard that," Carmelina said. Bonita had told her that. She wondered how Bonita and her grandsons had made out, and where they were. "Dora and I were talking about that yesterday."

"Yes," Maria said, piercing Carmelina with her gaze. "Don't trust anyone. Ever."

"Sadly, I've learned that lesson already. All too well."

SEVENTY-SIX

November 7, 2019
Rio Bravo-Rio Grande, Mexico-U.S. Border

Water rushed along the scraggy shoreline, small eddies swirling among the swaying reeds. The man standing at the end, shined a weak beam of light on a small inflatable rubber boat. The boat bounced and bucked against the current. Two families had already entered and sat at the back.

"You next," he said, flashing the light in Carmelina's direction.

Carmelina blinked, her chest heaving. The river stretched before her, representing hope. *EL Norte* was on the other side. She and Dora had made a pact—neither of them swimmers—to look out for each other while they crossed. Clutching Katya, Carmelina stepped forward and slid on the slope, her foot losing purchase in the glassy mud. Dora reached out and grabbed her arm to steady her. They were both frightened by the rushing water. Dora nodded, a small gesture filled with encouragement.

Carmelina stood at the bow, her heart pounding. The first boat was already halfway across the river carrying Maria and her family, and several others, to a new life, a better life.

A hush pressed down on the area, the only sound the relentless path of the river pushing west. Her heart pounded against her chest. The water wasn't deep, she knew that—they'd talked about it—but the churn of the current against the boulders lurking out of the darkness scared her.

Tentatively, she stepped into the boat. The little craft bobbed under her weight and she was thrown off balance again. Dora placed a steadying hand on her back.

"Put the baby down until you get on the damn boat," the man said.

"Carmelina, pass me Katya."

Carmelina turned back toward Dora, hesitating.

"Get on." The man's hand drifted toward his back where he'd jammed a pistol in the waistband of his jeans.

"I'm right here," Dora said. "I'll be right behind you. All for one, remember?"

"Come on." One of the men in the back hissed at her to get on. Tensions ran as high as the river, the threat of immigration as tangible as the mist wetting the sides of the boat. This was the last leg of a very long journey for all of them.

She relinquished Katya to Dora's waiting arms. Turning her attention to the bobbing craft, she pulled her other leg in, her feet unsteady against the soft bottom, and lurched toward the back when the bow was pushed off shore.

She fell into one of the other passengers and the woman held her arm until she regained her balance.

"Wait," she said, turning. "We're not all on yet."

The man stared at her and plunged a long pole against the current to guide them.

"Wait!"

On the shore, Carmelina could make out Dora's silhouette.

Dora in motion. She scrambled up the slope and disappeared into the scrub with Katya.

Carmelina jumped over the side. Her feet hit the bottom for a few seconds, then her legs were pushed from beneath her by the raging current. She flailed against the water, screaming for Katya.

"She'll drown," someone said.

"Not my problem," the man said. The voices receded as her head was tugged under the water.

She thrashed and surfaced, took a large breath and slammed into a large boulder. It knocked the air out of her, her stomach felt hollowed out. She clung to a notch at the top of the rock, her nails digging into the unforgiving surface. She held on long enough to catch her breath and get her bearings.

The shore was a couple of yards away. So close, but with the current trashing her efforts, she'd never make it.

Downstream, a large branch had fallen into the water. She let go of the rock, and dug for the bottom with her feet. When she crashed into the branch, it cracked against her weight. She gasped, reaching for something to hang onto. The solid limb held. Hand over hand, she dragged herself to shore, the water pushing her into the jagged, broken branches. She ignored the stabbing pain in her abdomen, the deep scratches against her legs.

She clawed at the muddy shore, fingers desperate for purchase, trying to push herself up and scramble to her feet.

Behind her, the water rushed on.

"Katya." She screamed into the dark of the night and raced up over the slope, the long grass slapping at her legs.

SEVENTY-SEVEN

Carmelina raced to the spot where they'd been dropped off earlier. The van and the SUV they'd come in were gone. She stood rooted to the spot, water dripping off her, gasping for breath.

Think. Had it all been a set up from the beginning? Did Dora leave with the people who had brought them? If so, how was Carmelina going to get back to town without being seen and find the house again? Even if she did find it, there was no guarantee Dora would be there. Could she call Ana to get the address? Would she help?

Most of the sky overhead was black as wet bulls, any light from the moon or stars obscured by heavy rain clouds. A sliver of light flashed against the scalloped top of a thunderhead, an edging of quicksilver deftly drawn by moonlight.

Katya's cry pierced the air. To the right. She held her breath. Some instinct deep in her belly urged her to stay quiet. She didn't call out. She ran, a mad woman with no thought for her own safety, in the direction of her child's cries.

As she drew closer, she heard muffled screams. If Dora hurt

her baby, she'd beat her senseless. Adrenaline surged through her and she pushed her legs faster, pumping her arms.

Another scream. It was Dora. She was close. She edged forward quietly. The low guttural voice of a man stopped her in her tracks. Up ahead, the brush gave way to a clearing. She crept forward, keeping her body low, until she came to the edge of it, hiding herself behind the trunk of a scraggly mesquite tree.

On the far side of the clearing, was a tree hung thick with women's torn underclothing. Bras and panties hung slack and wasted from the twisted limbs. A bra tree. It's where many women migrants were raped near the borders—one final payment cruelly extracted. Rumor had it that hundreds of these trees lined the border from east to west.

"Hurry up," a man grumbled. He stood facing away from Carmelina, hands jammed in his back pockets.

"Shut up," the other man snarled. His body sprawled over Dora, he pumped his bare ass, his hand clamped over her mouth. "You'll get your turn."

Dora's eyes were wild. The man's other hand pinned one of her arms to the ground, with her free hand she beat at his shoulder and tried to claw at his face.

"She's a feisty little thing," the man said, his breath ragged. "Come over here and hold this bitch down."

"Just punch her in the face again, that'll keep her quiet."

The man paused mid pump and turned his head toward his friend. "You know I like them alive and kicking. Where's the fun if there's not a little fight? Get over here and hold her arm."

When the second man moved, Carmelina spotted the small bundle on the ground. Katya. She'd been set down close to a patch of scrub brush.

Heart thudding against her chest, Carmelina edged her way around the outside of the clearing, scrambling from one clump of scrub brush to the next.

When she was within a few yards of Katya, she dropped to her belly and pulled herself slowly along the ground. Both men were focused on Dora. For now, Carmelina was out of their sightline.

Her blood pounded in her ears, the constant whoosh drowning out all other sound. Her heart raced, crashing against her chest so hard she feared it would escape.

The man on top of Dora quickened his movements, his grunts punctuating the assault. It wouldn't be long until he would finish and her moment would be gone.

She gulped in a breath and raced to her baby's side.

SEVENTY-EIGHT

Carmelina pressed her hand over Katya's rosebud mouth and lifted her from the ground. The baby was tightly wrapped—she'd swaddled her in the scarf before the river crossing—so there was no struggle, no flailing of her chubby little arms. Katya's lids flew open, her pupils wide. With one smooth movement, ground to neck, Carmelina pressed Katya against her, her familiar smell quickly calming the baby.

The man straddling Dora cried out.

Step by careful step, her eyes glued to the men and Dora, Carmelina backed out of the clearing, back into the scrub. She turned and picked her way across the ground for several more yards, farther away from the clearing.

"You're done. Get off." The sound of the second man's impatient voice cut through the night. His friend protested and the two of them started to argue.

Under cover of their bickering voices, Carmelina ran. She ran like the devil was at her heels, back toward the spot they'd been dropped off.

In her panic, she ended up on a different path and spied a beat up, black pickup truck. Did it belong to the men who had Dora? Or did it belong to the men with the rafts? Wouldn't they have parked closer to the river?

She'd never learned to drive, but it didn't look so hard. If it was an automatic, she could do it. She and Diego once drove their uncle's old truck at his farm. She crept toward the vehicle. The bed of the pickup was lumpy, filled with sleeping bodies? With sacks of corn? Inching forward, the items started to take shape. Life jackets. The truck was filled with them yet none of them had been offered one before boarding the raft.

Hoping to find the keys, she moved down along the side of the truck toward the door. Through the open window came the sound of clothes rustling, followed by a grunt, then rhythmic snoring.

Someone was sleeping inside. Heart in her throat, she backed away several yards then turned and raced on toward the river.

If this truck belonged to the men with the rafts, they'd be coming back to this side of the river.

Determination and hope pushed her forward. Minutes later, the roar of the river filled her ears. Standing on the edge of the slope, she waited for her eyes to adjust to the darkness of the broad river valley. On this side, there was nothing. Nobody stood along the shore that she could see. The water burbled and glugged its way west, swirling around large boulders near the shore.

There. One of the rafts, fighting against the current, making its way back toward her on the southern shore.

She knew she risked being raped herself by going down to the water on her own. Raped, robbed, killed even. Her feet rooted in place, she forced a full breath into her lungs and looked up into the sky. Clouds blotted the stars. From somewhere behind her came a man's voice shouting.

She scrambled down the slope toward the water's edge, then, reason intercepting her state of panic, she hid in a clump of brush and reached for the money—her Ernesto money—and grabbed a fistful of bills.

When the man reached the shore, nosing the raft up onto the mud, she was waiting.

"You're late." His eyes narrowed and his gaze ran the length of her. Her clothing was soaked through, mud and brambles stuck to her shirt, her pants were torn from the branch that had saved her from floating farther downstream.

"You're the one who went overboard."

"I need to get across."

He shook his head. One sharp turn to each side. "Had your chance."

"I can pay." She held the bills out to him. "Please."

Palm outstretched, he waited while she counted bills into his hand. He whistled, an eerie sound against the raging waters. "You got more?" He peered up at her, greed shining in his eyes.

"That's everything I have. Please." She started to say he'd been paid twice for her passage, but reason didn't seem a logical approach.

Whose voice had she heard shouting and how long did she have until someone else showed up? Until Dora and the two men noticed Katya gone and came looking for her?

She folded to a kneeling position, her knees slapping into the mud. "Please, I beg you. I'm someone's sister, I'm my father's daughter. If you have family, if you have someone you love and care about, think about them. Help me. And hope that someone will help them someday."

His eyes met hers. He stared at her for a long time. Finally, his gaze softened and he jutted his chin upwards. "Come on."

He grumbled all the way across the river: the cost of taking only one person should be more. She didn't point out she was paying him more than the full fare, and no middleman or coyote was taking a cut. No, at this point, it was best she said nothing, grateful he was taking her at all. She sat quietly, rocking Katya, intent on the far shore as it loomed before her.

El Norte.

A better life.

The land of opportunity was now within her reach.

PART THREE
LAND OF OPPORTUNITY

SEVENTY-NINE

Carmelina ran through the night, her feet once again on foreign soil. This was her third foreign country since she'd left her suburb, her mother, her sisters, and life as she'd known it behind.

And this foreign soil should feel sweet, since it was her final destination and hard won through all the troubles she'd experienced on the road.

But these things weren't on her mind. Maybe later, she could entertain these thoughts. For now, she pushed aside the stabbing pain in her abdomen and her shredded legs and dug deep within to maintain a single focus and keep moving forward.

A single dirt track guided her way. She calculated the group had a forty-five-minute start. They were somewhere ahead of her. There was a chance the smaller children with the families might slow them down. It gave her a small glimmer of hope. There was an equal chance they'd taken an alternate route or had already been picked up.

Her breath rattled against her throat, lungs bursting. Katya mewed against her, the constant, unsteady movement unsettling the child and making her restless.

Overhead, the hovering clouds parted. Moonlight shone down and a weak platinum light shimmered over the land. She stopped, took a breath, and stared into the sky above. Her eyes scanned the clouds and haze until she spotted the light of the North Star—Ricky's star. Using it to navigate, she raced on.

Ahead on the horizon, she spotted a dark clump. Was it trees or could it be a group of people? Carmelina dug harder, thighs burning as she pounded across the uneven ground, closing the gap. There. Movement. Trees didn't move. It was people. She was making progress.

The ground stretched before her. For as far as she could see, it was scrub grass. An occasional dip or rise threw things into shadow, but mostly the landscape remained uninterrupted by anything of interest. The people represented her chance to ride into civilization and not be left in the desert to fend for herself.

A set of headlights flashed twice into the night. It took her by surprise. She crouched, low to the ground. The headlights cast a brief light over the people, a quick flicker, and yet, enough for her to be sure it was her group. She called out, her air-starved voice a shredded thing, her words lost beneath the engine of the oncoming vehicle.

It advanced toward the group then rolled to a stop. The large truck stood silhouetted against the horizon.

One by one, the group climbed up into the back of the truck. She was closer now. She recognized the Honduran man passing his children up to his wife, Maria.

She screamed her name, but nobody heard her. With all the willpower she had left, she pushed forward. Now more of them were on the truck than were left waiting on the ground. Harder, faster, thighs burning. Bumping against her shoulder Katya started to cry.

"Wait!" Carmelina yelled again. Only four people remained

on the ground. One of them turned his head in her direction. She yelled again. "Wait."

They all turned to her now.

A man in a baseball cap prodded them to hurry. "Get in," he said. "We're not taking anyone else."

The remaining three people clambered up over the bumper and into the truck.

The man in the cap slapped his hand against the side of the truck and reached to swing the wide wooden door shut.

"We know her." Maria stood in the opening of the door, her hand outstretched to prevent the door from closing. "She's with us."

Carmelina reached the truck. The man in the cap raised his brows. "We weren't paid for this one."

"Yes," Carmelina gasped. "I'm..." She bent over, one hand braced on her thigh, coughing.

"She's with us." Maria's husband jumped down and put his arm around her back to support her. "She got separated, that's all. Go ahead, count. She's with us."

Maria reached out and Carmelina grasped her hand. Maria pulled while her husband pushed Carmelina up into the truck.

Depleted of energy, relieved beyond prayers, tears streamed down Carmelina's face. She fell into Maria's arms and sobbed. Knees shaking, she crumbled to the rough wooden plank floor of the truck, Katya cradled in her arms.

Maria's husband climbed in and the man in the hat grunted, slammed the heavy wooden door behind them, and slid the heavy bolt into place.

EIGHTY

The truck rattled and rolled through the night. Everyone sat on the rough planks, jostling against each other each time the truck dipped, or hit a rock, or, at times, it felt like the vehicle was sailing as it left the ground after a particularly high bump. Airborne, all went silent and Carmelina held her breath, bracing for the inevitable crash and slam back onto the dirt.

A couple in the corner chattered, excited about finally being in the United States.

"It's not over yet," one of the single men said. "We've still a long way to go."

"Perhaps," said the woman. "But there's a long way behind us, too."

The man shrugged, conceded her point, and fell silent. Carmelina agreed with him, but said nothing. Thanks to Diego, she knew what lay ahead. It was far from over.

She ached for news of Ricky. Before she could call Diego, she'd need to change money and buy a new SIM card. She knew it was far from over, and yet, a small flicker of hope grew in her belly, each passing kilometer fanning the flame.

WITHOUT WARNING OR SLOWING, the truck braked. It spun in a large circle, tires sliding in gravel, before lurching to a stop. Carmelina was thrown against Maria. Bags and bodies shifted and slammed into the sides of the truck and each other. The child next to her landed on her, his elbow digging into her thigh. She knew she'd have a bruise later—she could add it to the others.

A high-voltage spotlight lit up the night, the white light leaking through the slats in the planks that made up the side of the truck's box.

The front doors of the truck opened and the men in the front bolted.

A man's voice yelled. "Go after them." Footsteps pounded the ground outside.

Maria's husband scrambled to his feet and peered between the slats.

"What is it?"

"The light's too strong, I can't see anything," he said.

Men's voices surrounded the truck, shouting against each other. Someone slammed a hand against the side of the truck. The heavy bolt slid out of place and the door swung open. A bright flashlight danced over them.

Carmelina shield her eyes. Cold fingers of fear snaked through her bones. She sought Maria's hand, Maria squeezed her fingers. For a brief instant, their eyes met.

And then chaos reigned.

Once again, her path was blocked.

"HOW MANY?" The question was barked out, authority infused the gravelly voice.

"Fifteen, maybe twenty."

"Don't guess. Count."

A man leaned farther into the truck with the light and rested it on each face while he counted aloud. "Fourteen adults, six minors."

"Twenty on the nose!" The man outside laughed and clapped the man with the light on the back. He turned and spoke to someone behind him. "Pay up, boys."

Somebody muttered, "Lucky son of a bitch."

The man standing in the open door swung to the group of men behind him, his light pointed at their feet. It cast eerie shadows up their bodies, the creases in their pants darkened, their faces still in shadow.

Grumbling, the circle of men reached into pockets, pulled out wallets, passed bills to the largest of the men who pounded the ground with his heel each time someone paid him. "Whoo-ee," he said. "Good payday, boys."

A whisper from a man in the corner of the truck whipped Carmelina's head on her shoulders. His whisper was then chained from person to person, heads nodding, spirits dampened, hopes quashed.

The big man shouldered his way past the man with the light. He took his time, carefully aligning and folding the bills he'd collected before stuffing them deep into the front pocket of his pants. Placing his hands on his hips, he worked his mouth while his gaze swept over Carmelina and the others. The crest on his uniform confirmed the whispers.

Migra.

Immigration.

EIGHTY-ONE

RICKY GONE 179 DAYS

November 9, 2019
Customs and Border Protection Detention Facility,
Del Rio, Texas, United States

The lights never went out. There was no escaping them, no way to distinguish day from night. It was a special kind of torture. Twenty-four seven the ugly fluorescent tubes flickered overhead, shining down on them and illuminating the deplorable conditions in which they were held. The cell they were in had a capacity for thirty people. The beds had been removed. Over a hundred women crowded the small space. A few lucky ones edged the walls, graced with a place to rest their backs and several inches of floor space to call their own. Everyone else jostled, shoulder to shoulder, climbing over each other when it was necessary to move, sandwiched into slivers of space on the damp concrete floor.

A lone toilet and sink, encrusted with dirt, open to the room, stood in the corner. Filthy, it reminded Carmelina of the bathroom in the safe house in Piedras Negras. Except for the distinct lack of privacy, a luxury not extended to them here.

At seventeen, Carmelina should have been housed with the minors. Without bothering to check her papers, Immigration and Customs Enforcement had thrown her in with the adults. In part because of Katya, and in part because it was easier to lump them together than process her correctly.

When they'd been discovered in the desert, when they'd all filed out of the truck and into the waiting U.S. Customs and Border Protection vehicles, her companions grumbled about their bad luck. Carmelina, on the other hand, experienced growing hope.

She was a minor and her clock was ticking—she wanted to be processed into the system as quickly as possible. The sooner they got her and Katya into the system, the sooner she could be reunited with Ricky.

She pulled the thin foil blanket tighter around her shoulders and folded it over Katya. She and Maria huddled together, for security as well as warmth. Despite the press and stench of human bodies in the small space, the air was frigid.

On arrival in Del Rio, ICE had separated Maria from her husband, sending him to the men's wing. Her children slept up against her legs, the smallest with his head in her lap.

"How long will we be in the *hielera*?" Maria spoke to an older woman sitting beside her who chewed methodically on her fingernails.

"Been here two weeks," the woman said.

"In the icebox? I thought they could only hold us here seventy-two hours?" Carmelina knew the rules, but also knew they'd broken them when Diego had first been held.

The woman laughed, spit a jagged sliver of nail into her palm, and studied it like a gold nugget before discarding it on the floor.

"What they're supposed to do and what they actually do is two different stories." She grunted and stuck another finger in her mouth. "Anyway, count yourself lucky you're here and they didn't send you back across to Mexico to wait."

"Almost three weeks for me."

Carmelina turned toward the new voice. The girl looked to be in her late teens, not a lot older than herself. Her jet black hair, cropped close to her head, stuck out in uneven, oily clumps.

"Oh, this?" She scratched her fingers along her scalp. "I hacked it off myself with a penknife. It used to be longer than yours."

"You still have the knife?" Maria asked.

She shook her head. "No. I hacked it long before I got here."

"But the knife?" Maria persisted. "The guards took it?"

The girl lowered her voice and darted a look toward a group lounging in one of the corners closest to the door. They sprawled out, relaxed, taking up more than their share of space. Several of them had prominent tattoos. "No, *they* took it."

Carmelina recognized the type. Tough girls, banded together before arrival or after, it didn't matter. They would create the rules and take what they wanted.

"I'm Luz."

"That's Maria," Carmelina said, before introducing herself. "Are you Mexican?"

"Yes, from a small town in Tabasco, near the Guatemalan border."

"Oh." She fell silent. "Did you come up that way? I mean, I know things are rough through Tamaulipas. With, um..."

Luz leaned in and lowered her voice. "With the mass graves?"

"Yes." How much was she willing to tell this girl? At this point, it didn't seem to matter, given they were already here. "My brother came before me and when I saw the news, I thought he might have been taken."

"I didn't know that," Maria said. She patted Carmelina on the leg. "Was he?"

"*Gracias a Dios*, no."

Luz's eyes brimmed with tears. "My uncle was taken. My aunt had to go and identify the remains. She came home with a small box of bones." Luz bit her lip and struggled to control her emotions. She splayed her hands over her face and lowered her head.

Carmelina and Maria looked away to give the girl time to compose herself. After a few minutes, she sniffled and looked up at them.

"I took the train."

EIGHTY-TWO

"You took the train? I've heard it's so dangerous. Were you alone?" Carmelina's questions tumbled over each other. She took a breath and leaned back. "Sorry."

"It's fine," Luz said. "I was with a couple of friends. Guys. They're in the other wing now."

"Tell us about the train," Carmelina said. "I know someone who decided to go that way."

"You didn't want to go with them?"

"Too dangerous with the baby," she explained. "I walked from Mapastepec."

"We didn't take the train all the way." Luz picked at invisible lint on her leg. "Once we got into Tamaulipas, the cartel started coming aboard more often and taking the women. We got off at the last minute and fled into the woods. We were almost caught."

"Me, too," Carmelina said. "I went out the back window of an abandoned Pemex and hid in the woods."

"The train is faster, sometimes, but we waited ten days before we could board. Once you get on, you're a moving target. There's nowhere to run. Bandits get on all the time to try and steal your money. And then the cartel will show up and take women. The night they came, the train stopped in the middle of nowhere—always a bad sign—and then the trucks arrived."

"White trucks," Carmelina said.

"Yeah. It was definitely planned. The train knew exactly where to stop. They buy everyone." She paused. "But that night, there was a guy from El Salvador, you're from there right?"

Carmelina nodded.

"He'd been at the tracks with us almost the whole ten days we waited. Nice guy, always helping out. Anyway, Jaime saw it all happening ahead of time. He was at the back of the train and ran forward warning women to get off."

"This guy, Jaime, was he traveling with his brother and wife? Flora and Manuel? Flora has a little boy, about six."

"Noooo." Luz drew out the word in a way that made it sound like a yes. Or at least a maybe. Her brow knit together. "He was traveling with a group of Guatemalan guys. They sat at the rear of the train with pieces of rebar and big sticks to run off the bandits."

She tapped her finger against the side of her mouth. "But I did hear a story about him when we were waiting for the train. Keep in mind, ten days is a long time to wait, and people make up stuff to pass the time."

"Go on."

"Apparently he'd already been on the train, somewhere farther south. But got off when the little boy he was traveling with fell off the train."

"What do you mean he fell off the train?"

"Again, the train was stopped somewhere, but in a town, and the cartel showed up to take the women. Jaime and his brother's family tried to get down but the train lurched forward and the little boy..."

She met Carmelina's gaze. "I'm sorry, but the little boy was sucked under the train and lost his leg."

Maria gasped and instinctively reached out to touch her son's back. Carmelina's hand flew to her mouth. Images of Ricky tunneled through her brain, followed by images of Beto.

"Oh God," she said, her stomach queasy. "Did he live?"

"Yes. Jaime stayed with them at the hospital for a while. But then... Oh, I'm just full of bad news. Remember this is all hearsay. I don't even know if these are the people you know."

"Just tell me."

"His sister-in-law left the hospital one day to pick up tacos and was never seen again. Someone said they saw her picked up in the main street by the cartel."

"Oh, no." Carmelina exchanged a look with Maria.

"They take the women and put them into tolerance houses near the Guatemalan border. Especially young, thin Salvadorans, and Hondurans," she glanced at Maria, "because they're lighter skinned than the Guatemalan girls. They don't always send them south though, sometimes they send them other places. Basically, they enslave them and force them to work in the brothels."

Poor Flora. "And what of her husband? Jaime's brother? I mean, why wasn't he with Jaime?"

Luz shrugged. "I suppose he stayed behind to look after his son."

Of course, Carmelina thought. She wanted to throw up. For everything Flora and her family did to her, stealing her money, leaving her stranded, and the pain she'd felt from their betrayal, she wouldn't have wished this on them.

"Jaime was coming north to work so he could send money for the hospital bills. And, I think his brother went a little mad. He's with his son all day in the hospital and then at night he goes to the brothels hoping to find his wife."

"Flora."

"What?"

"His wife's name is Flora. I have a photo of them on my phone."

A tear slid down Carmelina's cheek and she dashed it away. For a few days at least, Flora had been like a sister to her. She remembered the night Katya was sick, and how Flora had helped bathe her to bring her temperature down. She remembered the countless kindnesses extended to her by Jaime.

And, she remembered Manuel's temper: quick to anger and often irrational. He'd beaten that junkie to a pulp and later killed the man who'd assaulted Flora. God help whoever had taken Flora once Manuel found them.

"Wait." She bit her lip. "When did you last see Jaime? Is he one of the guys you were with when you got here?"

"Garcia! Carmelina Garcia!" A female ICE agent stood in the open doorway.

Carmelina jumped to her feet and picked her way across legs and reposing women toward the hall.

EIGHTY-THREE

"The baby's in good shape." The doctor made a few notes then set the clipboard on the counter. "Good job, mama."

Carmelina felt her cheeks flush.

"You're what? Eighteen? Nineteen?"

"I'll be eighteen in January."

The woman's brows shot up. "You should be in the minor's facility."

"I know." Carmelina clasped her hands in her lap.

"Hmph, we're so overcrowded these days." She rocked her head to the side, stretching out her neck. "Let's have a look at you now, Carmelina."

Her instruments were cold against Carmelina's back. She tapped on her chest, checked her blood pressure, asked her countless questions.

"I'm going to do a swab for STDs."

Carmelina prepared to lie back on the exam table.

"You can stay sitting up for now. We'll do the throat first."

"Throat?" She swallowed.

The doctor stood with her back to her, snapping on a pair of latex gloves. She turned holding a culture kit. "Happens a lot. Have you had any symptoms?"

"Like what?"

"Ulcers in your mouth, sore throat?" She peered at Carmelina who shook her head. "Most women don't have symptoms. We'll take a swab for the lab."

When she was done, she said, "You can lie down now, put your feet in the stirrups." As she turned back to the counter, she said, "Were you assaulted on the way here?"

"You mean by Border Patrol?"

"No." She turned to Carmelina. "Were you sexually assaulted during your trip?"

"No."

"Well, it wouldn't be uncommon. The stats are pretty high. Some say six in ten, but what we see here is closer to eight in ten."

She settled onto the rolling stool near Carmelina's feet. Carmelina heard a sharp intake of breath. "What happened here to your legs? These are deep scratches."

"I had a disagreement with a tree in the river."

"It's a little infected. I'll give you some ointment. Anything else?"

"One of the branches dug into my belly. It still hurts."

"Now, this might pinch a bit." She slid the speculum into Carmelina. When she was done with the swab, she removed the speculum and leaned back in her chair. "Are you sure?"

"That my belly hurts?"

"No, I mean, about being sexually assaulted. Are you sure?"

"Of course I'm sure." Katya stirred in the crib the doctor kept by the exam table. Carmelina turned her head to shush and comfort her.

"I see quite a bit of trauma and scar tissue. Maybe the trauma is not recent?"

Recent? There was a time in Carmelina's life when she was

convinced she would forever live the hell of being Flaco's *niña*, and later, the worse hell of being Memo's. What was recent? Did most of her adolescent years count? She felt like it had been months since she'd left, years since she'd been separated from Ricky, and yet—

"Roughly," the doctor said. "An estimate."

Right. Overcrowding. The doctor was busy. She was kind, but she couldn't spend all day with her.

The words built up in Carmelina's mouth until, like projectile vomit or insects escaping, they tumbled out of her all at once. "I was sexually assaulted regularly, almost daily, since I was thirteen." She blinked and stared at the ceiling. Someone had taped a poster of a cat with a panicked look on its face hanging from a branch by its front paws. The caption, in bright yellow, said "Hang in there, baby."

The wheels of the doctor's stool scraped across the floor. Carmelina took a breath, assuming she planned to examine her more closely, ask her more questions, but the woman rolled up beside her, stripped off her gloves, and put her hand gently on her arm.

"Carmelina." Her voice was quiet and warm, steady, grounded.

Carmelina turned her head and when she saw the look in the older woman's eyes, and realized—that at this moment, in this small exam room, with this woman—she was safe, a dam inside her broke. She sobbed, her face soaked with tears. The doctor gripped her hand and she let go, bawling her head off, stomach clenching, until she was almost cried out. She continued weeping. She wept for her lost girlhood, for her missing son, her brother Diego, for Flora, and even for Dora. She blurted out all of it, until there was nothing more to say.

With blurred vision she watched the doctor wipe at her own eyes before passing her a tissue.

Carmelina blotted her eyes, and gulped in large breaths.

"Let me check your abdomen and then you can sit up." She prodded her gently. "Some bruising, I think, but no lasting damage." She helped her sit up.

"Oh, Carmelina." The doctor shook her head and rolled her eyes to the ceiling. Then, using her fingers to tick off her thoughts, she started to talk.

"I'm going to set you up with a social worker. You're a minor. You shouldn't be in this center." She glanced at her watch, pulled the chart toward her and scribbled something down. "I'll insist she see you tomorrow. She can help you find your son."

Carmelina opened her mouth to thank her, but the doctor continued.

"I'm going to write up a report that details your abuse over the past years. The social worker will help you start your application for asylum. You're a prime candidate for that." She looked up from the paper. "Understand?"

She nodded, not trusting herself to speak. After so long, everything seemed to be going so fast.

"I want to see you again when the tests come back. Although, it's possible you won't be here by then."

"Really?"

"If your application for asylum is taken care of, you could be out in a few days. They'll release you until your court date."

"Wait. So that means I'll be able to go and get my son?"

"Where is your son?"

"I don't know." Her lip trembled.

"Did they take him when you came in? Usually children stay with their mother."

"No, he traveled up with my brother almost six months ago. They were separated when they were picked up, and then he was moved, and..." It was no use, she couldn't hold it back. Large tears rolled down her face as she started to cry again.

"Nobody knows where he is." Carmelina sniffed and wiped at her nose.

The doctor jumped to her feet and paced the length of the small room, fisting and unfisting her hands. After a few minutes, she leaned against the counter, staring into the sink, fingers clenching the stainless steel rim and shaking her head while she muttered under her breath. When she turned back to Carmelina, her face was red but she'd composed her features.

"Look, I know Sandra, the social worker. She's good. She cares." She sat again, rolled the chair up to Carmelina and repeated her words. "She cares. She'll do her very best for you."

She nodded solemnly. Her life had been filled with broken promises but she wanted to grasp onto this small ray of hope with all of her heart.

The other woman reached for her hands and looked up into her eyes. "Things are going to get better, Carmelina. I promise."

EIGHTY-FOUR

RICKY GONE 180 DAYS

November 10, 2019

For the first time in weeks, perhaps months, Carmelina passed the night without the threat of unknown danger looming over her. She'd made it. She was in the United States and she felt she'd found an ally in the doctor and the doctor's friend who would help her find Ricky.

The possibilities running through her mind excited her. Tomorrow she'd see Sandra, the social worker. She felt like she knew her already, and tried to imagine what she would look like. Would she be tall like a Texas cowgirl in the movies? Or petite with closely cropped highlighted hair and big blue eyes?

It didn't matter. Sandra could get her moved to the minor's facility and.... It all swirled around in her head, a psychedelic kaleidoscope of hope.

The tears she'd shed in the doctor's office and the release she'd felt, combined with the stress of the last weeks caught up with her, and she nodded off.

She didn't sleep exactly, but she did drift in and out, catnapping through the night. Curled on the cold concrete against Maria's back for warmth, she cradled Katya in her arms and kept her eyes shut tight against the overhead lights.

———

THE SOUND of metal clanging against metal startled Carmelina out of her slumber and she bolted upright. Beside her, Maria tried to untangle herself from the heap of her children, their arms and legs thrown over her limbs and lower body. Luz was already sitting up and cast a look to Carmelina.

A tall guard swung a baton between the bars, hitting each side rapidly, creating a clanging less pretty, but not unlike a loud church bell. "Wakey wakey," he yelled, a cruel laughing tone in his voice.

Around them, the other women stirred. Some were already sitting, others were extricating themselves from the thin silver blankets they'd cocooned themselves in. The women in the corner, the gang girls as Carmelina thought of them, didn't move. They stayed stretched out on the floor, under a pile of clothing and blankets they'd stolen from others. The guard ignored them.

A senior guard, Carmelina recognized her from when she'd arrived and been processed, stepped up to the door. The woman had thin, colorless lips and pale skin, unfettered by any smile lines. Her neutral expression seemed carved in beige stone. She ran her finger down the side of a clipboard and started shouting out names.

"That's me," Luz said. She grabbed Carmelina's hand. "Maybe we're going to the minor's facility."

"When your name is called, stand up." The first guard yelled into the room. Luz sprang to her feet. His boss continued calling out names.

At each name, they waited for someone to stand before continuing. One of the older women got up, then two or three definitely older than Carmelina, probably in their early twenties.

Luz's brow furrowed and she glanced down at Carmelina. "Not all minors."

"Quiet," the first guard yelled.

Two more names were called and then, "Garcia, Carmelina."

Carmelina stood. Luz threaded her arm through hers.

Maria stared up at them then focused her attention on the guard with the clipboard. She started to scramble to her feet. "I'm coming with you."

"If we haven't called your name, sit back down." The guard pierced Maria with a look and banged his baton fiercely against the metal door.

Maria protested. "I'm going with them."

"You single?" The woman with the clipboard raised one of her brows in an expression of disgust and looked at the children clinging to Maria's legs.

Maria shook her head. "No, my husband is—"

"Families will be moved later. Sit down."

"They can't move us." Fear snaked through Carmelina. She was supposed to see the social worker today. "They can't move us."

"Quiet!" The guard rapped the baton against the metal bars again.

Maria reached up for Carmelina's hand. "*Cuidate mucho*," she whispered.

"You take care, too," Carmelina whispered. "You'll be with your husband soon." It seemed like the right thing to say, but she didn't know if it was true.

"*Gracias por todo*," she added, remembering Maria's kindnesses, her attempts to warn her about Dora that day on the roof, the way she and her husband spoke up for her in the desert. If this trip had taught her anything, it was that she needed to appreciate kindness where she found it and it was unlikely she'd see Maria again.

"*Gracias a ti, hermanita.*" Maria's eyes crinkling as she smiled up at her. She blew a kiss to Katya.

"Move. Everybody standing move into the hallway. Let's go." The guard rapped the baton on the metal for emphasis.

Luz grabbed Carmelina's free hand and they stepped through the throng of bodies and out into the hall.

EIGHTY-FIVE

The two guards led the group single file, about forty of them in total, down the cinder block hallways. Absurdly painted bright pink, the halls stretched past countless cells, each filled beyond capacity with slumbering women. The multiple intersections created a maze.

The large black D painted at the juncture of two hallways announced they were in Cell Block D. This facility, once a women's prison, was old and crumbling despite the pathetic attempt to freshen things with the Pepto-Bismol hue of the walls. The musty smell of damp concrete permeated the air.

Everywhere large fluorescent tubes burned and flickered overhead, the unforgiving white light bouncing off the glossy paint and illuminating the smallest of corners. It was stark. All sharp edges.

"What time is it?" Carmelina whispered to Luz.

"Hard to know. Early morning?"

Katya hadn't wanted food yet, that was her only guideline. Perhaps five or six in the morning. With the constant lights and no view to the outside, it was almost impossible to tell.

"Where are they moving us?"

Luz shot a look over her shoulder and shrugged.

The knot in Carmelina's belly grew colder. If they moved her out of this facility, she'd lose her chance to meet with the social worker. This idea manifested and grew until it overtook any rational thought and shouted into her brain that all would be lost. Sandra, the magical social worker she'd yet to meet, was her link to Ricky. The doctor, too. She started to hyperventilate. She couldn't leave here.

Would it be a new facility? Another processing and another icebox? Maybe a doctor who wouldn't give a rat's ass about her? Someone who had seen it all before and would treat her like a number. Or worse, like she was less than human. She'd heard some of the other women talk and she knew she'd won the lottery with the doctor she'd seen yesterday.

For the most part, her experience with border patrol and with ICE had run true to stereotype. To a man, and woman, they were callous, cruel and uncaring, processing them without seeing their individual humanity. She knew not all of them could be that way. She could appreciate, in the smallest of ways, that they had a job to do, a job that probably required them to remain emotionally distant from the migrants they worked with.

And yet, there would be the unprovoked, unseen kick in the back of a shin. A smirk while doling out the meager portions of instant noodles or sandwiches of stale white bread and processed cheese. Or worse, the neutral, unwavering expression worn by the woman with the clipboard leading them down the corridor.

Apathy. It was hard to come to terms with the fact that apathy, after so much overt cruelty, might in fact be the end of her.

Carmelina! Her mother's voice rang through her head. *Pull yourself together, mija. You've come this far. Keep going, mi amor. Ricky needs you. Find my grandson.*

Carmelina straightened her shoulders. She could do this. She'd come this far. Whatever they threw at her next, she would find a way. Put a boulder in her path and she would find a way over it, around it, or under it. If she had to go through it, break it down piece by piece with the tiniest hammer—like she'd seen in the movie about the prison escape—she would do it.

She would find her son.

ROUNDED UP LIKE LIVESTOCK, the women crowded into a large gymnasium. They'd been ordered to stay inside a large circle painted on the floor for some game or sport played here in better days when it had been a justice facility. At least the prisoners had yard time and social time. So far Carmelina had only spent time in the one frigid, crowded room and the doctor's office.

Other groups of women were being led into the room by other guards and ordered to stand in their own circles. Soon there were eight groups.

"There's over three hundred of us here," Luz said. "What the hell is going on?"

One of the women nearby turned to them. "We're being moved to another facility."

"Well, that much is obvious."

The woman sneered. "Do you remember a few days ago that there were some people here touring the facility and asking us all questions, about food, and conditions?"

"Sure." Luz glanced at Carmelina. "It was before you got here."

"Those people made a big stink in the media about the overcrowding and the conditions here. So right now, what you're seeing, is the government covering their damn asses and moving us somewhere else."

"But where?" Carmelina's steady voice belied the anxiety building inside her.

"I don't know. But they may send us somewhere... I don't know. Somewhere they can hide us is my guess."

"Hide us from what?" Carmelina said.

"From all of it. Do you think the world isn't watching this? We may be here illegally, but nobody deserves this kind of treatment."

"I believe they're watching," Luz said. "I just don't believe anyone can do anything to change it."

"We're not here illegally, you know." Both women turned to Carmelina. She continued. "We have the right to enter another country to ask for asylum. We're not illegal."

"They damn well treat us like we are," the woman said. Her friend grabbed her arm and she turned away.

"Is that true?" Luz said.

"According to my brother, yes. Diego's already met with a lawyer." She chewed at her lower lip. It felt like so long since she'd been able to talk to Diego. She missed him.

"It's not illegal. And they're talking about charging the U.S. President with crimes against humanity."

"How is that going to help us?" Luz stared at Carmelina, her eyes dark and sunk deep within the heavy circles under her eyes. Her skin was sallow and acne crawled up one side of her cheek.

Carmelina had noticed the longer women were here, the more pronounced the effects of bad nutrition, lack of sunlight and exercise, showed on their gaunt faces. And it wore them down, quashed their spirits. She grabbed Luz's hand and stared into her eyes. "I don't know. But we have to believe that it will. Don't give up hope."

Loud voices at the front door, interrupted them. Everyone in the large gym turned toward the commotion.

EIGHTY-SIX

"The vans are ready, let's go!"

"There's two more groups to bring down."

"Leave them. The media is already outside the gate. Sunrise is minutes away. We go now."

Two large double doors were opened to the hallway where the officials were arguing. Several more guards rushed into the room. Luz held tightly to Carmelina's hand. In the span of only a few hours, their roles had reversed, Carmelina now the strong one.

Starting with the circles closest to the open doors, the guards guided the women out the doors and out of sight. Straining to see over the crowd of bobbing heads, Carmelina counted as the women filed through the doors.

"Already over two hundred." She and Luz stood in a circle in the far back corner, the woman around them shuffling nervously.

Everyone was grumbling and throwing out ideas about where they would be taken.

"Look, if the media is outside, maybe we can get some attention," Carmelina said.

Luz shook her head. "No, they'll file us onto buses here. Don't you remember, the main gate is down the drive. The whole goal here is to get us out of sight."

"Still, we could yell out a window."

"Are you still asleep?" Luz tapped Carmelina's forehead with the tip of her finger. "The bus windows don't open, they're prison buses, they probably have grills over the glass. Trust me, there won't be a chance to talk to anyone."

The circle to the left of them started to shuffle toward the exit. Around them, women jostled and talked among themselves.

"Quiet." A guard came up to the left of them. "This group next. Slow and orderly to the exit."

Another guard fell in behind the group and they were guided to the door like sheep. The pit in Carmelina's stomach knew no end. She felt like she was being led to slaughter. She wanted to scream out that she couldn't go, that the doctor needed to see her again, that Sandra was waiting to see her.

"Wait," she said to the guard. "I'm—"

"Not special," the guard said, shutting her down. "Shut up and keep moving. All your questions will be answered later."

"But, I'm—"

"Shut up. Keep moving." His brows pulled down over his eyes, his pupils black as coal. He jutted his chin toward the exit.

Luz poked her and held a finger to her lips.

"What do I have to lose here?" Carmelina whispered.

"I don't know. And I don't want to find out," Luz said. "Keep walking."

Each step Carmelina took closer to the door tightened the fist in her stomach. She couldn't just leave here. Not when she was so close.

She now estimated almost four hundred women filing from the gym to the buses waiting outside. How many buses would that be? Would there be a chance for her to slip away from the group? Maybe hide somewhere until the buses had left?

She reached the double doors and her group spilled into the hallway. The smell of diesel and a waft of cold air filled the air. The guards kept them moving straight ahead, two by two, like school children being corralled back inside after recess, or some kind of twisted ark story.

Katya woke, hungry, and started to cry. Carmelina tried to quiet her but she would not be stilled. She opened her little mouth and wailed.

To her right, Carmelina thought she heard her name. She turned and spied the doctor hustling toward her down the long hallway.

She yelled again. "Carmelina."

Carmelina's feet rooted her in place. The woman following behind crashed into her, knocking her off balance. She released Luz's hand and stepped out of line.

A guard appeared at her side. "Keep moving."

Katya wailed louder.

"No." She shook her head, her eyes fixed on the doctor.

"Wait," the doctor said. She sprinted toward them. She was dressed in street clothes, a tan leather jacket, blue jeans, black cowboy boots. Small in stature, she inserted herself between Carmelina and the heavyset guard. "This one can't go."

"Get out of the way," the guard said.

"I'm her doctor. She can't go."

The guard's gaze swept down the doctor's attire and he laughed. "Doctor?"

"I just got in, I haven't changed yet. You need to see my lab coat to believe me?"

"Uh, yeah I do. This one goes, they all go." He reached past the doctor and grabbed Carmelina's shoulder, using his arm to block the doctor. "Let's go."

God bless her, the doctor went around the other side and jumped between them again. This time she spread her legs for balance and dug into an inside pocket to pull out a security badge. She waved it in front of his face.

"You listen to me, you, you... Neanderthal. This woman and her baby are sick. Contagious. They shouldn't be in the general population at all."

Eyes wide, the guard released Carmelina as if she'd burst into flames. He backed away. Several women nearby stepped away also.

His eyes narrowed and he looked from Carmelina to the doctor. "She looks fine to me."

"Oh? And where's your medical degree? Why do you think the baby is wailing? She's in pain. You got kids at home? Cause you'll be taking this infection right to them. Better be sure your medical insurance is up to date."

The man took an involuntary step backward.

One of the guards farther down the hall yelled. "Let's go. We need to keep moving."

Relenting, he motioned back toward the hall where the doctor had entered. "Fine," he said. "Take her."

He turned on his heel and focused on herding the other women toward the buses.

The doctor grabbed Carmelina's hand. They raced down the hall and through another set of doors. Carmelina chanced one look back to say goodbye to Luz, but she was already gone from her sight.

EIGHTY-SEVEN

Sandra didn't look anything like Carmelina had imagined her. She was neither tall nor thin, neither petite nor blonde. The social worker was average height, for an American, and built like a cherub. Her smile was infectious and her dyed red curls bounced around her face as she talked.

Animated and cheerful, she was very direct in her actions. Carmelina liked her immediately.

The doctor had taken her to Sandra's office, where, after calling Sandra to come in early, she'd left her so she could feed Katya. Twenty minutes later she'd returned with hot coffee and stale pastries. It was the most appetizing food Carmelina had seen in days and she devoured it.

When Sandra came in, she also brought a sack of fresh *gorditas*, stuffed with cheese and *rajas*, which she encouraged Carmelina to eat while she grumbled under her breath that the pitiful crap they called food in the system wasn't fit to be fed to a pig.

"Honestly," she said, "how they expect people to survive on

instant noodles and white break is beyond me. Zero nutritional value. And to think they're feeding the children the same way."

She stopped talking when she saw the look on Carmelina's face. "Oh, Wendy told me you had a son lost in the system."

"Wendy?"

"Yeah, Dr. Wendy. You didn't know her name?"

"No, she never said."

"Yeah, I like to think of her as Wendy from Peter Pan." She chuckled and popped a stray *raja* into her mouth. They were sitting across from each other at her desk, eating the *gorditas* out of a greasy paper bag. It was the most normal thing Carmelina had done in ages.

"I saw that movie."

"Yeah, she likes to mother everyone. She chose a good profession, don't you think?"

Mouth full, Carmelina nodded. A few seconds later, she grinned and said, "Would that make me Peter Pan?"

Sandra braced her hands on her desk, threw back her head and laughed. A deep belly laugh. It was infectious and Carmelina laughed, too.

Brow creased, Sandra grew serious. "I wouldn't think so. Peter Pan never grew up. I have the feeling you had to grow up much too fast. Wendy said you're seventeen?"

"Yes." Carmelina sobered and stuffed the last of the *gordita* in her mouth. The change in mood had killed her appetite but it felt rude to waste it. Who knew when she'd eat decent food again?

"We might not have much time," Sandra said, shuffling through papers on her desk. "Once the boss comes in, the guards will let him know we pulled you out of the transfer group. Let's get going on this."

CARMELINA REACHED for a tissue to wipe the ink from her hands. Under Sandra's guidance, she'd completed a stack of forms. Katya napped quietly in the corner. An hour earlier, Wendy had tapped at the door to let them know the boss was delayed so they'd have a reprieve.

Sandra multi-tasked like a bandit. One minute she was on the computer, the next texting from her cell, and then she was punching numbers into the handset that sat on her desk. She put the receiver back in the cradle and clapped her hands.

"Great news. RAICE is going to take your case."

"What is RAICE?"

"It's a non-profit agency that provides free and low-cost legal services to underserved immigrants and especially unaccompanied minors. You definitely qualify."

"You mean like a lawyer?"

"Yes, a lawyer. Very few unaccompanied minors are successful in court without representation. With their help, you'll have a much better chance."

"I do have some money," she said. "Or at least I did when I arrived. They took my personal things."

"It will all be returned to you when you're released."

"When will that be?"

Sandra drummed her fingers against her desk. "Can't say for sure, depends on the asylum application. But it could be within a couple of days."

"A couple of days? I met several women who said they've been here for over a month."

"They're not minors. Look, in less than 2 months, you're going to be eighteen. Right now, we can process you as a minor. That makes things a whole lot easier for you."

"Do I have to stay here?"

"No, like I said, you'll be released."

Carmelina rubbed a scratch on the side of her hand. "What I mean is, can I go to Arizona or do I have to stay in Texas?"

Sandra grabbed the phone and started punching in numbers. "You'll be able to go to Arizona. You will need to return here for your hearing though."

"Sure," she said into the phone. "They're putting me on hold. RAICE is sending someone over to see you today."

"Wow." Carmelina sat back. She'd beaten the clock. How many times chopping onions and cilantro in the taco stand with Carlos and Paco in Mexico City had she almost given up hope of making it to El Norte before her eighteenth birthday? "I can't believe it."

"Believe it." Into the receiver she said, "Yes, I'll continue holding."

Sandra put the receiver down and hit the speaker button. She rested her elbows on the desk, steepled her hands in front of her mouth, then nodded to herself, red curls bouncing.

"It won't all be easy, Carmelina."

The tone in her voice had shifted from hopeful to a warning. She had Carmelina's full attention.

"You're going to have to prove, beyond a shadow of a doubt, that you face real danger if you were forced to return to El Salvador. It's called a credible fear interview and your lawyer will be there with you."

She nodded. "The lawyer who comes today, from RAICE?"

"Correct. He, or she, will walk you through it and prepare you but the questions can be quite difficult. A lot of people find the experience quite traumatizing. You'll have to recount and basically relive many of the things you've gone through."

Katya stirred and Carmelina looked over to check on her. She was determined to give Katya a better chance at life than she'd had. "I can do it."

"I know you can," Sandra said. "I just want you to be prepared. Like I said, the lawyer will prep you later today."

"Yes," she said into the phone. "I'm still holding. Okay, good, thanks."

"They're putting me through," she said to Carmelina, hand over the mouthpiece.

She introduced herself and then explained she was calling about a three-year-old Salvadoran boy named Ricardo, calling on behalf of his mother.

She waited, brows arching as she listened. Carmelina leaned forward in her chair, heart pounding.

A knock came at the door. Someone in the hall spoke loudly but Carmelina could not make out the words. Sandra pivoted in her chair to ignore it, pressing her free hand to her free ear. The visitor, more insistent, knocked louder. When Sandra did not answer, the door flew open. A man with bushy silver sideburns, wearing a blue suit and white ten-gallon hat, filled the open doorway, then entered the office with two large guards in his wake.

EIGHTY-EIGHT

"Garcia, come with us." The man in the hat loomed over Carmelina's chair and stared down at her.

She squirmed like a bug on a pin. Her eyes shot to the corner where Katya was napping. She rose to go to her but the man blocked her way.

Sandra's eyes were wide and she jumped to her feet but she was finally talking to someone. She shook her head wildly at the man. "No," she said.

"No, not you," she said into the receiver. "Keep talking, I'm listening."

"Get her out of here," the boss said. The guards flanked Carmelina and pulled her out of the office.

Over her shoulder she heard Sandra say, "I have a mother here looking for her three-year-old boy."

"I'm not leaving without my baby," Carmelina said.

"Someone will bring your kid," the boss said. "Take her back to holding."

"No. You already lost my son, I'm not leaving without my baby."

Carmelina tried to sit, dropping her butt to the ground. The guards held her up, their fingers digging into the sensitive area under her armpits. She yelled for Katya.

"You can't take that girl," Sandra called from inside the office. One of the guards reached back and slapped the edge of her door. It swung shut with a slam of finality.

Carmelina let her whole body go limp and the guard on her right lost his grip on her. She slid to the ground like water, fell on her side, then righted herself and crawled back on the floor toward the door. The guards scrambled to grab her legs. Someone pressed a foot on her kidneys and pinned her to the floor.

"What a hell of a morning," the boss said. The tips of his well-polished cowboy boots appeared in front of Carmelina's face. He raised the sole of one boot and brought it down to rest on her fingers. "One more who thinks she deserves special treatment."

She turned her head and looked up at him. "I just want my baby."

The guard with his foot on her kidney pressed down harder.

"Trust me," the boss said, "you're nothing special."

"She is." Sandra burst through the door. Hopping mad, she bounced from one leg to the other. The color rising in her cheeks matched her hair. As she hopped, her red curls bobbed like a rooster racing across a barnyard.

"She's a minor. She shouldn't be here at all. What the hell are you doing with unaccompanied minors in the general population?"

"General population," one of the guards repeated. The three men chuckled.

"This isn't a prison, not anymore," the boss said.

"Damn straight it's not, and this girl has rights. Stop treating her like a criminal."

The boss folded his arms and looked down at Sandra. "We're

taking her. If you want her to have the baby, bring him out here now."

"She's a girl," Carmelina said.

"Shut up," one of the guards said.

"You can't take her. She has an appointment with RAICE today. She needs to stay with me until her lawyer arrives." Sandra yelled into the face of the boss, her voice laced with a hint of hysteria.

Rapid footsteps tapped down the hallway. "What's going on here? Did I hear you say you're waiting for RAICE?" It was a woman's voice, calm and forceful.

Carmelina turned her head but could only see the toe of a tan shoe. The pressure on her back was relieved as the guard removed his foot. The boss lifted his boot from her fingers.

"Thank God you're here," Sandra said. "This girl's a juvenile. They're trying to transfer her out. I explained they can't take her until she sees her lawyer."

"Here I am," the woman said.

"You'll have to see her another time," the boss said. "You don't have an appointment and this detainee was supposed to be transferred this morning."

"Detainee?" Sandra reached for Carmelina's hand and helped her up. She brushed at her clothes.

"Take her," the boss said to the guards.

The lawyer stepped in front of Carmelina and Sandra, blocking the guards. "You know," she said to the boss, her chin tilted up, her gaze and tone not wavering, "it was a real mess getting in here this morning, what with the media at the gate and all. I'd hate to have to explain to them why I'm back outside again so quickly."

Their eyes locked, the big man staring down at the lawyer. Carmelina held her breath. Beside her, Sandra put her hand on her back.

Long moments passed. Finally, the boss relented. He shook his head in disgust. "Fine. One hour and then I want you out of here."

"I'll need more time with my client. You don't have the right to impose a time limit."

His eyes narrowed and his mouth opened, then he clamped it closed, turned on his heel and strode down the hall, the two guards at his heels.

———

CARMELINA WASTED NO TIME. She spun, entered the office, and rushed to Katya's side. Without ceremony, she scooped the baby up and pressed her against her neck, her nose in her wispy hair.

"I'm Rachel," the lawyer said. She and Sandra filed in behind Carmelina.

"Nice to meet you," Sandra said. "Thank you. That could have gone very badly. Your timing was amazing." She cocked her head. "We only called an hour ago, how did you get here so quickly?"

Rachel leaned against a battered file cabinet and folded her arms. "I'm not actually her lawyer." She looked to Carmelina, a sparkle in her eye.

"This is Carmelina," Sandra said.

"Nice to meet you," Rachel said, extending her hand.

"But you are a lawyer, right?" Sandra pinned her with a quizzical look.

"Oh yes, I'm with RAICE. I came in this morning to meet with my client but when I heard the commotion, and overheard you mention RAICE, I intervened."

"Thank God you did," Sandra said. She motioned to one of the empty chairs in front of her desk and edged around the side to sit down. "Coffee? This morning has already been too exciting for me."

"Please." Rachel nodded and Carmelina came to sit beside her in the other chair. "Beautiful baby."

"Her name's Katya," Carmelina said, suddenly feeling shy. "*Mil gracias.*"

Rachel waved her hand. "Look, I better call RAICE and come up with a plan so we can move forward with Carmelina's case."

Sandra, in the middle of pouring coffee from her thermos into three cups, motioned to her phone. "Feel free," she said.

"Thanks, I'll use my cell. I don't want to chance any of this being recorded." Rachel stood and moved to a corner of the office.

Carmelina exchanged a look with Sandra, accepted the hot coffee she pushed across the desk, and let out a long, slow breath. Her body, still trembling, now infused with relief.

"Oh," Sandra said, "I have news about Ricky."

EIGHTY-NINE

November 12, 2019
Del Rio, Texas

"I picked up a SIM card for you." Rachel fished in her purse and passed a small cardboard envelope to Carmelina. Predawn traffic was sparse but Rachel's eyes never left the road.

"I don't know how to thank you." She popped the back off her phone, inserted the card, and watched the screen waiting for the network to activate.

"So you've said. You don't have to keep thanking me." Rachel pulled out around a tractor trailer, gunned the engine to pass, and then slid the car expertly back into the inside lane.

"I can pay you for this." Carmelina raised the empty envelope.

"Hang onto your cash, you'll need it."

After a tearful goodbye with Sandra and Dr. Wendy, Carmelina had received all her personal belongings back, including every cent of the cash she'd had left. The two women had brought in supplies for Katya, and she had a backpack filled with diapers and fresh baby clothes.

Rachel had even brought a change of clothes for her to wear to the interview. The clothes didn't flatter, but they almost fit. More importantly, they were clean and Carmelina thought the cut and style made her look like she belonged n the United States.

As both Sandra and Rachel had warned her, it had been tough reliving her experiences with Flaco and Memo. It was so common-place for her—and she'd assumed the officials heard stories worse than hers all the time—still, she'd been surprised to see shock on the man's face when talking about some of the things that had happened in the *LC-14 casa loca* over the four years she'd been a *niña* there.

The car slowed and Rachel guided it down an exit ramp. A hard right followed and she pulled into the parking lot of a large bus station. She stopped the car and turned to her. "This is it."

Carmelina reached down for her backpack.

"Don't forget about the court date. It's a long ways out. It could be almost two years. You'll have to come back to Texas for that."

She nodded gravely. A question had been plaguing her since the interview. "Do you think they'll accept the stuff about Kike?"

The Special Immigrant Juvenile Status required that she prove that she'd either been abandoned or abused by one of her parents. Her parents had done nothing but love her. She hadn't been able to slur them in any way, despite Rachel's strong recom-mendation.

"Kike does, in a way, qualify as a guardian. He did *sell you.*" Rachel took a breath. "I think the rest of your application is strong. I've sat through a lot of these interviews and there's no question your life would be at risk if you were returned."

Before the interview, Carmelina had been allowed to call her mother. She'd learned from Claudia that Memo had been threat-ening to kill her if she ever showed her face there again. She'd been expecting that. He'd even sent a letter to her mother.

"I know you're worried about your family, but him threatening you in such a concrete way really helped establish credible fear."

She shook her head. "I don't know where it will end."

Rachel reached out and took her hand. "For you it ends here. You have a chance at a new life." She squeezed her fingers. "Your bus leaves in ten minutes. Time to go and get your son."

"Don't forget, my card is with your documents. Call me if you need me. And my contact with The Florence Project in Arizona is listed on the back. Reach out to them."

They stepped out of the car and Rachel embraced Carmelina and Katya in a bear hug. For a petite woman, she had a lot of strength in her arms.

"I can never..." The words caught in Carmelina's throat and tears sprang to her eyes.

Rachel placed a finger on her lips. "You're so brave, Carmelina. We're all rooting for you. I may be able to stop that big bastard of a boss at the detention center for you, but I can't stop the bus." Her eyes sparkled. "Go. Get on that bus and go get your son. Live your best life."

Carmelina threw her arms around her again. Then, not trusting herself to speak, she turned and sprinted to the front doors of the bus station.

NINETY

Sandra and Wendy had packed a box of Pablum and small jars of baby food into Carmelina's care package. The baby spit out the first mouthful of apricot. The orange ooze plopped onto her bib. Carmelina stayed with it. A woman sitting across the aisle gave her a few tips. Carmelina tried them but for the most part Katya didn't cooperate. In the end, she had enough to eat and her lids slid closed.

Grateful for a few minutes to herself, Carmelina pulled out her phone. She found the number for Diego, that she'd gotten from her mother before she escaped, and hit dial. The phone rang six times then went to voice mail. She hit redial. After the third try, she sent a text asking him to call as soon as possible.

Both Rachel and Sandra had tried to get through to the detention center in El Paso but hadn't been able to get an update on him. When she'd spoken to her mother early yesterday morning, she hadn't heard from him either.

Scrolling through her contacts, she came upon Ana's number, the woman who had brought her safely to the border. She'd felt a bond with Ana and believed she genuinely wished her well, despite being paid to accompany her. She sent a text to let her know she'd arrived and all was good. It bounced back undelivered. Carmelina hit dial. The phone only rang twice before a tone played and a recording announced the phone was no longer in service.

Putting the phone down, she stared out the window at the endless stretches of light industrial buildings and flat fields of scrub grass rolling past. She couldn't contact José, she'd given his phone to his parents. She wished she had a number and could thank Ernesto and Estella. Their money was still easing her way. She felt certain they'd want to know she'd made it.

Switching over to a browser, she searched for the family name and found twelve listings for numbers. Using google maps, she eliminated four of the listings. When she called the fifth one, the number was out of service. On the sixth try, a housekeeper answered.

"Could I please speak to *Sr.* Ernesto or *Sra.* Estella?" she asked.

"*De parte de quien?*"

She told the woman who she was. "*Hablo* Carmelina."

"*Ay*, Carmelina. *Hablo Gaby*." It was the head housekeeper and she remembered her. "The house is in mourning. I'm sorry."

The phone clicked in her ear. Gaby hung up before Carmelina could say anything more. Did this mean José didn't make it out? Or had someone else died? Couldn't Gaby stay on the phone ten seconds more to tell her what was going on? She redialed but the call went directly to voice mail. She cursed under her breath.

Her hands shook as she once again opened the browser. If José was dead, what did that mean for her friends? Ernesto had said he had a plan, he'd been confident he knew what he was doing.

This is what she knew. Carlos and Paco came from somewhere near Tierra Blanca. They had a taco stand called Paco's Tacos. When she'd offered to contact their family, they insisted they didn't want to worry their parents and would be free in a couple of days. She didn't even know their last name. Frantic, she exhausted every idea she could think of and came up empty.

She redialed Ernesto's number. Once again it went immediately to voice mail. Sick with worry, she tried to ignore the cold fingers clutching at her heart.

A caravan of recreational vehicles passed the bus. She counted eight of the large, luxurious looking vehicles lumbering west. Traffic was heavy and towns were sparse on this part of the trip. Tractor trailers glided past like large ships. She settled in, knowing she still had a long way to go.

She was sorry she didn't have a chance to talk with Ernesto or Estella. She would like to pass along her condolences. Of course, it could be any member of the family who had died. It would be better not to picture the worst-case scenario.

She hoped Gaby would mention that she'd called. Hoped they would know that some good had come of their help and that she was safe.

Safe. The word was so foreign in her vocabulary it almost seemed too good to be true. And yet here she was—a broken girl from Central America, on a Texas bus whizzing down the longest, most featureless highway she'd ever traveled and she was grateful for every single bit of it.

In a few hours, she'd be reunited with her son. How she longed to see his little face, his trademark smile that crinkled the left side of his mouth more than the right. The giant Texas sky would be a perfect place for them to stare at the stars so she could teach him more about the constellations. She could easily imagine the feel of his little body in his arms, the sensory memory bringing a tear to her eye.

Hang on, mijo. Mama will be there soon.

Her phone rang. She snapped it up and said hello without bothering to check the screen.

"*Hermanita.*"

"Diego. Did you see my text?"

"I did. Plus Mama told me when I called her last night. I'm so relieved you and Katya are safe."

"Me, too. I'm on my way to get Ricky!"

"I know. Oh man, it's good to hear you feeling excited."

"I was starting to think I'd never get out of Mexico City alive. As soon as I get Ricky, we're coming back to meet you in El Paso."

The line hummed between them. Carmelina pressed the phone closer to hear ear. "Diego?"

"I'm not in El Paso."

"I don't understand. Where are you?"

"You won't believe it when I tell you."

Fearing the answer, she asked "Were you sent back?"

"No, I'm in New Hampshire. It's in the northeast," he added.

"In the northeast of the United States?"

"Yes, I'm going to cross into Canada in the next couple of days."

"What?" Her stomach tightened as her plans flew out the window. After all this time, she was going to be on her own here? "I thought you were still nearby. Why didn't you wait for me?"

"I'm sorry. I tried but things were getting complicated. They were starting to deport people either home or across the border into Juarez. I managed to slip away from detention with a couple of guys and we came north."

"So you escaped from Immigration?"

"It's a long story. Look, I want to hear your news. Fill me in on all the details."

She caught him up, watching the road as she filled in the details.

"Listen, once you get Ricky, come to Canada. It's easier there."

"Easier than what? I already have the visa, I can't skip out on my hearing."

"You could—"

"If I do, I'd never get legal status again."

"Well, screw the U.S.," he said. "If I stay here, I'll be undocumented. You know what that means? A lifetime of grunt work and looking over my shoulder. It's either this or getting deported back home." He paused and sucked in a loud breath. "*Hermanita*, say you'll come join me in Canada."

Canada. She couldn't get her head around another country, another immigration process, more traveling. They'd always planned to live in the U.S. together. It was unbearable to think her family would be in so many corners of the world, so far from her. She needed time to think.

"I can't make any decisions until I get Ricky." She paused, her next words a twisted echo of ones she'd spoken a few months ago when he'd called from Juarez.

"Will you let me know when you're safe on the other side?"

NINETY-ONE

The sun glowed bright orange, an over-sized globe burning through the haze above as the bus hurtled through the western edge of Texas. El Paso sprawled in every direction. Across the river lay Ciudad Juarez.

Rachel had emphasized how lucky she was not to be dropped into the Remain in Mexico program that would require her to stay south of the border until her asylum hearing. She didn't pull any punches, calling it unconscionable and a death sentence for migrants to try to survive with few resources in one of the most dangerous cities in the world where they'd be preyed on and constantly at risk while their immigration status was in limbo.

Was it only Juarez, Carmelina had wanted to know.

Also Laredo and Tijuana, but any of those cities close to the border were dangerous, controlled by cartels, and the new U.S. policy was straining the already over-taxed Mexican support system and privately run shelters.

Once again, being a minor had saved her. Diego had been right about that. He'd been right about all of it. He'd always been her strongest ally.

She missed him. Maybe once she had Ricky, she should head to Canada and they could all be together again. Canada could work for them.

After so many hours driving through Texas, New Mexico seemed to pass quickly. She cheered silently when they crossed into Arizona and opened her maps app to watch their progress.

She counted the minutes until she could get to her son.

———

AT THE FRONT door of the Tucson bus station, Carmelina queued up with other passengers waiting for taxis. When it was her turn, she got in the car and told the driver where she was going.

An older man with a bulbous nose and floppy ears turned in his seat and looked at her. "It's late to be going out there. They'll be locked up tight." His gaze landed on Katya. "Why don't you let me take you to a hotel and you can head out in the morning?"

"My son is waiting." She put her hand on the door handle. "If you can't take me, I'll find someone who will."

"Suit yourself. Just trying to save you a wasted trip." He started the meter and pulled away from the curb.

On the dark desert highway, wind licked at the low-riding car. She cracked the back window and enjoyed the feel of the fresh air on her face. It felt odd to be so close to the pavement after riding high in the bus over so many kilometers.

"What's your name, sweetheart?"

"Carmelina."

"Where you from?"

"You ask a lot of questions."

"Just making conversation. It's a long drive." He reached out and turned on the radio. Hotel California by the Eagles blasted out of the speakers.

Twenty minutes later, Carmelina asked him to turn it down. "I'm from El Salvador," she said.

He nodded and made eye contact in the rearview mirror. "You got papers?"

She fell silent.

"I'm just sayin' is all. If you don't have papers, they might detain you. I saw it happen two weeks ago when I was waiting for a couple who were there to pick up their children. They didn't have papers and the agents dragged them inside. They never did come out."

He paused. "I waited a long time."

"SO YOU'LL WAIT FOR ME?" Until the driver mentioned waiting, she hadn't considered how they'd get back. Her singular focus, the only thing she cared about, was getting to Ricky.

"I can. It's a long drive back into town, so yeah. You pay me a standby fee and I'll bring you and your kids back to town."

"Just one more. My son."

"Two, four, it's all the same to me." He chuckled and glanced in the mirror to catch her eye. "As long as they all fit in the car. No riders in the trunk or on the roof."

Carmelina found herself warming up to him. "How much longer?"

"Ten minutes."

THE DRIVER HAD BEEN RIGHT. The shelter was closed. A large sign on the gate, in both English and Spanish, stated visiting hours and the hours of business. She'd missed closing time by over three hours. Determined, she rang the bell until a voice crackled through the intercom speaker.

"We're closed."

"I'm here for my son," she said.

"Come back in the morning."

"I've come a long way. Please, he's only three." She gripped the metal gate and peered into the yard.

"I'm the night staff. I'm not authorized to open the door. Come back tomorrow."

The static fell silent.

"Please." Carmelina was talking to herself. She rang the bell again.

"Miss, if you don't leave the premises, I'll have you removed."

"Is there someone else here? Someone who can help me?"

"No. Come back tomorrow." The speaker crackled again and the light over the gate was turned off. Standing alone in darkness, sadness blossomed through her chest. She'd come so far. She hated to admit defeat but for now there was nothing to do, the man had been adamant and she believed he had zero intention of helping her or opening the door.

She leaned in the window of the cab. "I'll settle up with you."

"Pay me when we get back to town."

"I'm going to stay out here. Wait for morning."

He shook his head slowly. "You can't do that. It's dangerous."

She glanced around. They were on a lonely road in the middle of nowhere. "There's nobody here."

"Looks can be deceiving," he said.

"I'm going to sleep in that field so I'm here first thing when they open up. My son is waiting for me. He's only three." Except he wasn't. They'd been separated so long, impossibly long, over six months now and so he was older. Three years and four months. She'd missed his birthday.

The driver pushed his door open and levered himself—limb by

long limb—out of the car. He was tall and lean, his back stooped. In the car, he'd slouched so far down in the seat she'd had no idea what size he was.

"I have a niece about your age," he said, "and there's no way that I am leaving you and your baby out here overnight. I'll take you back to town, I know a decent cheap hotel. In the morning, I'll pick you up and bring you back out here. As early as you like. Before dawn even."

She opened her mouth to protest, but he grabbed her elbow, opened the back door, and guided her back into the car.

Moments later, they sped through the black countryside back toward town.

NINETY-TWO

November 13, 2019
Unaccompanied Minor Shelter, Tucson, Arizona

"Ricardo Garcia Sanchez. Ricky!" Carmelina shouted into the Intercom. "He's three." For some reason, this always seemed important, like a negotiating point. Her son was three. Who in their right mind would keep her from him?

True to his word, the taxi driver had returned to pick them up before dawn. The hotel he'd recommended had been basic, safe and clean. Excitement and fear had wrestled for her attention through the long night and she'd slept little. She'd been first in line, refusing to wait in the cab, standing at the gate under the sun, already hot as Hades at eight in the morning. Picking up on her distress, Katya shifted restlessly.

"We don't have him. Next."

"You do have him," she said. "My lawyer already got confirmation that he's here. Let me in. I have photographs of him. I have his birth certificate."

The intercom fell silent. One of the guards came forward and opened the gate a crack so she could slide through. He escorted her to the front door of the shelter and held the door open for her to pass through.

The taxi driver's warning rang in her ears: If you don't have papers, they might detain you.

Once inside, the smell hit her. That funky smell she'd lived with in the shelters and the icebox, unwashed bodies and soiled clothing. Here it was laced with the distinct tang of ammonia and urine.

Her son was living in these conditions? Had been living in these conditions for how long now?

"Wait here." The guard swung open a door to a small room with several rows of folding chairs. "Someone will come help you."

She sat. After a few minutes, she got up and paced. A small window looked out onto the yard she'd just passed through. A long line of adults had formed at the front gates behind her. One by one, they were questioned. Most were turned away, but others made it through and were brought inside to sit alongside her in the small room.

An hour crawled by. Finally, a woman with a clipboard entered and called her name. "Garcia, Carmelina."

"That's me," she said. "I'm here for my son."

The woman held up her palm. "Give me a second." Her finger trailed down the sheet of paper and she called two more names. A woman in her thirties and a squat man in his early twenties came forward. She motioned them to follow her.

They exchanged glances as they stayed close behind her down a narrow hallway. The building had a distinct institutional smell, like a hospital, too much disinfectant that didn't quite mask the underlying unpleasant smells.

"Sit here." Once again, they were left to wait. This time at a row of chairs tucked under a stairwell.

"What the hell?" The man sat, his heel lifting from the

ground, jostling his knee. It was something Carmelina did herself when she was agitated or nervous. "This waiting is going to drive me crazy. I just want my kids back."

"Me, too," the woman said. "They've had my niece four months." She turned to Carmelina.

"My son's been moved all over. They actually lost him for a while."

"*Ay, Dios.* I've heard about that. I was actually happy when they moved my niece here. It sounded a lot better than that hell-hole in Texas."

"Which hellhole was that?" Carmelina asked.

"Have you been living under a rock?" The woman cocked her head.

"Um, no. I've been on the road. Which place?"

"It was all over the news. There was a shelter just outside of El Paso that was horribly crowded. When they went in and saw the conditions—like I said it was all over the news—they moved a bunch of kids overnight."

"I bet that's what happened to Ricky," she said. "My brother said he was somewhere near El Paso. Started with a K?"

"With a C. Clint. About thirty-five kilometers outside of El Paso."

"It was horrible." The man's face reddened as he spoke. "Kids in cages, no soap, no showers, most of them hungry."

"Yep, they moved two hundred of them out right away. And didn't say where."

"Oh my," Carmelina said. She couldn't bear to think of her son in those conditions. "That must be how Ricky got here."

"Well, as horrible as this place seems to us right now," the woman wrinkled her nose, "according to the news coverage, that Clint shelter was much worse."

"Some of them went to a temporary tent in El Paso," the man said. "One of my kids did. They didn't even keep my kids together.

My youngest was separated from his two sisters until they moved him here. For a while it looked like they would deport him."

"Would you have gone home?"

"Going back would be certain death for me. My relatives would have to raise my son."

Carmelina's heart skipped against her chest. "That's horrible. I can't imagine having to choose between my children." Her final bittersweet memory of her son—that image of him bubbling over with excitement as he bounced up the bus steps—flooded her mind. She shivered as a wave of cold passed through her.

Her thoughts turned dark. Her precious son back in San Salvador? Subjected to Kike's cruelty or Flaco's rules?

Overwhelmed, she sat silent for several minutes. It was too much. Finally she spoke. "We're at the end now, right? They're going to give us our kids back."

"That's why we're here," the woman said.

"I'm not leaving without them," the man said. "They can burn this facility down around my ears, but until they hand over my kids, I ain't leaving."

NINETY-THREE

The ball of anxiety in Carmelina's belly grew with each passing minute through another excruciating hour of waiting. All three of them jumped to their feet when a woman in a green smock showed up.

She glanced down at a clipboard. "Ms. Garcia, come with me."

"*Suerte*," Carmelina said to the other woman and the man before following the woman down a long hallway. The pale olive-green color of the walls reminded Carmelina of spit up.

"How old is your baby?"

"She just turned ten months."

"She'll be excited to see her brother again." The woman flashed her a smile. Carmelina's heart pounded faster. *Ricky*. She followed the woman through a maze of narrow hallways, each time expecting to round the corner and spot her son.

After several minutes, they arrived at an intake room with a tall counter along one side. The woman made a checkmark on her clipboard. "I'm going to leave you here with Officer Smith. He'll take care of you."

"Uh, okay. Where's Ricky?"

The woman raised a hand and waved as she bustled back toward the door. "Officer Smith will help you."

"Ms. Garcia, we just need to complete a few details before we can reunite you with your son." He pulled a stack of papers toward him and started to flip through them. "Do you have the boy's birth certificate?"

"I do." She dug in her backpack and pulled out a plastic document sleeve. When she found the birth certificate, she placed it on the counter. The man pulled it toward him and filled in some of the boxes on the top form.

"Can you meet me at the end of the counter, please?" He stepped sideways and she followed. "Have a seat in the chair and look into this blue light." She did as she was told. Light flashed in her eyes, momentarily blinding her.

"You need my photograph?"

"Yes, we also need your finger prints."

"Finger prints?"

"It's our policy to ensure children are only released to their proper parents or guardians."

"I'm the boy's mother."

"I'm sure you are, Ms. Garcia. Bear with me please, it will just take a few minutes."

In El Salvador, Carmelina had been taught to ask no questions. Answers were rarely given and questioning authority was never a good idea. But both Rachel and Sandra had encouraged her to ask as many questions as she could. Ask until you get answers, Rachel had said. Nobody is going to lock you up for wanting information.

Fingers stained with purple, Carmelina used the tissue offered her to wipe off the excess ink. "Now can I see my son?"

"A few more details." Officer Smith shuffled through the stack of papers in front of him. "Sign here, please." With his pen, he indicated a blank line and slid the sheet of paper over to her. It was all in English.

"What does this say?" She could read the words but it would take her a while to puzzle out the meaning of them all put together.

"We have a translator on call," he said. "It should only take a couple of hours for them to arrive."

"Will I have to wait until then to see my son?"

He shrugged.

She was determined not to lose her patience. Not now. "Can you explain to me what it says?"

"It says you understand that your son is being released to you and confirms that you are his legal guardian."

Carmelina signed and pushed the paper and pen back to him.

"One final thing," he said. "I need to see your documents."

"Which ones?"

He tapped his finger on the counter top. "The ones that say you're in the United States legally."

"I have a Juvenile Visa." She opened the purple sleeve again and riffled through her papers. It wasn't there.

Don't panic. You can see the end line, stay calm.

Pulling open the top of the envelope, she slid all the papers onto the counter and went through them one by one. "It's here. It was here when I left Del Rio."

With great attention and care, she went through each piece of paper again, her hands shaking.

"I can wait." Officer Smith folded his arms and raised a brow in the direction of his colleague. The other man shuffled closer and cocked his head to someone standing behind Carmelina.

NINETY-FOUR

"Ms. Garcia."

Carmelina turned to face a short, squarely-built man with rounded shoulders, his rumpled gray suit shiny at the knees and elbows. "If you can't find your paperwork, I'll have to ask you to come with me."

"I have a visa." She turned back to the counter, fingers flying through the papers. She had it when she left Del Rio. How could it have disappeared?

"I'm afraid I have to ask you to come with me now."

"No. Look me up in your system. Surely you have me in the computer." She turned back to Officer Smith. "Please. Look me up."

Smith grimaced. "We're so backlogged most of the recent data hasn't been input yet."

"Is that how you lost my son?"

The officer's eyes narrowed.

"Let me call my lawyer then. I have her number." She sorted through the papers and remembered Rachel telling her in the car that the card was with the visa. "She's with RAICE, in Texas. Can I call her?"

"Ms. Garcia. Right now."

She ignored the man standing behind her. Her voice rose. "I want my son. I'm his mother. He's three."

The man in the shiny suit grabbed her elbow. "Ms. Garcia, you're making a scene. I need you to come with me. If you don't calm down, we can't bring your son out."

That sobered her. She took a breath to calm herself, looked once again at Officer Smith, then let the other man lead her out of the room.

They'd shuffled her from one place to the next so many times this morning, she'd lost her sense of direction. She hadn't seen a window for a while and had no idea which way was out. As she forced herself to calm down, the man let go of her elbow and let her follow along beside him. He pushed open the door to yet another waiting room and asked her to sit inside.

"What's going to happen now?" she asked.

He closed the door. She reached for the knob, but the door was locked. She rattled it, trying to pull it open. "What happens now?" she yelled.

"It's no use."

Carmelina turned to see several people sitting in rows of chairs. They all looked as miserable as she felt. The woman who spoke gave her a weak smile. "We're locked in until they decide what to do with us."

"What do you mean?"

"If you don't have papers, they might detain you."

"I do have papers."

"Then why did they bring you here?"

"I couldn't find them."

"Like I said, without papers they could detain us, put us back into a detention center, or worse—"

"Right, these days they're sending people back across the border. We could all be back in Mexico by the end of the day," a man next to her said.

"But they'll send our kids with us, right?"

"Not usually," the woman said. "But I don't really know. This is my first time through this."

Another man with dark circles under his eyes spoke. "They've been sending kids to some office called the Office of Refugee Resettlement—it's in the Department of Health and Human Services—and putting them into foster care."

"They can't do that," Carmelina said, bolstered by the information Rachel had given her. "It's illegal for them to separate us from our children."

The man shrugged. "Some kids they tag as 'unclaimed' have already been adopted."

"Adopted?" The words slammed into her like a wrecking ball to her gut. The image she'd had of the woman reading the bedtime story to her son and Ricky calling her Mama screeched into her head. She slumped into an empty chair.

The determination and fight Carmelina had been riding on for the last few days deserted her. After coming all this way, and after all this time, she wasn't going to be able to rescue her son?

This couldn't be the end of the line for her. She fell silent, lost in her own thoughts.

In the corner overhead, on a small television screen mounted on the wall, the news came on. It was one of those news stations that loop the same stories over and over.

"Not this again," the woman grumbled. "Did you see this? It's horrible."

Early yesterday, authorities in Mexico City raided a kidnap express house in a northern suburb of the city. Unfortunately, the cartel thought to be responsible were alerted of the raid and killed everyone on site before the police arrived.

A video camera panned a gruesome parade of body bags being carried out the front gate and placed into waiting vans. Carmelina leapt from her chair and hurried to the TV, craning her neck to see the screen.

Almost a hundred people were found shot dead in the house. The people responsible had already fled. One man who said he'd been living in a tent outside the building for the last four months and forced to cook for the hostages, escaped with his brother over the back gate. The man has agreed to testify and this next clip protects his identify.

The video showed a man in silhouette. Carmelina held her breath.

We heard gunshots and screaming. The guards at the back gate left their post and ran inside the house. That's when my brother and I escaped over the wall.

Joy surged through Carmelina. It was Paco's voice! Paco and Carlos got out.

Did you both get away, the newscaster prompted.

My brother—Paco's voice faltered—was shot in the back. He died there. I was shot in the shoulder and stayed on the ground when I fell. They left me for dead.

Carlos was dead. She bit her lower lip hard, fighting back tears.

Across the street, the police raided a companion house that held almost as many hostages. One of the men found on site had been stabbed multiple times and his throat slit. Authorities believe he wasn't a hostage but someone working with the cartel.

The camera swung to the front of the other house. A jumpy video showed men zipping up a body bag over a flash of bright yellow.

Yonas? Could it be? She'd seen him go into that house. He'd been working with them all along.

The news story continued but Carmelina had had enough.

She walked back to her chair, cradled the baby's head against her chest, and lowered her head thinking about the brothers.

Paco had studied violin in Europe for a year and Carlos claimed he was a virtuoso. And Paco bragged equally about Carlos who had studied art at UNAM in Mexico City and was a renowned painter. Their lives thrown into chaos when the cartel took over their region and the two gifted artists fled toward El Norte with a rat trap taco stand to pay their way. Ironically, the thing they thought would ease their way had been their downfall.

At least Paco would make it home. Why hadn't she insisted they leave with her? Why had she trusted Ernesto to get them out? The whole thing made her gut-wrenching sick.

So much damn loss and for what?

So many innocents killed. People's throats slit. Her friend Carlos shot in the back. She couldn't help but wonder, when they sent her back to San Salvador—whether it was tomorrow or next week—would Memo kill her slowly or just get it over with? Would he make her suffer or simply make an example of her? Her mother would raise Katya but the idea that her daughter might be sold later by Kike or grabbed to be someone's *niña* shocked her back into action.

She unclasped the baby carrier and put Katya in the chair next to her, clasping the straps to the back of the chair to keep her secure. Fishing in her pack for the document holder she upended it and dumped all the papers on the floor. She rubbed the tears from her eyes and dropped to her knees, grabbing each paper violently from the pile and sorting them to the side.

"*Señora?*" A woman crouched in front of her and placed a hand on Carmelina's shoulder to get her attention.

She looked up, gulping back sobs.

"Can I help you?"

"I have a visa," she said, moving the papers under her hands. "I have a visa, they can't hold me, my son is here, I need to get him out—"

"Breathe, *chica*. Breathe. Let me help you."

Carmelina sat back on her knees and the woman reached for the papers. One by one she laid them carefully on the floor, placing each piece of paper beside the other.

"These ones are stuck together," the woman said, holding them up. Indeed, the paperclip had attached itself to one of the other papers and as she slid them apart, Carmelina's visa and Rachel's cards were revealed.

"Is this your visa?" The woman peered at the paper.

"*Que milagro,*" she breathed as the woman passed it to her.

"Well, that's at least one of us out of here," the woman said. She methodically piled the other papers together and slid them back into Carmelina's purple document holder. Carmelina was already on her feet and getting Katya ready to go.

She thanked the woman and spun to the door, yelling while she pounded on the mesh-reinforced window.

NINETY-FIVE

Carmelina banged against the window until it rattled against the frame and the pads on her hand hurt from the pressure. Distressed, Katya started to wail. The woman who had helped her find her papers tried to calm her and twice attempted to drag her away but she would not budge from the door.

The man with the shiny suit stepped into view, reddened cheeks huffing from exertion, and put his finger to his lips to shush her. She slapped the visa up against the window. He leaned forward, the tip of his nose almost touching the glass, and peered at the paper. The hairs in his nostrils moved swiftly like underwater reeds in a stiff current.

He motioned for her to step back from the door, unlocked it, and reached for the visa.

"No, this is not leaving my hands," she said.

"Very well. Follow me." Carmelina stayed closed on his heels as he hurried back through the maze of hallways to the intake center. Officer Smith glanced up from the counter.

"She found her visa."

"I'll get to her when I'm finished up here." The woman Smith was helping glanced over her shoulder at Carmelina then back to the counter and the form she will filling out.

"Ms. Garcia, can I trust you to stand here, quietly, until it's your turn? If you do not—"

"Yes, yes, I know. I won't see my son. And yes, I will wait quietly." She waved him away, surprised at her ability to dismiss him. The man's face turned a brighter shade of beet but he looked past her, nodded at Smith and then turned away.

When the woman's forms were done, a female employee in a green smock led her away. Carmelina stepped ahead and placed her visa on the counter.

Smith scanned it without looking up at her, then grunted. He punched a few keys on the computer and studied the screen. "Huh."

"What is it?" Carmelina tried to lean over the counter to see what he was reading. He put his hand down on the counter blocking her.

He lowered his chin and stared at her. "I don't want you to panic. Understand? I can't find him. But it's like I told you earlier, that's normal with our backlog." He turned to a colleague. "We're looking for the Garcia kid. Ricardo. Three years old."

The other officer grabbed a file folder with a large G stenciled on the front and flipped through the pages. "No Garcia, Ricardo. Did you check the other files?"

"Other files?" Carmelina said.

Smith looked sharply at his colleague. "He means he might have been moved already or sent to foster care or—"

"Or to Refugee Resettlement?" Carmelina's voice pitched higher. Smith glared at her. She took a breath deep into her lungs forcing her panic down and braced herself against the counter.

"I know he's here," she said, her mouth tight. "The lawyer already confirmed he's here. Wait. Maybe you have him under Martinez."

"Why would we?" Smith fisted his hands against his hips, his patience clearly wearing thin.

"His father's name was Martinez and he's listed on the birth certificate." Flaco had insisted on being on the birth certificate. His first son. Never mind he'd never even seen the boy and had contributed absolutely nothing to his upbringing.

"Was? Is the father dead?"

"No, but he's not in the picture."

The men glanced at each other. That old story their look said.

"Look, he's only three, Ricardo, Ricky, can you look again? Under M?"

The other officer pulled another file and flipped through a stack of papers. "Wait, is that the star kid?"

"The star kid?" Smith said.

"Yeah, pretty sure we had a Martinez yesterday. Kept babbling about the North Star. I think it was the only English he knew." They laughed.

Carmelina's heart fluttered. "That's him. He loves the North Star." She leaned into the counter again.

"Oh, well..." He closed the file and picked up another one bulging with papers with a large red stamp on the cover that said Released.

Carmelina's breath caught in her throat. He thumbed through the papers and pulled one out. "Here it is. Ricardo Angel Martinez Garcia."

"That's him!"

"Yep. Released yesterday."

"What?"

"Yeah, someone picked him up yesterday."

"Wait, how is that possible? You made me show documents and took my photograph and, and, fingerprints—"

"It says here that Enrique Garcia Sanchez, his legal guardian, picked him up."

Kike. Carmelina's knees felt weak. She grasped the edge of the counter. The official turned to another page and flipped it around so she could see his photograph and fingerprints. That cold glint in his eye, mocking her, like he knew she would see this photo, like he knew it would destroy her. "But he's not my son's legal guardian. I'm the boy's mother."

Smith grabbed the papers from his colleague and ran his finger down the page. "I processed this kid. Yeah, that's right, we have a document on file from a lawyer in El Paso giving us permission to release the boy to a legal guardian."

"But that was supposed to be to my brother Diego."

"The document doesn't specify names, only that he can be released to a legal guardian." Smith's eyes narrowed. "Do you not know this Enrique Garcia? He claimed to be the boy's uncle."

She nodded dumbly. "He is. But—"

"Here it is," said Smith. "He brought a notarized letter from the kid's father giving permission for him to pick up the boy." He placed the letter on the counter and turned it so Carmelina could see it. He tapped the name. There it was, in black and white. "Timoteo Tomas Martinez Lopez. You said that was the father, right? It's the same as the name on his birth certificate."

"But I have his birth certificate," she protested.

Smith sniffed and fanned the papers. "Here's a notarized copy of the boy's birth certificate."

The muscles in her stomach contracted and she tightened her grip on the lip of the counter. Kike had found the copies her mother had had notarized as a safeguard in case Carmelina lost the original documents during her trip. Her lower lip started to tremble. "When?"

"Like I said, yesterday. Late. Not long before we closed."

"Yesterday afternoon." Her voice sounded faraway, floating, like it belonged to someone else. Yesterday afternoon she'd been on the bus, only a few hours away, optimistic it was over and bubbling with excitement as she'd anticipated the reunion with her son.

Her legs turned to jelly. She instinctively wrapped an arm around Katya.

"Miss?"

Her vision grew misty and someone nearby stepped forward and grabbed her arm just before she lost consciousness.

NINETY-SIX

"Damn Kike to hell. Does his cruelty have no limits?" Diego's voice was tight. She recognized her brother was fighting to control his emotions.

"I don't understand why Mama didn't warn me."

Diego grunted. "She probably didn't know. Have you talked to her?"

"No, I—there's been no time for that."

"They're probably not back yet. Mama wouldn't think much of him being away a couple of days."

The taxi driver veered across three lanes of traffic on the expressway throwing her off balance. Instinctively, her arm shot out to hold Katya in place. Glancing out the back window, she spotted the car he'd cut off fish-tailing behind them.

"Lina?" Diego asked.

The taxi driver made eye contact in the rearview, his brows raised in question. "You did say you're in a hurry, right?"

Carmelina tipped her chin up and settled back into her seat. "How would Kike even know about those notarized papers?"

"Because he's a sneaky and devious bastard. Don't blame Mama for that."

She paused, mute. Part of her was still in shock, grappling with the details while trying to blot out the reality of the big picture.

Close to a minute passed before Diego asked, "Are you still there?"

"I fainted when they told me."

"Ay, *hermanita*. I wish I could be there for you."

"They put me in the infirmary for an hour and made me eat and drink before they let me leave." She stared at the overhead expressway signs announcing exits for places she'd never been. "How much longer?" she said to the driver.

He shrugged. "A few more exits. Not long."

"Listen to me," Diego said. "We'll get him back. If you can't sponsor him into the U.S., I'll sponsor him into Canada. He won't grow up there, hear me?"

What kind of life would Ricky lead in San Salvador constantly under Kike's cruel influence? Or worse, Flaco could take a more active interest in the boy. Her son's education would be on the streets if he wanted to survive. She'd wanted so much more for him. A childhood free of worry, free of crime and violence, a chance to finish school, gain a skill, get a job. Such ordinary dreams torn out of her reach.

"Diego, they might still be at the airport. Rachel said their flight out is probably a red-eye."

"A what?"

Carmelina had never heard the term before either. For that matter, she'd never been on a plane or even set foot in an airport. "I guess it means it goes overnight."

The line hissed between them. When Diego spoke, his voice was monotone as he carefully chose his words. "They might already be gone, Lina. By now they could be out of the country."

She shook her head. "No. Rachel said--"

"Who is Rachel?"

"The lawyer in Texas. I just spoke to her and she's calling a lawyer who works nearby to help me."

"What if they went to a different airport?"

She scoffed. "Kike's lazy. He'll do the easiest thing. I have to bank on that." Her voice quivered. "He thinks he's in the clear now. Hopefully, that will give us an advantage."

Diego cleared his throat. "And if they're gone?"

"Then I'm going back. Ricky can't be there on his own."

"No." Carmelina could easily picture her brother shaking his head. How she missed him—he always had her back. If only he were here right now. "Memo has already threatened to kill you. And clearly Flaco did this out of spite. It won't be safe for you back home."

"He's my son. I'll have to go."

"No. Think of Katya. You can't take that little girl back there and leave her orphaned."

Carmelina choked on a sob. Diego was right. She'd be no good to either of her children if she ended up dead. Still, how could she let go of her son and sentence him to the life he'd have to lead there.

"You have the Juvenile Visa. You'll never have this chance again. Please *hermanita,* listen to reason. You have to stay in the U.S."

"But Ricky—"

"I want you to look into Katya's face right now. Do it. Look."

Carmelina looked into her sleeping baby's face, her soft features angelic, and tears welled up in her eyes. "But you're gone. I'll be alone here. I don't know anyone... I barely speak English."

Diego's voice came through the line—calm, steady. "You speak a lot more than I do and I'm getting by. All those hours you studied on the bus ride to work, it's all going to pay off. Look, you're smart, you're strong. You're free now, Lina. You're so brave—you've saved Katya and you've saved yourself."

"But Ricky—"

"Mama will love that boy and protect him like a bear. And I promise you, we'll get him out."

She loved Diego with all her heart and she didn't blame him for losing her boy—it wasn't his fault Homeland Security had ripped him away—but she knew his promises may never come to pass. And as much as she loved her mother, she'd hadn't been able to protect her, or Claudia, from Kike or Flaco or Memo. Well-intentioned or not, her mother would be powerless to protect Ricky.

She bit her lip and swiped the tears from her eyes. "No," she said, her voice calm.

"No, what?"

"For right now, I have to believe that there's still a chance. That he's not already gone. This is *not* the end. It simply can't be."

The driver jerked to the right, roaring down an exit ramp. "International or domestic?"

"I don't understand. What?"

"Where are you going? International or domestic?"

"El Salvador."

"International it is then." He shook his head, maneuvered to the inside lane and pulled up behind another taxi parked at the curb.

"I'm here." Carmelina unbuckled Katya's carrier from the harness and slung her pack over her arm.

"Lina. *Hermanita*, wait—"

She ended the call and leaped from the cab.

NINETY-SEVEN

The cavernous space of the departure terminal bustled with activity. Carmelina stood rooted to the floor inside the automatic glass doors while a sea of humanity pressed and veered around her like a storm-swollen river rushing around a granite boulder. The majority of them pushed forward toward long lineups in front of a long row of counters. She studied the airline names and logos but had no idea which one would be flying to San Salvador.

"Miss?" A tall but stooped elderly man with the bushiest brows she'd ever seen appeared near her elbow. "Do you need help?"

"I'm... uh, I'm looking for a flight to El Salvador." Her heart fluttered against her chest. The whole thing was so disorienting. She felt like an idiot. And—more important than her bruised ego—she was wasting time.

"Do you know which airline?"

"I do not." Bewildered, she looked again toward the counters and various company logos that hung above them. *Focus.*

"What does your ticket say?" The man cocked his head and stared into her eyes.

"Um..."

"Let's have a look at the board, shall we?" The man grasped her elbow and guided her gently through the milling throng until they stood in front of a large digital screen lit with departures.

Oh, that looks familiar. Similar to the bus station departure board. She smiled at the man, her breath starting to regulate itself. She scanned the board. "I don't see anything."

"What time is your flight?" His remarkable brows knit together above the bridge of his nose. "Are you all right?"

"Yes, just... The flight is a red-eye. So, midnight?" She peered at the board while the rows cascaded and the list of flights updated.

"It might be too early for it to be listed," the man said. "Or, no, there it is." He pointed to the flight as it moved up the board. "See it?"

"Yes."

"Do you have luggage to check?"

"No, actually..." She let her words trail off. Better to keep her business to herself for now. "I'm meeting someone else who is taking that flight."

"Well, you have plenty of time. Keep track of the gate number and you can probably meet them near security."

She glanced over her shoulder, anxious. "Security?"

The man's brows inched down his face again. "If you don't have a ticket you won't be able to go through to the gates or boarding areas. Anyway," he glanced at his watch, "I think you'll be okay now. Just follow the signs for security."

To the left of the departure board hung a sign with a range of gate numbers. She noted the number she needed and started to turn away.

"You'll be okay now?" the man said.

"I will." Gathering her wits and her manners, she flashed him a smile she hoped emanated more confidence than she felt. "Thank you so much for your help."

The kindly gentleman tipped his chin and bowed slightly at the waist before turning away.

CARMELINA HURRIED along the brightly lit passageway. Shops selling purses and books, silk scarves and T-shirts, chocolates and enormous bottles of liquor displayed in elaborate glass pyramids flanked both sides. She took it all in without registering the details or slowing her pace, determined to get to security. If Ricky and Kike had already passed through security, she would need a ticket in order to follow them. With no idea what a ticket would cost—or whether the cash she had left would cover it—intercepting them was her best chance.

She slowed then came to a complete stop as people ahead of her bunched into a large crowd. Rising on tiptoe, she tried to see around the man in front of her but he was too tall and she couldn't see past his shoulders. To the far left of the corridor, a man scurried past going in the opposite direction. Spotting an opening, she shuffled to that side and skirted along the long line of people until she reached the entrance to security. People also lined the wall of the corridor from the opposite direction.

An older woman, holding a young child about Ricky's age, stood in a dead zone waving to a woman who was stacking her belongings into a plastic bin. Carmelina watched her slide the bin along a set of moving metal rollers then step through what looked like a metal door frame when the security officer waved her forward.

From what the man with the eyebrows had said, security would be her last chance to spot them. Her eyes scanned the area carefully. Though the crowd was large, the security officers worked through the passengers efficiently, scanning the items in the bins and occasionally waving some kind of baton over people after they passed through the metal frames. At the end of the conveyor belts, travelers gathered their things before rushing off and quickly rounding a corner out of her sight.

Methodically, heart pounding against her chest, she worked her way back over the crowd, her gaze lighting on each figure before flitting to the next. They weren't in the hall. Still, she had to be sure. Kike was tall. He should stand out. She swept the area once more. She trained her eyes on the people at the nearest end of the conveyor belts. There. A young child with jet black hair. Would Ricky have grown that much since May? Her heart fluttered. The small boy turned, his face in profile, a thumb jammed firmly in his mouth. Her stomach dropped. Not her son.

Scanning the line to the right as far as she could see, she satisfied herself that she had time to take a closer look at the line to the left. Walking down the corridor toward the east, it soon became clear that Kike and Ricky were not in that line. Retracing her steps, she reached the same conclusion with the other line.

She backed up against the wall again. After several minutes, she realized if they did approach, they would also be able to see her. This wouldn't work. She was too exposed. She needed to keep the element of surprise in her favor.

NINETY-EIGHT

Carmelina ran her finger around the edge of her over-sized coffee mug. The dregs of her drink, cold and filmy at the bottom of the cup, perfectly reflected her mood. A plate with the remnants of her meal had been pushed to the side, the cold french fries soggy from soaking up the juice from the under-cooked burger. Her first American burger hadn't thrilled her. She wondered aimlessly how she would feel about apple pie.

Exhausted, she lay her hand on the table top and slanted a look to Katya sleeping soundly on the bench seat beside her, then her gaze returned to the corridor. From her vantage point, she had a clear view of the people moving in two connecting corridors toward security.

The stress of the last few days threatened to overwhelm her. A low, throbbing pain at the base of her skull competed with the tightly clenched muscles in her jaw. Her entire body thrummed with fatigue. She'd hoped the food would give her a second wind but it had only made her drowsy, her eyes itching to close as she struggled to remain vigilant.

There. Something in the crowd approximately ten meters along the west corridor caught her eye.

Bouncing along the corridor in a lime green T-shirt that slipped off his shoulders and hung almost to his knees came her son. Taller—he'd shot up like a bean sprout, almost a head taller than when she'd last seen him--but it was definitely him, her impossibly beautiful son. She jumped up and navigated a path through the tables toward the restaurant exit.

"Miss!" came a voice behind her. "Your baby."

How could she possibly manage this on her own? It was impossible for her to be two places at once. She turned, nodded, and raised her palm toward the waitress before turning her gaze back to her son.

In the wide corridor outside, a family passed by and behind them followed several couples, a group of young business men and a trio of flight crew, and tucked behind them, strolling leisurely in the direction of security, came Kike and Ricky. To run out now would surely cause a scene, and what if Kike took off? She inhaled deeply into her lungs willing her body to stop trembling. She'd come this far. For now, there was time and she didn't want to alert Kike to her presence.

Sprinting to the table, she collected Katya and her backpack and tucked a twenty-dollar bill under the coffee mug. Nodding a quick thanks to the waitress, she remained hidden behind a post waiting for Kike and Ricky to pass by the restaurant exit.

But they never did. Where could they have gone in only a couple of minutes? Had Kike seen her? Her stomach dropped. She raced ahead but they weren't there. It wasn't possible. He couldn't disappear into thin air. She raced back, dodging through other passengers until she passed the restaurant again and then she spied the water fountain and the sign for the washrooms.

With her back flat against the cool tiled wall, she waited for them to exit, her heart pounding so hard in her chest the rush of blood in her ears drowned all sounds around her to a low drone.

A flash of lime green. Ricky skipped into the hallway and bent his head over the lower fountain, humming and laughing as the water spurted into his mouth.

Carmelina stepped forward. Placed her hand on his bony shoulder. He turned and looked up at her, eyes widening as recognition crumpled his features into a smile. "Mama!" She bent to hug him and Ricky wrapped his arms around her and she gathered him into her arms and straightened with him clenched against her chest—he was not so much heavier now than he'd been—and then she twisted on her heel and raced away, bolting through the oncoming crowd.

"RICKY! RICARDO!" Kike's voice boomed over their heads, echoing off the tiled walls. Carmelina ran faster, pushing against her body's limitations. The straps of Katya's carrier dug into her shoulders. The baby, woken by the jolting movement, wailed. Ricky, arms tight around her neck, babbled in her ear.

"Mama, tio is calling me."

"Hush, *mijo*."

"Tio--"

Carmelina hushed him. "Ricky, quiet."

"But tio is looking for us. He told me not to get lost, he told me-_"

"Ricardo, please. Quiet." The corridor widened and opened around her into a waiting area. Comfortable-looking chairs and couches, most filled with people chatting or peering at their cell phones or tablets, clustered around several low tables. The crowd she was weaving through thinned out.

"I see you, Carmelina!" She glanced over her shoulder. Kike was closing in on them.

"Mama." Ricky started to cry. "Tio said he was bringing me home to you. Why are you running away from him?"

"*Mijo*, please." Carmelina panted, her arms ached with the weight of him, Katya's shrill cries pierced her ears.

Her only thought had been to run. But it was clear she couldn't outrun Kike—not with an infant on her back and a toddler in her arms. She needed a plan. Her eyes scanned the corridor, seeking a route through the loose groupings of people headed toward her. Among them, she spotted two men in crisp white shirts with insignia on the shoulders. They could be police. Or they could be military or even flight crews. Either way, she needed help.

KIKE RACED past her right shoulder and straight to the men in the uniforms. "Officers, this woman is stealing this child."

The men stepped around Kike's large frame and braced their bodies squarely in front of Carmelina. They stood shoulder to shoulder, the one with tousled blond hair and skin as white as weathered bone had blue eyes that glinted daggers at her. Her gaze slid past his shoulder to the open area on the right. Should she make a run for it? Dodge through the people playing with their phones? Leap over tables? Where would that lead her? It was still a long away to the exit and then what? A taxi would be miraculously waiting? Ready to whisk her away into the night while her pursuers stood milling helplessly around the doors staring at the retreating taxi as she escaped to safety?

No. She stood tall, shrugged off the sinking feeling she had of being cornered like a rat and chose to come out fighting, taking strength from the rise of adrenalin surging through her body.

"He's my son," she yelled at Kike. "Who do you think you are? How could you take him from me?"

The blond man held his palm up toward her. "Let's all calm down."

People started to give them a wide berth, their heads swiveling comically on their necks as they gave in to their curious natures before hurrying on toward their flights.

Kike stepped closer and drew a fold of papers from a small backpack. "I'm the boy's legal guardian. I'm taking him home on the authority of his father."

"His... father?" sputtered Carmelina. "Flaco doesn't care about him."

"Mama?"

Belatedly, she wished she'd chosen her words more carefully. Her arms tightened around her son. Her gaze darted between the two men. The bald man stared back at her, his demeanor more curious and somehow softer than his partner's. She appealed directly to him.

"This is *my* son," she said. "*I'm* his legal guardian."

"Where's home?" he asked.

"El Salvador," thundered Kike.

"I... For me, the United States." Squaring her shoulders, Carmelina stood up straight. The blond officer quirked a brow. "I'm legal," she said. "I have a visa to be here."

Reaching to his waist, the blond lifted a phone off his belt and glanced at his partner before skewering Carmelina with a dark look. "I'll get Immigration down here."

Behind him, Kike started to edge backwards. The bald officer responded when Carmelina glanced his way, followed her gaze and twirled in time to grasp Kike by the forearm as he was turning away.

"Let's wait for Immigration, shall we? We'll get this all straightened out."

He led Kike off to the side toward an empty couch and motioned for Carmelina to follow. Kiki slouched into the cushions, grumbling under his breath and shooting her dark looks—as usual his actions had been shortsighted and he was looking for someone else to blame. She ignored him and their small group huddled there until the other officer rejoined them.

"They're on their way."

CARMELINA SITUATED herself sideways in a chair, Katya sobbing softly against her back, Ricky wide-eyed and shaking on her lap. The bald man left them under the watchful yet dismissive eye of his partner but returned quickly with a bottle of water. As he offered it to her, she noticed the patch on his shirt above the chest pocket that said Airport Security. They weren't even police.

What did she know about authority in the U.S.? Only that if she somehow breached it, broke the law, strayed outside what would be considered normal behavior, then maybe her visa would not be honored. Maybe they would simply put her on the plane with Kike and send them all home. Then all of this would be for nothing and Memo—or perhaps Flaco— would kill her and her kids would grow up without their mother.

Carmelina took a long pull of the water and focused on trying to calm herself.

"Want a drink, *mijo?*" It was incredible. After all this time, her son was in her arms. She held the bottle to his lips but he twisted away and slid off her lap. She reached for him and guided him to the chair beside her.

Kike fixed her with a hateful stare. "You've always been such a troublemaker," he hissed.

"Troublemaker," she echoed. "Because I wanted an education for myself? A better life for my son?" Her eyes never left her older brother's. "Cause I didn't want to be sold, or raped daily, or live in constant fear?" Her voice rose, attracting attention from a couple sitting nearby. "All because I was unfortunate enough to be born a girl? And to have such a *pendejo* for a brother?"

Kike's upper lip twisted into a satisfied sneer. "You deserved everything you got, little sister."

Red hot energy burned in her belly. She lunged out of her chair but before she could reach him, the blond officer stepped between them leaving her no recourse but to sit back down. Not for the first time, she wondered why she'd had the misfortune to be born into the same family as Kike. Aside from her mother, she didn't know a single person who cared for him.

NINETY-NINE

Carmelina's phone pinged. Reluctant to take her eyes off her son for even a few seconds, she lifted the phone so she could see the screen and still keep Ricky, behind the large plate glass window, firmly in her view. It was a text from Rachel.

Where are you? My friend from the Flores Project is there. Immigration.

She kept glancing at the screen but nothing came back. In the small room, an Immigration officer and social worker about her mother's age were interviewing Ricky. The woman, her face all hard angles with cheek bones that looked razor sharp, had introduced herself as Janet before leading Ricky away and reassuring Carmelina she would be able to see her son at all times.

Another text from Rachel.

Hang on. He'll find you.

Carmelina breathed air deep into her belly and exhaled slowly. Help was on the way. Beside her, Katya stirred. She checked her forehead—it was stifling in the offices with zero airflow—removed the small blanket and fanned her reddened face with her hand. The baby's lids fluttered and she slipped back to sleep. The chaos earlier had worn her out.

They planned to interview her when they were finished with Ricky. Kike had been taken farther down the hall to be interviewed almost an hour ago. She wondered what vicious lies he would be spin.

Ricky hunched forward in his seat, his rounded back to the window. The poorly fitted T-shirt gaped slackly at the base of his neck revealing bony vertebrae. If only she could see his face. Another Immigration officer entered the room from a second door on the far wall. He left the door standing open, placed a sheet of paper on the table, and leaned down to consult with his colleague. Janet listened intently, pulled the paper toward her and quickly scanned the contents.

As she watched, Janet slid a bright, foil-wrapped candy across the table toward Ricky. His small hand flashed out for it. The woman put her head together with the Immigration officer, shook her head with a grim twist to her thin lips, then stood and came through the door into the hall.

"We'll just be a few more minutes," she said. Without waiting for a response, she turned back into the room closing the door behind her.

Ricky stood up. The other officer edged toward the door he'd arrived through. Wait! Would they take Ricky out that back door? Would she never see her son again? She jumped to her feet and put her nose up against the glass.

"Garcia." Someone from the end of the hallway called her name. She ignored it and knocked on the window.

"She's there," someone said. Footsteps approached but Carmelina's eyes remained fixed on her son. He was edging around the end of the table toward the social worker. The second Immigration officer stood with his hands on his hips waiting by the open back door.

She pounded on the window, both palms flat against the glass. Ricky's head turned toward the noise but he didn't see her. She realized it was a two-way glass and while she could see in, her son could not see out. *He couldn't see her!*

"Carmelina? What's going on?" A young guy in a button-down soft pink shirt and tight black jeans touched her on the shoulder. He looked like someone ready to serve her a trendy drink in an upscale cafe. Or launch an Internet search engine.

"My son--" She banged again on the window.

"Carmelina," he said, "I'm Rachel's friend." Carmelina couldn't focus on him, her whole body was shaking now. He gripped her forearm. "I'm the lawyer from the Flores project."

"They're going to take my son again," she wailed. "Look, they're going to take him out that back door."

Ricky stood beside Janet. Janet took his hand. Carmelina stepped past the young lawyer and reached for the door handle.

"Wait," he said. "Let me. I'll be right back." He slipped inside the door and closed it behind him. Carmelina watched the adults shift their attention to the newcomer.

Janet settled into her chair and motioned to Ricky to return to his seat. He skipped back around the table with another candy in his palm. Head down, he concentrated on opening the bright wrapper.

Carmelina shifted her weight from one foot to the other. Behind her on the floor next to the chair where Carmelina had sat, Katya gurgled. She glanced over her shoulder long enough to be sure she was secure, then turned her attention back to her son.

Rachel's friend now stood beside Ricky, his palms flat on the table. The officer who had brought in the paper backed out of the far door and closed it behind him. Several minutes passed, the Immigration officer scowling while Janet and the lawyer talked. Janet exchanged a look with the officer, nodded to the lawyer, and he stepped back into the hall.

"Let's sit for a few minutes," he said.

"I'm not leaving this window," Carmelina said.

"They told me they only have a couple more questions for Ricky. The social worker assured me they'll be bringing him back out in a few minutes."

"And you believe them?" Carmelina felt like her eyes were about to bug out of her head. She leaned closer to the window, her hand still against the glass.

"I do." He cocked his head slightly to the right and peered at her. He had dark brown eyes. Kind eyes. "I'm Matthew," he said. "Matt. I'm sorry it took me so long to find you."

"I'm just glad you're here. Are they going to keep him? Are they going to take him from me again?"

"I don't know, but I don't think so. They asked me to give them a few more minutes and they'd bring him out. Like I said. That's really all I know for now."

Her head jerked away from him and back to her son.

"Let's give them that time, and we can stay right here and watch them."

A shadow darkened the end of the hallway, followed by a low growl. Matt and Carmelina turned toward it. Kike walked toward her with two officers looming behind him. His stare was filled with such hatred that she sucked in a breath.

"You know him?"

"It's my brother. The one who tried to take my son. Can you watch Ricky?" Without waiting for a response, she stepped across the hall and shielded Katya with her body.

Kike's face twisted into an ugly sneer. "You bitch," he said.

"Keep moving," said the officer behind him.

Her brother's face reddened, his eyes darkened and he glared at her. As he drew alongside, he hissed at her. "Flaco will kill you. If I don't do it first."

Carmelina sucked in a breath, and the blood drained from Matt's face.

"That's enough," said the officer, pushing Kike's shoulder and propelling him forward. Kike's arm shot out and Carmelina lunged away, his fist landing against her upper arm. She bit her lip to keep from crying out. She wouldn't give him the satisfaction.

"Can you get him out of here?" Matt said.

The officer in the back shot a dirty look at him over his shoulder. They took Kike into another room several doors down.

"Are you all right?" Matt moved to her side.

Carmelina rubbed her arm and nodded.

"Will you be okay for a minute?"

She nodded again and he strode toward the door, but before he could reach it, it was flung open. Janet stepped into the hallway.

"What's going on out here?"

"That was Carmelina's brother," Matt said. He pulled the door closed behind Janet, tipping his chin in Ricky's direction to indicate he didn't want the boy to hear the conversation. "He threatened to kill her."

Janet's head swiveled toward Carmelina. "He did?"

Carmelina huffed. "Nothing I haven't heard before."

"Did anyone else hear him threaten her?"

"Sure, the officers would have heard him." Matt was in his element now, just getting warmed up, his voice steady and firm.

"Give me a minute." Janet stepped back inside the room and a couple of minutes later the door opened wide and Ricky flung himself across the hall and into her arms.

"Mama! Mama, the lady gave me candy." He held up his hand, his fingers sticky and yellow.

A few feet away out of earshot, Matt and Janet conferred in low voices.

Carmelina snuggled her son to her chest. "I see that, *mijo*."

ONE HUNDRED

"It's really not necessary," Matt said. They were standing in the hallway near security where Carmelina had stood hours before waiting for Kike and Ricky to arrive. Except now, she was waiting to watch Kike depart. "Immigration will escort him to the plane. They'll be with him until he boards."

"It's necessary for me." Carmelina shifted Ricky's weight. He slept soundly, his head resting against her shoulder. Matt had insisted on wearing Katya's carrier over his own shoulders—the baby nestled peacefully against his back—somehow making it look like the most natural thing in the world. "I'm so grateful to you," she said. "Your timing was perfect."

"I'm glad I could help. Rachel and I go way back."

"I can't imagine you go way back with anyone." She laughed. "You can't be much older than me." She studied him for a few seconds then blurted, "How can you be a lawyer when you're so young?"

Matt smiled and his whole face lit up. "I'll be twenty-seven next month. Almost ten years older than you."

"More like nine. But you look much younger than twenty-seven."

"I get that a—"

"Carmelina, Flaco is going to kill me if I go back without that kid!" Kike was being led into the security area. "You don't care about anyone but yourself!" he yelled. "Flaco will come for you. You better watch yourself."

The officer pushed Kike forward.

Matt rested his hand on Carmelina's forearm. "You don't have to listen to more of this. We can go now."

"No," she said. "I need to see the back of him."

Matt stood quietly at her side while the officers accompanied Kike through security. Perhaps he would turn toward her again. A small part of her hoped he would. As much as she hated him, he was still her brother. Still her blood.

Ricky's arms tightened around her neck. "Mama," he mumbled. "I'm sleepy."

"Go back to sleep, *mijo*."

Her gaze didn't waver, her focus on the back of Kike's head until he rounded the corner and disappeared.

"There." Matt turned to her. "He's gone. You'll never have to see him again."

Her eyes remained fixed on the spot where her brother had slid from her view as she echoed Matt's words: "I'll never have to see him again."

Tears pricked her eyes. She would never be going home again. Would never again tickle her sister Angie or argue with Claudia, would never hug her father again or kiss the sweet face of her mother.

And never again would her life be dictated by someone else. She had fled her abusers, rescued her son, and persevered—dogged in her determination for freedom and a better life.

Her life was here now.

She gazed into the sleeping faces of her son and daughter. *Their* life was here now, too. She would nurture her own family and create a life for them here.

It might not always be easy but she did believe it could be better.

What happens to Flora after her son falls off the train? Her story is coming. To receive a note when it's ready (and other insider information), sign up for the reader newsletter at TheMigrantNovel. com/readers. You can also follow the author at Amazon: amazon. com/author/kate-fox

ABOUT THE AUTHOR

Kate Fox writes thrillers with an edge that will stay with you long after the final page has been read.

Visit TheMigrantNovel.com/readers to join the reader's group and receive insider news, previews, and cover reveals.

Coming soon, the next book in the Freedom Series. Follow Kate to stay up to date with new releases.

Made in the USA
Coppell, TX
19 February 2021